"There's something we need to discuss before riding any farther."

"What?" Her own expression was beginning to take on the quality of a cornered rabbit.

"My payment."

"Oh, but I can't possibly pay you now! I thought you realized that." She stared up at him in confusion. "I was expecting to wire funds from Abilene Station. I have no money with me."

"I wasn't thinking money."

He flashed her his third smile of the day and Dorcas suddenly felt as though she were wrapped in ice. Ice so cold it almost burned her. No . . . it was the gleam in his eyes that was burning her. So it had to come to this, had it? Her knight had become a dragon? She steeled herself to meet his look without wavering.

"What, then? What *do* you want?" she asked. *As if I don't know*, she thought.

"What do I want in payment?" He took a step forward. "It may surprise you."

"Really?" she said, struggling to keep her voice level. Was the man an idiot? Surely he didn't think she was *that* naïve. "Try it," she added ominously, "and *I* may surprise *you*."

He stopped dead in his tracks, threw back his handsome head and howled with laughter. "Dorcas Jeffries, after seeing you leap out of that tree in your underwear, I doubt there's *anything* you could do that would surprise me!"

I Do

MIMI RISER

LOVE SPELL      NEW YORK CITY

To impossible dreams . . .
and all those who dare to pursue them.

LOVE SPELL®

October 2003

Published by

Dorchester Publishing Co., Inc.
200 Madison Avenue
New York, NY 10016

Copyright © 2003 by Mimi Riser

ISBN 0-505-52561-5

The name "Love Spell" and its logo are trademarks of Dorchester Publishing Co., Inc.

Printed in the United States of America.

Visit us on the web at www.dorchesterpub.com.

I Do

Chapter One

A castle . . .

A Scottish castle . . .

A medieval Scottish castle dug into the dusty red plains of western Texas?

Staring out of the train's dirt-streaked windows at those endless, arid plains, Dorcas Jeffries slowly shook her head. Not that it was the castle itself that disturbed her so much—though that could have been enough, of course. A Highland castle ought to be in the Highlands of Scotland, oughtn't it? It seemed not only peculiar but impractical to construct such a monstrous edifice out on this scrubby terrain. Wherever did they find the stone for it?

Oh, that was right, she suddenly remembered—it had been built from those mud bricks they called adobe. That was some consolation, anyway, the girl supposed, shaking her head again without even realizing that she did so. It was one of those annoying little habits her late aunt

1

had never been able to quite cure her of. Another habit was the rapid jiggling of one knee or the other whenever she was agitated or engrossed in thought. At the moment it was her right knee that was bouncing up and down.

What was really bothering her, she decided, was the reason for this journey. How could a family send a girl nearly halfway around the world to marry a man she had never even seen? What kind of man would accept an unknown bride? This was modern day 1883 America, not 1483 Scotland. The whole idea was positively feudal! There was something almost indecent about such an arrangement.

She had to admit, though, that Lady Flora MacAllister didn't seem to think so. Dorcas felt she had heard enough about family loyalties and honor and tradition these past days to last her until doomsday. She had only met one of them so far, but she was already sick of the entire MacAllister clan. And she was sick of tartan wool, too. It was hot and scratchy, and Dorcas felt sure a paid companion should not be asked to wear her employer's clothes.

"But me spare trav'lin' gown fits ye sae well, Dorie dear. And ye look sae bonny in it," Lady Flora had chattered cheerfully every morning of their tiring trek west. "Ye wouldna be sae cruel as tae deny a poor, lonely lass such a wee bit o' comfort, would ye? It makes me feel less homesick tae pretend I've a countrywoman along side me. Why, wi' yoor fair hair an' those deep green eyes, I could a'most swear ye were a MacAllister. Leslie's been sayin' we could a'most be sisters. 'Tis th' reason I chose ye. T'other lasses yoor agency offered were awl puddin'-faced hens, they were. I didna fancy bein' cooped up wi' any o' them. But th' moment I laid eyes on ye, Dorie dear, I sed tae meself, now there be a Highland lass—whether she kens it oor nay!"

Thank goodness this was only a temporary assignment. *Dorie dear's* knees were stiff from virtually perpetual jiggling. And her neck had developed a distinct crick from all her unconscious head shaking. But she would soon be free of the fancies of Flora, she comforted herself. Their train would be rolling into Abilene any blessed moment now. Lady Flora MacAllister would be greeted and herded off by her Texas kinsmen, and her exhausted chaperone would have several well earned days all to herself before returning to Philadelphia and whatever needy damsel or matron the agency next assigned her to.

If it's another Scotswoman, I'll quit, Dorcas silently promised herself.

"This looks like the end of the line for us, ladies," offered an attractive young man with a military bearing and British inflection as the train screeched to a rocky stop. "Gad! You'd think someone would oil those wheels once in a while, wouldn't you? If I ran my ships the way these lads run their locomotives, I'd be fish food on the bottom of the ocean by now."

"Aye, Leslie, yoor a bonny, braw sailor an' Dorie an' I both ken it. Don't we, Dorie dear?"

"Well, you would have more personal knowledge of that than I, Lady Flora. Captain Armstrong is your family's friend, after all. But since he ferried you across the Atlantic without mishap, I believe I can safely assume that he's a more than adequate seaman," Dorcas said while moving about the private compartment, gathering the hand luggage together.

Leslie Armstrong rose from his seat to relieve her of the heavier pieces and was rewarded with one of her rare smiles.

"And I know for a fact that he's a most solicitous traveling companion," she continued, blushing slightly at his returned grin. "I'm sure Lady Flora has already thanked you for it, Captain Armstrong, but I should like to add my own gratitude to hers. It was most chivalrous of you to take a leave from your professional duties to see us safely here."

The handsome Englishman swept a small bow before her, deepening the girl's blush. "It was my extreme pleasure, Miss Jeffries, but I was not quite so altruistic as you seem to think, I'm afraid. You see, I was heading west, anyway. I . . ." He paused a moment, suddenly blushing himself for no discernible reason. "Well, the truth of it is, I've resigned my naval commission and accepted the captainship of the merchant schooner *True Love*. She sails for the Orient out of San Francisco at the end of this week. I've had to make special arrangements to arrive on time," he finished in an awkward rush.

"Oh," was all Dorcas could say. This was certainly a piece of news. Armstrong had had such a promising career, it had seemed. Lady Flora had confided that he would probably make admiral before he was forty. Whatever could have induced him to resign?

"Leslie! Why didna ye tell me?" Flora gasped, sinking into a swoon.

With Flora's faint came the answer to Dorcas's question. *Oh, dear Heaven, how awful,* she thought, hastily rummaging through her purse for the smelling salts she always carried. *Why didn't I guess this before?*

It was so obvious, now that she considered it. So obvious. And so pathetically ironic. Of course they were in love; Flora and Leslie had grown up practically in each other's pockets, to hear them tell it. They had probably been in love since childhood. But Leslie had been so ambitious. Flora had thought he was married to his career. That was undoubtedly the real reason she had agreed to this ridiculous marriage to her Texas cousin, Alan MacAllister—who must be one sorry specimen of a man to have agreed to such an impossibly medieval alliance.

"I wish he was here right now. I'd give him a lesson

in *modern* customs he'd never forget," Dorcas was muttering under her breath as she fanned some lavender water under Lady Flora's pert little nose. She hadn't been able to find the spirits of ammonia, so the lavender would have to do. It smelled nicer, anyway.

"Dearest, I wanted to tell you before now, honestly I did," Leslie began the moment Flora's eyelids started to flutter.

He had been kneeling beside her, chafing her wrists and staring at her with such an agony of love, Dorcas could almost have fainted herself, just from the backlash of his emotion. Except she really wasn't the fainting kind. The prim maiden aunt who had raised her never allowed such self-indulgent displays.

"I would have told you, darling, but I was afraid it wouldn't make any difference. You seemed so determined on going through with this *bloody* marriage—Oh, I beg your pardon, Miss Jeffries," he apologized with a sheepish glance toward Dorcas.

"That's quite all right, Captain Armstrong. I understand the provocation," she assured him.

"But Leslie dear," Flora said, her eyes filling with tears, "ye didna give up yoor commission fer *me,* did ye?"

That was too much for the young captain. His British reserve broke and he swept her into his arms like a tidal wave swamping the shore.

"My commission? Dear God, what's my commission worth without you? What's *anything* worth without you?" he choked. "Give up my commission for you? Flora, you little fool, don't you realize that I'd willingly give up my *life* for you?"

"Oh, Leslie . . ."

Dorcas discreetly turned her back on them and stood staring fixedly out the compartment's window at a row of wanted posters on a nearby wall. This was hardly the sort of behavior she approved of. But . . . well, she *could* understand the provocation. Or, rather, she thought she could *imagine* understanding it. It wasn't as though she had any actual, personal experience with such things—or wanted any, for that matter. But surely, under these circumstances, it was . . . wasn't it?

The little compartment suddenly felt like an oven, and Dorcas realized that she must be blushing all the way down to her toenails. *Oh, I don't know what I think!* . . . Except for the fact that she was thoroughly disgusted with herself.

Behind her, Lady Flora had begun to sob.

Don't tell me she's one of those silly girls who cries when she's happy, Dorcas thought, a trifle disgusted with Flora now, too. She need not have been concerned, however. Flora MacAllister was anything but happy at the moment.

"Oh, Leslie, ye foolish laddie, ye should've told me sooner. 'Tis too late now!" she wailed.

"Darling, of course it's not too late. It's perfect timing, if you ask me." Leslie was chuckling indulgently. "I've already hired a private coach to take us to El Paso. From there we can catch a train straight to San Francisco, where we'll have just enough time to be married before the *True Love* sails. Her owners are quite amenable to your sailing with me. They feel that a wife on board makes for a more stable captain."

Flora sobbed harder than ever. "But ye dinna understand. I'm *here* now! My people are meetin' this train an' they'll hold me tae me pledge. They'll ne're let me go wi' ye!"

"They will once I talk to them and explain the situation, gentleman to gentleman. This isn't ancient Scotland." Leslie was chuckling again. "We're a civilized world today and I'm sure your cousin Alan is a very reasonable man, dearest."

"Reasonable?" His dearest's voice cracked shrilly on the word. "A MacAllister—*reasonable?*"

Flora may actually have a point there, Dorcas suddenly thought. From what she had heard so far of the Texas MacAllisters, logic did not seem to be one of their dominant characteristics. Long before any other white men had entered this territory, several score clansmen and -women had arrived, fleeing the British persecutions that had plagued them in the decades following the Jacobite rebellion. They had rapidly built an adobe replica of their destroyed family fortress back in Scotland and had lived securely in it ever since, a world unto themselves—as though they honestly believed they had never left the Highlands. It was utterly absurd, but a fact that might have to be reckoned with, nonetheless. What was it the Scots themselves said?

"Wha' canna be cured mun be endured," she said aloud, imitating a brogue. The sound of her own voice surprised her and brought Flora's weeping face up out of her hands.

"Why, Dorie," she sniffled, "ye sounded a'most like me."

"Yes," Dorcas said softly. "I know." Very carefully, she turned from the window and confronted the couple. She had to move carefully because her heart had just begun racing so fast, she was afraid it might burst straight through her bodice if she made any too sudden gestures.

"Captain Armstrong?"

"Yes, Miss Jeffries?"

Dorcas glanced from him to Flora and back again. How could she put this to them? She could hardly believe herself what she was about to propose. "I . . . I think that Lady Flora is probably correct. Her relatives here still operate on ancient Highland law. They'll never allow you to simply walk away with her. The clan's honor

7

is at stake, and that kind of honor takes precedence over all else."

Armstrong gazed down at the petite, feminine form fairly quivering with resolve before him, a mildly bemused expression in his hazel eyes. He was still obviously unconvinced of the gravity of the situation. "What do you suggest we do then, Miss Je—" At that moment, a wild, weird wailing suddenly filled the air. "Gad! Is someone slaughtering pigs out there?"

Flora gave a little laugh, in spite of herself. "Ye daft laddie. 'Tis auld Highland tradition. Bagpipes tae welcome th' bride." On the word *bride,* she choked, and Dorcas caught her hand.

"Never mind, Lady Flora. We'll counter them with another old Highland tradition. *Stealing* the bride," she said, giving the girl's fingers a reassuring squeeze.

"How?" Leslie asked, his confidence apparently cracked by the wailing of the bagpipes. "It sounds like there's a regiment out there!"

"Oh, nay. They'd ne're send sae many," Flora said quite seriously. "A dozen, purhaps—nae more."

Leslie gave a wry grin. "A dozen or a regiment, it makes no difference, darling. I can't fight that many. And I doubt that I could slip you past them in your tartan. They'll be watching everyone who gets off the train."

"True," Dorcas said, straightening her bonnet and giving her borrowed skirt a quick shake to smooth the creases out of it. "But there are two of us here in tartan, and the MacAllisters will only be expecting one."

Flora's eyes flew wide. "Oh, Dorie—ye wouldna!"

"I most certainly would! It's already been commented that we could almost be sisters. Of course, you're a good deal prettier, but the MacAllisters have only your portrait to go by—they've never actually seen you."

And a man who would marry a girl he's never seen can't be that choosy, anyway, she added silently to her-

8

self, pulling on her gloves and collecting her large purse.

Disliking deceit in any form, she was not especially enthralled by the prospect of the switch. But it was a question of the lesser of two evils. Just like when her aunt's tragic death a year before had left her penniless and she had nearly lost a well-paying position because the service agency wouldn't hire anyone under twenty-one. In that instance, it had been either tack several years onto her age or starve. In this one, the choice seemed as obvious: either a few hours of embarrassment for herself or a lifetime of misery for Flora and Leslie. Once she'd reached that decision, an earthquake wouldn't have been able to jar her loose from it. That was another of Dorcas Jeffries's habits that her aunt had never been able to cure: pigheaded stubbornness.

She paused an instant to listen. "It sounds as though they're near the front platform. That's the one I shall use. You two will have to disembark at the rear, but give me a few moments' lead before you do. I'll need to draw them away."

"No!" Leslie Armstrong had moved quickly to block her exit from the compartment. "This is very noble of you, I'm sure, Miss Jeffries, but a gentleman can hardly allow a young lady to endanger herself on his behalf. You don't know what they might do to you at that castle!"

"Really, Captain Armstrong, I have no intention of playing this charade that far. I shall never even see their horrid old castle. I appreciate your concern, but I assure you, I am quite capable of looking after myself," Dorcas said, meeting his rigid gaze with iron in her own. "Now kindly move aside."

He crossed his arms solidly in front of his chest. "Absolutely not."

"Leslie is right, dear. We canna let ye do this."

Dorcas resisted the urge to stamp her foot. "Good heavens, Lady Flora, it's not as though I intend to *marry* the man! I'm simply going to distract them long enough for you and Captain Armstrong to get safely away. Do you two want to elope or don't you? We're running out of time."

"Time? Why th' time be near eight o' th' mornin'. . . . Who asks?" a heavy voice said from the corridor just outside.

" 'Tis too late!" Flora squeaked, and promptly fainted again.

Leslie tried to catch her but was sent sprawling as the compartment's door burst open and a haystack in a short plaid skirt muscled its way into the small chamber.

Oh, not a skirt. It was a kilt, Dorcas mentally corrected herself.

"C-cousin Alan?" she stammered out.

The haystack glared fiercely down at her, glanced at Flora and Leslie slumped motionless together on the floor, then fixed his bushy-browed gaze back on Dorcas. A big, beaming smile split open between beard and mustache.

"Florie MacAllister, I'd ken ye anywhere!" he roared. "Welcome tae yoor new home, lassie! Th' bonny bridegroom couldna come t'day. I be yoor Uncle Angus!"

Thank heaven for small favors, Dorcas thought as she fought for air in his rib-cracking hug. At least this wasn't Alan. . . . Though perhaps Alan would be worse? . . . She shoved that idea completely out of her head. Right now she had to get Uncle Angus off the train before the good captain and Lady Flora regained their senses (and herself along with them—in a different sort of way). Already Leslie had started to twitch and moan a bit. She watched in horror out of the corner of her eye as his lids fluttered open and he dazedly began to sit up.

"Uncle Angus, 'tis fair squeezin' the breath oot o' me, ye be," she giggled, neatly twisting out of his burly embrace and dropping her heavy traveling purse at the same

10

instant. It landed squarely on Armstrong's head. "Ah, th' poor laddie," she said, as his eyes closed and he slumped forward once more. " 'Tis exhausted he mun be."

"Aye," Angus agreed, glancing briefly downward. "Who be they, Florie dear?"

"I dinna ken fer sure," Dorcas lied, batting large, innocent eyes up at him. "They only boarded th' stop afore this one an' we had such a wee time fer speech."

Angus's eyes narrowed suddenly, drawing his brows together into one big, fuzzy, blond caterpillar creeping across his forehead. "Th' lassie wears MacAllister tartan!" he exclaimed.

"Oh, aye." Dorcas quickly laughed. "Th' poor dearie was splashed by a carriage just afore boardin' an' she hadna anuther gown, sae I made her take one o' me own."

"Ah, now there be a MacAllister fer ye—generous tae th' core!" Angus boomed. "Come alang now, Florie dear. Me lads be fair hoppin' oota their kilts tae see ye."

"Aye, Uncle Angus." Dorcas beamed up at him.

I must be completely mad, she thought to herself, following his broad back off the train.

"They're mad!" A disheveled tartan-clad feminine fury stormed to the opposite end of the dim, dusty chamber, flailing cobwebs out of her flushed face as she went.

"All of them—mad!" She fumed back to the thick wood door, kicking through a pile of ancient straw on her way and startling a family of rodents.

"Every last man Jack of them—completely and utterly stark raving *Mad*!" Grabbing the door's heavy iron handle with both hands, she braced her feet, threw her weight backwards, and tugged with all her might.

It refused to budge.

Which was pretty much what she had expected, since she had already tried to open it eleven times and had gotten exactly the same result with each effort. She hadn't been able to resist a twelfth attempt, however, just in case it wasn't actually locked, but merely stuck, and a really solid pull would jar it loose. A fancy born of desperation, of course, because she knew well and good that the horrid door to this horrid tower prison was horridly locked. She had very clearly heard its horrid latch scraping horridly into place when they had thrown her in there barely thirty horrid minutes before.

It took two of them to do it, though, Dorcas mused, studying the blood under her fingernails—none of it her own. That was some satisfaction, at least. The tartan gown was rather the worse for the tussle, her long hair had tumbled loose and was probably looking like a banshee's at the moment, but other than that—and a few definite dents in her pride—she was basically intact, she supposed . . . so far.

Which was more than anyone would be able to say for Duncan and Douglas. Or had it been Donald and Dunstan who had imprisoned her up here? Douglas and Donald, perhaps? . . . Dorcas shook her disheveled head. Angus's four sons all looked so alike, how could anyone be expected to tell them apart? Probably it made no difference. They were four peas in a pod—all insane, like their father. Some kind of congenital defect, obviously. Only insane people could be thinking what they were.

After all, they knew the truth now. She had admitted who she was long before they had come within sight of this adobe monstrosity. She'd had to hold off a while, naturally, to ensure Captain Armstrong and Lady Flora an adequate head start, but she hadn't waited a moment longer than necessary. Scarcely three hours out of Abilene, she had told all. It had been right as they were passing that other wagon, the one with the pleasant-looking Mexican family. It had seemed such a providential time, because, once the MacAllisters realized she wasn't Flora, they certainly wouldn't want her anymore, and she should have been able to beg a return ride to Abilene with the Mexicans.

Except . . .

"Ah, well, wha' canna be cured mun be endured," Angus had said with a shrug after listening silently to the confession.

"Thank you so much for your understanding, Mr. MacAllister," Dorcas had said, twisting around in the wagon seat, straining to see whether the Mexican family was still within earshot. The explanation had taken far longer than she had intended. "I must say, you're being very gracious about this."

Where was that other wagon? That couldn't be it, could it? That pinprick on the horizon?

"Oh, dear." She had turned back toward Angus. "I'm terribly sorry about this, but I'm afraid I'm going to have to ask you to drive me back to Abilene."

"Why?" He had flashed her a big, toothy grin. "Florie oor Dorie—'tis such a wee dif'rence. Dinna ye fear, lassie. Alan'll still wed ye."

A high-button shoe stomped furiously onto the filthy wood floor. *But I've no intention of wedding Alan!* Dorcas raged inwardly. *I don't care if he's Prince Charming himself, I don't even want to meet the man!*

The truth of the matter was, she had no intention of wedding anyone. Ever! Her aunt Matilda had always preached that marriage was little better than slavery for women. Dorcas wasn't sure if that was entirely correct; she had known some girls who seemed to be quite contented in their chains. But they were generally the type of Lady Flora—girls who hadn't much stored in their attics, so to speak. She agreed with Matilda Jeffries that she, herself, was not especially well suited for it.

"You are too intelligent and far too independent to

tolerate such a union," she could almost hear her aunt's voice saying. "For you, Dorcas, marriage would feel like being nibbled to death by ducks—a slow torture. Leave it to the girls who can think of nothing else to do with their lives. You will be far better satisfied if you forge your own way in the world, as I have."

"Right," Dorcas answered aloud, moving determinedly away from the locked door. "But the only way I'm interested in right now is whatever way will get me out of here!"

Stopping in the center of the circular tower room, she peered about, trying hard to determine her options, and harder to ignore the fact that there didn't seem to be any. Except for the gloom, the must, and the dust—of which there was plenty—the cell was practically bare. Nothing but one heavy door with a small iron grating letting in scant light from the passage beyond . . . one narrow, deep-set window letting in a bit more from the nearly full moon outside . . . one torch in a wall bracket, offering no light at all, because it was unlit . . . one comforting manacle dangling from a short chain in the wall (the comfort being that it wasn't dangling from her) . . . one foul-smelling heap of straw . . . one small, scarred wood table . . . Was that all?

But there had to be *something* here. Something she had missed. Something she could use.

Swallowing down anger, frustration, and rising panic, she forced herself to make another deliberate inventory. Table. Straw. Manacle. Torch. Window. Cat. Door . . .

Cat?

She rushed to the window. There on the floor below it, stately and dignified, like a king holding court, sat the biggest, blackest, most magnificent tomcat she had ever seen. He was almost too beautiful to be real.

"Why, you marvelous creature," she breathed, carefully dropping to her knees before him. "Wherever did you come from? I'm sure you weren't here a moment ago."

The cat stared solemnly up at her through large golden eyes as she slowly reached a hand out to him. He sniffed her fingers, rather with the air of a courtier kissing a damsel's hand, and then began a deep bass purr while she stroked between his ears.

"I wish you could show me how you got in," she said. "Because maybe I could get out the same way."

Instantly, the cat stood up, gave a long, regal stretch, and leaped neatly into the window crevice.

"Oh, now don't tell me you came in through there." She shook her head at him. "We must be at least three stories high. Did you scale the tower, or simply fly? I don't see any wings on your back."

"Nor I on yours. And I thought angels always had wings," said a low voice behind her.

Her heart in her throat, Dorcas whirled about to confront a tall, lanky man in his early thirties lounging against the closed door and studying her with obvious amusement. He was fair-haired, like most of the Mac-Allisters, but he spoke with a distinctly American accent and wore trousers instead of a kilt. Which meant—she allowed herself a discreet sigh of relief—he wasn't Alan.

"Who were you talking to just now?" he asked.

The fellow might not be Alan, but he was someone with an apparent vision problem. Dim the cell might be, but her feline visitor was hard to miss.

"The cat, of course," she answered warily. "Don't you see him?"

"I'm afraid not."

"But you must." She glanced over her shoulder and suffered a sudden, weird tingle down her spine. "Oh! It . . . it's not there anymore."

"Well, don't let it trouble you," he drawled slowly.

Though Dorcas wasn't sure exactly what he meant by

it—the cat's disappearance, or the fact that she had seen it when he had not. Either way, she didn't particularly care for the man's tone, nor the idea that he had somehow gotten into the cell without her hearing him.

"Who are you?" she demanded.

"At the moment, I rather wish I was Alan." He grinned, and she found herself not caring much for that, either.

Her eyes slid over him like a glacier. "No, you don't," she told him.

Her reply broadened his grin. "Perhaps you're right. I saw what you did to Duncan and Dunstan. I'm Simon Elliott," he offered, looking as though he thought the name might mean something to her. When it obviously didn't, he gave a slight shrug and continued a bit cryptically, "You could call me a . . . a friend of the Mac-Allisters. I'm engaged in some . . . well, let's just say some research here at the castle. Among other things, I'm studying old Highland customs," he added with another irritating grin. "Angus has been telling me all about you, Miss Jeffries. A fascinating situation you've landed yourself in, I must say."

"I'm so glad you find it amusing."

Her expression, which must have looked anything but glad, seemed merely to increase his amusement.

"Oh, come now, buck up." He chuckled. "I'm sure things aren't nearly as bad as you think they are."

"How would you know?" she asked, deliberately turning her back on him.

"I'm a wizard. Wizard's know everything."

Marvelous. He was insane, too.

"Look at it this way. Perhaps, when you two finally meet, Alan will decide that he doesn't care for you—as unlikely as that seems. Or you may decide that you *do* care for him," Elliott suggested amiably. "I don't, of course. He's a little too odd for me."

Dorcas gave a strangled laugh as she spun back to him. *"All* the MacAllisters are *odd!"*

"Perhaps," Simon agreed lightly. "But Laird Alan is the oddest of the lot."

Double marvelous.

"Did you climb all the way up here just to tell me that?" she asked icily.

"I came to cheer you up," he replied warmly.

"Well, I'm sorry to inform you of this, Mr. Elliott, but you have been *anything* but cheering."

"How unfortunate. I must try to do better." He grinned, stooping to retrieve a black wood box from the floor near his feet. "See? I've brought you a gift to brighten your stay here. It's one of my latest toys."

Curiosity driving back her distress for a moment, Dorcas reached for it. It was a little heavier than she had expected from its size, and it had a glass globe covering a wire coil sticking out of its top.

"How do you work it?"

Her interest appeared to please him. "Place it on the table and I'll show you."

When it was positioned, Elliott touched something on its back with one hand while flourishing the other in the air, declaring, "Let there be light!"

And there was. While she stood blinking in the glare of it, he quickly and quietly left.

"I told you I was a wizard," she heard him whisper just before the lock clicked back into place.

"Yes, and I'm Cleopatra," Dorcas muttered, unable to take her eyes off the contraption. What an annoying man. Rather ingenious, though. This was a very serviceable electric lantern. It was smaller than the one Mr. Edison of New Jersey had come up with a few years earlier, but it produced even more illumination. The compact size with the increased brightness, in fact, were two of the improvements her aunt had been trying to perfect right before she died. If Dorcas had been older at the time and had had the funding to continue the work, she might have devised something like this herself. But the investors had been appalled. A woman scientist had been dubious enough—regardless of her sterling credentials— but a girl?

She shook her head. There had been nothing to do but lie her way into a decently paid position with that prestigious service agency, ignore the foibles of the wealthy women she companioned, and plan for the day when she had enough money saved to continue her aunt's research. It was a bit aggravating, naturally, to realize that someone had beaten her to the punch on this lighting device, but modifying Mr. Edison's idea had only been one of Aunt Matilda's lesser projects. Everyone and his brother had been working on the same problem, it seemed. And there were so many more interesting and original discoveries waiting to be made.

"I'll never get a chance at any of them, though, unless I get out of here!" the girl fumed aloud. Reaching around the back of the box—obviously some sort of power storage unit—she felt for the trigger . . . ah, there—a small lever. She flipped it, and the bright glow popped out with a distinct crackle.

"That didn't sound good. The voltage is unstable," she muttered. "You had better be careful with your toys, Mr. Elliott. I don't believe you're quite as clever as you think you are."

Something nudged the side of her foot. She jumped, sure that it was one of the members of the rat colony from the straw, and then began laughing with relief. "Oh, you're back, are you? Where did you disappear to before?"

The black cat stared unblinkingly up at her and gave a long, resonant yowl.

"Goodness! You sound just like an alarm siren, and I

entirely agree. This predicament *is* alarming. But what can I do? I know it seems absurd, but I'm like one of those fairy-tale damsels in distress. Complete with an imprisonment in a genuine towered fortress." Kneeling by the cat, Dorcas stroked him from the top of his satin head to the tip of his long tail, his purr rumbling like a steam engine at full throttle.

"I don't suppose you know of any knights in shining armor who could come to my rescue, do you? You'd think a castle this size would have at least one Sir Lancelot or Galahad . . . or a Robin Hood, perhaps?" She sank back on her heels. "Right now I'd even settle for Friar Tuck."

Studying her intently, the cat yowled again and leapt onto the table. He sniffed the lantern, arched his back, and gave a ferocious hiss.

"Yes, I agree with you there, too. Mr. Elliott won't be any help. I'd already discarded that possibility myself. Any other ideas?—Oh! Be careful, you might hurt yourself!"

Her four-footed confidant had just lashed out and batted the lantern clean off the table. The glass globe shattered and the box split open, spilling wires and coils all over the dusty floor. Dorcas stared at the mess, her eyes suddenly like two full moons. There, in the center of the jumble, was what must have caused the unstable current. A long, curious iron key . . . The key to her prison? The key to her freedom?

She looked at the cat, sitting motionless in the center of the table like a big, furry black Buddha. "Oh, my," she breathed. "Do you think we could possibly have misjudged Mr. Elliott?"

The feline's only answer was to abruptly leap off the table, snatch the key in his mouth, and dart pell-mell across the cell.

"*No!* Bring that back!" She raced after him, but he

had already disappeared through the narrow recessed window. "I thought you were my friend!"

She could almost have sat down and cried, but that certainly wouldn't have solved anything. So she found herself, instead, sliding into the window crevice after him. Due to the thick walls of the tower, it was nearly three feet deep and a bit of a squeeze, but she thought she could manage it. *However is he getting up and down from here, anyway?* she was wondering as she did so.

"Heavens, what a monstrous tree! Why didn't I notice that before?" she asked aloud, staring in fixed fascination at the massive branches grazing the outside of the tower.

"Because you didn't check the window before, you nitwit," she answered herself.

It was true. The window was so deep set that it was difficult to see out of it unless one actually climbed into it. And she had known that she was too high to make escape that way a possibility, so she simply hadn't bothered to look. Also, she just happened to have an absolutely ghastly horror of heights. It was the one habit her aunt had never even tried to cure her of, because Aunt Matilda happened to be horrified of heights, too.

Probably an inherited trait, Dorcas mused, clutching the adobe sill with a white-knuckled death grip and trying desperately not to be sick as she peered out into the April spring leaves. There sat the cat among them, just out of reach, with the key jutting jauntily out of the corners of his mouth and what appeared to be a highly amused expression in his large amber eyes.

"Oh, you think this is funny, do you? Don't you dare yowl and drop it, you little imp! Bring it here to me," she ordered.

He stood upon his branch, stretched, and casually padded a few steps toward her.

"That's right—that's a good boy—come here—one more step—come on, angel," she coaxed. "Oh! You naughty little devil!" she hissed as he abruptly spun and flitted back the way he'd come.

Key in mouth, he strolled about the nearest branches, pausing here and there to sharpen his claws, stopping occasionally to level that warm, golden gaze on her. "I'll give you the key if you'll come here," he seemed to be saying. "Come on, it's perfectly safe. Look at me. It's easy."

It's insane, Dorcas thought. *The whole situation is insane. This castle is insane. The MacAllisters are insane. The cat's insane. . . .*

"And I am the most insane of all! Oh, how I hate heights," she groaned, sliding herself through the open window.

It was a heart-stopping scramble from the sill to the first branch. Dorcas never was quite sure how she accomplished it, because she had her eyes squeezed shut during the whole process. A crowbar wouldn't have been able to pry them open. When she finally did dare look, there was the cat sitting two branches below and staring encouragingly up at her, as if to say, "You did that very well—for a human."

"Thank you," she said. "Now may I *please* have that key?"

"No. I've changed my mind," he said. "It's a cat's *purr-ogative,* you know."

At least, that was the way Dorcas interpreted his response. What he actually had done was turn his back to her and leap down four more branches.

"He's right," she realized, gazing mournfully from the cat to the window and back again. "I couldn't possibly steel myself to climb back up there, even if I wanted to return to that wretched room. The lesser of the two evils is to continue the way I'm going." The branches were large and sturdy and there were plenty of them. With the worst part behind her, she supposed it wouldn't be too terrifying to make it the rest of the way down.

She managed it surprisingly well, in fact (for a dyed-in-the-wool acrophobe who was certain she was going to pass out and plummet to her death at any second), except that the tree seemed to have developed a distinct hankering for her skirts. Anything the branches could catch on, they caught. And ripped. Leaving pieces of fabric fluttering festively among the new spring leaves like gay tartan streamers.

She tried not to think about it—it was too embarrassing—but by the time she had made it to the lowest branches she was down to hardly more than her corset, corset cover, plain white cotton drawers, and high button shoes. Even her modest black stockings had been shredded mostly away. Her long gold hair spilled wildly about her shoulders; she was scratched, bruised, hot, flushed . . .

And extremely perturbed when she reached the final position, where the cat sat waiting for her, and discovered that there were still nearly five yards between herself and the ground. Fifteen feet to go and no more branches. *Marvelous.*

"All right," she complained to the nonplused feline, "you got me into this. Now tell me how I'm supposed to get the rest of the way down."

Blinking his enigmatic eyes at her, he swiveled, crouched, and sprang, landing easily near the base of the giant trunk.

"Yes, I was afraid you'd suggest something like that." Dorcas sighed. "But are you sure that's the only possible way? I mean really, *really* sure?"

He stared silently up at her for a moment, pointed ears on alert, swishing his tail from side to side, then turned quickly (the now useless key still in his mouth), darted around the tree, and was lost to view.

"I guess that means he's sure," she muttered to herself,

shaking off a brief, uncanny feeling that she was, somehow, being observed. It was impossible, of course; there
wasn't a soul in sight. "I could call for help," she continued muttering. "But that would rather defeat the entire
purpose of an escape." Not to mention that whoever
came would find her in little more than her undergarments.

"I think I'd rather take my chances with the jump,"
she finally decided. It might prove fatal, but if anyone
saw her like this, she would undoubtedly die of embarrassment anyway. So, drawing a deep breath and clamping her eyes shut, Dorcas Jeffries leaned forward, let go
of her branch, and dropped—

Straight into a waiting pair of solidly muscled arms.

Her eyes flew open and the scream that had just been
about to burst past her lips shriveled instantly in a
scorching blaze of shock. She was too startled even to
breathe, let alone make a sound. The arms that had
caught her were attached to a . . . well, not a Mac-
Allister, at any rate. She supposed she ought to be grateful for that. But . . . The girl blinked.

A Comanche?

The Comanches *were* the people who had once
roamed this part of Texas, weren't they? She had
thought they had all been moved onto reservations, but
one, at least, had stayed. That much seemed definite, because it was obviously a Comanche warrior who was
holding her.

A Comanche with cleanly chiseled, motionless features and warm, tanned skin. A Comanche with thick
black hair grazing what would have been his collar if
he'd been wearing a shirt. A tall, powerful Comanche in
the prime of manhood, with shoulders like a gladiator's
and deep amber eyes. Eyes that were fixed on her with
the solemn, penetrating gaze of a cat. They seemed to be
boring straight into her soul. It was worse than distract-

ing. It felt weirdly intimate, almost invasive somehow.

He was holding her so closely, she was uncomfortably aware of every hard-muscled contour of his broad, bare chest, and the heat of his flesh pressing into her own was sending the most ineffable tingles shivering through her. Dorcas had never felt anything like them before, and she wasn't at all sure that she relished the sensation.

"Th-thank you," she finally managed to choke out. "I-I'm extremely indebted to you, b-but do you think you could put me down now?"

The Comanche apparently did not think so. All he did was shift her even closer, sending a fresh, hot wave of those disturbing tingles washing over her.

Oh! Perhaps he doesn't understand, she suddenly thought.

"Down. You—put—me—down." She spoke very distinctly, pointing to him, herself, and the ground.

"Are you sure you're able to stand?"

Dorcas almost laughed with relief. He did speak English! Quite well, in fact, in a rich, husky baritone, with just a subtle touch of some nebulous accent. "Yes, yes, I'm fine," she assured him. "Thank you, but it really is all right for you to . . . Really, I'm . . . fine . . ."

What was he doing? He had stopped listening and appeared to be engrossed in studying every inch of her rapidly flaming exposed skin, shifting her this way and that in his arms as though she were no more than a rag doll. A very confused and extremely unnerved rag doll.

"You've a lot of scratches," he announced, abruptly capturing her eyes again. "Not serious, I think, but they should be cleansed. I'll take you where they can be seen to."

"No!" Dorcas squealed, as he began carrying her toward the castle's towering main keep. "Please, not there!"

He halted in midstep, looking down at her with a slight frown. "Why not?"

"Because I can't let any of the MacAllisters see me!"

The frown deepened. "Aren't you a MacAllister?"

What? He thought she was . . . Well, it was understandable, she supposed. She did have the MacAllister coloring. And probably, to an Indian, all white people looked alike, anyway.

"Oh, perish the thought," she said with a shudder, and explained her predicament as quickly and coherently as possible, considering the circumstances. The Comanche's eyes never left her face and his smooth carved expression never changed.

"So, you see," she finished a little breathlessly, "it's imperative that I escape. Quickly! If you'll help me, I'll pay you whatever you ask."

"A tempting offer," the man said, staring down at her with a curious, unreadable look in his dark amber eyes. "But you should be careful about agreeing to a price before you hear what it is. You can never be sure what a person might . . . *propose.*"

"I don't have time for bartering right now!" she snapped, not taking the time, either, to wonder why she was so willing to trust this stranger. Not considering that she was, possibly, grabbing at straws, and not worrying that he might turn out to be as stable as a loose straw in a stiff wind. In simple desperation, she grabbed at him because there were too many miles of wild, open country between herself and Abilene.

Whoever he was and whatever he was doing at the castle, it seemed obvious that he wasn't one of *them*. If he had been allied with the MacAllisters, he'd have thrown her back to them already, wouldn't he? Much as her independent spirit chafed at the realization, she honestly did need some sort of knight-errant to help rescue her. And the Comanches were sort of like knights, weren't they, with their horses and long war lances? Gazing at his smooth, tanned skin, Dorcas imagined she could almost see the sheen of polished armor over it.

"Please! There's no telling how long I have before they discover I'm not in the tower. And the moment they do, they'll come searching for me. I have to be well away from here by then!" she said urgently. "Won't you help me? *Please?*"

That unfathomable amber gaze locked onto hers, holding her firmer, even, than the powerful arms locked about her slender, tense form.

"And you'll pay me whatever I ask?"

She forced herself to meet his stare unblinkingly.

"I promise."

The Comanche gave a short, low whistle and, out of nowhere, it seemed, trotted a giant gray Appaloosa stallion, snorting and shaking his head. There was nothing on him save a blanket and a simple leather halter.

Dorcas gulped. She wasn't sure exactly what she had hoped for, but this wasn't it. "I . . . I'm sorry. I do ride, but I'd never be able to handle *him.*"

For the first time since she had dropped out of the tree and into his embrace, the savage smiled. "Not to worry." He winked. "I *can.*"

With one fluid motion, he tossed her onto the stallion's back and leapt up behind her, immediately spurring past the kitchens and several other low buildings toward the rear of the castle's great inner courtyard. "We'll use the postern gate. I left it open when I rode in tonight," he called just a moment before they cleared the opening in the back of the massive bailey wall.

"What about the moat?" Dorcas gasped, seeing instantly that there was only a narrow footbridge spanning it at that point.

For answer, her knight-errant simply spurred his charger faster.

The moat was nearly twelve feet wide and waterless, due to the dry climate, but Dorcas had already determined that its bottom and sides were studded with long, deadly sharp, daggerlike stakes. Her eyes huge with horror, she watched it rushing toward them. He couldn't possibly be planning what she thought he was, was he? . . . She felt the Appaloosa gathering itself.

Oh, God—he was!

"Hold tight!" the Comanche shouted.

It was an absurd waste of breath. A dynamite blast couldn't have loosened her grip as they soared through the air and landed with a jolt on the opposite side of the moat. A second lunatic leap and they were flying over the outer palisade. The stallion never even broke stride as his hooves struck earth, but thundered off across the wild moonlit prairie like a giant, dappled bat straight out of the jaws of Hades.

Merciful heavens! He's a madman, too, Dorcas thought, fighting to regain her breath. She had a sudden mental image of something being thrown from a frying pan into the fire.

The something was her.

And the fire was in the Comanche's glittering amber eyes . . .

"We'll need to stop here," he finally said, some immeasurable distance later, as their mount slowed to a canter, then a trot, and finally an agitated walk. He pulled the animal to a halt by the side of a small spring, jerking the stallion's head up when it stretched toward the water.

"Why did you do that?" Dorcas demanded. "He's thirsty!"

"I don't doubt it. He'll get a drink as soon as he's cooled off," the savage said, jumping lithely to the ground and lifting her down beside him. "That spring is

27

fed from deep underground and the water is cold. If I let him drink now, it could make him sick."

"Oh," she said, quickly backing a few steps away. It had seemed to her that her rescuer's hands had lingered on her just a little too long when he'd lowered her off the horse. As much as she appreciated his help, his way of offering it was beginning to grate on her nerves. "I wish he could be solicitous without being so . . . so *tactile* about it," she muttered under her breath, watching warily as he harvested a handful of tall, dry grasses and used it to wipe down the stallion's froth-speckled flanks. Then, with a sharp slap, he sent the animal trotting off.

"Don't worry, he won't stray far from the water," he said, turning to Dorcas. "What was that you just said?"

Drat the man—he must have ears like a fox.

"Um . . . I was only asking if I should wait to drink, too," she improvised, instantly lowering her eyes.

"A few more minutes might be wise. We can use the time to bathe your scratches."

Her eyes flew back to his. *"We?"*

"You can't reach the ones on your back," he pointed out.

And for the second time since she had met him, the Comanche smiled. But to Dorcas, it suddenly looked like the hungry grin of a wolf.

"My back can wait until I reach Abilene," she said, turning that part of her anatomy toward him.

"Did you know there's a great rip in the seat of your drawers?"

With a gasp, she spun around again, hastily reaching behind herself. "Oh! You—There is not!"

"I know. I just wanted to make sure I had your attention," he replied, his expression abruptly turning to stone. "There's something we need to discuss before riding any farther."

"What?" Her own expression was beginning to take on the quality of a cornered rabbit.

"My payment."

"Oh, but I can't possibly pay you now! I thought you realized that." She stared up at him in confusion. "I was expecting to wire for funds from Abilene. I have no money with me."

"I wasn't thinking of money."

He flashed her his third smile of the day, and Dorcas suddenly felt as though she was wrapped in ice. Ice so cold it almost burned her. No . . . it was the gleam in his eyes that was burning her. So it had come to this, had it? Her knight had become a dragon? She steeled herself to meet his eyes without wavering.

"What, then? What do you want?" she asked. *As if I don't know,* she thought.

"What do I want in payment?" He took a step forward. "It may surprise you."

"Really?" she said, struggling to keep her voice level. Was the man an idiot? Surely he didn't think she was *that* naïve. "Try it," she added ominously, "and I may surprise *you.*"

He stopped dead in his tracks, threw back his handsome head, and howled with laughter. "Dorcas Jeffries, after seeing you leap out of that tree in your underwear, I doubt there's *anything* you could do that would surprise me!"

It snapped her tense control. An attempted assault was bad enough, but being made fun of was absolutely, positively intolerable. She flew at him like a five-foot, two-inch, hundred-pound freight train, knocking him several steps backward. She fought like a wildcat on wheels. It took him three full minutes to bring her even partly under control. And then another one to wrestle her to the ground.

"I was wrong," he panted, his breath hot on her face,

as she battled beneath him. "You do surprise me."

Dorcas responded by trying to spit at him, but her mouth had gone dry. "Wa-water," she finally croaked and suddenly went limp, as though she had swooned.

She felt his lean, hard torso relaxing against hers, and watched from beneath lowered lashes as his expression changed from suspicion to concern to genuine alarm. Then she was free of his weight and studying his muscular back in the moonlight as he knelt by the spring. When he rose and turned back to her, she was standing there, brandishing his own belt knife before herself like a miniature saber.

The Comanche heaved a long sigh, letting the water in his cupped hands spill onto the parched prairie. "Full of surprises, aren't you?" he said simply. "But enough for now. I'm tired. Give me the knife."

"Try and take it! Just try!"

"If you insist."

The next thing Dorcas knew, the knife was somewhere in the nearby brush and she was snug against the Comanche's solid, naked chest. His arms tightened about her like iron, pulling her completely off her feet and bringing her face level with his own.

"Any other requests?" he whispered, his lips grazing hers.

"Y-yes," she choked, experiencing an intensified replay of those wild, weird tingles she'd felt in his hold under the tree. "P-please don't d-do this."

"Do what?" His lips brushed hers again.

"K-kiss me!" she gasped.

"If you insist."

And his mouth covered hers, sending an electric shiver jolting through her like a lightning bolt. Her whole body went rigid for an instant and then abruptly melted into his, as she, amazingly, found herself kissing him back. Kissing him fervently and full and hard and deep.

30

He released her and she dropped back to earth, staggering slightly as he stepped away. Breathing heavily, he stood there staring at her as if she were a puzzle he couldn't possibly piece together.

"To think I believed there was nothing else you could do to surprise me," he said huskily. "I'm beginning to wonder if there's anything about you that *isn't* a surprise." Spinning on a moccasined heel, he whistled for the stallion. "We'd best go now."

What? He was still *going to take her to Abilene?*

Dorcas watched through a cloudy red haze as the Comanche led his Appaloosa to the spring. Gradually she let her breath and pulse return to normal. Slowly she shook her head. It was impossible to accept what had just happened. *I don't do things like that,* she thought distractedly. *I don't even consider them!* Maybe it was some kind of momentary hallucination?

"I must have hit my skull in the scuffle and imagined the whole thing," she told herself. "I mean, I know I've been up to some foolish business lately, pretending to be Lady Flora and all. But there was a good reason behind that." What possible motive could she have had for . . . for *kissing* him?

At the memory of his lips on hers, her recalcitrant body flooded her with so many reasons, she couldn't suppress a groan.

The reason for the groan glanced over his shoulder at her. "You'd best come drink. 'Tis a dry ride back."

Still dazed, Dorcas walked to the spring. "It never happened. I never did that. I imagined it," she repeated inaudibly over and over, while drinking and splashing cold water on her flushed face and arms.

That's right. You imagined it, a voice confirmed in her mind. *And you'll go on imagining it. If you live to be a hundred, you'll never forget it.*

"Oh, shut up!" she told the voice aloud.

The Comanche looked down at her, an odd expression in his mysterious amber cat eyes. "Who are you arguing with?"

"Myself," she answered testily. "I do it a lot."

His eyebrows rose slightly. "Interesting. You must always win, then."

"No, hardly ever." She sighed. "Can we go now, please?"

The moment they were remounted he swung the stallion's head in the direction from which they had previously galloped.

"Wait a minute!" The girl squirmed around to glare at him, her green eyes flashing like emeralds in the bright moonlight. "This isn't the way to Abilene!"

The arm about her waist tightened. "I know."

"But you promised!"

"So did you. Sit still or you'll startle the horse," he ordered, as she tried to throw herself free.

"This isn't fair," Dorcas fumed, pulling as far away from him as was possible in the short space on the stallion's back.

He yanked her back close against himself, sending a hot flush spiraling through her. "Isn't it? I kept my end of the bargain, didn't I?"

"You did not! You said you'd take me to Abilene!"

"I said I'd help you get away from the castle. And that I did," he corrected. "I never promised not to return you."

Dorcas strained around to glare at him over her shoulder, but all she could see clearly was his firm mouth barely inches from her own. She hastily faced front again.

"You never had any intention of taking me to Abilene," she said tightly. "Why did you go to all the trouble bringing me out here, anyway? Simply to . . . to molest me?"

A low laugh rumbled against her spine. " 'Twas only a kiss, dear. Don't tell me you've never been kissed before."

She clamped her mouth shut, but her sudden trembling gave her away.

"I never would've guessed it," he said more to himself than her. "One more surprise."

"Let me off this horse," she said darkly.

The arm about her hardened into hot steel.

"Let me off this instant! Or . . . or I'll spur him into that ravine ahead and kill all three of us!"

The Comanche laughed. "He can jump that ravine."

As her trembling spilled over into frustrated sobs, Dorcas was suddenly angrier with herself than she was with her captor. This was mortifying.

"Whoa." The Comanche reined them to a halt. "Listen, lass," he said, wrapping both arms warmly about her and lowering his head close to hers. "I'll admit 'twas a bit of folly to ride you off the way I did. You were so anxious to be rescued, I . . . I'm afraid I just couldn't resist." His voice purred softly against her ear. "But my intentions at the spring were honorable. I simply wanted to . . . propose something, you might say. You never gave me the chance to explain what."

"So explain now!" she snapped, her tears evaporating in the heat of a new anger.

"Later," he said. "You're too miffed now, I think, to give me the answer I—"

"Miffed?" Dorcas practically strangled on the word. "I'm a good deal more than *miffed*," she ground out, pulling uselessly against his snug hold. "Do you think I *like* the idea of being locked in a rat's nest? Because I promise that's what will happen if you don't let me go right *now!*"

"And if that's all that's bothering you, *I* can promise you'll not be shut in the tower again." He chuckled.

"*How?* How can *you* promise me anything?" she blazed back, straining around once more to glare at him. "Why should you even care? What difference is it to you whether I return to the castle or not?" she demanded. "Who *are* you?"

The Comanche answered by suddenly spurring the stallion forward into a furious gallop.

"I'm the laird of the castle!" he declared over the thunder of the hooves. "I'm Alan MacAllister—your future husband!"

Chapter Two

A battalion of water, wind, and hail blasted against Castle MacAllister's thick adobe walls and ripped through the great courtyards, shrieking like all the fiends of Hell out on a bloody warpath. It sounded like the end of the world.

Which was right in keeping with Dorcas's mood as she huddled in the center of a big four-poster bed listening to the assault. This was her second night in the fortress and she was depressingly wide awake, having spent her first night and most of the following day sleeping like a drugged person.

In fact, she was irritably certain that she *had* been drugged—probably just after the impossible lord of the place had carried her in and left her. It couldn't have been done before that, of course, because she had been kicking and screaming too much. Not that she had believed fighting would do her any good—the man was too

35

strong to escape—but she had seen no reason to make it easy for him.

There could have been some tasteless drug in the water, she speculated. Or, perhaps, a topical narcotic in the salve that little maid had brought for her scratches.

Whatever had caused her slumber, Dorcas had only the sketchiest impressions of the past twenty-four hours. She knew there had been people hovering over her at intervals. Chambermaids, she thought, but she couldn't really recall anything about them. There had been the queerest dreams, too. But she couldn't remember much of those either—except that they had been unsettling enough to make her grateful she couldn't remember them. And once she had awoken briefly to find the black cat curled up beside her. Though he wasn't there now, she noted, pulling herself upright and glancing around. An oil lamp burned low on a table beside the bed, bouncing weird shadows everywhere, but there were no cats hiding in them.

She was in a different room, a large, handsomely furnished chamber on a lower level of the keep. They hadn't shut her back in the prison tower, thank goodness. Alan had kept his word about that, at least. Not that she would trust him on anything else. Mr. Elliott had been right. Of all the odd MacAllisters, Laird Alan was definitely the oddest. To say nothing of the most aggravating, Dorcas thought, slipping out of bed and padding across the room. She had to see if the door was locked. After all, Alan had promised she wouldn't be shut back in the tower, but he hadn't promised not to imprison her elsewhere. And she had learned something about Alan MacAllister's promises. They were a lot like her favorite Swiss cheese—tempting, but loaded with holes.

She gave a small gasp when the heavy beamed door creaked open; it was so unexpected. But then she realized the reason. Her captor knew he didn't need to lock her in a single room; the entire castle was her prison. Even if she could find her way out of the keep, through the inner and outer courtyards, and scale the massive bailey wall, there was still the moat to cross and the outer palisade to get over. A classic medieval-style castle like this was one of the most efficient fortresses ever designed. Before the invention of gunpowder, a scant handful of men could have held such a place against almost any enemy save starvation, because it was virtually impenetrable. Which meant, unfortunately, that it would also be virtually impossible to escape.

"I couldn't try it in this storm, anyway." Dorcas sighed. "I may be desperate, but I'm not stupid."

Turning bleakly away from the door, she also realized how famished she was. Thirsty, too, but she wasn't about to drink from the jug on the table, just in case it was the water that had been drugged.

And that was another concern: *Why* had they drugged her? Simply to keep her quiet? Or had there been a more devious intent? Either way, it was a decidedly disconcerting form of manipulation. Of course, the MacAllisters lived in a different world, with a different set of rules from hers. Perhaps drugging a captive bride was an old Highland custom, she thought sarcastically, exploring the rest of the chamber with one aggravated, sweeping gaze.

It stopped on a small steamer trunk nestled against a wall, and Dorcas let out a second sigh, this time one of relief—a little relief, at any rate. They had returned her previously confiscated luggage. That was something, she supposed. It would be comforting to wear her own sensible clothes again after all those days in Lady Flora's annoying tartans . . . the tartans that had gotten her mired in this mess.

"I hope she and Leslie made it away safely. I'd hate to think I'm going through this for nothing," Dorcas mused aloud, and then caught her breath, the image of lovely Flora having given her an inspiration. Perhaps the MacAllisters were actually viewing her *as* Lady Flora. Sort of a six-of-one, half-a-dozen-of-another situation. When they saw her in her true colors, they might lose interest. After all, they had no idea what a severe little plain Jane she really was.

"Laird Alan," she announced softly, "I believe I have another surprise for you."

Opening the trunk, she frowned suddenly, muttering, "Honestly! If they had to search my things, the least they could have done was put them back properly." She quickly rummaged through the jumble, looking for one of her high-necked shirtwaists and sedate dark skirts.

"What the . . . These aren't my clothes! These are all . . ." Her voice was lost in rolls of thunder as she pulled out piece after piece of soft, frilly, frothy, exquisitely feminine apparel—all of it breathtakingly beautiful.

It was Flora's fancy French-made wedding trousseau, ordered and paid for by her Texas kinsmen. The welcoming wardrobe the Scots girl had bragged would be here waiting for her. *How awful.*

Still, one had to wear *something.* Heaving a resigned sigh, Dorcas hurriedly selected undergarments and what appeared to be the most modest of the gowns and dressed herself. It had to be near midnight, but she needed to find food and drink before she fainted from sheer hunger. It had been over a day since her last meal. Snatching a silver-handled brush off the bedside table, she turned up the oil lamp and moved to stand before the dresser's large mirror. A pair of large, luminous green eyes went larger with horror.

"Oh, no," she moaned, staring at her reflection. "I look lovelier than Lady Flora!"

It was true. The gown was an elegantly cut forest-green velvet with a rather provocative neckline, which she had chosen for its dark fabric and long sleeves. Unfortunately, the covering of her arms seemed only to emphasize the dip of the bodice, and the rich color accentuated the alabaster tones of her skin and made her hair look like spun gold.

Grimacing and making all kinds of faces at herself to try to dispel the enchanting image, she yanked the brush through her long locks, pinned them up into a tight bun—which was the most unattractive style she could think of—and stomped out of the chamber in search of sustenance.

It was then she discovered she was not the only soul prowling the castle that wild and storm-tossed night. Groping her way down a dimly lit, narrow passageway, she nudged something with her slippered foot and the something let out an eerie, blood-chilling wail.

"Oh!" Dorcas gasped. "I'm so sorry. Did I hurt you?"

The cat's large eyes glowed up at her like two amber coals. "Just my pride," he seemed to say, making a soft rumbling sound in his throat.

"You naughty boy," she murmured, stooping down to stroke him. "I really should be most annoyed with you over that incident in the tower, but how can I be angry with my only friend here?"

"I'm glad to hear you say so," spoke a low voice just behind her.

Dorcas jumped a foot in the air and whirled around. "Mr. Elliott! You do have a knack for appearing out of nowhere."

"As I told you, Miss Jeffries, I'm a wizard." He gave her a long, slow grin. "My, don't you look stunning tonight. Just like a fairy-tale princess."

"Yes, I know," she grumbled. "Isn't it dreadful?"

His eyebrows sprang up for an instant, then lowered to normal, and he chuckled. "Miss Jeffries, you are a very

39

unique young lady. Most girls would blush over a compliment like that."

"Most girls aren't in my predicament," she snapped. "I don't want to look like a princess. I'm not the princess type. If I have to look like anything out of a fairy tale right now, I'd prefer it to be the ugly old hag."

"Well, cheer up. Most women turn into hags eventually, don't they?" He grinned again.

"What an unpleasant thing to say. Even if it were true—which it's not—I can't afford to wait that long. And furthermore—" she paused for breath—"I do wish you'd stop trying to cheer me up. With cheering like yours, I'd never need anything to depress me."

"Why, Miss Jeffries," the man said, casting baleful gray eyes upon her, "is that any way to speak to a friend? I thought you just said that you couldn't be angry with me."

"I wasn't talking to *you*, Mr. Elliott. I didn't even know you were there," she said irritably. "I was talking to the cat."

"Hmm . . . the cat again. I see," he said slowly, giving her a look that made her feel he was measuring her for a straitjacket.

"Oh, don't tell me you didn't notice him this time, either," she groaned.

"Afraid not." He stared oddly at her for another moment and then seemed suddenly to brush the matter from his mind. "Say, as long as you're up, would you care to see some magic?"

"Only if it involves pulling supper out of a hat. I'm famished."

Simon Elliott chuckled and offered her his arm. "I'm sure I can materialize something for you. And then, perhaps, we'll have a Light Show."

"More electric lanterns?" She glanced up at him, mildly interested.

"Mmmm . . . sort of." He grinned slowly. "But these ones are a bit larger."

A bit? Good heavens, Dorcas thought, awestruck by the scene. These were the largest generators she had ever seen. They stood about fifteen feet high: two thick metal cylinders on wooden bases, capped by giant zinc spheres that were shooting out lightning bolts like a July Fourth fireworks display.

"What feeds them?" She had to shout to make herself heard over their ferocious crackling.

Elliott didn't even bother to shout back, but took her hand and led her to one of the narrow windows of the tower they were in. He pointed out of it to the stormy night sky, punctuated with slashes and flashes of brilliance.

"Lightning?" she mouthed at him.

He nodded, his attractive face looking inordinately pleased at her interest. She started to shout something else, but he gestured for her to wait, then strode over to a small control box and flipped a lever.

"That's better," he said, turning back to her. "The storm outside is loud enough for me at the moment, without having to deal with one in here, too."

"How on earth do you harvest it?" Dorcas asked him, staring at the now quiet behemoths.

"The lightning, you mean? That's the easy part. We've secured a lightning rod to the roof of this tower, with wires leading down from it to Jack and Jill, here. When lightning strikes it, the electricity runs down the wire and into the generators . . . until we let it out, of course."

Hmm . . . yes. That's the next question, isn't it? she thought, gazing curiously at him from under her lashes. What could he be working on that would require such tremendous voltage to power it?

"What are you going to use them for?" she asked.

"We haven't decided." Crossing his arms, he leaned casually against a wall and leveled one of his slow grins at her. "But I imagine we'll come up with something . . . eventually."

She met his grin with a small, knowing one of her own. "I didn't think you'd tell me."

"Oh, come on, Miss Jeffries, be fair." Simon sounded wounded. "You know how it is. Did your aunt spill her beans when she was cooking something big?"

"Never." Dorcas laughed. "And she was always working on something big. There were no small projects as far as Aunt Matilda was concerned. She used to say that the largest breakthroughs often grew from the tiniest seeds of discovery."

"Yes, and one should never discount anything, regardless of how insignificant it might first appear," the man quoted back to her.

Dorcas dropped her gaze beneath his, abruptly washed by a wave of memories—pleasant ones, however. Marvelous Aunt Matilda, so prim and proper, yet so powerfully independent. And such a genius! To say nothing of her drive and her heart. No matter how busy she was with her own work, she never had been able to turn away any of the young hopefuls of the science community who came to her for instruction or advice. The thought of that generous spirit gave her niece a slight twinge of guilt.

"I . . . I'm sorry I didn't recognize you before, Mr. Elliott," she said awkwardly, her eyes flashing back to his. "But so many students visited my aunt; I never could keep track of them all."

"Well, you could hardly be expected to," he said, smiling. "Anyway, I was only there once, and you couldn't have been more than seven or eight at the time."

"I was nine, actually—but only just. It was my birthday, in fact. That's why I should have remembered you," she admitted, unable to suppress a small smile of her own. "When you found out, you jumped the fence into our neighbors' yard and stole an armful of their prize roses for me."

He began chuckling. "Yes, I recall that, now. 'Beautiful blossoms for a beautiful little lady,' I said to you." The chuckling abruptly stopped and his brows shot up. "And you got angry! It quite startled me. Still does, in fact . . . Why don't you like being thought of as a beauty, Miss Jeffries?" he asked softly, letting his gaze drift over her.

"Because I'd rather be appreciated for the contents of my head, than what's on the outside of it," she declared, blushing almost as pink as the long-gone filched flowers. "Men think pretty girls are merely decorations to wear on their arms. They never take them seriously or consider them capable of accomplishing anything worthwhile."

Simon pulled away from the wall and came toward her with an easy, confident gait. "Well, then, let me assure you, Miss Jeffries, that I do appreciate your contents," he drawled, halting only inches from her and grinning. "But I hope you'll forgive me if I can't help admiring your packaging, as well. That gown does suit you, you know."

"Aye. 'Tis good to see how well it suits you, considering the money I had to pay for those frocks," came a low growl from behind them, wiping the grin from Elliott's face and sending him back a step.

"You can't blame a fellow for trying," he murmured to no one in particular.

Her blush flaming scarlet, Dorcas whirled toward the tower's doorway and nearly choked on her own surprise. This *was* the same person, wasn't it? That impossibly handsome face was the same, at any rate. But the rest of him had undergone a remarkable transformation. Remarkably disconcerting.

She battled back a brief—thoroughly illogical, of course—mental flash that she had liked him better as a Comanche. Bare-chested, in leggings, breechclout, and moccasins, he had seemed merely savage. In the civilized dress of a western gentleman, he looked . . . She groped for the right term . . . Sinister! That was it.

The golden brown leather vest accentuated the glitter in his eyes. The crisp white linen shirt accentuated the breadth of his muscular shoulders and chest. And what those form-fitting black trousers accentuated, she didn't even want to think about. *Drat the man! Why couldn't he wear a nice, modestly pleated kilt like his clansmen?*

Whipping up self-righteous indignation before herself like a shield, she bit out, "My, my, if it isn't Big Chief Thief-in-the-Night. I want my own clothes back, chief. You had no right to steal them from me!"

Those glittering amber eyes scarcely blinked. "As the laird of the castle, and your soon-to-be *personal laird,* dear, I'd every right," Alan replied, staring implacably back at her. "And I didn't much care for the cut of your clothes."

"Fine. Then I won't ask you to wear them," she said tartly. "I *do* care for them, however. And, laird or not, you've no authority over me. I'm not a MacAllister. I will never be a MacAllister. And I want my things back. Now!" she insisted, her angry blush climbing up the scale to crimson. "If you don't give them to me, I'll tear this . . . this adobe absurdity apart brick by brick until I find them! Do you hear me?"

"They can probably hear you in Abilene," Alan muttered, his gaze slanting sideways, as though something on the door frame had suddenly caught his attention. "Ah . . ." He cleared his throat. "I can't give them back. They've been burned."

They'd been . . . *"What?"* The crimson blush went

44

purple. "Why you miserable, egotistical, insufferable, thieving—"

"Simon! How can I be expected to concentrate with all this caterwauling? What the devil is going on out h— Good Lord, don't tell me this is the new Dorie everyone has been whispering about? I wouldn't have guessed it if you gave me a million years to try. . . . Dorcas Matilda, you astound me!"

Instantly all color drained from her face. *It couldn't be . . . Here? . . .* On legs suddenly become limp dishrags, the girl turned. A tall, dignified man with graying hair and penetrating green eyes was striding eagerly toward her from the inner door on the other side of the generators.

"Dr. Earnshaw!" she cried, and flung herself into his outstretched arms.

"Oh. You two know each other, do you?" Simon said, with a bit of surprise.

"Matilda?" Alan said, with a snort.

"There, there, no need for tears," the older man kept repeating, his own eyes suspiciously moist as she clung to him. "Stand back, child. Let me have a good look at you. . . . My goodness, can one year make such a difference?" he said wonderingly, holding her at arm's length. "Why, Dorcas Matilda, you look positively charming!" His mouth twisted into a wry grin and he clucked his tongue at her. "Though Matilda would hardly have approved of this gown, you know."

"Believe me, I know. I'm not overly fond of it myself." Dorcas laughed through her tears, suddenly understanding how a person could cry from pure simple joy and relief. Zachary Earnshaw was the classic absentminded professor, but he had also been her aunt's most trusted associate. Surely he could help her out of this dilemma.

"What are you doing here? I tried to find you after the funeral, but no one seemed to know where you'd disappeared to," she said, unable to pull her eyes away from his. He looked exactly like landfall after a long, treacherous trip at sea. "Oh, Dr. Earnshaw, you have no idea how glad I am to see you!"

"The feeling is mutual, child. . . . My goodness, but you've become the image of Matilda," Zachary breathed, his gaze and hands dropping from her at the same time as he turned awkwardly away. "Her death hit me hard, you know. Matilda wasn't only a valued colleague—she was my dearest friend. Philadelphia held too many sad memories for me with her gone. Everywhere I looked, all I could see was her absence," he confessed, turning back with a half shrug and a full sigh. "Perhaps the move out here was a little hasty, but I really wasn't thinking clearly at the time. I just knew I wanted to be near family."

"F-family? . . ." Staring up at him, Dorcas could feel her smile beginning to freeze. "B-but you're an Earnshaw."

"On my father's side, naturally. But my mother's people are MacAllisters," he said, his brows rising slightly, as though he was somehow surprised she hadn't realized that. "It's a large clan, you know."

Her brittle smile froze so hard it cracked and dropped straight off a suddenly ashen face. Dorcas thought she could almost hear the shattering sound it made as it hit the floor.

"Too large," she said hoarsely. She turned like a zombie and glided shakily to the door, only to find her exit blocked by an amber-eyed Rock of Gibraltar in a crisp linen shirt and trousers so tight, she wondered, even in her haze, how he was managing to draw air. Just the painted-on sight of them was making it difficult for her to breathe. Between that and the second regretfully large helping of boiled beef Mr. Elliott had foisted upon her earlier, she couldn't get outside fast enough.

"And where do you think you're going, lassie?"

"The bailey wall. I'm going to hurl myself off the top," Dorcas lied, regretting, also, the second helping of apple custard. "If that doesn't work, I'll try falling into the moat," she said tightly. "That's the nice thing about castles—they offer so many suicide options."

The Rock lounged casually against the door frame, his eyes glittering down at her. "Aren't we being just a wee bit melodramatic?"

"I don't know about you, but I certainly am. It's such an appropriate night for it—what with the storm and all," she half gasped, not sure how much longer her midnight supper would stay in place. "Now you'd really better let me by."

"No. Not if you're going to try something silly."

Good heavens! Couldn't he see she was just . . . just . . .

"I'm not going to be silly. I think I'm going to be sick!" she strangled out, clamping one hand across her midsection and the other over her mouth.

Instantly, Alan grabbed her by the elbow and steered her out into the courtyard. The rain had stopped only moments before and the wind gusted fresh and cool against her flushed skin, quickly blowing the queasiness away and bracing her up.

"Th-thank you. I'm all right now," she said, trying to step out of his hold.

The hands on her arms remained firm, setting her an entirely new problem: how to ignore the electric tingles their grasp was sending through her.

"You're sure? This is an awfully sudden recovery." There was just a hint of suspicion in that rich, husky voice.

Added to everything else, it rankled her nerves. "Yes! I'm fine. Now let go."

With a low laugh, Alan released her arms. Apparently,

just so he could slide his hands around her waist and draw her solidly back into his body. Dorcas's breath caught as his warmth wrapped around her and she felt his chest muscles rippling against her spine.

"Of course now, 'twas a sudden illness, too," he said thoughtfully. "Makes me wonder if you planned it to get me alone."

Her breath whooshed out in an angry rush and she tried first to elbow him in the ribs and then to stomp on his foot. Both blows went haywire.

"Easy, lass." He chuckled softly, spinning her around in his arms so that she was facing him. " 'Twas just a joke," he said, smiling down at her.

Her heart pounding wildly against his, Dorcas glared green daggers up at him. "Well, I'm not laughing. And big chief better takum hands offum pale face squaw before squaw knockum stupid grin offum big chief's face!" she ground out.

His expression darkened and he released her so abruptly, she staggered two paces backward before catching her balance.

"That wasn't funny." The chill in his voice sent an icy shudder down her spine.

She shook it off and drew herself up with all the dignity her slender, trembling frame could muster. "I don't see why not," she said stiffly. "If you can play Comanche, why can't I?"

"Because you're not a Comanche."

"And you are, I suppose?"

"Aye . . . I am." And his gaze dropped before hers.

Dorcas's eyes widened and then narrowed. Around her in the moonlit courtyard, puddles flashed and the tower ramparts loomed like shadowy giants, but all she saw was the tense, muscular figure before her. *Alan MacAllister thought he was a Comanche?* Of all the ridiculous . . . Wasn't being the lord of a Highland fortress on the flat plains of Texas eccentric enough for him? She shook her head. The man was obviously either a liar, a joker, or a lunatic. Probably all three. And she wanted nothing to do with any of them!

"Right. Of course you are," she answered coldly. "And I happen to be Shakespeare's Hamlet. Excuse me now, but I must go and look for my father's ghost." Gathering her skirts, she turned sharply and darted up a nearby stairway that led to the top of the bailey wall, completely forgetting her earlier threat.

"Dorcas—don't!" Alan caught up with her just as she reached the rain-slick path behind the parapet, grabbing her by the wrist and swinging her around to face him.

She skidded and gave a little shriek. Not because of Alan, but because she suddenly realized something that, in her anger, she hadn't stopped to consider from the ground: how high and exposed it was on the wall. The parapet shielded the outer edge, but the inside of the path was a twenty-foot, dizzying drop straight down to the massive, muddy courtyard below.

Dorcas took one look at it and, without stopping to reconsider, threw herself into his arms. It was the last thing he'd been expecting and it knocked him backward a pace, but he rapidly rebalanced, swinging her completely off her feet and tightly against his chest. She shivered, clutching his shoulders and burying her face against his neck to shut out the sight of the drop. Her hair had come loose and it hung about them both, shimmering like a gold veil in the moonlight.

"Now that *was* silly," he murmured. "You didn't really think I'd let you jump, did you?"

"What?" She let out a slightly hysterical laugh. "Good heavens, I was being facetious when I said that. Heights terrify me! You couldn't get me to leap off this wall if you lit a fire under me," she said with a shudder.

His arms tightened just a bit, but she was too unnerved

to notice. Nor did she see what Alan was gazing at over her head: the small audience gathering in the yard below.

"Opportunity knocks but once," he said cryptically, a sudden, odd lilt in his voice that slipped past her, too. "All things considered, then, dear, this looks like a perfect time for me to confess something," he whispered into her ear.

"Oh, no, you're not going to confess that you're also an Arabian sheikh, or a Russian Cossack, or something like that, are you?" Dorcas groaned into his neck. His answering chuckle had an ominous ring to it, but she missed that warning, as well.

"Dorcas Matilda, the only thing I've any interest in being right now is your husband."

"What?" Her head flew up and she glared at him.

"This is what I wanted to discuss at the spring," Alan explained, parrying the glare with insufferable calm. "I'm asking you to marry me . . . and if you don't say yes, I may become so downhearted, I'll go weak and accidentally drop you off the rampart," he threatened softly.

"You wouldn't dare!"

"I surely wouldn't. But then . . . I might not be able to help myself."

"No!" she gasped, and clutched at him as he took a quick, wavering step toward the path's open side. "Wait!"

"Aye, dear? You've something to tell me?" His amber eyes gleamed expectantly.

Hers blazed frightened fury back. "I don't think you really want to hear what I have to tell you," she hissed like a cornered cat.

"I'd better." With a wicked grin, he relaxed his hold slightly and took another step.

"No—Yes!" Dorcas shrieked over the pounding in her ears.

"Which is it, aye or nay? Make up your mind, lassie. My arms are getting tired."

He moved right to the edge.

She clung frantically to him, fighting down dizziness and frustrated rage. This was so unfair! So unbelievable! So MacAllister, she thought wretchedly.

"All right! Y-yes," she finally managed to choke out, though how she was able to squeeze the words past the suffocating lump in her throat, she had no idea.

"Yes, what?" he asked, in a voice that sounded like the business end of a saber.

"Yes, I . . . I'll m-marry you," she half sobbed.

"Louder. I want to hear you say 'I promise to be your wife, Alan MacAllister,' " that razor-edged voice instructed, as a powerful pair of arms slipped their hold just enough to make her gasp and clutch at him again.

The crisp, post-storm air blew against them, fanning Dorcas's hair out over the courtyard like a blond banner but doing absolutely nothing to cool the scorching heat in her cheeks. *Oh, what difference does it make?* she groaned to herself. *Engagements have been broken before. It's not like I'll ever go through with it.*

Drawing a deep, trembling breath, she discreetly crossed two fingers behind his back and repeated with as much volume as she could muster, "I promise to be your w-wife, Alan MacAllister."

He pulled her securely against his chest and stepped away from the edge. "And I promise to be your husband, Dorcas Matilda. . . . Did you hear that, Uncle Angus?" he called.

"Aye, lad, we all did!" the big man's voice boomed back. "Why dinna ye kiss th' bonny bride?"

Alan glanced down at the bonny bride's murderous expression. "A-hem . . . later," he said, with a slight flinch. Grinning a bit sheepishly, he quickly carried her down the stairs to those waiting below.

51

Roaring felicitations in Scots Gaelic, Angus snatched Dorcas up into a rib-crunching bear hug and planted a resounding, hairy smack on each flushed cheek before turning her over to the next in line.

"I . . . I'm not sure what to say," Dr. Earnshaw murmured hesitantly, gazing down at her with a curious mixture of bemusement and concern. "You're rather young for this, and marriage isn't like a math equation, Dorcas Matilda. There are no tried-and-true formulas you can follow to make it come out correctly. Are you certain you know what you're doing?"

I know I'm not *going to marry any overbearing, overmuscled, insane Scottish Comanche,* Dorcas thought, meeting the worry in his gaze with iron resolve in her own.

"Quite certain!" she told him.

Zachary Earnshaw's expression relaxed into a relieved smile. "Then you have my blessing, child," he said, leaning forward and kissing her lightly on the forehead. The smile went a trifle wry and he added, "Though I doubt Matilda would have approved." Chuckling to himself, he turned and walked briskly off toward the generator tower, a slight crookedness in his gait the only evidence that he still carried several annoying ounces of shrapnel from the Civil War in his leg.

"Aunt Matilda would have had a conniption!" Dorcas muttered, agitatedly slapping some creases out of her velvet skirt while pretending it was Alan. Suddenly, she froze.

"You must be losing your touch, Mr. Elliot. I heard you approach," she said, turning slowly around to meet him.

"I thought it would surprise you more this time if I didn't appear out of nowhere," he answered, staring steadily at her with an unreadable expression in his smoky gray eyes. "I'm afraid you've put your foot in it,

Miss Jeffries . . . or should I say Lady MacAllister?"

"Hah!" she snorted. "It's only an engagement, Mr. Elliott, and it hardly puts me in a worse position than I was in before. I'll be Lady MacAllister when they throw the first snowball out of you know where."

Simon Elliott opened his mouth as if to speak, then quickly snapped it shut again. He heaved a small sigh and shrugged. "Ah, well, far be it from me to disillusion you, dear girl. At least the situation affords me opportunity for this."

And without another word, he jerked her forward and kissed her. Kissed her warm and firm and full, in fact. And square on the mouth.

"Don't look so startled, Miss Jeffries," he said, grinning down at her when it was over. "I'm merely following the dictates of tradition. Who are we to argue with such things?" His gaze shifted, but the grin remained. "Isn't that right, Alan?"

"Aye. I daresay you wouldn't care much for the tradition I'm thinking of now, though."

"Probably not. But then, they can't all be this much fun." Simon chuckled. "You'll have to excuse me now. Dr. Earnshaw and I still have a lot of work to do tonight. You, too, I imagine. Hmm, Alan?" With a wink at Dorcas, the tall blond sauntered off in the wake of Zachary Earnshaw.

"I don't want you even speaking to him again." Alan's low growl rolled out like thunder.

Biting back her own aggravation at the incident, Dorcas glanced up into his black glare and asked evenly, "Are you giving me orders?"

"Aye! And you'll mind what I say, lassie."

"Aye. I'll mind you," she mimicked him. "I'll mind you when I see pigs circling in the air and building nests in the parapets. Now leave me alone! I've had just about all of the male species in general that I can tolerate for one night. I'm going back to bed. I'm going to drink that water in my room and hope that it is drugged, so I don't have to look at or listen to any of you for a good long while!"

She gathered up her skirts and raced toward the towering keep, only to find herself grabbed by the arm and spun around before she was halfway there. "Alan! Haven't you done enough to me for one night?" she raged at him.

He ignored the rage and shot back a question of his own. "What do you mean, your water is drugged?"

"It has to be! That, or some other damn thing I was given. Why the hell do you think I slept for twenty-four hours?" she shouted, and instantly clamped a hand over her mouth in embarrassed surprise. It was the first time she had ever cursed. *The way things are going, it probably won't be the last,* she thought dimly.

Alan loomed over her, his handsomely sculpted face in the shadows, so she couldn't read his expression. His voice, when it came, had a sharp edge of suspicion. "I didn't know about any of that. I was gone most of last night and all of today. I returned but a short while ago."

"How lucky for me," she said flatly. "What were you doing?"

The grip on her arm tightened. "One thing you'd best learn quickly, Dorcas, is not to question me. You might get answers you'd rather not hear."

Swallowing a sudden flutter of fear, she answered levelly. "Fine. I don't really care anyway. I only asked because I was hoping that wherever it is you were, it was someplace you'd be going back to soon."

"Not yet, lassie!" He jerked her back as she tried to shrug free, pulling her close enough that she could see the gleam of his eyes in the shadows. They glowed almost like a cat's. "I've one more bit of advice," he purred dangerously. "It'd be worth your while to at least try being pleasant to me. Your life could become a wee bit . . . uncomfortable otherwise."

"Otherwise?" Dorcas drew herself up to her full height. It allowed her eyes to reach the top of his shoulder. "Things can hardly be any worse for me than they are right now! My life has been *uncomfortable* ever since I left Philadelphia with that taxing little chatterbox, Lady Flora."

"If you didn't like her, why were you so willing to take her place?" he demanded. "I've been pondering that. What did Flora and that captain of hers offer you?"

"Don't be insulting. I wouldn't do something like this for pay. They tried to stop me, in fact," she threw back, stung by his implication. "And I never said I didn't like her. I simply found her a bit too fluffy-headed. Girls like that get on my nerves, I'm afraid. But I helped her and Captain Armstrong because they needed me. It seemed the only solution to their problem. And—" she paused a moment to gather her thoughts and dignity together— "and because the very idea of an arranged marriage in this day and age ruffled my feathers. It's uncalled for, unpleasant, and utterly archaic!"

"I agree."

"You . . ." Her eyes widened. Was that a smile she saw tugging the corners of his mouth? "Then why on earth were you going to marry her? Did the thought of her money mean so much to you?"

The smile vanished. "Now who's being insulting?" He gave a short laugh, but there was no humor in it. "Flora's family has little money, anyway. Didn't she tell you that?"

"No," Dorcas said softly. His words were beginning to paint a much clearer picture for her than the one Flora had presented. *Tradition and family honor my Aunt Fanny!* she thought. It had been nothing but a business deal. Though, naturally, Lady Flora wouldn't have cared to admit that. Dorcas hardly needed the rest of Alan's explanation.

"Money is the reason Flora's people wanted her to marry me. 'Tis this branch of the clan that has the wealth . . . for all the good it does us."

The bitterness of his tone surprised her. This man carried some grudge against his own family, it seemed. Because of the marriage arranged for him? What *had* been the purpose in that?

"If they weren't interested in more money, what were the Texas MacAllisters supposed to gain from the alliance?" she asked, staring intently into his shadowed face. Moonlight suddenly streamed out from behind a cloud, illuminating his features, and Dorcas caught her breath at the anger she saw there.

"They were hoping for a proper, civilized wife, I expect . . . to help tame their savage son," he bit out.

"And what did the son hope to gain?" she persisted, trying not to wince as his hand tightened on her arm like a vise. There was obviously more to this story, and she had to know the truth. If she could understand the motives at work here, she might be able to mold them into a bargaining point for her own release. "Why did you agree to the marriage?"

"I didn't! 'Twas all Angus's doing." Abruptly, the viselike grip on her arm relaxed, and he turned half away, his expression lost in the shadows again. "I'd no intention of wedding Flora. That's why I rode out the day she was to arrive. I didn't even want to see her."

Could this be the opening she had been looking for? If she offered sympathy and support, would he respond in kind?

"It must have been so horribly frustrating for you," she said softly. "Your uncle is a very difficult man, I'm afraid. Do you know he had me tied to the wagon seat when I tried to jump out on the way here?"

She quivered slightly at the memory. Then quivered more at the warm touch of Alan's fingers brushing her cheek when he turned back to her. His hand cradled her chin, tipping her face up to meet his eyes. Eyes that glittered mysteriously down at her in the moonlight. Eyes with such unfathomable dark amber depths, she had a sudden dizzying sensation of nearly drowning in them.

"No, I didn't know," he answered, his low voice rippling over her like smoke in the cool night air. "Though it hardly surprises me. Angus has used heavier-handed methods than that to get what he wants."

"Why is he so insistent about this marriage? And, more to the point, why are you?" she asked, a desperate edge creeping into her tone. Was it her imagination or was the night growing warmer? It was so difficult to keep her thoughts in order with that imposing form scant inches away and those mesmerizing eyes boring into hers. "You say you had no intention of marrying Lady Flora. Why, then, would you want me? It doesn't make any sense!"

"Doesn't it?" Alan said, gently drawing his fingers along the delicate line of her jaw. "Do you know, when I first saw you, I thought you *were* Flora?" The fingers started tracing up and down the side of her neck, making Dorcas feel as if flames were licking her where they touched. "I said to myself: *How interesting. Uncle Angus has found me a bride who jumps out of trees half-naked. He has more imagination than I gave him credit for. I may have to rethink this alliance.*"

"But I'm not Flora. You're breaking the law by keeping me here. When I get away—and I promise you I will—I can have the lot of you arrested for kidnapping!" Dorcas said, her voice sounding like sandpaper to her own ears. Alan had stepped so close, she could see the pulse throbbing at the base of his neck, feel his breath on her brow as he spoke.

57

"I think not. You left Abilene of your own free will, remember." His hand slid around to the back of her head and tangled in her hair. "You deliberately misled Angus as to who you were."

"Only for a few hours. It was necessary! But I told him the truth as soon as I could. And I was honest with you from the beginning," she argued, fighting down a wave of panic and heat. "Alan, this isn't right and you know it!"

Her breath caught in her throat with a ragged gasp as his free arm suddenly snaked about her waist, locking her so tightly against himself that their two lengths were almost molded into one. She could feel every solid contour of his body grinding into hers, hard in all the places she was soft.

"Are you a mind reader, Dorcas? You know what I know, do you?" he whispered, slowly drawing her up to her toes and pulling her head back so her eyes could meet his. "Tell me then, dear, what am I thinking now?"

For an answer, Dorcas squeezed her eyes shut against the fire in his. Already she could feel herself starting to melt into him, sense her body beginning its electric response to his, and she was powerless to stop it. It was maddening! She didn't know whom she was angrier with: Alan for doing this to her, or herself for suddenly wanting him to.

Then, unbelievably, she was free of him, and standing alone and trembling in the chill of the courtyard. Her eyes flew open and she drew in deep, shuddering breaths, like a drowning victim breaking through to the surface. Gradually, her pulse slowed and the flush receded from her skin. The burning haze she'd been blinded by lifted from her vision and she saw him poised, taut and watchful, a few paces before her. The last of the storm clouds had blown away and the yard was flooded with an eerie, incandescent glow, making the castle walls appear almost as though they were carved from green gold. Time seemed to dissolve into a distant mist as she stood, silent and shivering, waiting for . . . she wasn't sure what.

"I just wanted to convince myself our kiss by the spring wasn't my imagination. I needed to be sure that you reacted to me the way I remembered," Alan finally said, his husky voice wrapping around her like a velvet cloak. "But I'll not kiss you here. I might not be able to stop with just a kiss . . . and the courtyard's a bit muddy for anything more."

His words brought a hot new wave of color flooding into her face. And a rather chilling new concern prickling into her jangled thoughts. What, actually, was happening here? How could he have such a powerful effect on her? A mere word or look from this—this person, and she started to become someone she could hardly recognize. It went beyond confusing. There was something genuinely suspicious about it. Something almost . . . diabolical.

I have got to get away from here, she thought, quickly shaking the odd feeling out of her head. *This preposterous place is starting to give me too many preposterous notions. The next thing I know, I'll be suspecting him of black magic and worrying about demonic possession—and I've too many real concerns to waste energy on silly ones!*

"Go to bed, Dorcas Matilda. We'll finish this business later," that husky voice said as its owner stepped forward.

"The hell we will! My business with you is finished as of this moment!" she declared, gluing her feet to the ground when a masculine hand reached to brush back a wild wisp of hair from her cheek.

Chuckling softly as he tucked it behind her ear, Alan answered, "That's what you think, dear. Our business has only begun."

59

Taking her by the shoulders when she refused to budge, he turned her gently around, propelling her toward the keep with a not-so-gentle swat on the bustle.

"Why, you—" She whirled back, intent on some serious swatting of her own.

"Later." He chuckled, catching her hand in midflight and kissing it before she could jerk it away. "Now to bed with you. But on your way there, I've a question for you to ponder."

"Yesss?" she hissed, glaring murder up at him.

"I want you to decide whom you're really afraid of. Me? Or yourself?" The chuckle deepened into a full laugh at the look on her face and he added wickedly, "Now you'd best leave. Before I decide to ignore the mud."

Almost strangling on her own tongue, Dorcas snatched up her skirts and beat a hasty retreat to the keep, his low laugh burning in her ears the whole way.

Chapter Three

"I should have scattered a trail of bread crumbs after myself when I left so I could find my way back. I think I'm just going around in circles; everything is starting to look the same to me," Dorcas was muttering to herself as she wandered wearily down what seemed like the hundredth winding passageway she had tried since reentering the castle's main living quarters.

"Honestly! This keep is laid out like an unfinished jigsaw puzzle. I'll never reach my room at this rate." She sighed when the passage abruptly ended in a small, semicircular alcove. The area was bare, save for a few stools off to one side and a large, ornate, three-sectioned Oriental screen standing near the back.

How curious, she thought, her attention momentarily distracted by the screen. It looked so incongruous. What could it be there for?

"Aahoooeeeeeahhh . . ."

The hairs at the back of her neck shot up as the sudden

61

screech rattled the musty air of the alcove.

"Death . . . death . . . Leave before it's too late!" a banshee voice wailed. *"Ahooeeeooahh . . ."*

Instantly, Dorcas's eyes narrowed, and she crept toward the screen as silently and stealthily as a cat stalking a mouse, then, with a single quick move, grabbed one of its panels and snapped it back. The screen wobbled, overbalanced, and tipped over, landing on the wood floor with a heavy thud.

"Oh! Now see what you've done!" A tall, willowy, young woman with extravagant red hair, piercing blue eyes, and an almost blinding canary yellow negligee stood glaring at the screen in dismay. Stamping her foot, she moaned, "If it's been damaged, Uncle Angus will hang me by my thumbs and then have me hurled into the moat! That screen belonged to his mother."

She glanced at Dorcas, her brows suddenly pulled together in thought. "Or maybe it was his grandmother's; I can't remember. Anyway—" she heaved a dramatic sigh—"he's very fond of it. Here, help me set it right. I'm Mary MacAllister, by the way. But I detest being called Mary—it's too mundane—so I've changed my name to Esmeralda," she chattered as the screen was carefully placed back into position. "What do you think?"

Dorcas was studying the three panels as best she could by the light of the candle she'd been carrying. "It looks all right to me," she said finally.

Mary-Esmeralda gave a disgusted snort. "I didn't mean the screen! Who cares about that silly old thing?" She gave it a kick that almost toppled it again. "I want to know how you like my *name*. Don't you think Esmeralda has the wildest, most romantic sound to it?" she breathed, closing her eyes in ecstasy.

"Why, yes," Dorcas said in the voice she reserved for

62

small children and fussy lap dogs. "It makes you sound like a flamenco dancer."

The blue eyes snapped open. "Oh, no! That will never do. I can't sound like a flamenco dancer. They make far too much noise. All that heel clicking and those castanets—they sound like a herd of stampeding crickets!" She turned slightly away, her brow furrowed with furious thinking. "I know! I'll call myself Ophelia," she exclaimed, spinning triumphantly back to face Dorcas. "What do you think of Ophelia? Or . . . wait!" She flung out an arm for attention. "Flavia! . . . Or maybe Angelique? Sophia? Desdemona? . . . Oh, it's so difficult to decide! What do you think?" she demanded, stamping her foot and impaling Dorcas with her gaze.

"How about Cassandra?" Dorcas suggested, thinking of the beautiful, mad princess from Greek mythology.

"Cassandra?" The young woman's head tilted to the side, as though she were listening intently to some distant melody. "*Cassandra MacAllister* . . . I like that very much, I think. It'll look good in print, too. I'm going to be a famous playwright, you know. And star in all the productions myself. Cassandra, it is then! Thank you, Dorcas." She smiled sweetly. "Oh, wipe that silly shock off your face. Everyone here knows who you are. Didn't you see your audience the other night when Alan dragged you in here? That was quite a show you put on. I almost applauded. It didn't fool me any, of course—I knew what you were up to—but it was entertaining, nonetheless. I may use it in my next play," the redhead finally finished, because she had run out of breath. She stared down at Dorcas through narrow blue slits, a sly grin curling the corners of her mouth.

Dorcas stared back through equally narrowed eyes, the opposite of a grin tightening her expression. "What are you talking about, *Cassandra*?"

"As if you didn't know," the new Cassandra chanted,

wafting dreamily across the alcove and seating herself on one of the stools in a billow of screaming yellow silk. "But enough of that. Here I am boring you with all this talk about yourself when you must be dying to hear all about me."

"Not really," Dorcas said, still staring icily.

"I'm from Boston and my father sent me out here last month because he thinks the theater is a scandalous career for a woman," Cassandra cheerfully began, ignoring the ice. "He's hoping I'll marry one of Uncle Angus's sons instead. But I don't like any of Uncle Angus's sons. They're all toads. And not the kind you could turn into princes with a kiss, either." She grimaced. "If I kissed any of them, I'd get warts."

"So why don't you go back to Boston?" Dorcas asked pointedly.

"No." Mary-Esmeralda-Cassandra immediately clamped her lips into a firm line and her eyes became slits again, flashing blue fire in the candle's glow. "You won't trick me that easily, Dorcas. I know your game, but it won't work." She jumped haughtily to her feet, shaking out her negligee like a queen shaking out her robes of state. "And I'm not going to tell you any more about me. You can perish of curiosity, for all I care." Chin in the air, she billowed out of the alcove and was a dozen catlike steps down the darkened passage when she suddenly whirled and flew back.

"By the way, speaking of perishing, I'd keep my eye on Alan if I were you. He may be a murderer," she said brightly, gazing down at Dorcas's stunned face with an angelic smile illuminating her own. "A murderer and a widower, to be specific. The two terms go together, you see, because he supposedly killed his wife. Her name was Heather, in case you're interested." Still smiling, she turned and drifted into the darkness, like yellow smoke vanishing in a midnight breeze.

Dorcas fell, rather than sat, on the nearest stool, having abruptly discovered that her legs wouldn't support her. She was remembering the story of the original Cassandra and hoping that she had not chosen too appropriate a name for her new acquaintance. The first Cassandra had been a princess of Troy during its long-ago siege. She had asked for and received the gift of prophecy from Apollo. But she had also spurned the god's advances, so he had turned his blessing into a curse by declaring that no one would ever believe her. To all who heard them, Cassandra's words sounded like the ravings of a madwoman; yet the poor, doomed girl had spoken nothing but the truth.

This Mary MacAllister was obviously unbalanced, but that didn't necessarily mean she was a liar. Lunatics had been known to be accurate about some things before now, Dorcas thought. The entire atmosphere of the castle had suddenly shifted for her. Whereas previously it had simply seemed dim, dusty, impractical, and eccentric, it now felt eerily malignant and menacing.

She glanced warily around the silent alcove, the flickering glow from her candle making the curved walls appear almost as if they were pulsating. Even her own shadow looked, somehow, threatening. Steeling herself against a creeping, escalating panic, she rose cautiously to her feet, every nerve trembling like a touched fiddle string. Something hit against the hem of her skirt and the small shriek she let out nearly hit a high C.

She was that happy to see him.

"Hello, angel. You always appear just when I need you the most, don't you?" she murmured, kneeling down to pet the cat. "You're my little knight in furry armor."

He dug his warm head into her hand, that deep, throaty purr of his vibrating like a hive of giant bees.

"You must know this castle like the back of your paw. Do you think you could show me the way back to my room? Not that I really want to go there, mind you—I'd rather be far away from this dreadful place—but if I have to be anywhere here, I think my room is the safest. At least there I can lock the door and barricade myself in. Don't you agree?" Dorcas asked, gazing wistfully down into his glowing amber eyes.

The eyes blinked once and the cat suddenly gathered himself into a tight crouch beneath her hand. Then, like a spring unwinding itself, he shot around her and darted behind the screen. She heard a wild scrambling, a muffled woosh, like something large and soft hitting the floor, and then . . . complete, breathless quiet.

Now what was that all about? she wondered, slowly rising and shaking her head. "Did you hear a mouse?" she called out, her voice echoing oddly in the silence.

As if in answer, the candle flame flickered frantically for an instant and abruptly wisped out, leaving her in a darkness so dense it almost suffocated her.

But not quite. From somewhere a steady, stiff breeze was blowing. A draft that had not been there before. With her heart trying to pound through the bodice of her gown, she groped her way toward the source of the moving air and found, not only an opening, but also a surprisingly bright light in the passage beyond. The cat must have uncovered it when he'd clawed down the tapestry that had hung behind the Oriental screen. It was rather strange she hadn't noticed the tapestry before, Dorcas was thinking, as she stepped into the passage. But then, her meeting with Mary-Cassandra had been more than a little distracting.

She stooped briefly to retrieve the light that the red-haired distraction must have left behind when she'd entered the alcove. It was one of Mr. Elliott's electric lanterns, and Dorcas stood blinking and puzzling a moment, waiting for her eyes to adjust to the glare and wondering, suddenly, why the catty Cassandra had been there in the first place. *It was almost like she was waiting for me,* the girl thought. *And what was she doing with one of Simon's lamps?* Did he present one to every prospective bride who came to Castle MacAllister?

Dorcas heaved a small sigh. This was hardly a concern, considering all else she had to deal with—such as kidnapping, imprisonment, and a murdering fiance—but it did smell a bit suspicious.

A *bit?* The whole fortress and everything in it was beginning to stink like a kettle full of rotten fish!

Shaking her head, Dorcas glanced down the passage. Her black furry knight was nowhere to be seen, but that was all right because she realized where she was. This was the corridor directly off the one where Mr. Elliott had startled her earlier that night. Placing the lantern back on the floor, Dorcas hurriedly retraced her previous path back to her room.

She was a little breathless by the time she reached it. And more than a little dismayed to find no key in the door's lock.

"But I'm sure there was a key here when I left. I should have taken it with me," she muttered as she quickly dragged her trunk several feet across the floor and shoved it against the door's base. "No, that won't work. It's not heavy enough." She panted, hastily pushing it aside and beginning a determined wrestling match with the large mahogany dresser that stood against the wall directly to the right of the door. "Ugh!" she grunted. "This weighs a ton. I defy anyone to get past this monster."

"You're absolutely right. We don't want to be disturbed tonight. But that's far too heavy for you. Let me do it," said a low voice, as a powerful pair of arms reached around her and easily slid the dresser into place.

Dorcas let out a scream that would have tumbled the

entire castle down if Alan hadn't instantly clapped a hand over her mouth.

"Hush." He laughed softly, close to her ear. "They'll think I'm murdering you."

It was a poor choice of words from Dorcas's standpoint.

"Argh!" Alan bit out through clenched teeth as her teeth bit into one of his fingers. He stared down at her with a mixture of surprise, amusement, and something Dorcas didn't want to think about. "What's the matter with you, lassie?"

"N-n-nothing's the matter with me. Get out of here!" she gasped, her back pressed frantically against the far wall where she'd retreated. "What are you doing in my room?"

"*Our* room. 'Twas mine, in fact, but now 'tis ours," he corrected, flexing his hand a little to make sure everything was still adequately connected.

"*Our* room?" Dorcas choked out, unable to pull her gaze away from him. She felt pinned, like a butterfly on a mounting board.

Alan began a slow, languid approach toward her, looking as though he couldn't understand what all the fuss was about. "Aye. Husbands and wives generally share the same room, don't they?" Grinning like a cat, he removed his collar and vest and started unfastening his shirt.

Dorcas watched in horrified fascination as more and more of that massive, rock-hard, tanned chest came into view. The fact that she had seen it before offered not a whit of comfort. A bare chest had seemed . . . well, natural on a Comanche. It had been easier to deal with then. Now it seemed somehow improper. Indecent. And nerve-wrackingly sensual. She gulped as the shirt hit the floor. He casually pulled off his belt and her knees started to quiver.

What difference does it make what husbands and wives do? "We're not m-married," she strangled out, thinking that if he reached for his trousers, she would probably faint.

"Aye, but we are," he said. And reached for her instead.

Her knees buckled, but she quickly caught herself, swiveled, ducked under his arm, skidded across the floor, and plastered herself against the opposite wall. "We are *not!* We're merely engaged!"

Alan heaved a small sigh and turned slowly to face her, the muscles in his torso rippling like burnished copper in the glow of the oil lamp. "Look, dear, according to old Highland law, two people are married simply by saying so in front of witnesses. That's what you and I did on the rampart, if you'll recall. And that makes us man and wife," he explained, stealthily closing the distance between them. "At least, that's the tradition the MacAllisters generally follow. And, for once in my life—" a sudden grin lit his face—"I find myself most glad to be part of the clan."

Pausing two paces away, he raked her with a look that nearly set her hair on fire and ordered softly and deliberately, "Now come here, Dorcas. Stop acting so frightened. What do you think I'm going to do to you, anyway?"

Judging by his expression, Dorcas didn't know. Strangle her? Kiss her? In her current state, all possibilities seemed petrifying and probably fatal. She doubted if she could survive any of them.

"You're not going to do *anything* to me," she declared, dodging sideways and back to her previous wall. "Because I won't let you get close enough to even try. And I won't accept this so-called marriage, either. It's preposterous!"

"What's preposterous is the thought of me spending

our wedding night chasing you around the room," Alan replied, his rich voice something between a growl and a purr. "Now come here."

He took a single step toward her and waited.

"Dorcas . . . ?" He took a second step, then a third and a fourth, his eyes pulling at her like amber magnets. "This is your last chance. Don't make me come get you, lassie," he warned softly. "You might be sorry for it when I catch you."

"You might be sorry for it, too," she whispered hoarsely, watching him approach the way a caged canary watches a cat. He moved with an easy feline grace that sent disturbing, hot tingles shooting deep into her abdomen. "Whatever you're planning, I . . . I won't make it easy for you."

Alan halted in midstep. "And what do you think I'm planning, dear? I can understand a new bride being nervous on her wedding night, but aren't you being just a wee bit extreme?" He chuckled.

Infuriated, Dorcas glared straight into his eyes. It was a mistake, because they nailed her right to the wall, sucked the air and the movement right out of her. She stood totally transfixed for one breathless moment, just long enough for him to cover the last several feet between them, sweep her up into his arms, and toss her firmly into the center of the room's large four-poster bed.

"And now, bonny lassie," he purred, "the next question is, are you going to unfasten your gown? Or am I?"

The bonny lassie snapped instantly alert, only to find herself securely trapped between the mattress and Alan's warm, solid, utterly masculine weight. It sent a shudder down her whole length and she went rigid beneath him in a desperate attempt to make her recalcitrant body stop wanting to mold itself into his. Closing her eyes didn't help a bit. She could still sense the heat of his gaze on her face, feel his breath as his lips hovered just above hers. He was going to kiss her, and it would be all over. With a dismayed groan, Dorcas twisted her head to the side and his mouth touched the soft spot just below her ear instead.

"All right. If that's the way you'd prefer it," he whispered. "I'm going to taste every inch of you before this night is over; it makes no difference to me where I start."

He began planting a long, lingering trail of extremely distracting kisses down the side of her neck. Dorcas caught her breath a little more sharply with each one. *Heaven help me,* she thought. This was not going to be easy to ignore.

It grew less easy, in fact, as the kisses started smoking over the exposed part of her shoulder. By the time they were en route to her cleavage, it was absolutely impossible.

Gasping for air, she felt her hands moving almost as though they belonged to someone else. They slid over Alan's amazing back, across his shoulders, and tangled fiercely in his thick black hair. In a steamy haze, she realized that, somehow, her skirts had become bunched up around her thighs and her legs were twining themselves with his.

This is impossible, the small part of her mind that still belonged to her spoke from far away in the distance. *Dorcas Jeffries does* not *do things like this.*

But Dorcas hardly heard it. She was too busy listening to the groans of pleasure Alan was making over all those things she was not doing.

The groans rolled into words—soft, throaty, passionate words in a language she couldn't understand. What was it—Scots Gaelic? She didn't think so; but then, what other language, besides English, would he speak?

Suddenly she froze. Really froze. She went as cold and stiff as an icicle. *Oh, my God,* her inner voice wailed, loud and clear this time. Alan was whispering endearments to her in Comanche. Or something that he thought was Comanche, at any rate. He hadn't been joking before. She was lying there tangled up in bed with a Scottish madman who honestly believed he was a Comanche. Who also believed they were legally married. Who was probably also a murderer . . . and who knew what else! It made her almost physically ill.

"Dorcas, I can explain why I'm speaking Comanche," he said, gazing down at her with an intensity that merely tightened her fear.

"I don't want to hear it," she answered, struggling unsuccessfully to keep the hysterical edge out of her voice.

"No. You have to listen. This is something you need to understand," Alan insisted as calmly as he could under the circumstances.

This was unfortunate timing as far as he was concerned. That much was blaringly obvious to Dorcas, but she didn't care. She had her own concerns at the moment. Such as staying alive and in one piece.

"I understand already," she said, trying to squeeze out from under him.

He pulled her back. "No, you don't. Now let me explain. Just five minutes," he pleaded. "Then, if you still want me to let you go, I will. I promise."

"Oh, yes. We know all about your promises, don't we?"

"Damn it, lass, listen to me!" he exploded, pinning her wrists to the bed.

It was the worst possible move he could have made. It blew near panic into full-scale terror. Blinded by her own hysteria, Dorcas began shrieking and thrashing as if all the fiends of hell were upon her. Hardly surprising, since that was pretty much what she felt was happening.

Suddenly having a genuine battle on his hands to quiet her and keep her from injuring herself, Alan overlooked one small detail: to watch out for himself. A frantic knee came up and hit him squarely in what was, probably, the only place that could have stopped him.

With a groan that had nothing to do with pleasure, he rolled off her and onto his feet, clinging to one of the bedposts for temporary support while he caught his breath . . . and a couple of other things that were rather important to him.

Having no idea what she had done to prompt such a reaction, Dorcas quickly rolled off on the other side and stood staring at him in amazement, rapidly replaying her last few moves and trying to figure it out, just in case it was a defense she could use again in the future.

Worry about it later, you nitwit! Get out now, while you can, that inner voice urged.

"Right," she answered it aloud. She scurried to the barricaded door, pressed her back against the side of the mahogany dresser, and, painstakingly, began inching it away. There was an abrupt, scraping whoosh, and she felt herself flying backward, only to be caught by a pair of strong hands a hairbreadth before denting her gown's bustle (not to mention what lay beneath it) on the hardwood floor.

"I should have let you fall," a low voice growled as the hands hauled her to her feet.

"Then why didn't you?" she said, with a tartness that was meant to mask her fear. It didn't quite succeed. Nor did the aggravated shrug she gave trying to free herself from his hands.

Alan merely released her long enough to grip her by the upper arms and spin her around to face himself. "Because I've a certain fondness for that part of your anatomy. I'd hate to see it damaged," he ground out.

Trying not to tremble in his angry grasp, Dorcas determinedly kept her gaze riveted on the floor. There was nearly an arm's length of space between them, but it was almost as if she could feel the hard contours of his body still pressing into her, making it difficult to breathe and virtually impossible to think clearly—though she was doing her best.

"Look at me!" he ordered, his hands tightening on her.

Stubbornly, she shook her head, unwilling to trust her voice at that moment and definitely not daring to meet his eyes. The man *did* have some sort of Svengali quality, she was thinking. She hadn't imagined it down in the courtyard. He *had* been mesmerizing or hypnotizing her or some such thing. That was how he had managed to transfix her before. That was why she had been behaving so oddly, doing things she never would have dreamed of on her own. He was more devious than she had realized. And a lot more dangerous.

The worst of it was, she seemed to be powerless against him. It was horrible to feel so vulnerable. And infuriating not to be able to hide her fear any better than this. She groaned inwardly as an uncontrollable shivering shook her body.

Alan instantly pulled her close, his arms wrapping around her like warm steel. "Dorcas, you have got to stop this," he sighed, his tone suddenly quiet and almost tender. He rested his chin on the top of her head. "I can't have my wife too terrified to even look at me. What kind of a marriage would that be?"

She nearly strangled on a surge of hysterical laughter. "I'm not your wife and this isn't a real marriage!" She gasped against his chest as the icy shivers began turning hot.

"It *is* and you *are*. But I'll not stand here arguing that now," he said, swinging her up into his arms and striding toward the bed. "You've just got a bad case of the wedding-night jitters . . . and I know the cure."

Dorcas gasped again as she landed on the mattress with a slight bounce. Before she could draw breath, she was pinned, with her arms held immobile over her head and both legs locked securely beneath one of his. She went stiff as a statue, and blind as one, too, clamping her eyes shut against the danger in his. But there was no way to shut her ears against the deep, soothing purr of his voice. And that was one of the most maddening things of all: that the one who was tormenting her should also be the one trying to comfort and calm.

"Easy, lass, you're safe," Alan said, placing a light kiss at the corner of her trembling mouth. He followed it with a matching one on the other side. "I'm not going to hurt you," he murmured, letting his lips trail along her jaw.

She groaned as he gently nibbled her earlobe, sending an electric tingle all the way down to her toes.

"You have to relax now, dear, because we're going to finish what we started before. I'll take it very slow and you'll see that there's nothing to be frightened of," he whispered against her throat. "Men and women do this every day, Dorcas, and I've never known anyone yet to die from it."

"There's always a first time," Dorcas moaned as he laid a row of soft, smoky kisses down one side of her neck and started working his way up the other. Her body's response was rapidly moving beyond the boundaries of her mind's control. If she couldn't halt this soon, she realized, she wouldn't even want to.

"Alan!" she gasped in a frazzled effort to make him take his lips off her for a moment so she could think.

"What, dear?" he asked against the top of her shoulder.

Damn him. How could he kiss and talk at the same time?

"You . . . you seem to know a lot about this sort of thing," she choked out, desperately searching for the words that would make him stop.

"Aye, a bit." He half chuckled, releasing her hands so that his would be free for other activities. Her heart skipped several beats as he began doing them.

Oh God, do I dare? she wondered as the idea entered her mind. *It might tip him into a homicidal rage. . . .* Alan started to hoist her skirts and she took the chance.

"Is . . . is it because Heather had the jitters, too?"

His whole body froze and she pressed home her advantage, raising her lids at last and staring hard at him. "What happened to her? How did your wife die?" Her voice sounded like ice to her own ears, but not as chilling as Alan's when his answer finally came.

"She was stripped, beaten, and staked to an anthill," he said, returning her gaze with eyes that had become blazing amber slits. "Any other questions?"

"Yes," Dorcas breathed, battling down a violent wave of nausea. "Did . . . did you kill her?"

The man never moved, never even blinked. He might have been carved from stone.

"Aye," he said flatly. "I'm responsible."

Suddenly the room was empty of air and the bed was tilting like a cork bobbing about in the ocean. Alan's face was swimming dizzily above her; she couldn't tell where the rest of him was. Everything was fuzzy . . . dim . . . dark . . . and growing darker. She struggled for a wild moment, then gave up and sank deep into the blackness.

When she rose to the surface again—how much later, she had no idea—the room was still dim, but only because the oil lamp had been turned down to a tiny, smudgy glimmer. She was still in bed, though under the covers this time, she noticed, and there was a soft, cool smoothness drifting all around her. These weren't the plain cotton sheets she'd slept on the night before, she thought hazily. These were satin. *What an absurd extravagance.*

Inwardly shaking her head, she glanced down at them, sat bolt upright, and let out a shriek that rattled the rafters in the room's vaulted ceiling.

"What happened to my clothes?"

"Hush. I had to loosen your corset after you fainted," came a low purr from the foot of the bed. "And once I'd gotten that far, I decided I might as well finish the job."

Dorcas quickly snatched the top sheet all the way up to her chin, glared across at Alan . . .

And shrieked again.

"This is becoming a wee bit monotonous," he said, strolling around to the empty side of the bed, turning the lamp up a bit, and gazing calmly down at her. "You know, dear, it doesn't do much for a man's self-esteem when a woman screams the first time she sees him minus his trousers."

"I-I-I'm s-sorry," she stammered, suddenly remembering why she had fainted in the first place. He was a wife murderer. And he viewed her as his current wife. And—

Keep him talking! she ordered herself. "I—I didn't mean—it's just—just that you startled me. I've never seen a man completely un-undressed before."

"Oh, well, in that case, I forgive you," came the disconcerting reply. And the mattress sloped as he, even more disconcertingly, sat down beside her.

Ripping the top sheet out from under him, she hastily wound it about herself and started scooting as far away as she could get. A warm hand shot out and grabbed her wrist before she could slip to the floor.

"You're going the wrong way, lassie. I'm over here." He tugged on the wrist to draw her closer.

She latched on to the nearest bedpost with her free hand and held on for dear life. A crowbar couldn't have pried her loose.

But Alan managed it anyway. One stiff yank and she was sliding across the slippery satin and staring, with a sort of dazed fascination, at the broken piece of bedpost clutched in her white-knuckled fist.

A club? she was wondering.

A pair of amber eyes read the expression in hers and the post went sailing through the air, bounced once as it struck the floor, and rolled under the dresser.

"Don't worry about it, dear. I'll have it mended later," Alan said, in response to the dismayed look on her face. "Now come here. There's something I want to tell you."

I'll bet it's something I don't want to hear, Dorcas thought. She immediately countered with a quick, "Actually, that's not true, what I said before. You're not the first naked man I've seen."

The grip on her wrist tightened and his eyes narrowed suspiciously. "Another surprise, Dorcas?"

"I-I've seen pictures of Michaelangelo's *David,*" she admitted weakly.

His expression relaxed and a small grin began twitching at the corners of his mouth. "Oh? And how do you think I compare?"

A hell of a lot better, she realized with a gulp, and changed the subject again.

Or at least tried to. His arm snaked suddenly around her waist, hoisting her over and onto his lap before she could utter another word.

"That's better. But don't you find this sheet a bit constricting? I know I do," he remarked, casually inching the satin away from her breasts.

She caught her breath and the sheet at the same time, yanking the latter away from him and clutching it frantically against herself.

"You are a nervous Nellie, aren't you? I'd have thought you'd be getting at least a little used to me by now." Alan sighed, settling her more squarely into himself and tightening his embrace, as though that would still the trembling that had overtaken her. It increased it, in fact, making him sigh again and tuck her head against his shoulder.

"Listen, lass—I do appreciate why you've been frightened of me. But you can't possibly understand the whole story, and you've given me no chance to explain."

"So explain now!" she said, trying to push away.

It made him cradle her even more closely, and she broke off the fight. Struggling didn't help, she was beginning to realize. It only made her more intensely aware of the devastating masculine form pressing against her. Of course, not struggling didn't work either. There was simply no way to block the feel of his hot, almost electric energy wrapping around her, holding her fast. She suddenly had a great empathy for all the little creatures who had ever been snared in a spider's silken web.

"Another time. I'm hardly in the mood to discuss it now," Alan answered her. "I only want to point out that if I wanted to harm you, I've had ample opportunity to do it before now." His hand began tracing the length of her bare arm, stroking from the wrist to the elbow, the elbow to the shoulder, and over the shoulder 'til it tangled in the long, sandy locks at the nape of her neck.

"I'm not going to kill you. I'm going to make love to you," he whispered.

What's the difference? she wondered half hysterically. The one would end her life, but the other could end everything that made that life worth hanging on to.

"You're only frightened because this is your first time. Would it set your mind at ease if I told you what to expect?" Alan offered, sounding suddenly almost fatherly.

The tone set her teeth on edge. "Good heavens! I'm hardly a child. And I have an extensive background in science—including biology! I fully understand the human reproductive system and how it functions," she grumbled into his neck.

"I'm relieved to hear that. It makes things so much easier if we both know what goes where." He chuckled.

And instantly had to tighten his grasp as she tried to lunge away.

One hand still buried in her hair, he pulled her head back to face him. Before she had time to resist, she was trapped, drowning once more in those smoldering amber pools.

"Dorcas, *what* is the problem? I've been most patient with you so far, but I am fast reaching the end of my tether," he said slowly and deliberately. "I don't want to force you to do something you're uncomfortable with, but if you can't give me a good reason for all this fuss, I may end up doing just that."

The threat snapped something awake inside her, sudden outrage and indignation giving her the strength to tear free from his gaze.

"I'll give you at least three," she hissed. "Number one—regardless of how you view this mock marriage, I do not consider it valid. And I was raised to believe that intimate relations between unmarried people are wrong. Number two—even if none of that were the case, I simply do not want to be married! I have a life that I am very satisfied with. A life that does not include domestic servitude, men, or children! I have other plans for myself. Important plans!"

"Don't let Uncle Angus hear you say that," Alan blithely broke into the tirade. "He's expecting a new heir nine months from tonight."

"To hell with Uncle Angus and to hell with you!" she spit out, giving such a violent twist that she threw herself completely off him, landing face up on the other side of the bed, her sheet torn half away, exposing her to the hip.

She grabbed for it, but not fast enough. His weight was upon her, holding her flat on the mattress before she could blink or gasp. The indescribable raw force of that naked torso pressed hotly into hers stampeded all other sensations and concerns instantly out of her head.

Alan gave a thick groan and buried his face against her neck for several choppy heartbeats as both their pulses began to climb skyward.

"That's only two reasons." He panted, his breath searing her flesh. "What's the third?"

Dorcas had no idea. "Um . . . I . . . ah . . ." She choked, dizzily trying to pull her wits back from wherever they had fled.

He raised his head up slightly and stared down into her eyes with an intensity that drilled deep into her core, opening an aching void within her that demanded to be filled.

"Never mind. It can't make any difference," he said hoarsely. "None of your reasons can stand against this one!"

Almost fiercely, he tore the rest of the sheet from between them, and his mouth closed hungrily over hers.

"Alan! Ye awake, lad? Yoor needed!"

The shout was accompanied by the banging inward of the door and brought a blast of curses from the bed that would have blistered a better man than Dunstan MacAllister. Or a smarter man, anyway.

"Have you forgotten how to knock, you half-witted Scottish buffalo?" Alan growled, springing off the mattress like a cougar about to pounce.

Dunstan slouched lazily in the doorway, a stupid grin pulling his thick features into a lopsided caricature of contrition. "Sorry, cousin. I reckoned ye'd be finished wi' th' lass. Hell, ye've been in here lang enoof. I coulda serviced 'er ten times o'er by now," he defended himself, glancing openly at the bed, where Dorcas was frantically rewrapping the satin sheet about herself. "Perhaps nay, tho. She's a bit scrawny fer my tastes." He frowned slightly, then the grin twisted itself back into place. "Ah, well, breedin' an' nursin' bairns'll fatten 'er oop."

Dorcas turned pink, then red, then scarlet.

And Dunstan turned an amazing shade of chartreuse as Alan, with thumb and forefinger, jerked him to his toes and jammed him hard against the wall by his nostrils.

"What are you here for . . . *Dumb*stan?" he asked, impaling his cousin with a lethal look before letting him drop.

"Ow! Dinna be mad at me, laddie, I'm just th' messenger," the beefy blond grumbled, rubbing his swollen nose. "Yoor wanted in th' yard. 'Tis Mary."

Alan let out a deep, gut-wrenching groan. "I'm going to ship that little lunatic back to Boston on a mule train! What's her folly now?"

"She's climbed oot on th' ledge o' th' wizards' tower an' promises tae jump if ye dinna come," Dunstan said as Alan angrily yanked his clothes back on.

"Why couldn't one of you get her down?" he snarled, fastening his trousers with a slight wince. "Haul her in through the window above, or use a ladder. Don't tell me you're all afraid of one moon-mazed lassie!"

"Aye, when she's got a loaded revolver, we are," the blond answered. "Malcolm did try th' ladder, tho. She waited 'til he wuz nearly up, then gave it a stout kick." He paused a moment to scratch under his arm, adding thoughtfully, "Molly says 'tis a good, clean break—his leg ought tae heal."

"I'm glad to hear it," Alan said, as though glad was the very last thing he was. "How the devil did she get a revolver, anyway?"

"How should I ken? She's a witch, maybe." Dunstan shrugged, blinking at Alan through bloodshot eyes. "Air ye comin', oor ain't ye?" The eyes flashed over to Dorcas, huddled small against the large bed's headboard. "I can keep th' bonny bride amused whilst yoor gang," he offered, with a leer that curdled her blood.

"You can find yourself flayed and staked out on the prairie, too," Alan said, with a grin that curdled Dunstan's. "Wait for me in the yard. I'll be there directly."

He watched until his cousin had lumbered sulkily out of sight, then swung, snatched Dorcas's clothes off a chair, jammed them into her trunk on top of the others, slammed the lid down, turned the trunk's key with a vicious twist, tore it out of the lock, and shoved it deep into his boot.

"Just making sure you won't want to go anywhere while I'm gone," he ground out, stalking across to the bed and nailing her to the headboard with an iron glare. "When I return I expect to find you *exactly* where I left you. This night is not over for us yet, lassie. As far as I'm concerned, it hasn't even *begun!*" he hissed. "Now, come here."

She couldn't, Dorcas realized. Her whole being was paralyzed by the hot fury radiating from him. She had seen him angry before, but not like this. This was a real temper. It was suddenly too easy to imagine him killing someone.

She gave her head a little shake, simply because that was the only response she could manage, but it seemed to infuriate Alan even more. With a low, guttural sound, he reached forward and jerked her firmly into his arms, capturing her mouth with his, as though he would devour her in one bite.

It rocked her like an earthquake. The eruption of a volcano was nothing compared to what that kiss did to her. It turned her blood into molten lava and her breath into fiery steam. And it burned every last thread and thought of resistance clean out of her, leaving nothing but a deep, driving, devastating need.

"There! That should hold you for a bit," Alan growled as he abruptly released her.

She landed back on the mattress in what seemed to

her a shower of electric sparks and lay there gasping, staring at him through a red-hot haze as he strode for the door.

"I'll be back!" he flung over his shoulder. And then he was gone.

And she was all alone with a quivering, unquenchable desire . . . and a shivering, unspeakable fear.

Chapter Four

Turning the lamp up high didn't help. It brightened the room, but Dorcas's thoughts were growing blacker with every erratic beat of her heart. Alan had been gone nearly forty minutes, she estimated, yet it was a passing of time that might just as well have been seconds, so intensely could she still sense his body scorching against hers, taste his lips, and feel his energy. It was like being branded, she thought, furious with him for marking her and herself for letting him. Even if she escaped now, she would never again be totally free. Wherever she went, whatever she did, she would have to carry his memory with her . . . the rat.

Shaking her head in a hopeless effort to clear it, she paced about the room: from end to end, side to side, corner to corner, and back again. Wrapped up in the sheet, wrapped up in anxiety, glancing at the door and dreading his return, glancing at the bed and longing for what she dreaded. Watching, waiting, worrying, dreading, longing . . . Utterly confused, frightened, miserable, and boiling in such an emotional stew, the sudden crack of the door banging open hit her almost like a gunshot.

She jumped, tripping over a trailing corner of sheet, and stumbled forward and sideways before catching herself with both hands on the edge of the dresser by the door. Left to its own devices, the sheet slipped down off her breasts and she stumbled again in her rush to pull it back into place.

"Need sum help?"

The offer was made cheerfully enough, but the reek of stale sweat and fresh whiskey that came with it almost turned her stomach inside out. And the meaty hand that latched onto her arm sent a polar chill through her veins.

"Don't you ever knock?" she snapped, jerking away from the grip with a sharp twist.

"Why bother? 'Tis all family here, Cousin Dorie. We've nuthin' tae hide fray one anuther. An' we share an' share alike." Dunstan grinned, staring at the swell of her breasts beneath the satin and licking his thick lips.

Dorcas clutched the sheet higher as a disgusted shudder racked her. *Don't even speak to him,* she ordered herself, watching him the way a cornered cat watches an advancing dog, every fiber tensing for fight or flight, whichever opportunity came first. The moron ought to know she wasn't easy prey. He still wore the scratches she'd given him when he and Duncan had locked her in the prison tower.

"Aye, tha' reminds me," he said, not so drunk that he couldn't read her expression. "I owe ye sumthin' fer t'other day!"

A heavy hand lashed out, giving her a vicious slap before she could dodge it. The blow hit her painfully on the jaw, sending her hard into the dresser. She grabbed at it for support, trying to spin clear, but the back of the hand instantly cracked into the other side of her face, driving her to her knees. The room started to tilt and she struggled to maintain consciousness, barely aware that Dunstan was dragging her down beneath himself by her hair. He let go of it to clamp down on her throat, his other hand roughly tearing the sheet away.

"Here's sum o' yoor own back, ye wicked cat!" he snarled, biting into her shoulder with enough force to draw blood.

Dorcas scarcely noticed. The grip on her windpipe was choking her more than Dunstan in his drunken anger realized. Grappling with him in a desperate attempt for release, she managed to hit his sore nose with the heel of her hand.

He yelled, drew back, and gave her several more blows, but her lungs expanded with the needed air, because to strike her, he'd had to let go of her neck. He grabbed her wrists instead, locking them tightly together in one huge, sweaty hand, straining them high up over her head, while his free hand fumbled his kilt aside and his hairy knees began forcing hers apart.

"This be fer Alan. Stake me out, will he? I'll stake his bride tae th' floor!" He panted, his foul breath making her feel as if she had her face stuck in a sewer.

She gagged and then, as something ungodly grazed her thigh, started screaming for all she was worth.

Not half so loudly as Dunstan, however, as a yowling black fiend landed on his back in a furious frenzy of fang and claw. He bellowed like a wounded bull, rolling over in an attempt to crush the cat beneath his bulk, but it scrambled free, clawed its way over his head, and drove straight for the terrorized man's throat.

Dunstan lumbered to his feet and floundered about the room, wildly trying to tear the creature loose. And having a wildly disastrous lack of success. For something that was really only a good-sized house cat, the animal fought with the studied ferocity of a full-grown panther.

It seemed to know exactly what it was doing and clung to him like some crazed, black-furred devil-leech straight out of the darkest depths of hell. It strained toward his jugular, as if it had done this sort of thing many times before, as if it reveled in it, craved it, and only a long drink of hot, spurting blood would be able to appease it.

Still flat on her back, Dorcas followed the struggle in horrified amazement, too stunned for a moment to move. Her arms had been flung up under the dresser and she realized with a start that her fingers had, unknowingly, fastened around something hard and smooth. Her breath coming in ragged snatches, she inched it out, got shakily to her knees, and gazed down.

It was a fancy carved piece of hardwood, about the length and thickness of a baseball bat. It was the broken bedpost. But to her, it was the end of this nightmare.

Struggling to her feet, she grasped it with both hands and staggered toward Dunstan just as he had finally managed to tear off the cat and hurl it into a wall. The animal dropped to the floor in a hissing and spitting crouch and the wild-eyed man lunged forward to stomp its head in.

But Dorcas lunged faster, swinging with all her might, and it was his head that cracked instead. Or almost, anyway. Glaring down at the burly Highlander's motionless but obviously breathing form, she decided that, since he had mostly rocks between his ears, all she had done was to rattle them a bit.

She hovered above him another moment, poised like a batter awaiting the next pitch, just in case he needed another crack, but his lights had been well and truly blown out. So, dropping her weapon, she raced to the cat.

Which was, astonishingly enough, sitting there carefully washing its face, as though nothing the least bit unusual or unsettling had happened.

Dorcas scooped him up, hugging him tightly against

her chest with almost hysterical relief. He snuggled into her, purring like a miniature locomotive.

"You brave, foolish little angel, you," she choked out, uncontrollable tears splashing onto his sleek fur. "Thank you! But that was an awful chance you took—he's so much bigger than you."

The cat immediately fussed his way out of her arms, padded over to Dunstan, sniffed him, then turned his back, lifted his tail, and sprayed the unconscious man square between the eyes. It was, apparently, his way of saying, "The bigger they are, the harder they fall."

Blinking solemnly up at Dorcas, who was suddenly torn between laughter and tears, his glowing eyes seemed to suggest, "Don't you think you should be leaving now? We won that battle, but let's not press our luck."

"You're absolutely right," she sniffed, and stumbled back across the room to collect what was left of her sheet.

It wasn't until she was tucking it about herself again that she realized she was angrier with Alan than she was with Dunstan. The latter was only a drunken fool, whereas Alan was the one who had deliberately stranded her in such a dangerously vulnerable position in the first place. If she had been adequately dressed, she thought, she probably would have been able to dodge Dunstan before he'd even laid a finger on her.

"It's this damned sheet that caused the whole thing! It keeps slipping and tripping me," she complained to the cat.

He gazed at her a thoughtful moment, then snagged Dunstan's monogrammed kilt pin with a neat front paw, ripped it loose, and batted it across the floor to her. "Will this help?" his eyes asked.

Dorcas stared from the cat to the pin and back again in wide-eyed wonderment. "You are utterly extraordinary," she breathed.

The cat's glowing gaze narrowed into a smug, feline sort of grin. "Yes, I know. It's a specialty of mine," he seemed to say. "Now run along. I'll catch up with you as soon as I've repaired my weaponry." And he instantly began a very industrious sharpening of his claws on Dunstan's thick shoe leather.

Securing her makeshift toga with the gilt pin, Dorcas threw the longest edge over her shoulder and awkwardly groped her way through the dark passages that led out of the keep and into the fresh night air. The cat didn't follow. But then, she was beginning to get used to that.

By the time she reached the outside door, she had barely enough strength left to shove it open and stagger down the ramp to the inner courtyard below. Her knees gave way in front of a narrow bench deep in the shadow of a wall, and she collapsed onto it, suddenly feeling like a burst balloon. The adrenaline that had been keeping her on her feet and masking her pain had finally fizzled out, leaving her all too aware of how horribly she hurt.

There was something wet and sticky trickling down her face, and both her eyes were beginning to swell shut. Worst of all, though, was the pounding ache in her head. It felt like a battle was raging in there, as if someone was setting off blasting caps inside her skull, or cannon fire, or gunshots, or—

Pow! Pow!

It took two shots in rapid succession to alert her to the fact that the noise wasn't just in her head. Someone was firing a gun nearby.

Groaning slightly from the effort it took to sit up, Dorcas peered into the gloom and saw, for the first time, a small, buzzing cluster of people standing barely a dozen or so yards away in a circle of smoky torchlight. None of them had noticed her; they were all too engrossed in the surrealistic burlesque show being performed high over their heads.

Perched like a big yellow canary and singing like one, too, Mary MacAllister was balancing on the narrow upper ledge of the nearby generator tower, offering a lovely rendition of an old Scottish folk tune for—Dorcas could only assume—the amusement of her Texas cousin.

Except, judging by his body language, the Texas cousin didn't seem to be particularly amused. From his position on the long ladder roped against the tower so it couldn't be toppled, Alan was, apparently, either trying to climb onto the ledge with Mary or coax her into boarding the ladder with him. Neither endeavor seemed to be progressing very far. Dunstan had been wrong, Dorcas noted, squinting up at the torchlit pair. Mary did not have a loaded revolver; Mary had *two* loaded revolvers.

She was only holding one at the moment, though. The second was tucked securely into a holster on the heavy cartridge belt she had buckled jauntily over her billowy yellow negligee.

" 'O, ye take the high road and I'll take the low road, and I'll be in Scotland afore ye—' "

Pow!

Alan ducked as the third shot in several minutes whizzed past his ear.

" 'For me and my true love will never meet again, on the bonny, bonny banks of Loch Lomond,' " Mary finished plaintively. She glanced sideways at Alan as the top half of his head appeared over the ledge, and her elegant brows suddenly knit together with some sort of mental distress.

"Oh, dear, I'm so sorry, Cousin Alan. That wasn't right of me at all, was it?" she asked, gazing at him with fretful concern.

"Aye. But you missed me, so there's no harm done. Just hand over the guns and come down like a good lass and we'll forget all about it," he replied soothingly, as the rest of his head, followed by his shoulders, rose cautiously before her view. With painstaking care, he began hoisting himself onto the ledge.

Pow!

The fourth shot drove him back to the ladder in a hasty scramble.

"You silly thing. Men really are so stupid sometimes," Mary said, casually fanning the gun smoke away from her face with a graceful hand. "I was talking about the *song.* You're lower than me, at present, so I should have sung, '*You* take the *low* road and *I'll* take the *high* road.' "

And she sang the entire tune, with all its verses (including the twenty-odd she'd written herself) over again, making the necessary corrections, and keeping Alan glued to the ladder with the aid of two more erratically aimed bullets.

"There! That was much better and far more appropriate. Don't you think so?" she asked, as the last notes drifted eerily away in the storm-washed air.

"Aye," Alan agreed, a suddenly dangerous edge sharpening his voice. "And the best part is, you've now emptied both cylinders!" With a quick, catlike motion, he swung himself onto the ledge and grabbed for her.

She skipped lightly out of reach. "Ahhh, you can count to twelve—I'm so impressed! But it hardly matters. I've lots more cartridges." She giggled, and then bit her lip in concentration as she fumbled with the revolver in her hand, apparently trying to determine how it opened for reloading.

Alan made another grab. "Give me that! You don't know what you're doing."

"No, no, no—don't help me. I want to figure it out for myself," Mary said, dancing three more steps away.

Easily working her way around the ledge, she continued fussing with the weapon, always staying just beyond Alan's reach and cheerfully chortling to herself. "Ah-ha!

92

So that's how it opens. How cunning. Now I wonder which end of these is the front?" she mused, slipping one of the cartridges out of the belt and squinting at it.

"Mary, those aren't toys. Give them to me!" Alan demanded, doing his best to overtake her. But the narrowness of the ledge put a man of his size at disadvantage compared to the slender redhead.

"Don't call me Mary." She pouted, turning the bullet this way and that. "I told you before—I'm Cassandra."

"Cassandra, then," he half growled.

"No . . . After hearing you say it, I don't think Cassandra will do, either. It's too cumbersome." She paused briefly, and he thought he had her, but it was only a tease. "I think I'll call myself Monique instead. That way I can keep the same initial so I won't have to change my monogram. I do believe in being practical."

"Then be practical now and come down from here. You shouldn't be playing with Geordie's Colts. He's going to be very angry with you," Alan warned, almost slipping as he missed another grab.

"He's angry already. But it won't do him any good. These aren't his Colts any longer. They're mine." Mary laughed, pausing again to let Alan make up the distance he'd lost by slipping.

"How do you figure that?" he bit out.

"Because last night I had three aces and he only had two."

It was Alan's turn to pause. "Five aces total? You cheated him?"

"Don't be absurd," she said, deciding at last how the bullets loaded. "No one has to cheat Geordie at cards. It's too easy to beat him honestly." She clumsily began to fill the Colt's chambers. "One of my aces was a one-eyed Jack. One-eyed Jacks were wild last night," she explained, and gave a startled shriek as part of the tower wall abruptly fell away behind her and she toppled inward.

Several moments of tremendous banging, scuffling, and crashing ensued, punctuated by enraged feminine screams and a few genuine shouts of pain—none of them from a woman's throat.

Inching carefully along the outside ledge, Alan peeked through the opening, winced at what he saw, hastily retraced his steps, and hurried down the ladder.

He made it to the ground only seconds before Simon Elliott staggered through the bottom door of the tower with Mary-Monique slung over his shoulder. The lanky blond's tie was gone, his jacket was torn, and he was sporting a bump over one eye, a cut on his chin, and a bruise on his cheek. His cargo was hissing and spitting like an alley cat and furiously trying to reach one of her two revolvers, both of which were jammed into the waistband of his trousers.

"I'm afraid not, little girl. I'll give them back to you when you're old enough to learn how to use them properly," he said smoothly, landing a swat on her upturned derriere.

"I hate you!" she hissed from her inverted position.

"That's quite all right. You're not one of my favorite people either," he replied, swinging her down to her feet with a little jolt. "Now, why don't you go to your room? It must be way past your bedtime. Would you like me to come along and tuck you in?"

She shot him a glare that would have stripped the flesh from his bones if eyes were razors, stormed several paces toward the main keep, saw the figure huddled on the bench, and went whiter than the satin sheet it was wrapped in.

"Oh, my God! Dorcas, what happened to you?" she gasped, racing to her side.

Dorcas glanced up at Mary's blurry, stricken expression and tried to smile, but the current state of her face wouldn't quite allow it. "I enjoyed your performance. Almost applauded," she joked weakly through swollen lips.

With a laugh that sounded more like a sob, Mary quickly sat next to her. "Honey, I'm so sorry. I wasn't quick enough," she whispered, gathering the shivering form into her arms.

Too fuzzy to figure out what she was talking about and too shaky to sit upright, Dorcas let herself collapse against the silk-clad shoulder. Its owner might be as nutty as a fruitcake, but at the moment she was also acting sweeter than one. Why? Dorcas didn't know and didn't care. It was simply a relief to have the comfort.

She felt Mary tense suddenly and didn't even have to hear that angry growl to know Alan was looming over them.

"I thought I bid you stay in the room! What the devil are you doing here—dressed like *that?*"

Dorcas choked back a scream. *Oh yes, dressed like this,* she thought half hysterically. *The way you left me— naked and defenseless—a sitting duck for the first drunk who decided to try his luck!*

With a furious moan she buried her battered face deeper into the billowy negligee. "Make him go away," she mumbled.

Mary's already tense form stiffened into steel. "With pleasure," she muttered under her breath. And Dorcas felt one of the young woman's hands shift and close around something small and hard beneath the folds of canary silk.

How funny, she mused vaguely. *I was as wrong as Dunstan.* Mary hadn't had two guns, after all; she'd had at least three, apparently. The third one felt like a der-ringer in a garter holster. Was that what the well-dressed Boston belles were wearing this season?

"I think you've already done quite enough for one night, Cousin Alan," the redhead said with a curious, glacial calm. "Leave us alone now. I'm going to take Dorcas to my room." She pulled both of them upright, holding Dorcas against herself with a lithe, athletic strength that was almost as surprising as the hidden weapon.

Alan bit back a low curse, obviously fighting to control himself, and just as obviously losing the battle. "Listen, lassies, I've had all I'm going to take from either of you. Enough is enough! Mary, you can go to your room or go to blazes. I don't care, just so long as you go there now and go alone. And Dorcas, you are coming with me!"

A hand flashed out, yanking her away from Mary, his fingers not rough exactly, but digging into the bite wound on her shoulder with enough pressure to make her cry out. Mary flew forward and pulled her back, shoving her half behind herself and steadying her with her left hand, while the right was still buried somewhere in the froth of yellow silk wafting about her in the cool, predawn air.

"If you want her, you'll have to get past me," she said quietly and deliberately, and with an icy poise that made her sound as though she faced situations like this regularly, for sport. "Beating an innocent girl . . . I should have shot you when I had the chance," she added in a tone softer than death.

The innocent girl heard it, but the assumed beater of women's full attention was suddenly riveted elsewhere. He was staring at Dorcas's now exposed swollen and bloody face—with an expression of unspeakable black rage fast darkening his own.

"Who?"

One word. That was all he spoke. The sound of his voice sliced through her like a knife. His figure towered before her, fuzzy and wavering, his face a dim blur with two sparks of deep gold searing out of it. Squinting at them, Dorcas felt a furious wave of adrenaline wash over her.

"You! You did it!" she hissed.

Alan scarcely acknowledged the answer. He seemed to view it as mere hysterical raving. "Never mind. I'll find out for myself," he growled, his gaze burning over her, reading every mark, every drop of blood, as though it were a volume of information, while she glared defiantly back at him.

Neither of them noticed that they had become the new show for the audience in the courtyard. Only Mary was aware of the growing number of people clustering about them. Her piercing blue eyes never left Alan, but she knew the position of every kilted clansman, every tartan-shawled woman hovering nearby. The only person she missed, somehow, was Simon Elliott, who suddenly was just there, brushing against her right side and startling her so much that her hidden hand nearly jerked free.

"You're right," he whispered, grinning down, as she quickly caught herself, shoving the hand and what it was holding farther into the yellow folds. "That probably would not be a wise move."

"I don't know what you're talking about," she breathed, blinking up at him with wide-eyed innocence and just the right amount of feminine pique.

"Yes, you do." He grinned again. "And you know I'll be watching you closely from now on, too, don't you?"

She managed a very attractive little blush. "All men watch me. They can't help themselves." She pouted prettily. "My beauty attracts them, like moths to a flame."

"Mmm . . . yes," Simon murmured, stroking her from head to toe with a visual assessment that turned the blush genuine. "That's another good reason for it."

He sauntered past her into the shadows, leaving Mary looking like a gambler who had just accidentally dropped all her cards face up on the table and was trying to convince herself that no one had seen them.

Beside her, Dorcas was struggling to keep her uncooperative legs under herself and marveling that it could be so hot and so cold at the same time. She realized that she was probably suffering from shock, but somehow that knowledge didn't make the symptoms any easier to deal with. The only silver lining in the cloud was that she could hardly see Alan anymore. The courtyard and everyone in it were merging into one big swirling patchwork haze.

"Please, d-don't let me pass out," she gasped to Mary. "I don't trust what will happen if I faint again."

"Stand back! Someone get her some water!" Mary ordered, and immediately resettled her charge onto the bench and began fanning her.

Dorcas felt her hair being pushed back off her face and shoulders and the cool air stinging the now exposed bite wound. She also felt Mary almost drop her and heard the redhead's enraged shriek:

"Oh, my God—He's *bitten* her! She'll get rabies!"

The noise brought her back enough to be disturbingly aware of Alan kneeling before her and glaring hard at something golden fastened in the sheet just below the wound.

The kilt pin.

"Dunstan!" Alan snarled the name as if it were the vilest of curses.

He snarled it just as its owner happened to be lumbering his way out of the keep in an absolute idiocy of bravado. Dunstan had tidied himself up a bit and decided, apparently, that if he acted as though nothing had occurred, no one would be the wiser. He was that stupid. Or that drunk. Or both.

"Aye, cousin?" he said, staggering toward the cluster

of people like a big, smelly, unknowing lamb on its way to the slaughter.

Though slaughter was, perhaps, too pleasant a word for what it might have been if two men hadn't instantly leapt on Alan to hold him back.

And then two more.

And two more . . .

In the end, it took seven hearty Highlanders several long, hellish moments to drag their laird to the ground. Even then an extra one was needed to keep him there. That one was Uncle Angus.

"Hold, lad—hold!" he bellowed, doing a powerful bit of holding himself, with a heavy hand buried deep in Alan's thick hair. "If he's guilty, Dunstan'll be duly punished. But by MacAllister law, nay by yoors!"

Straining furiously against the kilted tonnage pinning him to the damp earth, Alan gave a single inhuman cry of defiance. It slammed through the great courtyard like the scream of a wounded panther, nearly splitting the walls and hitting Dorcas with the force of a bullwhip. In the dazed, dizzy state of her nerves, she felt, suddenly, as if she was reliving some ghastly, heartrending experience. But she couldn't remember exactly what it was. She only knew that it was something that had happened right where she was now, in the castle's inner yard, and that, somehow, she had heard that cry before.

"Even the laird canna change this! D'ye understand me, lad?"

Dorcas heard Angus's question and Alan's answering hiss of, "Aye," as if the voices were coming from another world. She stumbled through the next moments feeling as if she was barely in them, as though the whole thing was some weird, wavering masque and she was simultaneously one of the players and one of the spectators.

Dunstan was led forward, mumbling some sullen, fretful nonsense about her being a witch and cursing him with her evil eye. Which had made Mary spit, "No, you idiot, *I'm* the witch! And if you don't shut up, I'll turn you into something worse than the disgusting toad you already are!" He had ended by accepting his fate stoically, however, not even trying to argue against the accusations Dorcas had been required to state in front of all.

That had been the eeriest part for her—having to stand and recite what he'd done while that sea of curious eyes engulfed her. That and Dunstan's abrupt rousing to deny the part about the cat. His wounds were from her, he had insisted. She had fought him like a cat, that was all. Even in her haze, Dorcas had found that unnerving. Why would he lie about the cat, of all things?

"That's not true! I was in no position to fight. That's why he got as far as he did," she insisted, trying to make someone believe her. Good heavens, they were all staring at her as if she'd just sprouted whiskers and pointed ears.

Mary had quickly guided her back onto the bench. "Forget it, honey. What difference does it make? You must have been so frightened, you didn't realize everything that was happening. Listen, you vultures, can't you see what you're doing?" she demanded of the small crowd. "Dorcas doesn't need to think about this any longer. Shoot that oaf, hang him, chop off his head, or whatever you do with mad dogs and get it over with, so she can be tended to and rest!" Storming to her feet, the redhead hauled Dorcas up beside herself and started steering the girl toward the main keep. She let out a startled little cry as a quick hand stopped them short.

And Dorcas let out a yelp as she felt herself being swung up into a muscular pair of arms.

"Take it easy, Miss Jeffries. I'm merely offering some gentlemanly assistance. You don't look in any shape to navigate the ramp," sounded a familiar drawl, as a lazy grin beamed down at her.

Dorcas heaved a relieved sigh and sank back against the man's solid chest. "I never thought I'd hear myself say this, but it cheers me tremendously to see you, Mr. Elliott," she breathed, as he chuckled and carried her up the ramp to the keep's second-floor entrance.

"At least one of us is happy about it," Mary muttered, and promptly choked on a second cry as the trio's way was abruptly blocked by the figure Dorcas had least wanted to see.

Burning amber eyes glinted dangerously into Simon's cool gray ones. *Like fire and smoke,* she thought distractedly, as her heart threatened to skip the next several beats.

"If you're really a wizard, Mr. Elliott, prove it to me now by making him disappear." She groaned into his lapel.

Both men seemed to ignore the request. They looked a bit like two stags about to do battle. Except they were locking gazes instead of antlers.

"Thank you for your trouble," Alan said to Simon, as though gratitude was the last thing on his mind. "But I can handle things from here." His arms lifted to take her.

"You're welcome, but it's no trouble at all. I'm happy to be of service." Simon grinned, swinging his armful to the side and preparing to step past.

" 'Tis a service she doesn't need," Alan said, blocking them again. And he was not grinning, the armful noted.

"Yes, I do!" she insisted, locking her own arms around Elliott's neck as Alan started to pull her away.

An ear-splitting whistle pierced the air and three heads turned with a start, just in time to see Mary withdrawing two fingers from her mouth, her eyes blazing blue sparks.

"What do you think she is, a rope in a tug-of-war?" the tall redhead demanded, thrusting herself between Alan and Simon. "Cousin Alan, be reasonable. Leave

Dorcas with me tonight. She needs a woman's care. You'll only upset her more."

"I'll upset you, lassie, if you don't step aside," he warned, latching onto Mary's arm with an intimidating grip.

The grip jerked open. And so did his eyes, in astonishment, as her free hand shot out and landed a chop to his wrist that rattled his teeth.

Too late, Mary realized her mistake. She glanced over her shoulder to see Elliott's smoky gaze narrowly studying her, and her own eyes immediately began blinking, as though fighting back tears. "Oh, ow!" she sniffled. "I hurt my hand."

"I'm so sorry. Would you like me to kiss it for you and make it better?" Simon offered with a grin.

"No. But I'll tell you what you *can* kiss, if you're not careful," she answered with a sinister sweetness.

His grin broadened. "Mmm . . . if it's what I hope it is, I'd enjoy that even more."

"Eeuh!" Mary gagged, a horrified blush staining her cheeks. "You're disgusting." She pivoted back to Alan. "So are you! Both of you are disgusting! All men are pigs," she told Dorcas, neatly prying her loose from Simon and helping her to stand. "We don't need any of them." Holding her chin firmly in the air and her arms protectively around Dorcas, she tried to guide the girl through the keep's smaller, foot passage entrance.

Alan swiftly back-stepped, yanked the door shut, and held it fast with one hand while he reached toward Dorcas with the other. The sudden tenderness in his voice hit her harder than if he had shouted. "Please . . . let me take care of you. I'll not do anything to hurt you further. I just want to be with you. 'Tis the only way I can be certain you'll be safe."

"She'll be safer with me than she will with you!" Mary argued, feeling Dorcas start to shiver against her. "Why do men have to be so blind? She's been too long without care already, and you're standing here wasting more time! Stop being an idiot, Alan. Stand aside!"

The door suddenly started to rattle on its heavy iron hinges. "Did I hear someone say Alan? Be that ye, Alan MacAllister, holdin' this door shut?" a voice on the other side called. "Ye'd best open it, laddie—afore I take me stick tae ye."

"Molly? Thank heavens that's you! I was just coming to find you. That miserable toad, Dunstan, attacked Dorcas, and she needs help," Mary called. "Probably your charm for warts, too," she added thoughtfully.

"Dorcas, is it? Be that th' lassie I sent th' salve fer t'other night? Th' one they say has just wedded Alan? I've nay seen her yet."

"Yes, that's her, and she's ready to collapse. Make Alan let us through. He's being a pigheaded lout!"

The voice chuckled softly, then said sternly, "Alan MacAllister, I bid ye once to open this door. Now I'm biddin' ye again. If I hafta bid ye a third time, I ken someone who's gang tae be a very sorry an' a very sore laddie. D'ye hear me, son?"

Alan heaved a tremendous sigh. "Aye, Grandmother," he said, and reluctantly stepped aside. "What are you laughing at?" He glowered at Simon. "Don't you have somewhere else you need to be right now?"

"Actually, now that you mention it . . ." The other man grinned. "No."

"Well, go there, anyway!"

It was Elliott's turn to sigh. "Oh, all right. If you're going to be that way about it." He dipped a slight bow to Mary and Dorcas. "Ladies, I'll see you later."

"Not if we see you first," Mary muttered.

"Ah, but that's just it, isn't it? No one ever sees me first. I'm a wizard," he told her, that lazy grin spreading slowly across his face. "I can appear in a puff of . . .

smoke." He watched a moment as every last scrap of color drained from her, then turned and moved casually off with a long, lanky stride.

"Damn. And here I'd been thinking he was just some nosy tenderfoot," Dorcas heard Mary hiss under her breath. "I'm going to have to rewrite this show."

"Be ye makin' a new play, dear?" inquired a female Leprechaun from the doorway.

A female Leprechaun? No, that couldn't be right. Leprechauns were Irish. This was a Bodach, a Scottish pixie, perhaps. One of the Wee Folk, anyway, Dorcas decided in her daze. The white-haired woman smiling up at Mary was less than five feet tall and as wispy and delicate as a blade of grass.

"You know me, Molly, I'm always working on some drama or other," Mary murmured, looking as though she was deep in the middle of one right then.

"Aye, dear, yoor a bonny, braw play actress." The old woman chuckled. "An' this be me new granddaughter?" Her eyes crinkled for an instant as she seemed to read the whole of Dorcas's injuries and half her thoughts in one practiced glance. "I'm sorry ye've had such a rough welcome tae yoor new home, dear, but 'tis nuthin' I canna heal. . . . Wipe that ugly frown fray yoor face, Alan MacAllister, an' make yerself scarce. Mary an' I'll tend yoor bride. Yoor black looks be fearin' th' lassie," she said. "I'll send if yoor needed."

"You won't have to send far," Alan growled. "I'll be right outside your door."

"Oh, 'tis one o' them moods, is it?" Tiny hands on her narrow hips, Molly stood squinting up and clucking her tongue at him. "Ah, well, wha' canna be cured, mun be endured. . . . Bring yoor bride alang, then, ye blackguard. But mind ye go gentle. 'Tis a wicked knock on her head. If ye worsen it, I'll give ye one tae match on yoor own." Thumping her short staff on the floor with every step, Molly led the way deep into the heart of the keep to her stillroom, filled with sweet and pungent potions, powders, and salves, and heady, fragrant bunches of herbs drying from the ceiling rafters.

Dorcas rode the entire way in Alan's arms. And in agony—too weak to lift her head off his chest and having to listen to the steady beat of his heart throbbing a counterpoint rhythm to the painful pounding in her skull. There wasn't a single part of her that didn't ache. But the sharpest ache of all was the one that stabbed through her with the dreadful realization that part of her, at least, wanted this. She wanted to feel his warmth and his strength wrapped around her, holding her together, keeping her from flying into a thousand desperate fragments.

It was worse than horrible. It was ridiculous. It made no sense. She distrusted him, feared him, hated him even. Yet being held by him was like being held by a rock. It felt like coming home after fighting a war in some frightful, alien land. How could that be? How could it feel so right when she knew the whole thing was so utterly, awfully wrong?

She didn't even realize she had been moaning aloud until she felt his lips grazing her brow and heard his low voice murmuring, "Dorcas, I'm sorry. I'm trying not to hurt you."

It was the final blow. It burst the dam of her control and hot, salty tears flooded down her cheeks, stinging the open cuts. "Damn you! Everything you do hurts me!" she sobbed. "Why can't you just leave me alone? Let me go!"

A brief shudder ran through him, as though her words had been a knife thrust, and she felt his body tighten.

"I'm sorry," he repeated, the tenderness of his previous tone hardened into raw steel. " 'Tis not my intention to wound, but if that's the way you feel, you'd best get used to it, because this infantile resistance changes nothing. You're mine, whether you like it or not. I'll ride into Hell before I'll let you go!"

I'm almost in Hell now, Dorcas thought, struggling to choke back her sobs before they grew uncontrollable. His declaration had sent chills down her spine. Because he could be right, she realized in a near panic. Her fear, hurt, anger, and confusion might not make much difference at that. None of this was the least bit logical—but none of it really changed anything, either. She was beginning to feel that being in his arms was the only place in the world she was supposed to be.

Chapter Five

It was like placing one picture over a similar but not quite identical one, so that the lines blurred together and it was difficult to tell where one image ended and the other began. That was what the dream had been like, Dorcas was thinking as she lay between the sheets (fresh, sensible cotton ones, thank goodness) straining to remember it, her bruised eyes weighted shut with the effort.

Alan had brought her back to their room, as he called it, after Molly's skillful doctoring of her injuries. She had been too drained by then and too woozy from the pain-killer the herbwoman had given her to care where she was. She had barely even noticed Alan unwrapping her improvised toga, slipping a nightgown over her head, and tucking her under the covers as if she was a small child. Then he pulled off his shirt and boots and slid in with her, cradling her against himself until she had fallen fully asleep.

Which certainly proved the worth of Molly's potions, she mused. It was outrageous to think that she ever would have been able to sleep in such a position otherwise—no matter how exhausted she was. Especially given the way he had spent the fuzzy interval before slumber rubbing her shoulders and stroking her back through the nightgown, whispering soft words into her hair. Words she couldn't remember now.

That tender side of Alan seemed the most devastating of all to her. It rattled her to the core, because it was so incongruous with the rest of him. And because she was so defenseless against it, Dorcas thought. His growling and bullying was something she could lean into, brace herself for, and at least try to resist. But how did you fight gentleness? It was like one of those snares that used your own weight against you. The harder you struggled to loosen it, the tighter it became. She could feel the whole frightening situation closing in on her almost as if it were a noose around her neck. And her dream had only served to pull the rope more snugly.

It had been so weird; more like a memory than a dream, really. But a memory of something that had never happened to her. She had been someone else in the dream, a girl slightly older than herself, who had been locked in the tower room as she had, but during some earlier time. Dorcas had realized that, because the tree outside the window had been so much smaller. She had been squeezed into the window, staring out over the branches and waiting for someone, her heart pounding with a desperate longing and terrified dread at the same time. Who, exactly, she had been waiting for in the dream, she wasn't sure, but she had known it was a man, and that he was coming to rescue her. Though from what, she couldn't remember.

The rest of the dream was a blank, except for the last part of it. In the last moment before waking, everything had been pitch black around her and heavy with the odors of smoke and blood. She had felt frozen, unable to move, and she hadn't known where she was anymore. But there had been the horrible noise of someone or something screaming in rage. It had sounded almost like Alan's cry when they'd pinned him in the yard. And she had awoken with a jolt, the agony of it still ringing in her ears.

"Dorcas? I can tell you're awake by the way you keep jiggling your knee under the covers. Do you feel well enough to sit up and eat something?"

"Wh-what?" A pair of bruised green eyes popped open with a start, saw who it was, and crinkled at the corners, as Dorcas's sore face managed a half normal smile. "Oh, it's you. Good morning, Monique."

"It's afternoon," said the redhead, smiling back. "And you can forget about Monique. I'm going back to plain old Mary for a while."

"I'm glad. I always liked the name Mary. What time is it, anyway?" Dorcas asked, cautiously pulling herself upright in the bed. *So far, so good,* she thought. *My head hasn't fallen off yet.*

Mary rose from her chair in a rustle of lavender muslin and started fussing with some covered dishes on a nearby table. "It's about a quarter till two. You missed Dunstan's noontime flogging, but I enjoyed it enough for both of us. He got twenty good ones with a cat-o-nine-tails. His back looks like a freshly skinned buffalo carcass. And the rest of him is starting to look like an over-boiled lobster. He has to hang in his ropes in this blistering Texas sun until nightfall. Do you want scrambled eggs, porridge, or both?"

"Neither." Dorcas gagged, pressing both hands to her suddenly churning stomach. "That . . . that's barbaric! Poor Dunstan."

"Poor Dunstan, nothing!" Mary stared at her in disbelief. "How can you say that after what he did? He's getting off lightly. I'd have given him at least fifty lashes and left him hanging for a week!"

"Oh, Mary, you don't mean that. The poor fool was drunk. He didn't realize what he was doing. And he'd been punished enough, anyway, between the mauling and me cracking him with the bedpost." Swinging her legs over the side of the bed, Dorcas dropped unsteadily to her feet and staggered across the room to fumble her way into a lacy pink dressing gown she'd spotted draped over the top of the steamer trunk. There were matching slippers on the floor in front of it and she half collapsed onto the trunk to slide them on.

"Where do you think you're going? Molly's orders are for you to stay in bed all day," Mary said sternly.

"I'll be back as soon as I've cut Dunstan down," Dorcas said, having no idea how she was going to accomplish that feat, but wobbling toward the door to do it just the same. "It's too cruel to leave him hanging in the heat all day. On top of his other wounds, it could even kill him! And, if he dies, I'll feel guilty about it for the rest of my life."

Mary caught her before she was halfway out of the room. "Honey, that's not going to happen. Dunstan's a toad, but he's an iron toad. You couldn't dent him with a battle-ax. He'll be fine . . . unfortunately." She put an arm around Dorcas and started steering her toward the four-poster. "Come back to bed. You're still hurt and you're not thinking clearly. They wouldn't let you release him, anyway. The toad had to take his full punishment. It's the MacAllister code. The only one who could possibly spare him at this point is Alan, because he's the hereditary leader of the community. But I think Laird Alan would cut his own throat before he'd cut lover boy down early. He's in the outer courtyard now, watching him with a look that makes my scalp feel loose. I can only imagine what it's doing to Dunstan."

It was hardly the most comforting image Mary could have picked. A view of Alan as she had first seen him—as the savage Plains warrior—flashed instantly before Dorcas's black and blue and green eyes, and she couldn't help shivering as she was guided back under the covers.

"You see? You're all weak and trembly from moving around," Mary chided, plumping up the pillows behind her.

Dorcas shook her head absently, making herself so dizzy for a moment that the bed felt like a raft riding over the rapids. "No, it's not that." She clutched at the mattress to keep from falling off it. Drawing a few deep breaths, she waited for the white water to calm and for Mary's three faces to merge back into one. "It's . . . it's . . ."

It's this insane business about Alan thinking himself a Comanche, she was going to say, but Mary cut her off.

"It's your head injury. That and Uncle Angus's annoying fixation on introducing new blood into his clan's *breeding stock,*" the redhead said almost too wryly. "His insufferable matchmaking has made this a pretty insufferable few days for you, I'm afraid. Not that I've helped the situation any," she added with a sigh. "I was trying to save you from Alan and I got you assaulted by toad Dunstan instead. I'm truly sorry about that."

Dorcas blinked up at the elegantly featured haze hovering above her. "You . . . you were trying to save me from . . . But you hardly know me."

"What difference does that make? You looked like someone who valued her vir—let's just say *virtue,* and I thought it might be amusing to help you hang on to it a while longer." The haze shrugged. "The storm woke me last night and I saw that two-bit sideshow on the rampart. Later I saw Alan come in here. I waited in the pas-

111

sage a bit, but when I didn't hear any screaming or
shouts, I realized you were either lost in this maze or
hiding, so I went looking for you, and that's when we
met in the alcove. I couldn't do anything then, because
I heard someone behind me in the passageway—spying
on us, obviously. Though I don't know who it was, for
sure."

"I think I do," Dorcas put in, remembering the electric
lantern. "It may have been Mr. Elliott. But I can't imagine why he'd be spying."

"I can," Mary said, more to herself than to her charge.
"But never mind that now. My point is that I was only
acting odd then to divert suspicion, as they say in the
dime novels. I thought it might be Alan watching us.
Seeing as how he expects that sort of behavior from me,
I rather hated to disappoint him. He thinks I'm quite a
loon, you know."

He's in no position to judge, Dorcas thought as she
watched Mary's face coming slowly back into focus.

"I cooked up that little tower act to draw him away
from you. Not one of my more original performances,
I'm afraid, but it was the best I could do on short notice,"
Mary finished. "I could have kept him there until dawn,
too, if the darn wall hadn't collapsed. That's the most
peculiar thing I've ever had happen," she muttered. "It
simply *dissolved.* I can't figure out how it happened."

Oh, my God, Dorcas suddenly thought. It was as if
one of Simon Elliott's electric lamps had just flashed on
inside her aching skull. *I believe I know what he and Dr.
Earnshaw are working on!*

"Honey, what's the matter? Are you feeling sick
again? You're whiter than the pillowcase. Do you want
me to fetch Molly?"

"Um . . . yes . . . that might be a good idea," Dorcas
half lied. Her head was throbbing, after all, though it
wasn't merely from the knocks she'd taken. She had been

given too much to think about too quickly. She needed some time alone to sort through it all.

"Thanks, Mary. I really am grateful for all your help," she added sincerely as the redhead rustled to the door.

Mary paused a moment to look back, an unreadable expression on her classic face—or perhaps it was just that Dorcas's vision was still a little fuzzy around the edges. "Don't mention it. I'd do the same for any girl who needed it. I know how . . . how irritating unwanted advances can be." Something in the tone of her voice made it sound as though she knew a little too well. "By the way, that's one thing you needn't worry about—for a little while, anyway," she added more cheerfully. "Molly has given Alan very specific instructions not to do anything to jostle you for a few days, if you catch my meaning." With a quick, catlike grin at Dorcas's sudden blush, she waltzed gracefully out of the room.

Dorcas gave her until the count of ten, then pushed back the covers and slid tentatively to her feet, hanging on to one of the bed's three remaining posts for support while she shuffled back into the lacy pink slippers. Along with everything else in her mind was the inescapable image of poor, foolish Dunstan frying in the blazing sun like a slab of bacon sizzling on a hot grill. That had been her other motivation for getting Mary out of the way; she was still determined to set him free.

After that, she could ponder her own release. And what she thought Elliott and Earnshaw had created. And how she could use the latter to accomplish the former.

On her somewhat wobbly trek out of the keep, she kept glancing about, peering into corners and staring at shadows, half expecting to see the black cat. And half disappointed when the enigmatic feline never materialized. But then, he was probably nocturnal, she told herself, and spent the heat of the day curled up in some shady, secluded spot, sleeping. The only times she had seen him, after all, had been at night.

Which was hardly surprising, Dorcas suddenly realized, because the only times she had seen the castle itself had been at dusk or full night. This afternoon was her first view of the place in daylight. How curious. She had been there for, what . . . two nights and almost a day and a half? Yet this was her first clear look at her prison. Or it would be, anyway, as soon as she was outside.

The passing of time meant little in the large keep. Its walls were thick, its windows narrow and scarce. Here, there was no morning, afternoon, or evening. Here, as far as she could determine, there was only dim, dimmer, and dark.

Outside, however, with the sun blaring down on the castle's inner courtyard, the glare was bright, brighter, and solar flare. It almost blistered her eyes in their bruised sockets. Squinting and blinking into the light, Dorcas grappled her way down the long ramp and into the yard, paused a moment, and then started shakily across it. She had no idea where she was going, but it didn't seem to matter much; she couldn't see where she was going right then anyway. The abrupt glare had hit her so sharply, she had closed her eyes briefly to block some of its sting.

That was how she managed to wander into the open shed, trip, and fall face-first, full-length into the horse trough someone had left inconveniently lying about.

Or was it a horse trough?

Gasping, sputtering, surprisingly sticky, and trying to figure out what she had just landed in, she felt several sets of not particularly gentle hands hauling her out of it.

" 'Tis Alan's bride!"

"What's she doin' here, then?"

"Lookin' fer Alan, maybe? There's a joke fer ye."

"Nay. Spoilin' th' brew, 'tis whut. An' 'tis nay joke."

"Aye, Geordie. Ye can kiss this batch g'bye."

Beer? Oh, dear, what a mess.

Feeling like an imbecile, Dorcas hastily wiped the stuff out of her eyes and glanced nervously around at the four faces staring at her. They belonged to three stocky, kilted men and a plump, middle-aged woman in a tartan skirt, white blouse, and stained apron. None of them seemed overly pleased to see her and, under the circumstances, she could hardly blame them.

"I . . . I'm so sorry." She coughed, streaming brown puddles all over the floor. "The sun was in my eyes and I couldn't see where I was going. . . . Er . . . I hope you'll excuse me now. There's . . . there's something I need to do. . . ."

Hair sticking to her head like wet string, her lacy dressing gown plastered against her like a second skin, and smelling like a brewery, she had backed clumsily through the open door, turned, and gone about three steps into the yard when the woman called out irritably, "Laird Alan's in th' *outer* court, m'lady."

"The outer courtyard? Is that where Dunstan is, too?" Dorcas asked, glancing timidly at the glowering quartet.

"Aye!" the man called Geordie spat. "Throo th' gate yonder, ye'll find him, an' can gloat yoor fill." He gestured toward a gap in a high wall about twenty yards in front of her, then swung roughly back to his ruined beer.

"I'm not going to gloat. I want to—" she began, but she was cut off by grumblings of "Strumpet!" and "Witch!" filtering angrily out of the shed. Her face burning, she flung away from them as fast as her clinging garments and oddly fuddled head would allow, and squished the few dozen paces to the entrance Geordie had pointed out, leaving a wet, snaky trail behind her.

The beer had been only partially fermented, but she had swallowed enough of it on an empty stomach and on top of her head injury and the residue of Molly's pain-killers to make her what was sometimes referred to as loaded and ready for bear.

Not that she realized that. Having never had a drop of alcohol before, Dorcas had no idea what its effects felt like. She only knew that her squishing slippers and sticky, sopping dressing gown were uncomfortable, con-straining, and far more trouble than they seemed worth. Kicking off the former and ripping free from the latter just as she reached the wall, she tottered through the gap in it wearing nothing but her soaking white silk night-gown, which hugged every curve of her body as though it had been painted onto it.

A rear view of Dunstan stopped her dead in her tracks. He was several paces forward on a rough scaffolding, wrists lashed to an overhead beam and looking much like a raw side of beef hanging in a butcher's window to Dor-cas's blurry eyes. With a horrified cry, she dashed dizzily around to the front of the scaffolding, in plain sight of a dozen or so people who were milling about the great yard on business . . . and Alan.

"Oh, Dunstan! This is awful!" she wailed.

Shouting something a bit more colorful and a lot less printable, Alan lunged toward her, snatching the shawl right off the shoulders of an alarmed matron who hap-pened to be passing by just then and bundling it about Dorcas.

"What the devil—" he began.

"Cut him down!" she demanded, glaring defiantly into his amber eyes and realizing, with a start, that there were four of them staring furiously back at her. "Both of you!" she added, getting another start as her gaze swung to Dunstan and then back to the Alans. "Both of you cut both of him down right now!"

The look in the amber eyes went from fury to astonishment. And there was suddenly a whole sea of them swimming before her.

"No, wait!" Dorcas flung up her hand. "You can't all go up there. You'll collapse it. Just you, the one in the middle—you cut the Dunstans down. And be quick about it!"

"You're drunk," Alan said with amazement.

"I am not!" she declared indignantly. "I merely shlipped . . . I mean, splipped . . . I mean . . . Oh hell, I tripped and fell into a damn vat of—*hic!*—beer."

"An' had tae drink it, I'll wager, tae keep fray drownin'," Dunstan mumbled from the scaffolding. "Ye can hardly blame her, Alan. 'Tis whut I'd a done."

"You shut up or you'll find yourself hanging there 'til Christmas," Alan snarled up at him.

"No, you won't, Dunshtan," Dorcas told him. "Thish has gone far enough!" she told the Alans. "Cut him down now or . . . or . . ." She thought feverishly for a moment. "Or I'll hold my breath!" And her bruised cheeks promptly puffed out like two little balloons.

"Dorcas, stop that," Alan ordered.

Her cheeks puffed a little further and her eyes stared fixedly ahead.

"This is utter folly! You're behaving like a child."

Her face began to turn pale blue beneath the bruises and her knees started to tremble.

"I'm warning you . . . Do you hear me, lassie?"

Her knees gave out and she sat down hard on the ground but still refused to release her breath.

"Dorcas . . ."

She could feel her eyes crossing and the sun going dark.

"Bloody hell, I'll cut him down! Now breathe, for God's sake."

All the old air whooshed out of her lungs and she sucked in a big, fresh breath, noticed her bare toes sticking out in front of her, and asked abruptly, "Where are my slippers? Oh, thash right, I had to get rid of them," she answered herself. "They were squishing too loudly."

"Squishing?" Alan asked, staring down at her, his lips beginning to twitch.

"Yes, squishing. It was getting on my nerves," she said, shrugging off the shawl. "Sho is this. It's too hot."

He reached down and quickly wrapped it more tightly around her. "No. Leave it be."

"You leave *me* be!" she fussed, awkwardly untangling herself from the tartan folds the moment Alan had turned his back on her and mounted the scaffolding to free Dunstan.

"This is your lucky day, cousin," he growled softly to the half-baked man.

"Aye." Dunstan grinned crookedly, gazing over Alan's shoulder at the shawless Dorcas, who had just struggled to her hands and knees and was crawling away from the men toward an enticing little cluster of wildflowers she'd spotted a few yards away.

Alan sliced through Dunstan's last bond, swiveled slightly, saw her, cursed, jumped off the scaffold like a charging panther, grabbed the shawl, and managed to wrap her into it and his arms all in the same motion.

"Put me down!" she complained. "I want to pick some of those flowersh."

"I'll pick them for you later, after you've had a bath and are back in bed," he promised, carrying her toward the gate to the inner yard.

Dunstan had just finished painfully lowering himself to the ground as they passed the scaffold. "Thank ye, lass," he mumbled, glancing shyly at Dorcas and then hastily lowering his eyes beneath Alan's black glare.

"You don't have to thank me. I only did what had to be done. It washn't a fair punishment. You didn't mean to hurt me. It was the whishkey," she told him. "People aren't re . . . reshponsible for themshelves when they're drunk. You should remember that," she slurred sternly to Alan.

"I'll try," he said very solemnly. "Now it's back to bed with you, my tipsy lassie."

"I'm not yours. I'm not tipshy. And I don't want to go back to bed! I'm not shleepy."

"You don't have to sleep. Just lie there and rest. I'll stay and keep you company."

"Then I'll never get any rest. All you want to do ish . . . ish play footshie."

"Play *footsie?*" Alan paused in midstep to gaze down at her, an amused curling at the corners of his mouth.

It irritated Dorcas tremendously. "You know what I mean," she grumbled against his chest. "And I'm not intereshted! I won't like it. I take after my Aunt Matilda. She washn't intereshted in it, either. Sho there!"

"If you've never tried it, how do you know you won't like it?" he argued amiably.

That irritated her even more. "What'sh that got to do with anything? I've never been hit by a train, but that doesn't mean I think I'd like it. Both posshibilities sound too . . . too *messy."*

Alan suddenly laughed so hard he had to clutch her tightly against himself to keep from dropping her. "You may be right," he said, struggling to contain himself, as her look nearly blistered him. "Sometimes it can feel a bit like being hit by a train, I suppose. But I promise you, when the time comes I'll be as neat as I can." And he had to clutch her again as she tried to throw herself out of his arms on their way through the inner courtyard.

"Dorcas . . . shhh . . ." Quickly dropping onto a nearby bench, he held her snugly on his lap, pressing her head against his shoulder to keep her from angrily tossing it about. "You have to be still. You've had a near concussion. This fussing could make it worse. Please, dear . . . easy . . . 'Tis all right . . . quiet now . . . shhh . . ."

Dorcas trembled slightly as the hypnotic quality of his deep, musical voice forced her to relax in spite of herself. The exertion had made her blurry and dizzy all over again, and she was still decidedly drunk.

"That's better," Alan said softly, rising and carrying her carefully toward the single foot ramp that led into the keep.

"Wait!" She suddenly strained against him. "Not the middle one. It looks too wobbly. Take the ramp to the left."

"Whatever you say, dear. Just relax . . . That's a good lass. You'll be fine."

"I'm fine now," she snapped. "The only problem I have ish you. Stop trying to be sho . . . sho nice to me. I hate it when you're nice! It makesh me wonder what you're up to."

"I'm not going to be *up* to anything 'til my grandmother says you're well enough for it."

Muddled though she was, the innuendo was enough to turn Dorcas scarlet and clamp her lips shut until they were back in the bedroom and two shy little chambermaids in crisply starched aprons were carefully filling an ornate brass bathtub that had just been dragged in. A third maid was unloading several covered dishes from a tray onto the small table. Dorcas, who had been consigned to a burgundy armchair in one corner of the room, had become studiously engrossed in trying to pluck her beer-laundered nightgown away from her skin. It wasn't one of her luckier endeavors. The silken sheath seemed to have become glued to her, and the more it dried, the stiffer it became.

"Now I know how a moth musht feel in its cocoon," she was muttering as she did the only thing she could think of to loosen it.

"Dorcas!"

Alan soaked his shirtsleeves to the elbows hauling her upright in the tub in which she'd just completely submersed herself. "That was very silly," he chided her.

"I know," she sputtered, haphazardly wiping the water out of her eyes. "Beer'sh s'posed to be good for your hair. I washn't planning on rinshing it out . . . but I forgot." And then she promptly forgot about Alan, too, as the sight of her nightdress billowing up around her in the warm suds caught her undivided attention.

Sighing, as though it had only then dawned on him what a long afternoon this was turning out to be, Alan went to dismiss the giggling maids. It was just long enough for Dorcas to pull off her nightgown and drop it in a puddle by the tub. In the next instant, a new face appeared in the half-open doorway, and she stood cheerfully in the bath to greet it, like Venus rising out of the sea foam.

"Hello, Dr. Earnshaw—I fell into a vat of beer!" she announced, as if that explained everything. And, in a way, it did.

Cursing, Alan snatched up a large towel, bundling her into it and then the bed, where he yanked the covers to her chin, ordering, "Stay there!" before turning to the steamer trunk to find her a fresh nightdress.

"Oh, now, don't mind me, son. It's nothing I haven't seen before. And very true to form." Zachary Earnshaw chuckled, stepping into the room. "You couldn't keep clothing on that girl when she was tiny. It used to drive Matilda to distraction. She'd have her all dressed, as neat as a pin, and the moment your back was turned, the little minx would be prancing about, naked and free as a pixie."

"That can't be right. You musht be thinking of shomeone else. I'd never do anything like that," Dorcas declared, slipping clumsily out of bed, dropping her towel, and wobbling halfway across the floor, as naked and free as a pixie, before Alan managed to catch her and wrestle an ivory satin nightgown over her head.

"So like Matilda," the older man muttered to himself. Shaking his head slightly, as though suddenly rousing from a dream, he reached into his vest pocket and fished out a small, leather-bound notebook and gilt pencil. "Here; I know what may quiet her." He wrote for a moment, then handed the notebook and pencil to Dorcas, who had been re-deposited in the bed and was now stridently resisting having her tangled, wet hair combed. "Dorcas Matilda, can you focus clearly enough to work these for me?" he asked.

She halted in mid-squawk and squinted at the pages in sudden interest. "Of course I can. A chimpanzee could work these," she said a trifle indignantly. Gripping the pencil, she began scribbling with a vengeance.

Alan stared over her shoulder, his dark brows lowered in mild confusion. "What language is that?"

"Algebra." Earnshaw grinned. "An old trick of mine. Matilda used to bring Dorcas to my lab quite often when she was small, and I'd set her long lists of equations to solve to keep her out of mischief. Algebra was more fun for her than toys. The girl's something of a mathematical genius, you know. . . . It's in her blood."

"No, I didn't know," Alan said, sounding quietly shocked by the information. He was gazing intently at Dorcas while she flew through the equations, never missing a beat. "Why should I suspect that a lady's companion was even interested in mathematics?"

"A paid companion? Good heavens, is that what she's been doing?" If Alan had been quietly shocked, Dr. Earnshaw was loudly aghast. "Dorcas Matilda! Whatever possessed you? That's not the work you were raised for. Matilda would have wanted you to finish school and continue her research."

"Mmm . . . That's what I wanted, too," Dorcas muttered, never looking up from the equations. "There was the little matter of eating, however. You may recall that Aunt Matilda didn't trust banks. Most of our money went up in flames, along with the house and . . . and everything else." She glanced up into Zachary Earnshaw's eyes and found a look that sobered her even more than the algebra had.

"Child, forgive me," he said weakly. "I've been a selfish old fool. I was so wrapped up in my own pain, I never even stopped to consider anything else. I should have made certain you were provided for before I left the East."

"Why? I'm quite capable of providing for myself. It's not as if I was your responsibility, Dr. Earnshaw," she stated simply, and quickly returned to her algebra. At least with that she understood what was happening.

"Spoken just as Matilda would have said it." The man chuckled, although there was little humor in the sound, so far as Dorcas could tell.

She rapidly finished the last calculations and handed him back his notebook. "Aren't you going to check them?" she asked, when he slipped it into his pocket with scarcely a glance.

He gave her a small shrug and a smaller dry smile. "Why bother? I'm certain they're correct. Matilda taught you very well . . . almost too well," he added to himself, as he turned slowly and shuffled toward the door, so lost in some private, inner world that he was nearly bowled over by Mary, who came rolling in like a lavender storm cloud.

"Sorry, Dr. Earnshaw," she offered absently, heading straight for Dorcas, who had just yanked a comb away from Alan and was shakily attempting to fix her own hair. "Finally! Do you know I nearly had kittens when I came back here and found you gone? I've been charging all over creation trying to find you. I had visions of you fainting and falling into the moat," she fumed.

"No, just a vat of beer," Dorcas said, fumbling with the comb and her tangle of damp curls.

"So I heard. About Dunstan, too. You may live to regret that," Mary answered with a sudden grin. "Here, let me do that. You're making it worse." Elbowing Alan aside, she relieved Dorcas of the comb and rustled down beside her on the bed.

"Regret what?" Dorcas asked, wincing slightly as the comb hit a snag.

"Sorry," Mary apologized, deftly smoothing that handful of golden locks and moving onto the next. "I'm referring to Dunstan, of course. I hate to be the one to break this to you, but I'm afraid you've turned that revolting toad into your devoted, doglike admirer and the defender of your good name. . . . You may be a witch, after all." She grinned again. "Do you want to hear what your new champion did in your honor?"

"Do we have a choice?" Alan grumbled.

Ignoring him, Mary tossed the comb aside and began braiding Dorcas's hair into a long, loose plait, never missing a beat in her running monologue. "He was on his way back to the keep when he overheard that idiot Geordie and one of his idiot chums outside the brewers' shed. They were saying . . . um . . . some rather rude things about you, apparently."

"I'm not surprised. I did ruin a lot of their work." Dorcas sighed, wishing that Mary would hurry up and finish so she could find somewhere to lay her head before it tumbled off her shoulders. The drunkenness had finally played itself out, leaving her with another new experience—her first hangover. On top of everything else, it made her skull feel like it weighed more than the rest of her did all together.

"Well, Dunstan ruined some more work for them,"

Mary continued cheerfully. "He grabbed Geordie in one hand and the chum in the other, dragged them into the shed and spoiled a second vat by holding them in it until their legs turned blue. That was all you could see of them, I mean—their legs sticking out from under their kilts. The rest of them was under beer. It was the funniest sight! I was watching from the door of the shed and started laughing so hard, I almost—

"Mary, thank you for your help and your entertaining news." Alan cut her off. Grasping the redhead by her puff-sleeved shoulders, he hoisted her to her feet and firmly steered her to the door.

"Dorcas needs some rest now. Why don't you climb out on the tower ledge again and practice the balcony scene from *Romeo and Juliet*? Maybe Simon will help you with it."

"Euck! If I were Juliet and he were Romeo, I'd drink *real* poison, instead of a sleeping draught!" Mary spouted as the door closed in her face. "Dorcas, honey, I'll try to look in on you later," she called through it.

"Uh," Dorcas said. It was the best response she could manage at the moment. Huddled at the top of the bed, with her lower back braced against the headboard, her arms locked around her legs, and her heavy, throbbing head balanced on her knees, she fancied she could actually feel the heat from Alan's eyes as they glittered down on her.

"For a lass who wasn't even supposed to get out of bed, you've had a very busy day so far," he said, his husky voice stroking over her almost like the touch of a hand.

The sensation was the last thing she needed.

"Leave me alone," she mumbled into her knees. "You were right when you said I need rest. Just go away and let me die in peace."

"You'll rest easier if you lie down," he said, his voice caressing her again.

"I can't. If I move, my head will explode."

The mattress tilted slightly as he sat beside her. And her stomach tilted even more as his arms slid around her waist, drawing her gently back against himself. "Here, lean on me. Does that feel better?"

If Dorcas had had a gun right then, she might very well have shot herself. Because she realized, with an electric shiver, that it did feel better. It felt so incredibly much better, she couldn't prevent herself from sinking farther into him and letting her head nestle under his chin. His face dipped down and she caught her breath as he kissed her warmly on the sensitive spot where her neck met her shoulder. And then caught it several times more as he slowly and carefully nibbled his way up to her earlobe.

"Mmmm," he murmured thoughtfully. "You taste a bit like beer."

"I-I'm s-sorry," she stammered. What else was there to say?

"Nothing to be sorry about. I happen to enjoy good beer," he said, nuzzling her temple. "And Geordie's a flaming idiot if he thinks you could spoil any of that swill he generally produces. If he hasn't poured it out yet, I'm going to order him to keg the vat you toppled into for my personal use. It'll be the sweetest batch that scoundrel has ever brewed. Mmmm . . ."

Dorcas's stomach turned several somersaults and her heart skipped a few beats as Alan's lips slid back down to her shoulder and his hands slid up to her breasts. "Don't! Stop that!" she gasped.

"Don't stop? All right," he said agreeably as his hands tightened gently over their marks and his thumbs started doing something unbelievably distracting.

It sent a jolt through her that nearly melted her toenails and surprised him, apparently, with the intensity of her reaction. His hands dropped and he eased out from behind her, lowering her carefully to the pillows and bracing an arm on either side of her.

"I wonder if you'll still feel that way about me after we've been married for fifty years," he murmured, gazing down at her through smoky amber slits.

Her hand lashed out, striking him sharply across the cheek before he knew what hit him.

Those amber eyes never even blinked. "Satisfied now?"

"No!"

"Too bad, because you'll not get another chance to try that," he said, a hard edge creeping into his voice. "Be still now, or I may be tempted to forget my grandmother's warnings. If you've survived everything else you've done today, I don't think the loss of your maidenhood will kill you."

Dorcas almost strangled on her anger. Anger at him for threatening and humiliating her. And fury with herself for the tears that were suddenly stinging her face. "Stop playing games with me!" she bit out between sobs.

The dangerous glint in his eyes instantly dissolved. "Please don't cry. I'm not playing with you, dear." He sighed, collapsing onto his back and pulling her over on top of himself.

For some reason, the tenderness of his tone made the tears flow all the faster. She clamped her eyes shut and held her breath to stop them, while he did nothing but wrap her snugly in his arms and wait for the main force of the trembling to still.

"I was trying to help you relax . . . to take your mind off your headache," he finally said. It brought an hysterical burst of laughter out of her. "I know. Not one of my brighter ideas . . . I'm sorry. I let myself get carried away. 'Tis an easy thing to do with you."

Gently rolling her off himself, he leaned on an elbow to gaze down at her. "This is partly your own fault, you know. It's that way you have of looking at me like I'm some sort of devil," he said. "It makes me want to behave like one."

Her heart pounding so feverishly she wondered that it didn't break right through her ribs, she stared up at him, her eyes like a cornered doe's.

"You see? You're doing it again. You should really watch that," he warned.

"I . . . I don't view you as a devil," she choked out, as his face seemed to dip a fraction closer to hers. "But what you're doing to me is . . . *is* diabolical."

The words pushed him several inches back. "Excuse me?" he said, that hard edge sharpening his voice once more.

"You're trying to steal me from myself. You're keeping me from everything I've worked and planned for—as though none of it has the slightest meaning or value!" she said raggedly, her breath coming in short gasps. "Do you have any idea what that's like? Can you possibly understand how it feels to have your whole existence ripped out from under you?"

The laugh he let out could have rivaled a rusty saw blade for harshness. It cut through Dorcas about as roughly as one, anyway.

"I understand better than you could possibly imagine," he ground out. And then swung away from her with an explosive curse, as a light tapping suddenly sounded at the door. "I thought I left orders I wasn't to be disturbed any more today!" he growled at the unfortunate little maid who peeked timidly into the room.

"I'm sorry, sir, but 'twas a messenger fer ye just now. He said fer me tae give ye this. 'Tis urgent, he said."

Alan took one glance at the crumpled scrap of paper she had thrust at him before quickly curtseying her way out of sight, cursed again, and simultaneously began ripping his shirt off and snatching different garments out of the dresser.

Oh my God, he's going Comanche again, Dorcas thought, and dove face first into a pillow, until the mattress sloped with his weight and a strong hand rolled her over to look at him.

"It's safe to come out now," he said, caging her neatly between his arms and staring down at her with an expression that seemed anything but safe.

"I wasn't hiding," she told him, trying not to swallow too loudly at the sight of that naked, tanned chest rippling above her. This was the way she had first viewed him, all savage, primeval strength and sensuality. But it had been a little easier to deal with then, before she'd known who he actually was, when she had thought this guise was real. Now it only reminded her of all the things about him that confused and unnerved, even frightened her. "I was just . . . just resting," she added lamely.

"Aye," Alan responded, obviously knowing better but not considering it worth a contradiction. "Now listen to me—I have to leave you for a bit, but after Dunstan's punishment today, I doubt that anyone will even consider troubling you. You're to stay in this room, however, while I'm gone. I don't want to return and find that you've been getting caught in trees, or tripping into vats, or any other nonsense. Do you understand me?" he demanded, his eyes pinning her to the bed.

Staring motionless up at him, Dorcas gave the ghost of a nod, feeling her indignation rise along with the color flooding her face.

"Not good enough," Alan growled softly. "I want your promise that you'll stay put. Or I'll be forced to—"

"You'll be forced to what? Stake me to an anthill?"

His expression went black and his voice, when it came, sounded like cold steel. "That was uncalled for."

"The hell it was! I don't have to promise you a blasted

thing!" she hissed, anger making her reckless. "Since when does a prisoner owe her jailor anything? I'm being held here against my will, damn it! Have you forgotten that? I don't want to be here!"

"That may be. But you *are* here and here you'll stay. So you'd best learn to like it."

"That's preposterous!" she spat, too filled with a seething self-righteousness to heed the warning in his expression. "You can't keep me a captive much longer, anyway. And even if you could, there is no way you can possibly make me like it!"

"Can't I?"

Too late she realized what she had prompted. Alan's weight was pressing her into the mattress and his lips were on hers before she could even think of resisting. And once the kiss had begun, she didn't want to try. It held her like a silken snare—soft and slow and exquisitely sweet. Even from the center of the bonfire it lit within her, she could tell what infinite care he was taking not to hurt her bruised face. For some reason, that awareness made the experience all the more devastating.

And not just for her, it seemed. Alan's expression, when he finally raised his head to gaze down at her, was almost frightening in its emotional depth. Dorcas nearly drowned in it. It was hunger and passion and longing and a sort of desperate tenderness all crystallized into a single heart-stopping look. It shot deep into her, and then was gone so abruptly, she wondered if she had imagined it.

"Did you like that?" His low voice smoked over her.

Like? . . . How could he apply such a simple term as *like* to that sweet, soul-shattering kiss?

"No." She tried to answer truthfully, but she could barely get the single syllable out.

A small, satisfied grin touched the corners of that wickedly sensuous mouth. "That's what I thought." Rolling off her, he stood by the bed, staring down at her for several long breaths, his powerful chest rising and falling with each one. "No more nonsense now. You'll mind me and stay put while I'm gone," he said, swinging away and striding for the door with a lithe, catlike grace. "I should be back before dawn."

"Don't hurry on my account," Dorcas drawled, finding her voice the moment his eyes were off her.

The only sign that he heard was a slight tensing of his shoulders and spine as he paused an instant in the doorway. "You're not fooling anyone but yourself, you know." His whisper filtered back to her as he stepped into the passage.

Huddling deeper into the pillows, she heard the door shut behind him with an ominously decisive click.

Chapter Six

Alan did not return to the castle before dawn, as he had said he would. Nor did he return after dawn. He didn't return at all, in fact.

It had been midafternoon when he'd ridden out, but by the time the sun had disappeared in rosy flames behind the western ramparts the following day, there was still no sign of him, and Dorcas had begun to feel oddly concerned. Although she couldn't imagine why she should be. It made about as much sense as a condemned prisoner worrying over what had happened to his executioner. She could only assume her head injury had rattled her reasoning more than she'd realized.

It had kept her in bed the remainder of the previous day, at any rate. Despite her outer aches and inner turmoil—or, perhaps, because of them—she had fallen into a heavy doze shortly after Alan departed, and she hadn't roused until the sun was low and the food that had been set on the table hours before was stone cold and barely edible. She had eaten some of it anyway, because she'd awoken ravenous. Then she'd promptly fallen into a second sleep and a long, muddled series of dreams that had kept her tossing in the big bed until late morning.

She had been able to remember little about them on waking, but they had left her with that same confusing sense of overlapping images the former night's dream had triggered—that uncanny perception that she was herself, yet someone else, too, someone who had lived at Castle MacAllister decades before. It was an extremely awkward feeling, and one that was not made more palatable by the fact that half the castle's community seemed suddenly and perversely determined to treat her as if she had always been a valued member of the clan.

"It's your own fault. I warned you that you'd regret making Alan free Dunstan. They want to court your favor now, because it seems you have such a powerful influence over their laird," Mary teased.

She and Dorcas were slowly walking the inside perimeter of the outer courtyard, looking like a couple of spring blossoms in the last rays of the setting sun, with the redhead in a vivid blue linen creation that intensified her eyes and Dorcas in a ruffled confection of peaches and cream organdy that made her feel like a French pastry. She hated it—but no more than the rest of Flora's criminally feminine trousseau. At least the organdy was cool in the warm evening air. She managed a stiff wave and a stiffer smile as several men returning from some outside labor hailed her with big, toothy grins and a bushelful of unwanted compliments on her "bonny frock."

"Maybe I should have worn the lime taffeta. It would have set off my bruises better," she grumbled to herself.

"Actually, your bruises are fading already. In a day or two they'll hardly be noticeable. Molly's cures work like magic," Mary answered blithely, as though the grumble had been directed at her. "Are you sure you don't want to go in now? I know Molly said it would be all right for you to have some exercise today, but we've walked the whole castle from end to end nearly five times over. Aren't you tired?"

Mary had a point. From end to end, as the crow flew, the interior of the castle complex measured over three hundred yards. And the two females had been tracing the perimeters of both the inner and outer courts, more than doubling that distance. It had been a prodigious amount of legwork. But tiring?

"Hardly," Dorcas murmured absently. She had had enough sleep the previous day to fuel her for a week, she mused. But even without that, nerves alone would have kept her feet pumping. She had too much to think about. And for Dorcas, thought and motion had always gone together. Her brain seemed to be inextricably connected to her legs. "You can turn in, though, if you like," she added.

"No, I'll stay with you. But we'll have to give up soon. It'll be too dark for this in a bit," Mary said. "You're not going to find what you're looking for out here, anyway."

That comment brought her companion up short for an instant. "And just what do you think I'm looking for?"

"An escape route, naturally. But it can't be done from out here. I know; I've already investigated all the possibilities."

Of those three statements, it was the last one that Dorcas nearly stumbled on. "Why should you have been checking escape possibilities?" she asked, her voice barely more than a whisper. She scarcely needed an answer. It was too easy to guess.

"That's right," Mary said, seeing the awareness flash in Dorcas's green eyes. "I never intended for things to go this way, of course, but I'm almost as much a prisoner here as you are. Except my position is a little safer, because Uncle Angus hasn't decided yet which one of his toads—I mean, sons—he wants to inflict upon me. I suspect it may come down to a hurling contest . . . with me as the prize," she added.

"How can you be so calm about it?" She shuddered. "Can't your father do something? Does he know what they're planning?" Perhaps he was as bad as Flora's folks—though one would have thought that a Bostonian would have more sense of propriety than that.

"My father?" Mary said a little vacantly. The notion seemed to surprise, or at least confuse her for a second. Then she gave a quick laugh. "Oh, yes, dear old Papa. He'd be rather put out about it, I suppose. But, you see, he's . . . he's touring Europe this spring, so I haven't been able to get word to him," she explained, recovering her wits almost too smoothly, Dorcas suddenly thought.

Something was odd here. Mary wasn't being completely truthful, but why should she feel the need to lie? Unless her father was in on the arrangement and she was too embarrassed to admit it. It was probably disheartening enough to discover that your parent would sell you off to a high bidder without having to bandy the knowledge about, Dorcas decided, shaking her head.

She was embarrassed to admit something herself. More than embarrassed, actually—she was ashamed. The fact was, the idea had bolstered her own spirits tremendously. Not because she was happy about Mary's position, but because it was such a relief to know she wasn't the only captive at the castle. With two of them, their chances of escaping increased exponentially—sort of like one plus one equaling two hundred. With a little luck, they could be out of there and nearly to Abilene before the next sunrise!

And I have to be gone by then, Dorcas was hurriedly thinking. It had just occurred to her that she might have misunderstood Alan the previous afternoon. He might have meant that he would return before *this* dawn. And she had no intention of being on hand to great him.

"You're wrong, Mary," she said quietly. "We can get out through the wall behind the stables, I think, if we wait until full dark. It's the most sheltered area. No one will notice a hole there until daylight."

"A hole through six solid feet of adobe? Do you have some dynamite hidden in your flounces, honey?" Mary laughed, never missing a step. She seemed to find the notion a very amusing joke. "Or maybe you are a witch, after all, and can simply make it disappear." She gave Dorcas's fingers a friendly squeeze.

Dorcas squeezed back. "No, I'm afraid I'm not," she said, a small grin twitching the corners of her mouth. "But I happen to know of a nearby wizard who has a device that will do the trick."

The tall redhead stopped short, dropping the hand she'd been holding as if it had suddenly burst into flames and scorching the air with a blast of phraseology Dorcas doubted she had ever learned in Boston. "So that's how he got me off the ledge!" she steamed, offering a few more descriptive but less than ladylike phrases. "Are you trying to tell me that Smo—I mean, Mr. Elliott and Dr. Earnshaw have invented some sort of a . . . a disintegration gun? That's impossible!"

"Not as much as you might think. More than one person has researched the possibility already. It's a valid concept, based on the principle of vibrational pitch. Sort of the way some singers can shatter a glass by hitting a particular note. Not exactly, mind you, but that's the simplest way I can explain it. Understand?"

"No. And I'm amazed that you do. What are you, Dorcas, some kind of a . . . a scientist?" Mary's blue eyes pierced her as though she was wondering if the girl really was a witch.

It was by no means a new experience for Dorcas. She

had dealt with looks like that since childhood, when she'd first realized that many otherwise intelligent people regarded the modern era's fast-paced scientific research as little better than hocus-pocus.

"I'm not much more than an amateur at the moment," she admitted. "But my aunt was a top-notch professional and I grew up helping her. One of the last projects she was working on before she died was a form of disintegration device that could be used in mining operations. I think what Dr. Earnshaw and Mr. Elliott have come up with must be something similar. Aunt Matilda and Dr. Earnshaw were close colleagues. I know she discussed the basic concept with him. That's probably what gave him the idea for what he's developed here."

"Well, if it could be used for mining, the MacAllisters would certainly be interested in it. There's at least one mine on the property," Mary muttered, beginning to walk again, but only a few steps this way and that, back and forth, a little like a duck in a carnival shooting gallery.

Dorcas joined her in the pacing, hardly realizing what she was doing. She just needed to be moving. "I didn't know that. Lady Flora told me that they raised horses," she said.

"Alan is the horse breeder. The rest of the clan are craftsmen, farmers, or miners . . . gold miners. That's what the family fortune is built on," Mary explained absently. It was obvious that she was still trying to reconcile herself to the idea of a disintegration device. "Um . . . Dorcas, I hate to bring this up in case it's painful for you, but . . . how did your aunt die?"

"There was an explosion in her lab. It took most of the house with it," Dorcas answered with a small, shaky sigh.

Mary heaved a larger, shakier one. "I was afraid you'd say something like that. Was . . . was she working on this

. . . this disintegration thing when it happened?"

"I honestly don't know. She always had several projects going at once. But that might have been the one that triggered the blast. There wasn't enough of anything left to tell for sure."

"I'm sorry," Mary said quietly. Then she pulled up so abruptly, Dorcas almost smacked into her. "No! I don't like it! It sounds too risky. Too weird!" she muttered, shaking her head so violently, her luxurious curls dipped dizzily to one side. With a lightning gesture, she shoved them back into place, leaving Dorcas blinking and wondering if she had just seen what she thought she had. "Anyway, there's a simpler way out—through the dungeons. There's a tunnel that leads under the moat and the palisade and comes out near the horse corrals," Mary offered almost reluctantly. "I learned about it from Molly my first few days here. It's been my ace-in-the-hole . . . but I'm not sure I want to play it yet," she added vaguely, gazing pensively over Dorcas's sandy blond hair as she stood staring openmouthed up at her.

Mary knew of an escape route, but wasn't sure she wanted to use it? Dorcas didn't even bother shaking her head. She knew it wouldn't rattle that information into any kind of sense. *And just when I'd been thinking she was almost sane, too . . .* Oh, well; Boston bred or not, Mary was a MacAllister, she reminded herself, as though that explained everything. Which, in Dorcas's mind, it did.

"All right, Mary, you don't have to leave yet if you're not ready. Just tell me where the tunnel is so I can use it," she said, careful to keep her voice calm.

"Don't be silly, honey. You wouldn't last an hour on this wild prairie by yourself," Mary replied, still staring off over the girl's head, as if the answer she was searching for was written on the wall between the two yards.

"And you could, I suppose? What makes you think a

Bostonian could handle it any better than a Philadelphian?" Dorcas argued, a little more sharply than she'd intended. She didn't want to antagonize Mary, after all.

Fortunately, Mary didn't seem the least bit ruffled. The only change in her expression was a slight curling of the corners of her lovely lips. "Oh, you'd be amazed what a gal can learn in . . . Boston," she murmured, her cultured accent softening a bit around the edges.

"I don't care! I'd rather take my chances with the prairie than with Alan!" she snapped, abandoning all pretense of careful self-control. "I'm leaving here tonight— either through the dungeons or through the wall. Do you want to come with me or don't y—"

"Shhh!" Mary hissed so abruptly Dorcas almost bit her tongue as she bit back her last word.

"My, my . . . You two look as pretty as picture postcards," a pleasant voice drawled from somewhere behind her. "I'd like to put stamps on both of you and mail you home to Mother. You'd be so decorative in her curio cabinet."

With a startled gasp, Dorcas turned just in time to see Simon Elliott stepping lithely out of a nearby patch of shadows.

"How sweet," Mary said, beaming him a smile he could have read by. "But I'm afraid that would hardly be adequate compensation to the poor dear for the aggravation of having a son like you."

Answering her with a low chuckle that could have meant anything, Elliott turned his smoky gaze on Dorcas, who quickly moved closer to Mary. "Oh, now, don't look at me that way, Miss Jeffries. You ought to know by now that I'm not the big bad wolf around here."

"You could have fooled me," Mary muttered under her breath, wrapping a protective arm around Dorcas's tense shoulders.

Simon ignored the remark and said, "I was hunting

you, however. We've just had a runner at the postern gate with a message from Alan. He said to tell you that he's sorry he's been detained, but . . . but he'll make it up to you when he returns."

The words were delivered with such an air of apology, Dorcas was half inclined to forgive Simon for startling her. But the other half won out.

"How sweet," she said, mimicking Mary's smooth sarcasm. "Did the messenger give any indication when Alan will be back?"

"Probably around sunrise. But cheer up; sunrise is still hours away. You're safe for the moment," Simon answered, that slow grin spreading lazily over his face.

"I've asked you before, Mr. Elliott, to stop trying to cheer me up," Dorcas told him with an icy glare.

He pretended to shiver under it. "Brrr . . . point made," he conceded, and then suddenly hit her with a stern look of his own. "I'm quite serious, though, Miss Jeffries. This is very dangerous country, with all sorts of wild animals on the prowl. You are safer here right now than you'd be outside these walls. Especially tonight. Please don't try anything foolish. That goes for you, too," he added, shooting an even steelier gaze at Mary.

She returned it with an angelic smile. "How nice of you to be concerned. But unnecessary. I never do foolish things. I'm a very practical lady."

"Well, let's hope you're practical, anyway," Simon said, his smile returning.

Mary's disappeared. "Why don't you play wizard for us and vanish? Before I forget my manners and do something . . . *catty.*"

A little amazed, Dorcas glanced rapidly from Simon to Mary and back again. It took barely an instant, and by the second time she looked at him, the man was his usual, enigmatic self. But she knew she hadn't been mistaken. For the briefest moment there, the unflappable

Mr. Elliott had been swinging wildly in the wind, like a loose shutter.

And Mary was grinning like a kitten who had just stolen a pitcher full of cream. "I merely wanted to make sure we understood each other," she purred sweetly.

"Very kind of you, I'm sure," Simon said softly. "I appreciate your having enough confidence in my chivalry to let me know."

"Oh, I have no confidence in you whatsoever. I was simply demonstrating how much confidence I have in myself," she replied pleasantly. "Come along now, Dorcas dear. I'll help you get ready for bed."

Elliott moved quickly to block their path as Mary tried to usher Dorcas through the gate to the inner courtyard. "A word of warning Miss . . . ah . . . MacAllister. As confident as you are, even a cat has only nine lives, and you must have used up several of yours already. I'd be extremely careful if I were you. . . . Unless you're looking to get burned, of course." He grinned down at her.

She scarcely batted an eye. "And I wouldn't worry about me if I were you, Mr. Elliott. As you said, Dorcas and I are quite safe behind these walls. There's nothing here to burn us that I can see at the moment . . . just a little smoke on the wind."

His grin hardened into a tight line. "Ah, but where there's smoke, there's also fire."

"Yes. And where there's fire, there's always a lot of hot air," she spat, swishing past him with Dorcas in tow. "Come on, honey. I don't know about you, but I am exhausted. I think I'll sleep late tomorrow," she announced with just a bit more volume than seemed actually necessary.

Pulled steadily along behind her in the growing gloom of the yard, it took Dorcas a minute to regroup her slightly scattered wits. "What on earth were you two talking about?" she finally managed to ask.

141

"Shh! I'll explain later—when we're in the dungeons," Mary whispered.

If the redhead's hand hadn't kept her moving, Dorcas might have tripped over her own skirts. "You . . . you're going to show me the escape tunnel?" she whispered back.

"Show you, hell—I'm coming with you! This game is over," Mary hissed softly. "I've played enough poker to know when to fold 'em and walk away. It's time to cut my losses. That man infuriates me so much, I'll have a murder charge added to my handbills if I stay here any longer. No amount of gold is worth that!"

Handbills? Dorcas tripped for real this time, landing on her knees just as they reached the bottom of the keep's entrance ramp. She was suddenly remembering the row of wanted posters she'd been nervously perusing through the train's window back in Abilene, while Leslie and Flora had been playing footsie behind her in the tiny compartment. Even in the awkwardness of that moment, one of the drawings had particularly caught her eye because it was of a woman. An obviously young, attractive woman, too, despite the roughness of the sketch.

"Oh, my God," she breathed, gazing wide-eyed up into Mary's face. "You . . . you're Cat Kildare!"

"In person." Mary winked, glancing quickly over her shoulder to make sure they weren't being watched as she helped Dorcas to her feet. "Only the true name is Kathleen. You can call me Kathy . . . that is . . ." She hesitated, her usual composure suddenly cracked by doubt. "That is, if you still want to come with me. You're a decent girl, Dorcas. The kind of girl who's not supposed to associate with . . . um . . . I mean, I wouldn't blame you if—"

"Are you joking?" Dorcas interrupted. "The way this world is set up in men's favor, it's a wonder more females don't turn to crime. Good heavens, how you manage your life is your business. I'm not here to pass judgment on you," she said, grabbing the young woman's hand and taking the lead as they rustled up the ramp. "And quite frankly, I'm too relieved right now to learn that you're *not* a MacAllister to worry about anything else. . . . Wait a minute." She pulled them to a halt before the door. "Fix your wig. It's slipping again."

"Damn," Kathy muttered. "It's been doing this all day. I couldn't find my hairpins this morning."

Watching her tug the coppery mass back into place, Dorcas asked curiously, "What's your real hair like, anyway?"

"Appalling. Redder than this wig, in fact. And curlier than a corkscrew. I think that's why I became a con artist in the first place—to give me an excuse to cut it," the redhead quipped. "I have to keep it short, because in my work, I often wear wigs. Molly wasn't far wrong, you know. In my own way, I *am* a bonny actress." She grinned as they cautiously entered the keep.

"I won't argue with that," Dorcas murmured, feeling she could breathe freely again, after days of an almost suffocating tension.

The free feeling didn't last long, however—only until they were back in the bedroom, where Alan's clothes still lay on the chair where he had tossed them the previous afternoon. Just the sight of them was enough to conjure up hot, vivid memories. Or maybe her tranquillity was destroyed by the sudden awareness that she'd never again see what had been in those clothes. Whatever triggered the reaction, she found herself battling back both heat and a chilling, unreasoning sense of loss as Kathy's voice elbowed its way into her thoughts. "I . . . I'm sorry. What were you saying?"

"That this is outrageous!" Kathy repeated, buried up to the shoulders in Dorcas's trunk. "There are no riding togs in here at all! I thought those British noblewomen

were supposed to be such avid horsewomen. What kind
of a wedding trousseau is this anyway?" she muttered,
slamming the lid down and jerking to her feet.

"Lady Flora didn't ride. She told me she was afraid of
horses," Dorcas said. Instantly she felt the heat and chill
again, as the simple word *horse* conjured the very unsim-
ple image of a wild appaloosa stallion and its wilder rider
galloping full tilt across her mind's eye.

"Well, in that case, Flora certainly would have been
the perfect match for Alan," Kathy offered sarcastically.
"He's practically a centaur. How about you?"

"Wh-what?" Dorcas asked, her face growing red and
her pulse galloping faster than the image of the stallion.

"Relax, honey. I only meant, can you ride? Or are you
bothered by horses, too?"

"Oh . . . I'm no expert, but I can usually stay in the
saddle. I like horses," she answered. *It's Alan who both-
ers me,* she added silently.

"The problem with that is they don't keep any saddles
near the corrals, and we won't be able to risk raiding the
tackroom near the courtyard stables. We'll have to make
it seem like we've gone to bed and then slip through the
dungeons in a couple of hours, when all's quiet. If we
leave the keep any more tonight, it'll look too suspicious
. . . Have you ever ridden bareback?"

Dorcas swallowed a burst of slightly hysterical laughter. "Only once," she managed to choke out, remembering a little too clearly the furious gallop across the prairie
with Alan's arms locking her tightly onto his Appaloosa
and even tighter against himself. "But I . . . I wasn't on
the horse alone."

Kathy took the news with far more ease than Dorcas
had had in reporting it. "Fine. You won't have to do it
by yourself this time, either. You can ride behind me. It
shouldn't slow us down. The two of us together don't
weigh much more than a good-sized man," she said half

to herself. "And you can wear my riding skirt. I believe I'll be a boy for a while. It'll give me a good cover when we reach Abilene, and be safer for us on the prairie. I doubt we'll meet anyone tonight, but if we do, we'll be in a stronger position if they think one of us is a male."

"Then I should be a boy, too—if I can find the clothes," Dorcas put in. She was darned if she would let Kathy think she was some helpless little ninny.

But that was, apparently, more or less what Kathy thought. "Honey, that's silly. I do have an extra pair of britches with me that you could use, but you'd never pass for a boy. You're way too pretty—too delicate and feminine-looking."

Now that stung. And Dorcas was glad that it did. The irritation was exactly what she needed to help fasten her resolve in place until they were far away. Otherwise, there was the extremely unsettling possibility that she might not be able to go through with this escape. The castle—or one of its occupants, anyway—seemed to be holding her there.

But that was silly, Dorcas told herself. The moment she was back in Philadelphia, in staid, familiar surroundings, she would forget this experience as if it were nothing but some hellish bad dream.

You may be able to do that, the voice in her head put in, *but will you ever be able to forget the heavenly parts of that dream?*

"Shut up! You don't know what you're talking about," she muttered under her breath.

"What was that?" Kathy asked, too deep in her own planning, fortunately, to have heard.

"Ah . . . I was just saying, don't let these ridiculous ruffles fool you," Dorcas stammered. "Underneath, I'm quite a plain Jane—not your feminine type at all. I can probably make a better boy than you can."

"All right. We'll both be boys then. At least it'll make

it easier for you to move about in this rough terrain."
Kathy laughed. "But don't say I didn't warn you if you
don't fool anyone."

It was just the sort of challenge Dorcas needed to distract herself from the unending, unwanted images in her
head and that exasperating little voice that kept whispering, unbidden, that it made no difference how far she
ran. She could escape the castle, escape Alan . . . but she
would never be able to outrun her own heart.

Chapter Seven

The metamorphosis took most of the two-hour wait for the castle to fall asleep, along with some savage scissors work, a bottle of black ink, and some brown boot polish she had found tucked away in a small cabinet of the bedroom. But the effort was worth it—if only to see Kathy's eyes widen into blue moons and her jaw drop down to her fancy silver belt buckle when they met in the passage outside the upper dungeons.

"Good Lord, Dorcas, you honestly are a witch! You've turned yourself into the cutest *muchacho* I've ever seen."

"*Gracias*, señor, but my name ees Pedro," the brown-skinned lad replied, giving his short black curls a little shake. "It was these loose, cotton britches of yours that spawned the idea. They looked sort of Mexican peasantry to me," Dorcas added in her own voice. "If we meet one, I can be your servant. You need someone to polish those snakeskin boots and trim your phony mustache, after all."

147

"Hmm . . . I'll tell them I won you in a card game."
The black-clad gunslinger grinned back. "And you can
call me Señor Kid. This is my Kid Connors costume. I
use it for long rides over the prairie. The Kid's young,
but he looks sinister enough to make desperadoes think
twice about messing with him. Don't you agree?"

"*Sí*, señor, I shaking een my serape."

"Serape, my foot. That's a MacAllister tartan shawl.
But it's close enough, I guess. . . . Where did you get
those odd sandals? They're the same golden brown color
as Alan's good leather vest," Kid Connors said, his eyes
narrowing suspiciously.

Pedro blushed like a ripe cherry under his brown stain.
"*Sí*, Señor Keed. Ees same color, cause ees same leather.
You theenk Señor Alan mind I cut up heez clothes?"

"Not half as much as he'll mind what you've done to
your hair, if he catches us, *amigo*," the lethal-looking
outlaw quipped, shouldering open the heavy beamed
door to the first level of dungeons. It creaked and
groaned like a frozen river breaking up in a spring thaw.

Dorcas dropped her Pedro act like a hot tamale. "No—
he's not going to catch us! Don't say that! Don't even
think it!" she pleaded, grabbing onto the Kid's gunbelt
so fiercely that she jostled one of the pearl-handled revolvers half loose from its holster. "Oh, I'm sorry," she
breathed, shakily shoving it back into place. "Wait a minute—are these the guns you had up on the tower? How
did you get them back from—"

"I didn't. Mr. Wizard still has Geordie's Colts, so far
as I know. And I hope they backfire in his face," Kathy
said. "These pieces are mine. I never go anywhere without them. Though they've had to spend most of this charade hidden under the false bottom of my trunk. I
couldn't wear them as Mary MacAllister. They would
have clashed with her fashionable Boston frocks. My derringer had to suffice for her. It's in my sleeve right now,

by the way. I do enjoy the security of being armed to the teeth. And in case you're wondering"—she paused for breath and to flash Dorcas a wink—"I know how to use all three weapons. Quite well."

"Good," Dorcas said. "Because I have a very big favor to ask you."

Her companion's eyebrows rose slightly. "Yes?"

"If . . . if Alan *should* catch us," she said dolefully, "I want you to shoot me."

"Honestly! You Latin Americans are so emotional." Kathy sighed, yanking Dorcas into the dark passage and dragging the door shut behind them.

The echoes of its groaning timbers seemed to follow them into the gloom, like a living thing panting at their heels. The air was musty but unusually chill, and Dorcas pulled her improvised serape over both shoulders in an effort to stop the shivering that had suddenly possessed her. Her eyes kept darting from side to side, searching the shadowy doorways that appeared every several yards along the narrow corridor. Most of them stood open, like long black mouths yawning in the wall, but a few were closed. And those were the ones that disturbed her the most, because it was too easy to imagine something lurking behind them.

"Pedro, stop breathing down my neck. You're going to drip hot wax on me if you're not careful," Kathy hissed. "This is hardly more than a root cellar. It's where they keep most of the castle's stores. Wait until we reach the lowest level. That's the prison area. The cells have manacles and chains bolted to the walls, and there's an authentic medieval-style torture chamber—fully equipped. You'll be thrilled."

"I can hardly wait," Dorcas muttered, clenching her teeth to keep them from chattering as the passage took a sudden series of turns and began dipping downward.

Nor was it simple nerves causing her trembling, but

the wash of emotions that seemed to be oozing from the very walls of the place. Old angers, pains, sorrows . . . She felt as though she was breathing them in along with the dank air itself. And the feeling closed in tighter with every step they descended, until, by the time they were passing the doors of the first cells, she was nearly choking on it.

"Comanche warriors taken in skirmishes—that's who the bulk of the prisoners were in the castle's early years," Kathy was explaining, as if she was some sort of macabre tour guide. "It was the old raid-and-trade game. The Comanches were constantly harassing them in those days, and the MacAllisters would capture as many as they could so they could exchange them for their own people whom the Comanches had previously stolen."

Dorcas scarcely needed the information. That odd overlay of images was all around her. It was like a waking dream. She was aware of herself and Kathy scuffling as quickly as they dared through the dust and cobwebs of the rat-infested passages, but she was also sensing the place as it had been decades before. She could almost hear the scraping of chains drifting out of the barred cubicles, smell the stench of scorched flesh permeating the torture room. Her tour guide's news that the chamber of horrors was more decorative than functional didn't lessen Dorcas's nausea one whit as they were forced to pass through it to reach the entrance to the escape tunnel.

"That's wrong," she whispered. "It *has* been used. Can't you see the blood?"

"Where? There's no blood, honey. Your eyes are playing tricks on you in the shadows. Angus told me these gruesome toys were mainly for show. The MacAllisters used them as scare tactics."

"Angus was lying, then. Comanches don't scare that easily. I know. Dr. Earnshaw used to tell me stories about them when I was small. He seemed pretty sure of his facts."

"You may be right about that. Our old Highland matchmaker may have felt Mary's cultured Bostonian ears were too delicate to tolerate the truth," Kathy supposed, a small grin stretching her false mustache tight. "But even so, there's no blood here. Any stains would have faded by now. This part of the dungeon hasn't been used in ages."

I wasn't referring to stains, Dorcas thought with a creeping chill. The blood she had spotted had seemed sticky wet and fresh. A vision from the past? Perhaps. But it couldn't all be visions, she decided, clamping her lips shut to keep from crying out over the one cell she had just dared shine her candle into. There was no point in alarming Kathy with the news that the dungeon was still in use—or, at least, had been until very recently.

Where was its prisoner now? Its obviously well cared for prisoner . . . That had been the shock of the empty cell—not its horrors but its lack of them. Even at a glance, it had shown signs of long occupancy, but an occupancy someone had tried to make bearable with creature comforts. The cell's furnishings were every bit as good as those in the upper chambers of the keep, and the remains of the supper on the table by the bed had looked better than the meal she herself had eaten that evening.

How very curious, she thought, her chill increasing not only at the mystery of this missing, pampered prisoner, but at the image of all the suffering souls who had been locked here before him—all the warriors who had been treated to the rack and hot irons instead of clean sheets and beefsteak.

"The worst torture, though, must have come simply from being confined down here in the dank and the dark," she mused aloud. "For a Comanche, used to open space and light and air, that must have seemed a living death."

"On that score, you *are* right," the slim, black figure ahead of her agreed. "But before you feel too sorry for them, remember that the Comanche made use of some pretty grisly torments of their own. The MacAllisters were only fighting fire with fire."

"Marvelous. That way everyone gets burned," Dorcas said hoarsely. "I've worked a lot of arithmetic problems in my life, but I've never been able to make two wrongs equal one right. Most people don't see it that way, however."

"It may surprise you to learn that at least one Mac-Allister did. A young woman named Elspeth. Molly told me the tale. That's how I found out about the escape tunnel. It's all wonderfully dramatic. Would you like to hear about her?" Kathy asked, and then plunged straight into the narrative as though her silently brooding companion had agreed.

Dorcas tried not to listen at first. The last thing she needed at the moment was more drama. There were too many tales already crowding into her consciousness as the dungeon relentlessly whispered its secrets to her. But the story Kathy related ended up eclipsing them all. The further it progressed, the less Dorcas felt that she was actually hearing it. It seemed more like a memory rising out of herself, and Kathy's words were there merely to illuminate the details she had forgotten.

"This all happened several decades ago, when Molly was still a girl," Kathy began. "Elspeth was the one who taught Molly herb craft, even though she was hardly more than a girl herself at the time. She came from a long line of Highland healers and was very skilled, apparently. Molly said she was also very beautiful, very headstrong, and impossibly independent. Sounds like my kind of a gal, in fact.

"Anyway, it didn't win her many friends within the clan, but she insisted upon traipsing down into the dungeons regularly to tend the Comanche prisoners. When the laird forbade it, she bribed the blacksmith to make a skeleton key for her and continued her ministering angel act on the sly.

"Most of the prisoners were freed in a matter of days, but the important exchanges sometimes took longer. And there was this particular warrior—some kind of a shaman, I believe—whom the MacAllisters considered too dangerous to release at all. He was known as the Panther, and even his own people lived in awe of him. It was rumored that he had the power to turn himself into a wild beast, and that he could control others with a mere thought.

"Superstitious rubbish, if you ask me. I mean, if he'd really had any special abilities, wouldn't you think he could have freed himself? But he couldn't. Molly told me that he languished down here for weeks on end, while Elspeth grew more and more worried. She didn't view him as a prisoner, you see. To her, he was a wounded, suffering man, and she took her responsibilities as a healer very seriously. When none of her usual treatments offered any relief, she did the only other thing she could to save his life. . . . She helped him escape through the tunnel we're about to use.

"It was all so neatly done, no one should even have suspected her, but the truth did come out somehow, and she found herself in quite a stew. Especially since her habit of helping Comanche wasn't the only black mark against her. Elspeth had also alienated herself from the clan by falling in love with a man outside of it—Jeremy something or other. Very dashing, but a bit on the intense side, Molly said. He was some sort of frontiersman or missionary who had drifted into the area to trade with and preach to the Indians. Because of Jeremy, Elspeth had spurned a marriage offer from one of the clan leaders—one who took her refusal as an unforgivable personal slight. Men are really so thin-skinned about things like that—they can dish it out, but they can't take it. At any rate, she was locked up. Not down here. The dungeons were just for male prisoners. Elspeth was shut in one of the towers. I don't know which one . . ."

I do, Dorcas thought, her hands trembling so badly, her candle flame nearly went out.

". . . and charges were brought against her. Not treason, as you might expect, but witchcraft. She had been suspected of it even before the Panther's escape—her cures often worked almost too well. Plus, there was the silly little matter of her cat, Caliban. He was the descendant of two kittens who had been brought over from Scotland by her mother—some rare Highland breed, I think—blacker than midnight and much larger than an ordinary tom. Caliban tagged after Elspeth everywhere, as if he was her shadow. Which led some to suspect that he was her demon familiar, rather than her pet. They were planning on killing the poor thing after she was imprisoned, but Molly told me he escaped them. And there's been this ludicrous legend floating around ever since that he haunts the castle, searching for her. Of all the ridicu—Oh, good grief! Here, relight your candle from mine. And mind how you hold it or it'll go out again. There are some queer drafts down here."

"Wha . . . what happened to her?" Dorcas stammered, her voice thinner than a moth's wing. This was the part that was all darkness in her own memory—except for that blood-curdling scream.

"Oh, that's the juiciest part. She was sentenced to be burned at the stake. But she was rescued at the last possible moment by her frontiersman lover and a band of Comanche led by none other than the Panther himself! Isn't that delicious? Some of them stole in through the

154

NAME:_____

ADDRESS:_____

_____

_____

TELEPHONE: _____

E-MAIL: _____

_____ I want to pay by credit card.

__ Visa __ MasterCard __ Discover

Account Number:_____

Expiration date: _____

SIGNATURE: _____

Send this form, along with $2.00 shipping and handling for your FREE books, to:

Love Spell Romance Book Club
20 Academy Street
Norwalk, CT 06850-4032

Or fax (must include credit card information!) to: 610.995.9274.
You can also sign up on the Web at www.dorchesterpub.com.

Offer open to residents of the U.S. and Canada only. Canadian residents, please call 1.800.481.9191 for pricing information.

If under 18, a parent or guardian must sign. Terms, prices and conditions subject to change. Subscription subject to acceptance. Dorchester Publishing reserves the right to reject any order or cancel any subscription.

escape tunnel, fought their way up into the outer court, and managed to raise the portcullis and lower the drawbridge to allow the main group in. They attacked in full force just as Elspeth was about to become the first Texas barbecue.

"Not that she could have known exactly what was happening. She'd been drugged, and a black hood had been put over her head. The MacAllisters aren't monsters, exactly—just avid traditionalists. They were doing what their private legal code demanded, but they were trying to make it as painless for her as possible.

"There was no similar regard for the Panther, however. He and Jeremy had been fighting their way together toward the stake when Jeremy suddenly stumbled, pulling the Panther down with him. He made it up again quickly, but the Panther lay dazed for an instant. By the time he'd staggered to his feet, half the clan was on him. He fought like his namesake, but they dragged him to earth through sheer weight of numbers. Molly said his final battle cry as he lay pinned beneath them was awful to hear."

"They killed him," Dorcas breathed, feeling that some long-dreaded question had finally been answered. But the answer brought no relief—just a deeper sense of sorrow and loss.

"Yes . . . and no. Molly was a little vague on that point," Kathy mused, the glow from the candles flickering eerily over her face. They had come to what appeared to be a dead end and she was reaching toward an unlit torch in an iron wall bracket. "His body was certainly destroyed, hacked to ribbons by claymores. And they burned his corpse in the pyre that had been meant for Elspeth. Very thrifty, these Scotsmen—waste not, want not. But . . ."

The tear-filled eyes staring anxiously up at her looked like green pools in the wavering shadows. "But what?"

their owner prompted, desperate to know the truth and dreading it at the same time.

"Well, Molly claims to have seen Elspeth's cat racing through the courtyard at the precise moment of that horrible scream. And she has this peculiar notion that the Panther escaped, in a way—by hurling his . . . his inner essence, if you will, into Caliban," Kathy explained, grasping the torch and giving it a sharp downward tug.

There was a raspy scraping and grating, and a narrow section of wall slid open, revealing something that looked like a pathway straight into Hades.

"Utter hogwash, of course," she continued. "That poor man was well and truly killed. But it wasn't entirely for naught. His sacrifice gave Jeremy the time he needed to reach Elspeth. He needed the extra time, you see, because, during the fall he'd somehow taken a nasty blow to the face and was reeling like a drunk when he arrived at the stake. Molly was horrified for a second that he would accidentally slice Elspeth's throat instead of her bonds. But that final cry of the Panther's put steel in his spine, it seems. Just as it sounded, Jeremy pulled himself upright, freed Elspeth, and carried her off. They got clean away."

Stepping into the tunnel, she beckoned Dorcas to follow. "We'd better move quickly and quietly now if we're to do the same."

Neither of them spoke again until they had reached the end of the dank, low, raw-beamed tunnel. It took 183 steps. Dorcas counted every single one to help steady her legs. She had simultaneously counted Kathy's longer strides and every support timber they passed. No mean mental feat to keep the three tallies separate, but the effort had served to drive all other thoughts and images into the back recesses of her consciousness—where she sincerely hoped they would stay. The only thing she wanted to concentrate on at the moment was getting as

far away from Castle MacAllister and all its occupants—
past and present—as possible.

Cat Kildare seemed to be of a like mind, the only difference being that she was obviously enjoying herself in
the process. Climbing through the trapdoor at the end
of the tunnel with an easy feline grace, she reached down
a hand and helped Dorcas scramble up into the moonlit
prairie, grinning like the devil behind her phony mustache.

"This will be a new experience for me. I've never tried
horse thieving before. Con-artistry's more my line. But I
do believe in expanding one's horizons whenever possible. And I know exactly the mount I want, too. She
doesn't belong to the MacAllisters, either," she said,
turning toward the nearby corral.

By the time she'd reached the closest horse, Kid Connors was in full control, complete with swaggering gait
and western accent. "Hey, yo sweet thang," he drawled
to a stunning black mare with four white socks and a
star on her forehead. "Yo look juss rarin' t' go an' thass
zac'ly whut we'alls need. Raht, Pedro?"

"*Sí*, Señor Keed," Dorcas mumbled, while determinedly counting the corral's fence posts and the horses
inside in a mental wrestling match with herself to keep
all other thoughts at bay. Especially the thought that she
was being watched.

Multiplying the number of posts by the total number
of horses, she rapidly began calculating the square root
of the resulting sum as her eyes peered warily into the
surrounding shadows. There was no one . . . nothing to
see except the prairie night and Castle MacAllister looming out of it, glowing in the moonlight like some mythical
El Dorado. When she glanced back toward the corral,
she realized with a start that she couldn't even see Kathy.

Kid Connors had vanished! And so had the black
mare.

But she wouldn't just ride off and leave me. Dorcas thought, her heart rising frantically into her throat.

And then plummeting straight down into her golden brown sandals, as a familiar voice from behind her said lazily, *"Buenos tardes, mí amigo.* Charming outfit—but I think I liked you better as a girl."

Drat the man if he wasn't a wizard, after all!

Heaving a gut-wrenching sigh, she turned slowly to meet his smoky gray eyes. Her own widened into big green lanterns and then quickly dropped, so he wouldn't see the shock in them.

"Buenos tardes, señor. Ees good night for ride, no?" she offered meekly.

"Oh, it's a grand night for riding." Elliott grinned, shifting the weight of the large silver-studded saddle and bridle he held easily in his arms.

"Finally! It's so nice to find something, at last, that we can all agree on," Kathy remarked pleasantly over his shoulder as she cocked the revolver she'd just jabbed firmly into the base of his skull. "And how generous of you to bring us such expensive-looking tack. Now, why don't you be a good little wizard and saddle Esmeralda for me." With her free hand, she drew the black mare forward by its rope halter.

Elliott's gray gaze went almost black as the gun barrel bit harder into him. It seemed obvious that this was a unique situation for him, one he had probably never experienced before.

"That happens to be my mare, and her name is Petunia," he said between clenched teeth.

"Then she'll be so relieved to become my mare and have it changed. She hates being called Petunia—you can see it in her eyes," Kathy told him. "Pedro, come hold Esmeralda's halter while Mr. Wizard saddles her. . . . You like the name Esmeralda, don't you? Why, she's as graceful as a flamenco dancer. Her hooves will sound like

158

castanets as we fly across the prairie on her back." She grinned at Dorcas.

"*Sí,* señor." Moving cautiously around Elliott to take the halter, Dorcas tried not to grin too broadly in return. The man looked steamed enough as it was.

"Okay! But get that damn gun out of my neck so I can move properly," he ground out.

Kathy obliged him by backing off half a pace, and he reluctantly hoisted the ornate saddle onto the mare's back, then swiftly spun around.

His eyebrows rose slightly at the Kid Connors costume.

So did the Kid's at the sight of the revolver Simon had been hiding beneath the saddle. Quick as a cat, she switched the aim of her own weapon.

And Dorcas's black-dyed brows popped up the highest of all.

"Drop it . . . nice and easy," Kathy purred, "or you'll have to explain to Alan how you happened to let me blow her head off."

Elliott's eyes turned to steel. "What makes you think I won't blow yours off first?" he asked in a tone to match.

"Don't be absurd. Everyone knows that the famous Smoke Elliott is far too much of a gentleman to shoot a woman."

"What woman? I don't see any *women* around here."

"All right, if that's the way you want to play it." She sighed, carefully sighting down the barrel of her revolver. "Pedro, *muchacho,* remember—you *did* ask me to shoot you if we got caught."

That told Dorcas all she needed to know. Her face went chalk white under the boot polish and her hands began trembling so violently, the mare nearly shied on her. "No! I never meant that! You know I didn't really mean it! Please, Mr. Elliott, don't . . . don't let her . . ."

It must have been the sheer panic in her voice that

decided him. With a blistering curse, Simon knelt and laid his revolver on the sunbaked red clay soil.

Like lightning, Dorcas ducked down and retrieved it.

"Very nicely done. For a moment there, you almost had me convinced I was going to shoot you," Kathy commended her. "If you can't spot a bluff any better than that, I'd stay away from the poker table if I were you," she advised Simon.

He responded with a lethal look and a few curses that made his previous one seem as cool and refreshing as iced lemonade.

"Spoilsport," she said. And promptly ordered him to remove his boots. Which was the easiest part of the next few minutes, because he turned out to be a good deal more attached to his trousers than he had been to his foot gear.

"Don't be shy, pahdnuh. Y'all sed y'self ain't no wimmin heah," Kid Connors coaxed. "Y'all think y' gots anythin' Pedro an' me ain't a seed afore?"

Pedro turned redder than a basket of ripe chili peppers at a sudden vivid memory. It wasn't of Michaelangelo's *David*, either.

"I just didn't want to overawe you." Elliott grinned wickedly.

As his hands moved to his belt buckle, Dorcas speedily decided that she was quite capable of finishing the saddling herself. There was no sense in embarrassing Mr. Elliott any more than was necessary, she thought. For that matter, there was a lot less sense in embarrassing herself.

One, two, three, four . . . Goodness, look at all the little silver conches decorating this leather . . .

By the time she had finished counting them, Elliott's trousers and boots had been hurled deep into the center of a thick stand of prickly pear cactus and the rest of him had been securely tied to the corral fence with his own belt. Oddly enough, however, he didn't look fit to be tied. Leaning against the corral as though he was simply pausing in the middle of a pleasant midnight stroll, he watched the Kid and Pedro mounting his mare, that characteristic grin playing lazily about his lips and his eyes glinting with a devilish satisfaction. He seemed to be expecting something.

The riders found out what it was before they'd trotted sixty feet into the scrub. A distinctive whistle fluted over the prairie, and the black mare began dancing under them as if she had suddenly decided to demonstrate the trickier steps of a fandango. Instead of fighting with her, Kathy instantly let the reins go slack. A sharper whistle sliced the air, and Dorcas had to tighten her grip as the mare spun about and cantered obediently back to push her soft nose against Simon's solid shoulder.

"Good girl, Petunia," he said, with a butter-won't-melt-in-my-mouth grin at Kathy.

She ignored it.

"Now listen to me, Esmeralda, honey—as one female to another, never come running when a man whistles. It makes them think they own you."

"I do own her!"

"You see what I mean? He thinks of you as nothing but his property," Kathy said, stroking the mare's sleek neck. "All men are like that, you know. The only thing they want from us gals is to be able to dominate us. Is that what you want, Esmeralda? To be some man's slave? I think you have more horse sense than that."

The mare's ears flicked expressively back, as though she thought so, too. But she was obviously a fair-minded sort and batted her big, beautiful eyes at Simon, giving him a chance for rebuttal, apparently.

He didn't take it.

"Do you have any idea how asinine you sound, talking to a horse that way?" he asked Kathy.

161

"There's nothing asinine about giving a strong, intelligent creature a chance to make her own decisions. Is there, Esmeralda?"

She was answered with an agreeable nicker.

"Her name is Petunia!"

He received an aggravated snort.

"I told you, she doesn't like Petunia," Kathy said. "Now which will it be, Esmeralda? Do you want to come with me and be treated with respect? Or stay here and be treated like you-know-what?"

The mare pranced a few steps sideways, tossing her head and whinnying.

"That's what I thought." Her rider grinned. And without another word or look for Elliott, she reined the mare toward the open prairie.

"Petunia!"

A shrill whistle brought the black head swinging back to the corral for an instant, and Esmeralda gave a final, long whinny. It sounded a little like an apology.

But a lot more like horsey laughter.

Chapter Eight

There was no way they could go on to Abilene after that—not dressed as they were. Anyone from the castle who came after them would be looking for a black-clad gunslinger and a Mexican youth. Of course, the tartan shawl would have given Dorcas away in any case, but she had been planning on ditching it before they reached the station. She had only worn it for the ride there, because April nights on the high plains could be as cold as the days were hot.

Crowded behind Kathy in the leather armchair known, sometimes, as a western saddle, she pulled the makeshift serape closer around herself as she considered the Plan B they'd chosen. It would delay her return to Philadelphia by another week or three, but she could live with that, just so long as she did get back. She could live with quite a bit, she realized, just so long as she could continue living, period. The threat of death had given her a brand-new perspective on life.

"I'm sorry. Maybe I shouldn't have told you. It was only card game gossip, after all. Geordie doesn't like Alan very much, you know. And he'd been drinking pretty heavily that night. Maybe he made the whole thing up," Kathy was saying. "Now that I think about it, I don't recall anyone else even mentioning that Alan had a wife—let alone that he killed her."

"I have. Alan, himself," Dorcas replied bleakly. "He admitted flat out that he was responsible for her death."

"Maybe he was merely trying to frighten you."

"If he was, he succeeded."

"And what I just added to the story has only frightened you more." Kathy sighed. "It's an old ailment of mine— hoof-in-mouth disease."

"Don't be silly. It's far better that I know exactly what I'm up against," Dorcas assured her.

It's a relief, even, in a ghastly sort of way, she thought. Because there had been a part of her that hadn't really wanted to leave in the first place. It might have, subconsciously, made her do something stupid—such as allowing herself to be recaptured. But now she knew that was completely out of the question. Going back wouldn't just mean the loss of her self-respect and independence, the things she valued most in life. It could well mean the loss of her life itself. What Kathy had just related was that Alan's wife had been killed because she had been trying to run away from him. And, according to Alan himself, the death had been horrible.

That was the confusing part. Beyond confusing, really. It was almost unbelievable. She could imagine him killing in self-defense or unthinking rage, as he might have killed Dunstan that night if they hadn't stopped him. But to do what he said had been done to that woman? It didn't seem possible. How could a man who was capable of the tenderness he sometimes displayed be able to commit such a cold-blooded atrocity?

Perhaps he *was* mad. Not just eccentric, like the rest of the MacAllisters, but genuinely insane.

It wasn't an entirely new idea, of course. She had considered it the night of that infuriating mock wedding. But Dunstan's attack and all that had followed had pushed the concern into the back of her thoughts. But that had been before she had heard the reason for Heather MacAllister's murder.

And now I've given him the same motivation, she thought, shuddering. Suddenly even Philadelphia didn't seem safe. With modern-day train travel, it was too accessible. And he would know that she was heading there. That he might not follow never entered her mind. If she was sure of nothing else, Dorcas was certain that Alan would pursue her. He had made it threateningly clear that he considered her his property, that no power in or out of creation could induce him to let her go. And that was just one more sign of insanity, wasn't it? It had to be. What else could prompt such an unyielding, unalterable fixation?

"Dorcas, you're going to hurt something if you don't relax. I feel like I've got Lot's wife riding behind me— *after* she was turned into a pillar of salt. You're stiffer than a new corset."

"I'm sorry, I know I am." Dorcas sighed, trying to unlock her spine. Kathy was right; if she didn't move with the rhythm of the horse, she could rattle her kidneys loose. And she might need them yet.

One step at a time, she cautioned herself. It was a philosophy that had gotten her through the dark days immediately following her aunt's death. Sometimes the only way you could survive was to take it one moment at a time. The first bit of business was to stay hidden for the next several days, until their trail was cold. After that? Well, she would deal with the future when it became the present.

"Are you certain these friends of yours will be willing to shield us?" A lot hinged on that, of course.

"Absolutely. The Garcias adore me. They're the ones who clued me in to the MacAllister money and Angus's search for brides, in the first place. They're bandido stock themselves. Maria and I ran some delightful cons together when I was in El Paso. But when things started getting a little hot for them there, and she told me her family had decided to go straight, I was the one who staked them to this ranch we're headed for. Took a long, grueling night at the poker tables to do it, too."

"How much farther is it?" Dorcas asked, glancing nervously at the gray, predawn sky. They had been riding all night, with only a few breaks to rest Esmeralda, but she wasn't sure how many miles they had actually come, because there had been such a tangle of circling and doubling back and detouring over rock-hard stretches of earth where hoofprints wouldn't show. Cat Kildare had left a veritable fox trail for anyone who tried to track them. Unless Alan was a bloodhound, or a genuine Comanche after all, he'd never be able to follow it.

She gave a short, humorless laugh at the thought, but quickly bit it back. She didn't want to laugh too soon. If he had returned earlier than expected, or Elliott had broken loose, there could already be an impromptu posse after them. Alan wouldn't have waited for daylight. And she doubted that Simon would, either. He was turning out to be just full of tricks—even for a wizard.

"The ranch is beyond that next rise. Not too far. We'll make it before full light," Kathy said, easing one of Dorcas's concerns, at least.

Regardless of how indecipherable their trail was, she had been thinking, a tracker would hardly be stymied by it if they were still on horseback come sunrise. On this open expanse of prairie, they could be spotted a mile or more away.

Which was how all three females knew there was trouble even before they heard the shots.

Picking her way gracefully through the scrub at the top of a low knoll, Esmeralda had pulled to a sudden stop, her velvety nostrils flaring and her expressive ears at full alert. Ahead and a little below them lay the Garcia spread, a rough, narrow house dug halfway into the red clay soil, surrounded by a couple of corrals and several large sheds, all lit by the first rosy rays of dawn peeking over the horizon.

And the last smoldering remains of what only hours earlier had been Esiquio Garcia and his three sons.

Before burning, they had been tied to the wheels of the wagon Dorcas had seen them in on her way to the castle that first day. Somehow she knew it was the same people and the same wagon, even though there was little left to identify.

In front of her, Kathy had frozen still as stone, except for the hand that had quietly unholstered and cocked one of her revolvers. "Damn! Maria was always afraid of something like this," she hissed, swinging her right leg over the pommel and slipping lightly to the ground. "It's why her family moved up here—they'd made some bad enemies in the south. This could be revenge for an old grievance. Or, more likely, the work of some bored prairie pirates. Either way, I've got to check it out. You stay here."

"Like hell I'll stay!" Dorcas cursed, half falling out of the saddle to land jerkily beside her. Sudden nausea had turned her legs rebellious and rubbery and she felt, for a moment, like a sailor who'd just touched land after weeks on a rolling deck. "I saw that family happy and smiling barely four days ago. I was going to try to hitch a ride to Abilene with them," she choked out. "I'm coming with you!"

Agitatedly disentangling herself from the tartan serape, she slung it into the waist-high weeds and began pushing through them toward the homestead, her heart pounding furiously in her chest, and the gun she'd taken from Elliott clutched tightly in her hand.

With quick strides, Kathy overtook her and moved ahead, the barrel of her own revolver parting the tall grasses before her like a hunting dog's muzzle. "All right then, we'll both check it out," she whispered, obviously not wanting to take the time to argue. "But keep behind me. And be careful where you point that thing. I hope you know how to use it."

I hope so, too, Dorcas thought, frantically trying to remember every scrap of information she had ever heard regarding the use of firearms. Those adventure yarns with which Zachary Earnshaw had regaled her childhood ears had been full of gunfights, hadn't they? One simply kept a steady hand, thumbed back the hammer, pointed, and squeezed the trigger, right? How difficult could it be?

"I've done some target shooting," she lied, to put Kathy's mind at rest, if not her own. "But I'm afraid I've never fired at anything . . . anything living."

Kathy let out an unexpected laugh. "If it comes to that, neither have I. At least, not with the intention of doing any serious damage. I can't stand the sight of blood—especially my own," she admitted. "Oh, well, hopefully neither of us will have to find out how good we really are."

"Nice hope," Dorcas muttered under her breath. She didn't have much faith in it, though. The closer they drew to the Garcias' home, the more she could sense the danger permeating the entire area. It stank worse than the charred remains still smoking in the front yard.

Left alone on the knoll and none too happy about it, Esmeralda waited several long, uneasy moments, tossing her head and snorting feathery wisps of steam into the cool dawn air. Then, at a sudden, suspicious crackling of brush behind her, the mare abandoned her vigil and began a rapid trot down the slope after her companions.

Neither of them noticed her tailing them. Their focus was locked on the scene ahead and the battle to control their stomachs as the sight and stench of fried flesh grew more atrocious the closer they drew to it. All four corpses were naked, and there were signs, even through the charring, that they had been mutilated before the burning. Worst of all, two of them were not even full grown.

An act of vengeance? A way to relieve the tedium of a dull night on the prairie? Neither of Kathy's suggestions worked for Dorcas. Only a madman would do such things to boys scarcely out of childhood, she thought as a violent new wave of nausea hit her. She suddenly found herself wondering where, exactly, Alan was, and what he had been doing these past two days and nights.

Kathy, meanwhile, was scanning the corral. "We're in big trouble. Whoever did this is still here. And there may be a whole hornets' nest of them," she whispered, her voice tense. "Less than half of these horses belong to the Garcias."

Following her gaze, Dorcas felt the blood in her veins freeze. Even from a dozen yards off, she could see that many of the milling horses bore what she recognized as the MacAllister brand. And, as if that wasn't enough, right in the thick of them danced and snorted an all-too-familiar giant Appaloosa stallion.

The bottom dropped straight out of her. It wasn't until that moment, when she saw the proof, that she realized how desperately she had wanted not to believe it, how fiercely she had hoped she was wrong about him. The overwhelming sense of loss slammed through her, nearly knocking her to her knees.

Just then, a series of wild shots shattered the air. And

with them, an old man's agonized pleas for mercy, and a small child's hysterical screams for help.

"That sounds like Rosa—Oh, dear God, *no!*" Kathy cried, and raced toward the largest shed, yanking her second revolver free as she went.

Dorcas sped after her. But both were overtaken and passed by the practically fire-breathing Esmeralda, who charged forward like a one-horse cavalry. A steely-eyed figure lay low in the saddle, clinging to her neck like a blond leech.

Or a wizard?

"Both of you—*stay back!*" Elliott ordered as he galloped past them.

"That idiot is going to get himself killed!" Kathy shouted, putting on an extra burst of speed as she tore forward.

"We're *all* going to get ourselves killed." Dorcas groaned, instinct throwing her flat just as she rounded the open front of the three-sided shed.

Blinded by dust, shots blazing over her head and shouts ringing in her ears, she snaked over the hard-packed earth, guided only by the higher-pitched notes of the child's wild shrieks. A spray of bullets tore up the ground to her right, and without thinking she rolled left, firing off one shot toward something she could barely see.

Good heavens, it worked!

The something yelped and sat down hard, dropping his weapon to clutch at what was left of his kneecap.

More shots sounded from another direction. Whether they were aimed at her or not, she didn't know and didn't wait to find out. Rolling again, she was brought up short against a cool, sticky mound and had to fight to keep her stomach from splitting apart when she realized that the mound was the naked bodies of Maria Garcia and her two older daughters, stacked roughly together like bloody cordwood. It didn't take a lot of guesswork to figure what had been done to them before death. The bottom corpse was still staked spread-eagled to the ground. Dorcas could feel the lash wounds on all three females almost as if the bullwhips that made them had bit into her herself.

Battling back cold horror, she scrabbled sideways, squinting into the early sun's glare and trying to get her bearings. Somehow she had ended up to the west and almost thirty feet away from her original destination, the open side of the long, south-facing shed. That was where the child's cries were coming from, though the erratic shrieks had leveled out into an unbroken stream of forceful wailing. Little Rosa had good lungs, apparently. That was something, at least, Dorcas thought, with a few seconds of relief. Wails like that were from fright and anger, not actual pain.

Which was more than could be said for the man she had shot. He lay where the bullet had dropped him, bellowing like a stuck pig. Even his cohorts were giving him a wide berth. Four of them were grappling for a hold on Esmeralda's bridle, while three more were trying to drag her rider out of the saddle.

Dorcas glanced over her right shoulder toward them just as Elliott hit the dirt. Before she could attempt any aid herself, a burst of gunfire cracked out from between two bales of hay at the east side of the shed's yard, driving two of his attackers backward several paces. He sent the remaining one even farther with a lightning fist to the jaw and dove behind the hay, leaving Esmeralda to her own fight.

Were those bales where Kathy had taken cover? Dorcas wondered distractedly, the enraged mare's screams adding to the cacophony.

"I thought I told you to stay out of this!" Simon's voice sounded furiously over it all.

"You're welcome!" Kathy's voice blazed back.

Yup. That's where she was.

Those two will have to take care of themselves for the moment, Dorcas decided, flattening herself into the rusty earth and beginning a torturous crawl toward Rosa's howls. No bullets had come her way since that first blast when she entered the yard, and she had just realized why. In her brown and tan dust-stained clothing she was almost invisible, so long as she stayed well down. Except for the gunman she'd already incapacitated, no one—probably not even Simon or Kathy—knew she was there. With a little luck, she was hoping to get the child out and away before anyone realized it. All the attention seemed, currently, on corralling the prize mare. Only the mare seemed more intent on demonstrating, with a vengeance, exactly why she was such a prize.

Amid the chaos of shouts and yells and scattered shots, Dorcas heard something that sounded like a basket of eggs being stomped on and instantly buried her face in the dirt. Someone's skull had just been smashed by a flashing hoof. His brains had landed inches from her nose.

Choking back bile, she made a scrambled detour around them, forcing herself to look at nothing but her destination, as she dragged her body forward over the rough ground, bit by painful bit. Between the glare and the dust and smoke, it was difficult to see, but something was definitely moving on the side of the shed, she noted, praying fervently that it was only an animal. Sometimes prayers are answered.

And sometimes they aren't.

Dorcas's heart nearly stopped cold with the rest of her as a tall, black-haired figure stepped out into the light and halted in obvious scorn at the fiasco before him. With the sun in her eyes, she couldn't make out his face, but she didn't need to. Moccasins, leggings, breechclout

. . . and, above them, that unmistakable bronzed torso. There was no doubt who it was.

Yes, he would be scornful of such bungling, she thought. From what she had learned of him so far, he didn't seem to have much use for others' incompetence. And the word *patience* wasn't even in his vocabulary. But what did he expect with dregs like these for followers? He had to be their leader, of course. He wasn't the type to take orders—only issue them. What was he playing at here? In his madness, did he view this horror as a way of re-creating his own private Comanche raiding party?

A real Comanche would be revolted, Dorcas decided. She knew she was. But perhaps it was a good thing, after all, that she had been able to witness what he was capable of. At least it had set her free from all the other emotions that had been tormenting her these past few days. Gazing up at him, her cheek pressed painfully into the rocky earth, the only emotions she had left to summon were a cold, nauseating disgust for him and anger at herself for having ever felt anything else.

Perhaps she moved then. She didn't think she had, but something drew his attention. His head turned and he seemed to stare straight at her. Her heart pounding furiously, she held her breath until she thought she would pass out. But he must only have been looking at something nearby, or some point over her head, because just as her eyes were about to pop from the strain, he pivoted sharply and strode off.

With a ragged gasp, Dorcas caved completely into the dust and gave in to several seconds of silent, violent sobs. She had never dreamed that a person could feel such intense, soul-shattering relief. Not relief that he hadn't spotted her . . .

Relief that he wasn't Alan.

If the man's face ever had had any of Alan's handsome

lines, cruelty had long since turned its features hard and grim. The jaw was too rigid, the expression of the eyes and mouth too severe, and the nose . . . There was very little of that left. Just a stub of the bridge over two gaping holes surrounded by puckered scar tissue. As grisly as he looked, however, she could almost have hopped up and kissed him, simply for not being Alan.

That was her first unthinking, emotional response. Her second, more cerebral reaction was to consider that the MacAllister horses in the Garcia corral had, perhaps, been rustled by these walking dungheaps. Maybe the reason Alan had left in such a hurry was because he had been heading out after horse thieves. That made a certain sense. It also made her flush so hot she marveled that the earth didn't scorch beneath her. Remembering his departure had reminded her of his parting kiss. Which segued into all the prior ones.

Third, and finally, she thought that none of this explained away any of her original fears. Simply because Alan wasn't responsible for these crimes, it didn't mean he was innocent of all others.

Realizing with a shudder that she was right back where she had started from, Dorcas rose up slightly, glanced quickly about to make sure no one was looking in her direction, then leapt to her feet and sprinted the last several yards to the shed. All other concerns had been knocked clean out of her by a sudden, ominous hole in the din.

Why had Rosa stopped crying?

Because her grandfather, Servando Garcia, had requested her silence while he prayed to St. Jude, the patron saint of lost causes. Who had, apparently, heard—thereby restoring Dorcas's faith in prayer. Even if she, herself, was the answer to this one. The real stunner of the situation was how the man could manage to get out words at all. She didn't think she'd be able to solve that mystery if she lived to be older than he was.

Small, frail, half-blinded by cataracts, and crippled by arthritis to begin with, he had been severely beaten and crucified against the west wall of the shed by a wicked-looking stiletto through each palm. She had no way of knowing it then—and it probably wouldn't have made much difference to her if she had—but the razor-sharp blades were his own. Servando, before the cataracts and arthritis, had been known far and wide as one hell of a knife thrower.

It was simple hard luck that his reputation had outlasted his skill. If he had been able to give his family's tormentors the show they had wanted, perhaps they would have let him and Rosa live, as they had said they would. He didn't really think so, but then, one never knew, he explained to the stricken-looking *muchacho* who wanted to free him.

It was surprising and a bit more hard luck, perhaps, that the young Mexican could understand little of what he was saying, but Servando was philosophic enough to accept that. What he could not tolerate was being released while his *angelita* was swinging from a roof beam like the prize in a turkey shoot.

Switching from Spanish to broken English, he insisted that the child must be freed first. He was so furiously adamant about it, Dorcas rushed to oblige, though it seemed to her that Rosa would be safe enough in her rope harness for another moment or two.

It wasn't merely an old man's whim, however. Servando had his reasons. Scarcely was Rosa in Dorcas's arms, with her own little ones fastened around the strange *muchacho*'s neck in an amazing stranglehold for a two-year-old, before one of their attackers showed up. He had bad teeth, worse breath, and a sawed-off shotgun in his filthy hands. Staring down the double barrel, Dorcas had to lock her knees to keep them from buckling.

With her own revolver tucked into the waistband of her pants and Rosa plastered against her like wallpaper, she was in an extremely poor position to argue.

"Whal now, *'migo,* how'd we miss yew?" he drawled, a congenial leer showing off his broken teeth to their best advantage.

"*Que? No hablo inglés,* señor," she mumbled, stalling for time and hoping like heck that the man didn't speak Spanish, because she had just used up the bulk of hers.

She never found out if he was bilingual or not. But she did have to execute some fancy footwork to keep herself and Rosa from being flattened by him as he crashed forward, his leer fixed forever on his crooked lips and a long, thin blade buried to the hilt in the base of his skull.

How? . . . Staring wildly over Rosa's dark curls, Dorcas saw Servando still hanging from the wall by one hand. The other hand he had unbelievably managed to drag free, along with its stiletto. And it appeared that he had not lost his skill after all.

"*Vamanos, amigo!*" he breathed, and died with a look of peaceful satisfaction on his battered old face.

Fortunately, *vamanos* was one of the Spanish words Dorcas understood. Not that she really needed the urging. Shifting her sobbing burden a little to the side so she could draw her revolver, and choking back a ragged sob, she hurried down the shadowy length of the long shed to something she wished she had spotted earlier. It could have saved her that torturous belly crawl over the jagged terrain. But better late than never, she thought, kneeling before the rough hole at the east corner of the back wall.

It wasn't very large, and climbing through it proved more ticklish than she had anticipated, mainly because Rosa refused to be disengaged from her even for a moment. The operation took some careful calculation, a lot of breath holding, and a fevered plea to St. Jude, but they arrived on the opposite side of the shed in one intact unit, having only gotten stuck twice in the process.

That was when Dorcas discovered that she was up the proverbial creek in a leaky canoe. And she had just lost her paddle. Or, rather, she had just lost the other three members of her rescue team. Which sort of amounted to the same thing.

There was the double-burdened Esmeralda racing pell-mell past the corral and toward the knoll, with only a halfhearted scattering of shots following her. Dorcas had no idea how Elliott had finagled the escape and didn't even bother trying to imagine. Chalk it up to wizardry.

It was obvious why he had done it, though. Even viewing them from a distance, she could tell that the smaller figure on the mare was slumped drunkenly askew and held in the saddle only by the strong arms of the larger one.

Heaven help her, Kathy was wounded!

"He had to get her away. It couldn't be helped," Dorcas told herself, staring at the rapidly diminishing black spot as if it was the last train out of town and she had just missed it. Which she had.

She didn't think he had meant to abandon her. Whatever else he was—and Kathy had been full of tales about the surprising Smoke Elliott on their moonlit ride—the man was definitely no coward. He hadn't even seen her in the yard, after all. He probably thought she was securely hidden somewhere and was planning on coming back with help the moment Kathy was safe.

Realizing that, however, did not make Dorcas feel any less like a deserted and sinking ship. It was a wretched sensation that was made worse by the guilty awareness that she ought to be more concerned about Kathy, who had become such a close friend in such a short time. And, in all honesty, part of her was anxious over Kathy's state—extremely anxious.

But the rest of her was huddled low in the dust with a small, helpless child in her arms and a bloodthirsty band of prairie pirates breathing down her neck. And that was all. There was nowhere she could turn for help. Rosa had her to depend on, but the buck stopped there. She had no one but herself to see them both through this.

Having decided that, Dorcas suddenly felt calmer, and her pounding heart slowed down to only double its normal rate. It was always good to know exactly where you stood, she told herself. This way she wouldn't waste valuable energy wishing for some knight-errant to ride in and save the day. They never turned out to be what you hoped they were, anyway.

"Hush, *silencio, niña*," she whispered, stroking Rosa's curls and rocking her. The child's sobbing had been climbing up the scale to the danger level, but she quieted quickly, bringing a lump to Dorcas's throat at the realization of how much the tiny girl trusted her. She really didn't deserve such confidence. It was hardly more than luck that had gotten her this far. And she couldn't expect that luck to hold much longer.

It seemed to give out, in fact, at that moment, as the entire homestead violently erupted in blasts and shouts, like the splitting open of Mt. Vesuvius—minus the lava. There were churning clouds of dust, instead, lit fiery orange by the early sun at their backs as they swept in from the east. Dorcas hadn't seen them before, because her focus had been on Esmeralda galloping away to the north, but the bandits apparently had. Which was probably how Elliott had been able to wrangle his escape in the first place, she realized, squinting feverishly into the center of the leading cloud.

Even with the sun in her eyes, there was no mistaking him this time. What an amazing double irony, she thought. To get what you need just when it was past hoping for, and to be so grateful to see the very thing you were running away from. Lancelot himself could never have looked any better or been more welcome! Her luck was still with her.

Or was it?

Biting back a scream, Dorcas leapt up from her crouch as Alan abruptly dropped from his mount's back. *He'd been hit!*

"No . . ." Without thinking, she pulled Rosa closer and began racing straight for the thick of the shooting, then skidded up breathless, staring in dumbfounded relief. The Comanche in Dr. Earnshaw's adventure tales had sometimes done this, but she had never quite believed those tales. She still wasn't sure she believed them.

Under heavy fire from the outlaws, Alan had slid down until he was almost under the horse's belly. How could he stay on in that position, let alone handle a rifle? It made her head spin just trying to imagine what it was like to gallop full tilt upside down. And sent hot flames curling up her spine to realize the incredible, raw power of the man. It was like trying to look at the sun, she thought. He almost burned her eyes.

And he definitely burned the Garcias' murderers—figuratively speaking.

There had been about twenty of them originally. Dorcas knew she had wounded one. (She was still feeling a little nauseous about it, even though he had deserved it.) Esmeralda had dispatched at least one other. (She was still nauseous over that, too, though for different reasons.) And Servando had taken care of a third. (Oddly enough, that one didn't bother her a bit.) How many Kathy and Elliot had been able to deal with, she didn't know, but she didn't think there had been more than thirteen or fourteen standing when she'd first spotted the dust clouds. By the time Alan's small cavalry was just short of the main yard, only six of those were still mobile, and they had, apparently, decided that discretion was the better part of valor.

Unfortunately for them, however, Dorcas had come to the opposite conclusion. She was smaller than all of them and burdened by Rosa, but she was also a good deal closer to the corral. Before they even realized she was there, the corral gates were swinging wide and so were all the horses, stampeded by her remaining five shots.

It proved to be a multifaceted maneuver. First, it more than doubled the general pandemonium. Second, it kept the bandits from escaping before Alan and his Comanche warriors could reach th—

Wait a minute—Comanche warriors? Dorcas wondered distractedly.

The distraction was from the third and last result of her little trick. Third, it had brought No Nose after her and Rosa. And he did not look as if he had the least intention of laughing. He looked, in fact, as if he had a major chip on his shoulder regarding the whole thing. Some people had no sense of humor. He seemed to be one of them—all the time.

So was Dorcas—at that particular moment. She wouldn't have been able to laugh then, even if she had wanted to. She needed every last shred of her nearly depleted energy for a mad, skidding and sliding dash in and around the corral, under flying hooves, with Rosa in her arms and No Nose on her tail. She had scarcely breath enough to stay ahead, let alone any to spare for laughing, crying, or calling out.

Little Rosa, however, appeared to have been born with an extra set of lungs. She had been making a valiant effort to contain herself, since being hushed earlier, but the instant the horses were stampeded, her two-year-old control cracked and she began shrieking like a band of banshees. It was astonishing that one small child could generate such a piercing noise. It cut above the shouts, the horses' screams, the gunshots . . . and it temporarily deafened Dorcas, who heard it right in her ear. But it, also, landed two stocky Comanche on her pursuer's broad back.

He shrugged them off like a dog scratching off fleas and swiveled, presumably to knock their heads together. He could have shot them, but he must have run out of bullets during the cavalry charge.

Alan had not.

He held his rifle on No Nose while the Comanche chained him to the others they had rounded up. Seeing the two men together, she marveled that she could ever have mistaken one for the other, even briefly. Despite the rather striking similarities in height, build, and coloring, they were not the same. It wasn't just the facial differences, but their whole bearing. Their energies were completely opposed. It was almost like the contrast between dark and light, between life and death.

The thought sent a creeping chill through her. Neither spoke a word, but there seemed to be some sort of a battle raging between them. She could practically see the sparks flying.

Standing several paces off, working to get her breathing and pulse under control, Dorcas dropped her gaze from them. She was having enough trouble with her own inner battle to worry about theirs.

What a mess. To be rescued by the very person you were originally trying to escape. It boggled description. She had been so relieved to see him at first, but now she was wondering if she had simply leapt from one fire into another. At the very best, she was out of the fire only to be back in the frying pan. But she was suddenly almost too tired to think, let alone care very much.

One step at a time, she reminded herself. There was always the possibility that he wouldn't recognize her—he hadn't yet, after all—and she could continue on to

Abilene as intended. But if she did that, she might never find out how Kathy was. That was unthinkable. And she had Rosa to consider now, too. The toddler had finally stopped crying, but she still refused to be set down. Dorcas had already tried it twice, merely to rest her arms, but each time had been nearly choked by Rosa's frantic hold.

It was good she was such a strong little thing, though. *She'll need strength to survive this experience,* Dorcas mused, shifting the child more comfortably against herself and resting her cheek against the dark curls. *So will I, heaven help me. I'm going to have to chance a return to the castle . . . a return to Alan . . . at least for a while. I need to make sure that Kathy is all right, and that Rosa will be safe without me.*

What on earth made her think she would be even half safe herself? Dorcas wondered.

Nothing.

She was walking straight back into the lion's den and she knew it; but for some reason, she felt a tiny lessening of that deathly sense of peril. *Why?* Was it seeing the difference between Alan and a cold-blooded murderer? There was nothing safe about Alan, but there was nothing cold about him either, she realized with a shiver.

As for his wife's death . . . Well, there could be more to that than she had previously considered. It suddenly occurred to Dorcas that he had never actually said he'd killed Heather. What he had said, exactly, was that he was responsible for her death. There was a difference between the two things. A difference that meant she could return to the lion without fearing that he'd tear her into bloody bits?

Marvelous. Because what he would try to do to her might be far more devastating, she thought, feeling his shadow almost like a tangible weight as it fell across her and the child.

182

Staring at his dusty moccasins, she bit back a slightly hysterical laugh as he questioned her in Spanish. Just her luck he'd be fluent in the language. She had spent enough time with the Mexican cook Aunt Matilda had once hired to understand maybe a third of what he was saying. He was asking if she and the *niña* were all right, and telling her that she was a brave boy for opening the corral and making his job of catching these wicked hombres easier. He was very sorry for what had happened here but would do whatever he could to help. Did the *muchacho* and his little sister have any other family or friends in the area to whom his *compadres* could escort them? Alan wanted to know.

Good heavens, he obviously hadn't seen the burned wagon yet and thought she was one of the Garcia boys. It made what she had to do that much harder; it would have been so easy to just give him a simple *gracias* and accept a fast ride to Abilene. But what would she do with Rosa when she got there? And how could she get word to Kathy—or even know if Kathy was capable of receiving word?

"No, señor—no *amigos*," Dorcas choked out, her emotions and the dust in her throat making her voice unrecognizable even to herself. Drawing a deep breath, she raised baleful green eyes to his and managed in a slightly clearer tone, "No family or friends . . . just the MacAllisters."

Alan went chalk white under his tan.

"Dorcas?"

The awareness was instant and almost agonizing in its force. All in a few seconds, his expression went from shock that it was her to anger that she was there to horror at what could have happened to her . . . and, finally, a nearly heart-stopping relief that none of it had. With a low groan, he stepped forward and pulled her tightly against himself.

183

"Don't say a word. I don't want to know anything about it," he whispered hoarsely. "So long as you're unharmed, nothing else matters. You're safe now."

The hell I am, Dorcas thought, hot tears stinging her eyes. Crawling through the dust with bullets whizzing over her head had been a cakewalk compared to dealing with the warm, sensual, utterly maddening feel of Alan's arms around her. This was going to be even worse than she had thought.

Trapped between them, Rosa began squirming and squawking up a storm.

"My feelings exactly," Dorcas mumbled into the toddler's curls.

Chapter Nine

The return to the castle was uneventful except for one moment of surprise that arrived at the end—the surprise being that the end arrived so soon. Guided only by two silent and curiously light-eyed Comanche, because Alan had stayed to supervise the apprehension of the bandits, Dorcas found herself back behind the adobe battlements before the morning was scarcely past its infancy. The Garcias had merely been leasing, it turned out. Their spread was on MacAllister land. Though she and Kathy had ridden all night to get there, the little ranch actually lay just beyond sight of the castle walls.

What a brilliant hiding place it would have been if it had worked, she thought tiredly. Who would have considered looking for them so nearby?

It was no wonder Elliott had appeared a tad out of sorts when she had met him on the ride back. It must have been less than amusing for him following endless tracks that ultimately led almost to where he'd started from. He had changed into a fresh shirt and was on a fresh mount, but nothing else about him was very fresh. He looked and sounded as if he'd just been through a small war. Probably because he had.

"Well, well, if it isn't young Pedro. I was just riding out to check on you, *muchacho,* but since you're obviously intact, I can continue on to Abilene with a clear conscience. If you'll forgive my hasty departure earlier, I'll return the favor by forgiving you for helping to steal my horse," he drawled, reining in alongside her.

"And while we're on the subject of crimes, *mi amigo,* you might care to inform Laird Alan that I'll be back with help by tomorrow. Warn him that, as impressive as his display was this morning, he's to do nothing else beyond keeping those vermin confined until we get here. Any signs of claymore justice and he could find himself confined—or worse. The MacAllisters have been under enough suspicion as it is."

"Spare me the lectures," Dorcas said tersely, her head too stuffed with her own concerns to have registered a word he had said. "Just tell me how she is."

"She? Are you referring to the desperado in black? The one with the hearing problem?" Simon asked. "That little lunatic is in better shape than I am right now. All she got is a slight flesh wound where a bullet grazed her shoulder—hardly more than a scratch. But it nearly gave me a heart attack. She was so still and cold on the gallop back, I thought I'd lost her. I didn't realize it was simply that she'd fainted at the sight of her own blood!" he exclaimed. "Thank God you had the sense to stay clear. Where were you hiding, anyway?"

"You're the wizard, you tell me," Dorcas retorted. "I'll give you a hint, though." She nodded toward Rosa in front of her on the saddle. "Where do you think she came from?"

Elliott stared blankly at the toddler, as though he had

186

only just noticed her and was trying to figure out what she was. Then realization struck home and he went pale green under his coating of grime.

"Good God," he breathed, "you're a lunatic, too."

He was probably right about that, Dorcas thought, seated in the burgundy armchair and staring over Rosa's damp curls at the big four-poster bed across the room. Her own short curls were damp as well, and sandy blond once more, after the long bath she and the child had shared. She hadn't been sure the ink would wash out, but it had, along with the boot polish, causing a brief flurry of confusion when Rosa hadn't been able to understand why Dorcas's coloring was scrubbing off and hers wasn't.

Regarding all else, however, the little girl had been almost too accepting. She gazed around with large, solemn brown eyes, but had offered surprisingly little fuss since they'd left the ranch. It had made it easier to wash her, dress her in borrowed garments, and feed her, of course, but it was heartrending. The cries for mama that Dorcas kept expecting never materialized. And she was afraid she knew why that was; Rosa had seen and heard enough to realize that mama couldn't come.

The thought sent sickening chills coursing through her, but there was nothing she could do about it except hold the child, rock her, and tell her, in broken Spanish, that everything would be all right. Those assurances were the most difficult part, naturally. She wondered, even while murmuring the words, whom she was trying to convince—Rosa or herself?

"How's th' wee lassie?"

Dorcas glanced upward with a start and then relaxed at the sight of the slight figure in the open doorway.

"She's almost asleep, I think. How's your patient doing?"

"Wide awake and madder 'n a wet hen. Angus has been tae see her." Molly grinned.

"Oh, dear. He's not going to press charges, is he?"

"Charges? Fer what, lass?"

"For pretending to be a relative and trying to run a con game on him," Dorcas answered. That was obvious, wasn't it? And she thought it was pretty darn unchivalrous of Simon Elliott to have told the MacAllisters who Kathy really was, without giving her the chance to confess on her own.

"Oh, Angus dinna care fer that," Molly said, stepping lightly into the room. "He came tae tell her that, since th' lads canna decide among themselves, he'll be holdin' a hurlin' match in three days. The winner'll be her bridegroom."

"What?" Dorcas's gaze widened over Rosa's little head. "He still wants her to marry one of his sons?"

"Aye. 'Tis most fond of her he's become—whether she be Mary MacAllister or Kathleen Kildare. He says she's a bonny, braw lassie. An' since 'twas MacAllister gold she was after, 'tis MacAllister gold she'll get . . . but she'll hafta take one of his lads alang wi'it."

Why doesn't that surprise me? Dorcas wondered, sinking deeper into the chair.

"I'll come see her as soon as I can." She sighed. "In the meantime, tell her I said welcome to the club . . . and to stay away from the ramparts."

Molly's brow rose slightly. "What club be that, dear?"

"Never mind. She'll know what I mean."

"Aye, dear, whatever ye say. I only came tae make sure 'twas nuthin' ye needed fer th' child—such a bonny, wee thing. . . . But she seems well enoof tae me, considerin' what she's suffered, the poor bairn," Molly said, turning back toward the door after a long, covetous look at Rosa. "I've sum more wounds tae be tendin' now. Word has just come that me grandson's returned, draggin' sum

188

sorry-lookin' brigands behind him. They'll be loadin' 'em inta th' dungeons, I expect. 'Tis a lang time since those cells've seen such business," she muttered. "Not since I wuz a lass. Not since Elspeth's day . . . Now there's one who had a dab hand wi' battle wounds—heaven knows she had practice enoof. I mun tell ye aboot her sumtime. Ye'd find her interestin', I'll wager," the old woman offered, gazing back over her shoulder at Dorcas.

"Now that be queer," she added, more to herself. "I dinna notice afore, but ye put me in mind a wee bit of Elspeth. 'Tis sumthin' in th' eyes."

Something in the eyes . . .

It was such a simple, offhand remark, but it choked Dorcas like a stranglehold.

"Something in the eyes," she repeated, watching Molly's tiny figure disappear into the perpetual shadows of the passage.

Something in the eyes?

It was more like something deep in her consciousness, buried just beyond her reach. It was dreams that seemed like memories—memories that couldn't possibly be her own. It was the feeling that part of her wasn't herself anymore, that she was turning into someone else, someone she didn't know and couldn't control. It was almost like some sort of possession. But not by the spirit of a girl who had lived here decades before. These odd sensations and almost-memories seemed more like a bizarre side effect of her mind being invaded, perhaps a mental suggestion to make her feel she belonged here when she knew she didn't.

Someone was trying to possess her, certainly, but it was definitely not some long-gone girl. It was someone who was, apparently, willing to use any means at his disposal to bring her under his control.

Physical force . . . emotional intimidation . . . hypnosis?

Was such a thing possible? Could one mind dominate another to that extent?

She had helped her aunt once with a research project involving mesmerism. Their findings had rattled both of them; they had set out to disprove the concept, but had ended up reasonably convinced that mesmerism—within certain parameters, anyway—was a valid phenomena. How far it could be taken was another question. Dorcas was beginning to suspect that it might be a bigger force than either she or her aunt had reckoned.

It was something in the eyes, she thought. Not her eyes, though. It was in a pair of mesmerizing amber orbs that seemed to sizzle clear through to the bottom of her soul every time he looked at her.

She was going to have to try to remember all the data from that study; there might be something there she could use to defend herself. Perhaps Dr. Earnshaw could help. He was the one person, besides herself, with whom Aunt Matilda had discussed all her research. He might be able to fill in any gaps in her own recollection. She would try to see him after Rosa had had a good nap. If she moved now, she'd awaken the child.

Unfortunately, her unconscious knee jiggling had already done almost that. And after it had taken so long to lull her into a sound sleep, too. Gently shifting the little bundle into a more comfortable position, she hushed and rocked the child back to sleep.

"Dorcas, you are such a nitwit," she scolded herself.

"Aye. A bonny one, though."

Automatically catching her breath and then forcing herself to let it out slowly so she wouldn't disturb Rosa again, Dorcas shot a wary glance at the dusty, bare-chested figure lounging against the door frame. She was careful to avoid those dangerous amber eyes.

"How long have you been standing there?" she whispered accusingly.

"Long enough to see that you'll make a good mother for our children," Alan answered softly, bringing a sudden blush to her freshly scrubbed face.

She tried to control the heat, as well as her tongue. It was better to ignore comments like that. Anger would only weaken her position. Wasn't that one of the findings of the mesmerism research, that a heightened emotional state sometimes made a subject more susceptible to outside influences? The trick to this game was maintaining a cool detachment.

Think icicles, she ordered herself, as Alan slouched motionless in the doorway.

"How I ever could have mistaken you for a lad . . . it boggles the mind," he murmured, staring intently at her. "Chalk it up to the stress of the moment. I must have been temporarily daft."

Temporarily? Dorcas thought, grappling to hang on to her composure. Ducking her head over Rosa didn't help. Even when she couldn't see that powerfully muscled bronze form, she could still feel his gaze flowing over her like molten lava. Her carefully envisioned icicles were beginning to melt. Rapidly.

"Your cropped hair poses a problem for me, you know. It makes you look so much younger. I'll be feeling a bit like a dirty old man 'til those lovely locks grow out," he said, hauling himself away from the door frame with a weary sigh. "And, speaking of which . . . is that water still hot, do you think?"

What? Hers and Rosa's bathwater? She glanced up to see where he was heading, relieved that it was toward the brass tub and not toward her.

"It may still be a little warm, but—"

"Close enough," he cut her off, kicked off his moccasins, and began peeling down his leggings.

Good Lord! He wasn't going to bathe right in front of her, was he?

"Alan, you can't use that water—it's filthy!" she protested, quickly ducking her face as his hands moved to his breechclout.

"So am I. Anything'll be an improvement. I haven't the energy to wait for fresh."

With a deep groan of contentment, he collapsed into the tub.

Dorcas spent a few breathless moments replacing her steamed icicles with the image of a massive glacier. By the time she dared look up, he was completely hidden, except for his handsomely sculpted dark head and granite shoulders—which were distracting enough—but at least his eyes were closed. His head was sunk back against the curved brass rim and she realized, with a surge of sympathy that quite surprised her, that he was knock-down-drag-out, through-the-wringer exhausted. Though why that should bother her, she couldn't imagine.

"How long has it been since you've had any sleep?" she asked with grudging concern.

"Hmmm . . . sleep? What's that?"

Good heavens, he must have been trailing those pirates since he left here. What was that? Nearly forty-eight hours without rest?

"Oh, honestly—this is absurd! You need sleep now more than you need a bath. Get out of that tub and go to bed before you sink from exhaustion and drown," she ordered, scarcely thinking what she was saying.

His eyelids flickered and she immediately regretted having opened her mouth.

"Spoken just like a wife," he said, grinning. "Your worry over me is touching."

"It's not worry! It's simply common-sense advice. And I am no—"

"Shhh. You'll wake that wee lassie in your lap."

"I am no one's wife!" she whispered furiously. Somewhere at the North or South Pole a glacier must have just broken up.

"Dorcas, dear—for the final time—our marriage is valid," Alan whispered back, his half-lidded amber eyes looking disturbingly feline and predatory.

"Maybe it would be in old Scotland, but we happen to be in modern Texas!" she hissed.

"For all intents and purposes, MacAllister land *is* old Scotland."

"Of course it is. And I'm Joan of Arc and you're the war chief Cochise."

Alan heaved a long sigh, creating a slight splash as he slid lower in the tub.

"No. Cochise was Apache. I'm Comanche, remember? My name is Eyes-of-the-Cat."

"Eyes . . . Eyes-of-the . . ." Dorcas didn't need any reminding to keep her voice low. A scratchy whisper was all she could grate out. Her emerald gaze darted furtively to the door.

"Aye, that's a rough translation, anyway," Alan said tiredly. "And if you move one inch away from that chair, I'll be out of this tub so fast—"

"You wouldn't dare touch me while I'm holding this child!"

Eyes-of-the-Cat proved the aptness of his name as a glittering, golden glare riveted her where she sat.

"Don't tell me what I'd dare or not, lassie," he growled.

"And don't you threaten me!" she spat, something inside her abruptly stiffening and giving her the strength to hold firm under that glare. Or maybe it was the other scenes still so fresh in her mind's eye that stiffened her resolve. "I've had enough of this! I'm tired of being tricked and bullied and manhandled. I won't tolerate any more," she whispered tensely, her eyes glinting like green ice. "Today I saw the bloodiest that humanity has to offer. Unless you're prepared to top it, there's nothing you can do to frighten me."

It was a good boast, but she had forgotten, in the anger of the moment, that his power to dominate had little to do with pain. It was the opposite, rather. His main force lay in the raw heat of his physical presence—and the sensual pleasure it promised. Too late she was reminded of that, as he rose up out of the tub like a bronzed Neptune striding forth from the sea.

"I thought there was nothing I could do to frighten you," he commented, trailing water across the floor as he moved deliberately toward her.

Dorcas hastily doubled over the sleeping bundle in her lap. "I'm not frightened. I . . . I was worried about Rosa," she murmured, her tightly shut eyes burning with the imprint of Alan's hard-muscled, glistening form. "You can't walk around here like that. There's a small girl present!"

"Two of them, apparently," he muttered, angling away from her to close the door to the room. It pulled to with a deadly decisive click. "Rosa's not the one who's bothered, though," he continued, turning back. "She's sound asleep. I doubt an earthquake could wake her at this point. Lay her on the bed. She'll be safe there, and I want to talk to you without any distractions."

"Get dressed and I'll consider it."

"Fair enough, I suppose." Alan sighed and retraced his steps to the dresser by the door.

Talk about distractions, Dorcas silently fumed. *What did he think he was, poised there wearing nothing but his arrogance?*

She kept her face down until he had dragged on a form-fitting pair of fawn-colored trousers, and then carefully rose from the chair and carried the sleeping child to the bed. There was one good thing about this, she reflected. With Rosa nestled securely in the center of the

194

four-poster, he wouldn't be able to use it for anything else. Leaving the tiny girl surrounded by pillows so she couldn't accidentally roll off the mattress, Dorcas drew a deep, slow breath and turned around.

She drew a sharp, quick one as she saw Alan relaxed in the armchair she had just vacated. *That* was his idea of getting dressed? He had gotten no further than the fawn trousers and his boots.

The man definitely has a grudge against shirts. She sighed inwardly, feeling somewhat underdressed herself. She hadn't been able to determine, after the bath, which of Flora's detested frocks to inflict upon herself, and had gone with the temporary compromise of a sea green silk dressing gown over her underthings until deciding. But when Rosa had started to fall asleep on her lap, she hadn't wanted to disturb her, and then . . .

"Come here," Alan ordered, his voice a low, sensuous purr and his eyes pulling at her like magnets.

Suddenly, her feet didn't seem to belong to her anymore. Gliding over the smooth wood floor, Dorcas couldn't resist the draw of that gaze until her knees bumped his. Then, like a sleepwalker snapping awake, she dug in her heels and stopped short, the look of a bird that's narrowly missed being snared clouding her lovely face—and a shocked awareness building in her active brain. That had gone a little beyond mesmerism as she understood the phenomena.

How had he done that? she wondered indignantly, jerking back a pace, almost as if she'd been burned. In a way she had been—by the scorching blaze of two amber eyes.

They never blinked. "Come here," he repeated.

Dorcas set her jaw, planted her feet, and tried to imagine a wall of ice looming in front of her.

"I have come here," she said, frost gleaming on every word.

"I meant all the way here."

The ice wall sizzled into hot vapor as Alan reached through it, pulling her squarely into his lap. The dressing gown popped open with one deliberate tug and his hands slid warmly around the slender, corseted waist beneath it, locking her hard against his naked chest before she could wrestle free.

"I thought you wanted to talk," she choked out as his lips hovered above hers for a few wild breaths.

"Well . . . *communicate,* anyway," he whispered huskily. "See if you can understand what I'm saying."

And his mouth pressed firmly down.

The kiss was sheer, unbridled eloquence. It spoke volumes to her body, but nothing Dorcas could translate into actual words. It was raw power and unthinking passion and hot, hungry desire—her own, amazingly, as well as his.

Suddenly not caring whether it was proper or sensible or safe, she dove headlong into that kiss, winding her arms tightly about his neck and nearly blistering his lips with the force of her response. She poured herself over him like honey flowing out of a hive, pressing so desperately against his muscular form, it was almost as if she was trying to climb right inside him.

The chair toppled backward with an unnoticed thud and they rolled together onto the floorboards in a fevered tangle of arms and legs—a wild, double-backed creature of groans and groping hands and panting mouths—all fire and frenzy and devastating, driving need.

Drowning in a flood of kisses, lost in the ecstatic feel of that masculine body burning against hers. Dorcas was unaware of the piercing cries for several seconds. But when realization hit, she twisted furiously away and stumbled across the room, leaving Alan grappling for breath and sprawled on the floor behind her like the victim of a dynamite blast. Which, in a way, he was.

Dorcas, too. But she had the inbred feminine ability to push personal concerns out the window when a young one was sounding an alarm call.

"Rosita, what's the matter, *niña? Qué es?*" She gasped, quickly gathering the trembling little figure into her arms. "Did you have a bad dream? A . . . Oh, heck, what's the Spanish word for nightmare?" she muttered to herself.

"*Pesadilla*," Alan offered hoarsely, slowly hauling himself to his feet, like a diver coming up from the deep.

"Thank you," Dorcas said absently. And then abruptly turned scarlet, as the sight and sound of the man reopened the window and let all the sensations she'd previously bumped out sweep back in on her. Good Lord, *what* had been doing? *Or, what had she been* made *to do?* she wondered, her eyes instantly narrowing and her arms tightening convulsively around Rosa as Alan came toward them.

He was brought up short when the toddler began shrieking hysterically.

"Bloody hell! What's the matter with her?"

"You." Dorcas breathed, her face turning white as she realized what had frightened the child. She hadn't thought that Rosa could have seen them on the floor, but the noise of the chair tipping must have woken her and . . . *oh, God* . . .

"I think Rosa saw what happened to her mother and sisters," she said, staring at him with dull horror. "And when she saw us, she must have thought you were trying . . . trying to . . ."

Her voice trailed off. Perhaps Rosa had been right. Was it any less of an attack if the victim had somehow been mesmerized into accepting it?

Uttering a low curse, Alan reached out and lifted the little girl out of Dorcas's arms before she even realized what he'd intended.

197

"Stop that! You're frightening her!"

"And the sooner she sees I mean no harm, the sooner she'll stop being frightened," he said, angling away as Dorcas angrily tried to retrieve the sobbing child.

"You're hardly harmless," she muttered.

"I'm not the one who toppled the chair," he replied smoothly, and began speaking softly to Rosa in Spanish.

The little traitor quieted almost immediately, staring intently up at him, as Dorcas stood fuming at them both.

"Now, if only I could convince you as easily," Alan murmured, glancing toward her with the ghost of a grin haunting his face. He jerked slightly as Rosa caught him off guard by grabbing for his nose, as though she wanted to make sure it was real.

Dorcas's breath snagged in her throat. The child had made the same mistake she had. That was why the little thing had been so panicked. Just like herself, Rosa had thought Alan was the man with the ragged holes where his nose should have been. Why was that realization so disturbing? she wondered, a weird chill crawling over her flesh.

Because it implied that the two men were more similar than she had decided earlier. Comparing them that morning, she had been struck by the opposition in their energies. But that was actually a rather subjective judgment, wasn't it? If you ignored the differences in bearing and expression—and the nose, of course—their overall physical similarities were a little . . . well, uncanny. It was difficult enough to imagine there being even one physique like Alan's in the world, let alone two. It was almost as if they were . . .

She gave her head a quick shake to drive the thought out. It was impossible. Wouldn't someone have spoken of it before now? Even Flora had mentioned nothing of the kind. Granted, the Scots girl really hadn't known that much about her so-called betrothed, but surely she would have been aware of something like that.

Possibly not, though. That whole overseas engagement had been such a preposterous thing to start with. Dorcas was on the verge of believing the entire affair had been arranged by some malicious quirk of fate simply to land her in the position she was now in—trapped in a make-believe marriage with a man who was more puzzling than the pyramids.

She couldn't even understand him based on the rest of his eccentric family. In many ways he was so little like them. His coloring was darker than most of the Mac-Allisters—not to mention his temperament. His accent was a good deal lighter. He was their black sheep and didn't appear to be overly fond of the rest of the flock. A feeling that might be mutual, Dorcas was beginning to suspect. Whether the MacAllisters liked their laird or not, it seemed obvious that most of them were intimidated by him. Hardly surprising, she supposed. He certainly intimidated her. Even if he had turned out to be remarkably good with Rosa. In a matter of moments, the exhausted child had drifted straight back to sleep in Alan's arms.

Watching him gently settling the tiny figure onto the bed, Dorcas tried to juxtapose that image with the one of him galloping down on the outlaws like an avenging angel of death. The two pictures simply wouldn't fit together. But then, neither did anything else about the man. He was a towering mass of muscle and mysteries. Mysteries that were only increasing, it seemed.

"Dorcas, what is it? You're staring as though you've no idea who I am."

"I don't." Instantly dropping her gaze, she began backing across the room. It was unnerving enough to be caught staring—especially when she hadn't realized she'd been doing it—but it was more unnerving to have him stalking toward her this way.

"I don't know who you are," she said, hastily trying to refasten her dressing gown as she moved. She had just noticed, with a start, that it was hanging open. *When had that happened?* she wondered right before she nearly tripped over the upended chair—which jogged her memory, of course. "I don't know anything about you," she added, blushing deeper than the burgundy upholstery she was awkwardly skirting.

"That's what marriage is for," Alan said, reaching down with one hand to set the armchair straight as he trailed her. "We'll have the rest of our lives to get acquainted."

Without thinking, her eyes flew angrily to his. "Is that supposed to be funny?" she demanded.

"No. It was meant to get you to look at me."

With a wrenching in her midsection at her own mistake, Dorcas realized that she had been caught in those amber snares again. Alan's gaze halted her in her tracks and held her motionless while he covered the last few steps between them.

"How do you do that?" she whispered as he stopped only inches away.

"Do what?" he asked innocently, his eyes barely allowing her room to breathe.

Damn him—he knows what I mean, she fumed, feeling herself slipping steadily deeper into the web those eyes were weaving.

"Why do you need me to look at you?" she countered, trying to use the words as grappling hooks to drag herself free.

They fell a little short of the mark.

"If you spent more time in front of a mirror, you'd know the answer to that," he murmured, still holding her with nothing but that glittering gaze. "Is it my turn now? I've a question or two myself."

I hope they're spoken ones, Dorcas thought weakly,

remembering his last attempt at communication. She doubted she could survive another discussion like that. Already her legs were starting to melt out from under her just from the sheer heat of standing so close to him.

"I'd like to know why you're so afraid of your own desire," Alan said suddenly, his hands like hot steel as they flashed forward and captured her shoulders. "Why do you fight so hard against something you obviously want so much?"

His question hit her like a slap in the face, twisting her out of his grip and driving her back several steps. *Amazing*... Here, she had believed that anger would make her more susceptible to outside control, but the opposite was true.

"How dare you! I'm not fighting anything I want. I don't want any of this! It's all your doing, not mine!" she blazed at him, cloaked in her outrage as if it were a suit of armor. "How dare you lay this at my feet. It isn't you who's been kidnapped and threatened and used. You're not the one who's the prisoner here!"

"Aren't I?" Alan asked quietly. His hands were still poised in front of him, as though he refused to acknowledge that she was no longer within them. "I've been wondering about that. I've been remembering how you dropped out of that tree into my arms," he said, an odd roughness snagging at his voice. "And I've been asking myself who was the one who was *really* caught."

"That's absurd," Dorcas breathed, as what she saw in those unbanked eyes gripped her heart like a fist. This was the dirtiest trick he had played on her yet. She couldn't possibly accept what that gaze was offering. It wasn't real! She knew it couldn't be real. And even if it was, she didn't want it ... did she?

Of course I don't! she told herself.

"You can't mean that. It doesn't make any sense," she told him.

His hands reached slightly forward. And his eyes dove straight into her core. "Why not?"

Why not? She had known the answer to that a moment ago, hadn't she? What had jerked it from her head? *Those amber magnets . . .*

"Because what you're suggesting is fantasy! It doesn't happen that way in real life," she blurted in a rush, desperation having jogged her memory.

"A week ago I'd probably have agreed," Alan said, moving a deliberate step toward her.

Dorcas moved a more deliberate one back.

"But a week ago I hadn't seen you," he finished softly.

"This is preposterous," she whispered, because that was the most volume she could force out of herself. "There's no such thing as . . . as . . ."

"Love at first sight?" he offered helpfully.

"Exactly!" She gasped, finding her voice and her legs as he grabbed for her. Struggling to keep them both working while backing down the length of the room in front of him, she argued, "You're mistaking an . . . an animal attraction for something more."

"I don't think so. I've experienced enough *animal attraction* in my life to know the difference," he said at the exact moment Dorcas felt the wall bump her spine.

Pressing into it, she held her breath as he leaned slowly forward, planting a hand near each of her shoulders and caging her between the cool adobe and the hot circle of his naked arms and chest.

"And I don't think you're finding this nearly as difficult to believe as you're pretending," he added.

What a horrible thing to say!

Horrible, she realized with a small, sick shiver, because in a way . . . in a way, it was true. Not true that she actually believed any of this nonsense; she didn't even think he believed it. It was merely the latest battle ploy—his diabolical version of what people usually called sweet talk, the sort of blarney men had been using to seduce women ever since Adam decided he needed to repay Eve for the apple episode. But why, in the name of sanity, she wondered wretchedly, did part of her, at least, suddenly *want* to believe it?

Those eyes . . . damn! He was doing it again!

"You don't know what you're talking about!" she bit out, shoving anger in front of her body like a shield. "You don't know anything about me!"

"Aye. Perhaps you're right," he agreed with the same innocence the spider must have used when inviting the fly into his parlor. "But that's part of the excitement, you see. 'Twill be such an adventure, probing into your secrets."

Dorcas's knee shot up so fast, he barely made the dodge away from it in time.

"Whoa! So you did know what you were aiming for the other night. I didn't think you'd realized where you hit me," he said, an insufferable amusement widening his eyes.

Her own narrowed into smoldering green slits. "I didn't then. This was just a lucky guess." She frowned, wishing that her aim and timing had been as lucky. "But as long as we're on the subject, what about *your* secrets? Care to tell me why your wife was running away from you? Or shall I try to guess that one, too?"

The question was out before she had time to consider how hateful it might sound, and how dangerous the answer might be to herself. It had been one of those unfortunate cases of the mouth being quicker than the mind. Why on earth had she asked it? Because the subject had been roiling in her consciousness since dawn? Or had it simply been a verbal attempt to slap that grin off his devilishly handsome face?

Probably the latter, she realized guiltily. It had been remarkably effective, too—even more unfortunately—

about as effective as using a battle-ax to lance an annoying blister. Alan's amusement had vanished faster than money from a drunken sailor's pocket. And with it went the space between them.

"I'm becoming a wee bit weary of your questions, lassie. And that one happens to be based on a lie. Heather'd no need to run from me. I'd have willingly let her go anytime she asked me," he growled, yanking Dorcas roughly into his arms.

Some girls have all the luck, she mused perversely, all the while feeling as if she'd just been hauled into a furnace. But as long as she was, apparently, going to be taxed for asking, she might as well get an answer for her trouble. The question did carry a certain relevance to her own safety.

Battling for breath in that crushing embrace, she gasped out, "All right! But she was murdered for some reason, wasn't she? If it wasn't because she was running away, why then? Why was she killed?"

Alan's whole body clenched, like a fist ready to swing, and then his arms abruptly dropped, releasing her so unexpectedly that she staggered back against the wall, catching at it for support.

"You'd do better to ask Uncle Angus that than me, since he's the one who found the body . . . with her murderer hovering near." He sighed, suddenly sounding more tired than Atlas had after his first millennium of holding up the world. "The old ox said that for one godawful moment he thought it was me standing there. But I was miles away at the time. That's why she was killed . . . because I'd ridden out before dawn that day, without telling anyone."

Angling away, he raked long fingers through his hair, adding, "Heather was running, you see. But it wasn't *from* me. Angus says that she thought she was running away *with* me."

He uttered the words so softly, Dorcas wondered for an instant if she had misheard. Then the meaning of all he'd said struck home and she landed back against the wall with a jolt, her legs feeling about as solid as shadows at noon.

So that guess had been right, too. . . . She didn't know why the realization stunned her like that, since it was, basically, what she had already assumed. But there is, sometimes, miles of meandering road between assuming a thing and actually knowing it for sure. Perhaps because certainty had such an inescapable, final ring to it . . . *like death bells,* she thought, her spine freezing rigid as Alan pivoted back sharply, capturing her eyes with his.

"No more questions now," he said. "I've run out of answers for today."

"I'll supply the answers, then," Dorcas said quickly, digging her fingernails into her palms in a painful effort to resist the draw she was feeling from those hypnotic eyes. "All you have to do is tell me whether or not I'm right."

She knew she was right, though. Extrapolating from the few clues she was sure of, she had just pieced the entire puzzle together in her mind with clean, mathematical precision, as if she had been working out an algebraic equation.

"Dorcas, I'm in no mood for games," Alan warned, his gaze pressing her farther into the wall.

"Neither am I. This isn't play!" she declared. "That man who came after me this morning at the Garcia ranch . . . he's the one who murdered your wife. Isn't he?"

The piercing amber gaze instantly narrowed into two glowing points. "Your surprises never cease, do they?" he murmured dangerously.

"That's how he was maimed," she hurried on, before her nerves choked her. "He pretended he was you to lure her away, but she discovered the truth, and while he was attacking her, she bit off his nose." *It's what I'd have done to Dunstan that night if I'd had the chance,* she realized with a shudder.

"Bit his . . . ?" His eyes opened slightly. "Are we talking about the same person?"

What? He wasn't going to quibble over details, was he?

"You know we are!" she spat, refusing to be sidetracked. "Forget about the maiming, if you want. That could have happened some other way, I suppose. The point is—"

"The point is, you were probably blinded by the sun this morning," Alan cut her off. "But since you obviously feel you've worked everything else out so neatly, why don't you finish the story for us? Explain why our murderer pretended to be me in the first place."

Dorcas drew a deep breath to steady herself. This was the part that had been the easiest to figure out, once she had been certain who the man was. It made such sense—such perfect, pathetic, painful sense.

"He wanted her because she was yours," she answered, conjuring up an image of two identical little boys constantly warring over toys. "I imagine he always wanted whatever you had. He grew up resenting you because an accident of birth made you the clan leader and laird instead of him," she elaborated, shaking her head. "By how much did he miss the honor? Minutes? An hour, maybe? It must have been too bitter a pill for him to swallow. He eluded Angus and ran off after the murder to escape punishment—right? And since then he's apparently formed his own band of criminal misfits. This way he gets to be a leader, after all—regardless of his unlucky birth position."

"What the devil are you talking about?"

"That you're the older, of course," she said, her brows pulling together with suspicion. *Surely he wasn't going to try to deny this, was he? Not when it was so obvious.*

"Older?"

There was something in that husky tone that made her skin crawl. What was going on here? She knew she was right. If the two men had been bronze statues, they would have had to have been poured from the same mold. They were replicas of one another. What else could they be but . . .

"He's your twin brother. He must be!" she insisted, a desperate edge sharpening her voice.

The muscled chest before her suddenly heaved with a sigh that sounded as if it could have come straight from the depths of hell.

"I wish he were. As difficult as that would be, it would still be easier to deal with than the truth," Alan said wearily. "But he's not my brother, twin or otherwise. . . . He's my father. And he hardly needs reasons for what he does. None beyond the tortured visions of his own mind, at any rate. He's insane."

Chapter Ten

I liked my explanation better—it made more sense, Dorcas mused darkly, as the news Alan had just dropped sat between them like a ticking bomb. She kept waiting for something to explode. Herself, perhaps? By rights, shouldn't she be stark-raving hysterical after what she'd just heard? But the only emotion she could seem to manage at the moment was a brooding annoyance with a world that put grim truth before good, clean logic.

Or was that feeling merely a protective dodge away from the little voice at the back of her brain that was beginning to whisper, a bit too reasonably, that none of this should surprise her? It was such a minor modification of what she had originally surmised—that Alan, himself, was insane.

So it wasn't Alan. It was his father who was the demented one. But wasn't insanity often inherited? And since the son had received so many other traits from the sire, wasn't it logical to suspect . . .

"Yes, that would be your next line of thought, wouldn't it? The only way you can explain this to yourself is to view me as a madman," Alan said quietly, as though he'd been reading her mind—or, perhaps, only her expression. He was staring down at her, the look on his own face an inscrutable mask. "Why is the truth so difficult to accept?"

They were back to that again? *Marvelous,* Dorcas thought, her eyes widening and the explosion she'd been expecting abruptly threatening to detonate smack in the center of her skull.

"What truth is that?" she demanded. "The truth that I've been kidnapped? Locked up? Galloped off? Galloped back? Drugged? Dangled from ramparts? Tricked into some ridiculous sham marriage? Beaten and nearly raped? Shot at? Chased by an insane murderer?" she strangled out, her tone climbing rapidly up the scale to shrillness. "You're right! I don't know why I should find any of this so difficult to accept. Forgive me for being dim-witted!"

"Keep your voice down. You'll wake the child," he hushed her, his gaze starting to darken like thunder clouds gathering on the horizon. "And I'd like to remind you that you've brought most of this on yourself. You left Abilene willingly. No one forced you to take Flora's place. And as for the ordeal this morning, if you'd stayed put in this room as I bid you—"

"If I'd stayed put, that child you're worried about waking would probably have died hours ago!" Dorcas cut him off like a lightning crack. "So we'd all better say a thankful prayer that I don't give a rat's red ass for your bloody bidding!" she cursed, storming past him on the high horse of self-righteous anger.

She was pulled straight off it as Alan's hand shot out, locking around her wrist and jerking her back to his side.

"That will be enough of that, lassie," he warned softly,

his voice stroking over her like a heavy caress.

Enough? The word snapped something inside her—something often called the last straw.

Fighting for air in a room suddenly gone stifling, she whispered raggedly, "You're right again. This *is* enough. I'm through with this whole impossible charade. I won't tolerate any more! As soon as Kathy can travel, I'm taking her and Rosa, and the three of us are walking out of here. And if you don't like it, you'd better be prepared to kill me. Because that's the only way you'll stop us!"

Alan's hand tightened convulsively until she could feel her own pulse pounding wildly into his palm.

"You don't mean that," he said with deathly calm. But his grip gave him away. It was the grasp of a man who was feeling something slipping from his fingers and was trying anxiously to hang on to it.

"The hell I don't." She breathed harshly, her gaze meeting his like a wall of green flames. "You cannot keep me here any longer. I am leaving—either on my feet or carried out in a box! Do you hear me?"

"Aye, I hear. But I don't believe it. And neither do you. You don't want to leave me, Dorcas." He spoke quietly, his thumb beginning a maddening caress on the back of her wrist. "This is just hysterics talking. You're overwrought from seeing horrors this morn' that no lass should have to witness. That's all this is."

"Rubbish!" she said, yanking free and retreating a quick step backward. She had suspected he was crazy, but she hadn't thought he was stupid, too. Who was he trying to convince with that nonsense?

Himself? she suddenly wondered, catching an unnerving glimpse of emotion in his eyes. It drove her another pace back. *No!* She wouldn't fall for it. She needed to get out of this snake pit too much.

"I am not hysterical! And for your information, I've been through horrors before. What I saw at the Garcias' was like a window into hell. But it was hardly worse than watching my home go up in flames while my aunt was still in it," she said, feeling a scorching wave of heat as the memory of that blast washed over her.

Or was the scorching from Alan's body as he gathered her protectively against his chest?

"Dorcas . . ."

She shoved him away.

"No! I don't need pity—especially not from you. Don't touch me! And don't call me hysterical! I am far beyond hysterics at this point. What I am is fed up! I mean it! I have had it up to *here*," she hissed, stretching her arms as far over her head as they would go. The action popped her dressing gown wide open, but she was too furious to notice.

Or realize how the gesture accentuated every sensuous curve of her body.

Or notice Alan's rough intake of breath as he stared hard at those curves.

"I will not be used anymore. You can knife me, shoot me, strangle me—even torture me to death in your dungeon—but you cannot turn me into your toy! Do you understand?" she demanded, quivering before him like a leaf challenging the wind. "This game is over. Now! You are through playing with me!"

"Through?" The storm that had been brewing in Alan's eyes abruptly broke, drenching her in a steamy torrent of unleashed desires.

"Through?" he repeated, his lips curling with impossible devilment. "Lassie, I haven't even begun."

His words ripped away the last wispy shred of her tattered self-control. Blinded by a red-hot haze, Dorcas struck out to slap that exasperating grin into the next state.

He caught her hand in midflight, jerking her half off her feet and full into his arms. Crushing her struggling form solidly against his chest, he brought his mouth down on hers, smothering her protests with an all-consuming kiss.

She resisted it for one . . . two . . . three furious heart-beats, but the kiss swept through her like wildfire. It was as though he had used a lightning bolt to set off a stack of sky rockets. Drawing a deep, shuddering breath, she suddenly exploded all over him, turning the previous fight to resist into a fight to see who could devour whom the fastest.

Alan almost lost his footing in the battle. With blistering force, Dorcas drove him a dozen paces backward into the nearest wall, her fingers raking through his hair, down his chest, over his taut stomach, and burying themselves deep in the waistband of his trousers, where she began a mad tugging at the already strained front closures.

He retaliated by pivoting sharply and locking her against the wall instead, her lacy undergarments and corset ties giving way easily beneath his tearing fingers.

Kissing her as if his life depended upon it, he grabbed her about the waist and began to lift her hips to meet his. She responded by clutching at his shoulders and raising herself the last few necessary inches before letting instinct guide her hotly downward.

The shield of her virginity brought the action to a sudden halt. And jarred Alan back into some semblance of reason.

"Dorcas—no—wait—not like this—not your first time," he groaned, painfully breaking off the kiss. "It isn't right. . . . Please, dear, not . . . not now . . . tonight . . . I want to be able to make love to you properly," he begged, trying to push away from her.

Nearly drowning in her own desire, she dragged him back. *Properly?* she thought wildly. *Who the hell worried about* proper *at a time like this?*

"Shut up, you idiot!" she gasped, and drove herself down.

The contact jolted through both of them like a high voltage shock, almost throwing her off. His arms tightened convulsively, holding her close while they waited a ragged moment for the smoke to clear.

Such an ecstatically sweet burning, Dorcas moaned inwardly, clinging to him as the sea hugs the shore. It had been more like the answer to an undreamed of prayer than an actual pain.

The movement, when it started, was like the dance of life itself. It was like the spinning of the world on its axis, gaining power with every turn. It filled her like a sunrise, all rose and crimson and golden glow.

Alan filled her. He was like a blinding light blazing within and all around her, she thought dizzily, right before the world spun crazily out of control and they collapsed in a panting heap together on the floor.

Ever so gradually her heart calmed and the spiraling room came back into focus. As the mist receded from her eyes, the first thing she saw was Alan's hypnotically handsome face looming over her. He looked as if he had just unraveled all the mysteries of creation and was both reverently awed and deeply satisfied by what he'd discovered.

"Are you all right?" he asked, his husky voice barely more than a whisper.

Staring up at him with enormous eyes and unable to trust her own voice at all, Dorcas slowly shook her head. Then she nodded it. Then shook it again. Then gave a half nod. Then . . .

The fact of the matter was, she didn't know if she was all right or not. At that instant she was still trying to figure out *who* she was, and what the term *all right* meant.

Seeing the unveiled confusion in her green eyes, he

cursed softly and tightened his arms around her.

"I hurt you, didn't I? I must have," he said almost harshly. "Dorcas, I am so sorry. I never planned for it to happen that way. I wish you had let me stop. I could have made this so much easier for you in bed, with time to—"

At the word *bed*, Dorcas's mind clicked into startled awareness. *Why hadn't they used the bed?* she wondered, and remembered all in the same horrified second.

"Dear God—Rosa!" she gasped, cutting Alan off and bowling him backward as she scrambled frantically out of his arms. Snatching the remnants of her dressing gown from the floor, she grappled her way into it and flew across the room.

She breathed a grateful sigh of relief when she saw that Rosa was still sound asleep. She was unscathed by the . . . the . . . by what had . . . Suddenly it was almost impossible to swallow or draw air into her contracting lungs.

Merciful heavens—what have I done? She shuddered spasmodically. Or rather . . . that frightful question once more . . . what had she been *made* to do? . . .

As if it really makes the slightest difference, she decided wretchedly, turning as sea green as the tattered robe in which she was huddled. The damage had been done. Irrevocably. And however it had happened, he was definitely the one who'd instigated it.

"Dorcas, I'm sorry," Alan said softly. "I shouldn't have let things get so far out of hand. But 'tis all right, dear. I'll make it up to you. I promise."

Make it up to her . . . Her eyes went from saucers to dinner plates. *Make it up to her?* If that meant what she thought it meant . . .

"Don't touch me!" she squealed, ducking past him and darting to the opposite end of the room as he reached for her.

"Dorcas—"

"I'm serious! Don't touch me! Don't look at me! Don't even breathe on me!" she spat, halting him in his tracks with a green dagger glare. "If you ever again even think of laying a finger on me, you're a dead man," she ground out. "I swear it! Touch me one more time and I will kill you. If it takes my last breath to do it, I will see you eviscerated. And don't tell me I don't mean it!"

"I'd not dream of it. I can see you're quite serious," Alan said in the same tones he had used to two-year-old Rosa. Raising his hands, palms up and out, he began a cautious, step-by-step journey toward her. "But you're also a wee bit hysterical, dear. 'Tis understandable, mind you. You're a high-strung lass to begin with, and—"

"You're damn straight I'm hysterical!" Dorcas snapped, grabbing an earthenware water jug off a nearby table. "But I still know exactly what I'm talking about! And I am telling you that this farce is finished. It's over! You've gotten what you wanted from me. You've had your fun now. So leave me be! And who the hell are you calling *high-strung?*" she hissed, as the jug went barreling straight for his head.

"My apologies. 'Twas a stupid thing to say." Catching the jug on the fly, he set it down on the dresser he was passing without spilling a drop, his face a smooth mask of carefully controlled emotion.

"But as for the rest of it, dear . . . didn't you get what you wanted, too?" he asked, one hand catching her wrist as neatly as he'd caught the jug. The other one clapped securely over her mouth. "Don't scream or I'll be forced to silence it with a kiss," he warned softly. He had to shift his grip to her waist as her knees buckled under her. "Don't faint, either—unless you want me to explore some creative ways of reviving you."

"Any other instructions?" she asked blisteringly.

"Yes. I want you to answer my question," he said, lifting her completely off her feet and moving toward the burgundy armchair.

"Put me down!"

He obliged by putting her into the chair—after putting himself in it first.

"I said, *put me down!*"

"You are down," Alan pointed out, settling her more firmly onto his lap as she angrily tried to shove free. "Dorcas, I am tired. I don't feel like standing any longer. And I definitely don't feel like chasing you all over the room. Now, sit still. If you don't stop behaving like a child, I may start treating you like one and tan that charming backside of yours rosy red. Do you hear me, lassie?"

It would have been impossible not to, with his lips warmly grazing her ear. Locked immobile in that maddening embrace and all but choking on her own rage, Dorcas clenched her teeth and squeezed her eyes shut against the frustrated sobs threatening to spill forth. Neither action helped.

Feeling her trembling in his arms like a miniature earthquake and having his shoulder spattered by hot, salty drops, Alan tightened his hold.

"My apologies, again." He sighed. "You go ahead and cry if you want to. 'Tis a natural enough reaction for a lass who's just lost her maidenhead. But the rough part is over, dear. It only hurts the first time. I can promise you nothing but pleasure from now on."

That helped even less.

Suddenly feeling like a waterfall and infuriated by her own lack of control, Dorcas was swamped by several drenching moments of gut-wrenching sobs. *I'm doomed,* she thought. This torment was never going to end. It was only getting worse. He was going to keep her here until there was nothing left of her that she could recognize—until she was sucked dry as an old eggshell. And he didn't even seem to realize what he was doing. He used ridiculous, mundane terms like *pleasure* as though that was all the experience meant to him. And he was an absolute idiot if he thought she was crying over a brief flash of pain that she'd scarcely noticed. Who noticed a simple sting when one's entire being was going up in flames?

"You don't know what you're talking about or you wouldn't say such asinine things," she choked out toward the end of the tears, and felt her spine stiffen as Alan had the cheek to actually chuckle.

"I know a good deal more than you seem to realize," he purred. "Thank you for answering my question, though."

"What question?" she sniffed irritably, trying to wrestle an arm free in order to wipe her face on her sleeve. It wasn't an especially ladylike maneuver, but it was more gentile than a runny nose.

"Here." Loosening his hold long enough to fish a handkerchief out of his trousers' pocket, he offered it to her.

Dorcas grabbed both it and the opportunity to scramble to her feet as he added, "You've just assured me that you wanted what happened as much as I—"

"I didn't!" she protested, halted in her flight by his words as much as the hand that closed solidly over hers. *I think I wanted it more,* the voice in the back of her mind groaned, while, at the same instant the front portion insisted aloud, "I keep telling you—I've never wanted any of this!"

"You could have fooled me on that a short time ago. I'm the one who tried to stop it. Remember?" he asked, deliberately bringing her hand to his lips and planting a warm kiss in the center of her palm.

She jerked as though burned. "You didn't try very hard, did you?"

That answer got her hauled firmly onto his lap again.

"Listen, lassie, I am not going to sit here arguing something we both know is a lie."

"It's the truth!" she flared, wanting, once and for all, to have everything out in the open, regardless of the consequences. "You know it is! I don't want any part of this miserable charade. I never have! It's all your doing. You've been making me act like . . . like I w-want . . . want these th-things," she stammered, forcing herself to meet his gaze without flinching. "You've been hypnotizing me!"

For a suffocating moment, Alan's expression looked as if it had been carved from wood, and then, with devilish slowness, the wood cracked into a grin that sucked the breath clean out of her.

"I didn't think you'd noticed."

The breath rushed back in—along with a renewed flood of fears. "Then you . . . you *admit* it?"

"Aye. 'Tis what the old Highlanders would call the come hither. Shall I tell you a secret, though?" he whispered wickedly, cupping her startled face between his hands. "My come hither only works on you."

"Wh-what . . ." she began, and then went rigid as fear swung suddenly into complete exasperation. "Oh! How can you joke about it?"

" 'Tis no joke. I'm telling you the truth," Alan persisted, his hands gripping her face a little tighter. "And I'll tell you something else, too. You've the come hither in your own eyes. But yours only works on me. We've been hypnotizing each other, dear."

If there was a come hither in Dorcas's green gaze, it instantly flipped into a freezing go-to-the-dickens.

"That is the most preposterous thing I have ever heard." Twisting her face free, she tried to lunge off his lap.

His hands slipped quickly to her waist, holding her square. "Not a bit of it. 'Tis quite logical, really."

218

"So was the theory that the world was flat. Let me go!"

"Dorcas, you know what I'm trying to explain. And somewhere in that thick, bonny head of yours, you know I'm right. You're not fighting me, dear. You're fighting yourself. The sooner you admit it, the happier you'll be."

"Let—me—go!"

The iron grip abruptly relaxed and Alan's arms dropped tiredly to his sides. "All right. You're obviously in no mood to be reasonable, and I'm too weary to argue further. Go on, lass, get up if it'll make you easier."

It won't, she thought darkly. But it was a start. Scrambling to her feet before he could change his mind, she retreated several rapid steps out of range and stood trembling and glaring at him like a dynamite blast waiting to go off.

"Now, then . . . let me go."

Alan's hands and eyes went pleading upward. "Is she daft?" he asked the ceiling. But when the rafters couldn't seem to provide an answer, his gaze leveled back on Dorcas. "Look where you're standing, dear. I *have* let you go."

"Not far enough. I mean, let me go away from here. All the way! Let me wake up from this nightmare," she pleaded, clenching her hands in an unsuccessful attempt to keep her voice steady, as his eyes raked over her. "Please, Alan—I can't take anymore. I need to get out of this Bedlam. I need to go back to my own life. *Please* let me go!"

The amber gaze crystallized into a hard glow. "Never. And that's the end of it. This is just foolish stubbornness and I'll hear no more. Do you understand me?" he said, the beginnings of exasperation roughening his voice. "And stop looking like a frightened child. It's starting to grate on my nerves. You're not Little Red Riding Hood and I'm not the Big Bad Wolf. If I thought you were truly serious, I'd put you on the next train East—regardless of what it cost me. I'm not one to force my attentions on a woman who doesn't want them. But that's not the case here; you *do* want them. You've proved that too well, too many times now, for either of us to doubt it. The fact of the matter is this, dear . . . there's only one real reason why you're still here. And it's the same reason why you'll stay," he said, leaning suddenly forward and riveting her where she stood with an iron stare. "You don't want to leave."

Didn't want to . . . foolish . . . stubborn . . . childish . . .

The man was amazing. How had he managed to fit so many actual and implied insults into one short speech? Dorcas wondered, her color rising up the spectrum from a pale, nervous white to a blazing, defiant crimson.

"Are you done?" she asked in a voice like a fuse being lit.

"Only if you are. And I'm warning you, lassie, that you'd better be."

"Oh, I'm done all, right. I'm so done that if I was a baking cake, I'd be burned to a cinder by now," she offered with a smile that ended at the lips. "I'm done with stupid castles and stupid traditions and stupid—"

"Dorcas . . ."

"And most of all"—she skipped to the finish as Alan rose threateningly from the chair—"I'm done with being told what I think by a half-dressed, no-brain, pigheaded, egotistical barbarian who wouldn't know a genuine thought if it jumped up and bit him on his stupid ass! I may not be quite . . . but . . . Stop that!" she snapped, as her train of thought was derailed by rich, low laughter. "This isn't funny!"

"Isn't it?" Alan chuckled, an insufferably amused sparkle replacing the warning in his gaze, as his hands rested warmly on her shoulders. "If you don't like me being so charmed by it, stop being so irresistibly adorable."

220

"And you stop treating me like I'm no bigger than Rosa! I may not be quite eighteen yet, but I'm certainly no child, and I am definitely old enough to know my own mind. So stop telling me what I think!"

The hands on her shoulders froze, along with his amusement. "What did you say?"

"You heard me! I said, stop telling me what I think," she repeated, a chilling confusion creeping over her at the odd change in his expression. Alan was staring down at her as though she had just slipped a knife between his ribs.

"No . . . before that. How old are you?"

"Eighteen. Almost, anyway—the beginning of next month," she answered, her eyes narrowing suspiciously. What difference did it make? Was this some new trick?

Alan apparently thought so.

"You're lying! You can't be only seventeen," he insisted as his hands bit into her shoulders. "I saw your contract with that employment agency when I emptied your trunk that first night. It lists your age as twenty-two!"

"What if it does?" she shot back, anger helping to brace her against his sharp hold. "They wouldn't hire anyone under twenty-one, and I . . . I was desperate for work," she admitted, her blush deepening at the memory of having to fib her way into a decent job.

His own color drained, Alan quickly pulled back, as if she had suddenly become too hot to hold. Perhaps she had.

"Good God . . . No wonder you've been as frightened as a child. You *are* a child," he breathed, a stricken look widening his eyes. "Heaven help me, I've been robbing the cradle. You're hardly more than a bairn!"

He was calling her a baby? Now that was pushing things a bit . . .

"There's no need to be insulting about it. You're acting

221

like you're Methuselah or something—when Lady Flora
told me you're only thirty yourself. There's barely twelve
years between us. That's scarcely any difference at all
between a man and a woman. Lots of husbands are that
much older than their wives," she spouted indignantly.
And immediately clapped a hand over her own mouth.
"Good heavens," she whispered, rapidly debating how
much effort it would take to bite out her tongue. "What
have I just said?"

"You were implying that we're man and wife," Alan
said wryly. "And I appreciate the thought, dear, believe
me. But it comes a wee bit late. We're not married." he
sighed heavily.

Why is everything still in place? Dorcas marveled,
standing and staring at him in weak-kneed shock. To
hear him actually admit that could only have preceded
the world grinding to a jarring halt, couldn't it?

Working to gather her scattered wits she blurted out,
"Well, of course we're not married. Tell me something I
don't know, for heaven's sake."

"Dorcas, you don't understand. A traditional
Highland handfasting—in other words, a marriage cer-
emony such as ours—is legally binding so long as it oc-
curs on MacAllister land," he explained. "When the clan
first arrived here years ago, fleeing British law in the
Highlands, my ancestors didn't simply homestead this
tract. They bought it outright from the Mexican government and set up what could almost be called a sovereign
state. When Texas became a republic, it changed nothing, since this land lay outside its boundaries. But when
the treaty was signed that turned the Lone Star republic
into the twenty-eighth state, and the acres around ours
started being settled, we nearly had a small war. There
was a fear, you see, that the United States wouldn't accept clan customs as valid—which would have defeated
the purpose of the MacAllisters emigrating here in the

222

first place. But the federal and state governments proved to be more interested in keeping the peace—and keeping this land securely within the Union—than they were in outlawing a pack of old Highland ceremonies. We have a special, written provision under Texas state law that approves the legality of the MacAllisters' private code and practices."

"No!"

"Don't argue with me, lass. Have I lied to you yet?"

It was the quiet assurance of his tone that drove her anxiety up the scale to panic—that and the inescapable awareness that he was . . . was right. Alan did have a rather exasperating habit of omitting pertinent little facts, of evading issues, and giving replies that sometimes created more questions than they answered, but . . . No, he had never lied to her, she now realized. And that could mean . . .

Unbelievably, her wave of panic gave way before a flood of . . . *relief?*

Dorcas shook her head. That couldn't possibly be right. Something must have gone haywire with her internal sensing apparatus. There was no relief, whatsoever, in the knowledge that Alan really was her husband. Only the relief, perhaps, that condemned prisoners felt when the noose finally snapped their necks and the awful wait for death was over.

Unless . . . He had also been right about . . . And she . . .

The blond head shook again. That couldn't be it, either, because this actually had nothing to do with Alan, as absurd as that seemed. The real heart of her dilemma was that matrimony, itself, was totally alien to her character. She had never, ever wanted to be anyone's wife—not in the slightest—not even in her remotest dreams.

Ah, but that's the whole point, isn't it? the little voice inside her head whispered. And for once in her life, Dorcas found herself unable to argue with it. The suggestion made such simple, straightforward sense. It was almost too logical, this possibility. This remarkable, sun-bursting-through-the-clouds possibility that the real reason she had never wanted marriage was because she had never in her wildest, most far-flung fancies ever realized there was anyone in the world like Alan MacAllister.

Oh, my God . . . has this actually happened? To me? she wondered, as rapid-fire images raced across her mind's eye. Alan the first time she'd seen him under the tree . . . Alan kneeling by the spring on the prairie . . . Alan standing in the moonlight of the castle's courtyard . . . Alan charging through the dust, lit by dawn's fire . . . Alan in her arms as they . . .

Good heavens, I have been hooked, haven't I? I've swallowed the bait—hook, line, and sinker.

"All right, Alan, it looks as if you'd better reel me in."

"What?" A sudden wariness darkening his eyes, Alan took three slightly stumbling steps backward.

Dorcas moved three fluid ones forward.

"What do you mean, *what?* Don't play dumb with me, you . . . you *husband,* you. What have we been arguing about? What have you been trying to convince me of?" she asked with youthful simplicity. "I'm informing you that you seem to have succeeded," she added, a new-found womanly huskiness creeping into her voice.

"Splendid. Your timing is astounding." He groaned, retreating until his spine nearly dented the wall. "Dorcas, haven't you been listening to me?"

"Of course I have. You were explaining why our marriage is legal," she said, the vocal heat increasing as she deliberately closed in on him. "You know, that really was a dirty trick you played on the ramparts, but I can forgive you for it now because I understand the . . . the provocation behind it. I'm beginning to understand a lot of things, I think. It's as if a door has been unlocked for me—a door I never even knew existed."

"And I'm extremely sorry about this, but we're going to have to close it again and hide the key. You haven't been listening, or you'd know that we're *not* married."

The words couldn't have stopped her more effectively if they had been a brick wall.

"But you said the MacAllister weddings are legal," she argued, a queer new anxiety suddenly prickling her skin into gooseflesh. "For heaven's sake, Alan, which is it? Are they valid or aren't they?"

"They are. But ours is not, because you're underage," he explained sharply. "A bride has to be at least eighteen, or have her guardian's consent. Do you understand the problem now?"

"No," she said, wondering why her anxiety was increasing when there was such an obvious solution at hand.

"Dorcas—"

"Well, I don't *have* a guardian, so maybe that rule doesn't apply to me. But even if it does, I'll be eighteen in a couple of weeks. Can't we simply restate our vows on my birthday?"

It was the eyes that clued her, even more than his silence. All of a sudden, the man who had been come hithering her front, back, and sideways, was having trouble meeting her gaze. Her gaze? Alan Eyes-of-the-Cat MacAllister couldn't look her in the face?

The idea was such an absurd turn-around, it brought a brief burst of giggles. And then, as the complete realization struck home, the giggles clogged her throat, swelled almost to the point of strangulation, and finally blew forth in a fit of full-fledged laughter. Laughter that was hard enough to ice skate on—or cold enough, anyway.

"Oh, my, I have been an idiot, haven't I? Alan, I owe

you an apology," she said with an amazing show of good sportsmanship, considering the emotional pratfall she'd just taken. "I've been thinking horrible things about you, and I'm sorry for it. I'm sorry I thought you were insane, and a murderer, and some sort of diabolical hypnotist. You're not any of those things. What you are—" her voice tightened—"is a plain, old, run-of-the-mill, garden variety rake!

"No, wait!" She shot out her hand as he tried to speak. "I have to take that back as well. There's nothing ordinary about you. An *ordinary* rake would have been content merely to claim the girl's virginity. But you had to go one step better, didn't you? You had to get a declaration of devotion, too. Well, guess what, Casanova? I lied! I was only playing along to see how far you'd run this silly game." She sniffed, crossing her arms quickly in front of herself, because she had just noticed how her abused dressing gown refused to stay fastened.

"But at least it's over now, thank God." She sighed, deliberately turning her back on him—partly to show that she considered the matter closed, but more because the sea-green silk robe was in doubtful shape to demonstrate the same principle. "I think we've both gotten about all that we can from this thrilling masquerade, don't you? Any more and it runs the risk of becoming tedious."

"Dorcas Matilda, I can't imagine the world ever being tedious as long as you're in it," his low voice said behind her. "And—just for the record, dear—nothing is over until I say so. And I don't recall having said anything of the kind."

Dorcas nailed her feet to the floor to keep from charging to the dresser and grabbing the water jug again. *This is so typical,* she thought bitterly, as understanding dawned fiery red in her new assessment of the situation.

"Honestly! If male egos had feathers, this castle would

be an aviary. You know perfectly well you're finished with your little frolic now. You just don't like me being the one to say it first." Striding primly across to her steamer trunk, she snapped the lid back and began dumping its contents onto the floorboards by the armful.

"What do you think you're doing?"

"Packing to leave."

"It looks to me as if you're unpacking, dear."

"You're right. The only thing here I'm interested in is the trunk. I'm taking it empty, so I can sell it when I get back to Philadelphia to buy myself a decent wardrobe. Until then, I'll wear feed sacks if I have to. They'll be better than these whorehouse frills!"

"Dorcas . . ."

Bunching the peaches-and-cream organdy gown in her arms, she swung furiously to face him, like Joan of Arc confronting the English. "Damn it, admit that you're through! If you don't let me go now, you'll be breaking your own word. You said you're not one to force a woman who doesn't—"

"Aye, but that has nothing to do with you because you're not a woman," he smoothly sliced her off. "You're a child—as this temper tantrum proves. Though I'll admit I *am* rethinking the idea of marriage. All things considered, it might be more appropriate for me to adopt you."

"Don't be patronizing," she said, frost crystals glinting on every syllable.

The expensive organdy creation in her hands abruptly split down one of its seams. It made such a satisfying sound, she ripped it again and again, letting it flutter about her ankles in wispy tatters.

"Keep it up, lassie, and you'll find yourself locked back in the tower," Alan warned, his eyes glowing like coals in a banked fire. " 'Tis either that or I'll be locking myself in the icehouse," he muttered inaudibly, as each rip

227

pulled Dorcas's robe open a little farther, unbeknownst to her.

The last of the pastel froth landed like a crumpled cloud at her feet. "I take back my apology," she uttered in a voice more shredded than the organdy gown. "You really are a madman if you think you can threaten me with that again. You're hopelessly insane!"

"Aye, I'm afraid you've pegged the truth square through the center there, dear—for I've no business thinking anything about a lass your age. But the damage is done and there's nothing can fix it now," Alan grated out, the iron of his usual tone turning to rust. Heaving himself away from the wall, he turned angrily toward the door.

"I am insane," he confessed, shooting a look over his shoulder that nearly stopped her heart. "I'm hopelessly and insanely in love with you."

Chapter Eleven

Love . . . in love . . . in love with . . .

He did look as if he meant it, didn't he? He sounded as if he meant it, too.

So why was that ragged declaration so difficult to accept?

I'm hopelessly and insanely in love with you. . . .

The words hammered in her head like something desperately demanding to be let in, but Dorcas found herself pondering almost abstractedly why she couldn't bring herself to even crack open that inner door again—the door she had flung wide and then slammed shut when those amber eyes had refused to meet hers. Why couldn't she believe him?

It was a curious question, and one she didn't have time to answer just then, because the hammering turned out to be not entirely in her mind. Just as Alan's fingers touched the door handle, a heavy pounding came, shaking the wood planks in their frame and sending Dorcas, in mortified awareness of the state of her robe, diving for the bed, next to little, sleeping Rosa.

"Alan, lad—we've a wee bit of a problem," an unmistakable bass voice boomed, sounding as if the problem was anything but wee.

"Why not? A perfect end to a perfect day," Alan muttered, swinging the door open so sharply, Angus's next knock might have knocked some teeth loose if either man's reflexes had been slower.

"Johnny on th' spot, ain't ye? 'Twoulda taken me langer than that tae reach me bedchamber door when I wuz new wed," the older one said, grinning slyly as his gaze rested on the motionless form huddled under the fourposter's quilted comforter. "Ah, worn oot an' sleepin', is she?" he chuckled, as though that explained everything.

"Aye. We've had an . . . active day. Full of surprises," Alan said with a straight face. "And now you've another for me?"

In no mood to be sucked into any Clan MacAllister business, Dorcas lay curled on her side with her back to the men, their words only half registering as she concentrated on feigning a sound slumber.

" 'Tis nay surprise, really," Angus began, his characteristic bellow rolling down to the nearest it ever came to a whisper. "Ian's flown his cage."

"Again? That makes the third time in less than a week! And you know he can't stand light anymore. Even this keep's too bright for him. Why, after all these years of clinging to the dark, has he suddenly taken to wandering?"

"How should I ken? Purhaps our demon's been haunting him."

"And has been witching him out of his cell, you mean? That's not funny."

"Yoor right, lad. 'Twas a sorry joke based on a load o' superstitious rubbish. There be sum 'round here still be-

230

lieve those auld stories, tho'. Did I tell ye that Donald says he's seen pawprints in th' dungeon again? Feline prints?"

"Before or after his nightly beer?"

"Scoff if ye like, but ye'd best warn Dorie tae say nay more aboot black cats. Dunstan wuz a loyal lad tae cover fer her that night, drunk as he wuz—but she could start sum worrisum gossip if she repeats that tale."

"Let her, then. Considering all else I've to deal with right now—including an insane father on the loose—gossip is the least of my concerns. Are any of our braves from this morning's action still on the premises? It'll save time if we can begin the search directly from here. He can't have gotten far."

"He's closer than ye think. 'Tis nay need fer a search."

"But—"

"I said Ian flew his cell. I didna say he'd flown th' castle. He's in th' great hall, demandin' th' right o' trial by combat . . . an', as full square daft as he may be, he's also got enoof MacAllister blood in his veins that ye'll hafta grant it."

It was the sudden flash of silence that pulled Dorcas's attention to the hushed debate. Scarcely daring to breathe, she lay motionless in the big bed, rapidly trying to recall what she had just heard while simultaneously straining to catch the rest.

"*Have* to grant it?" Alan finally asked in a voice that made her think of a sword being slowly drawn from its sheath. "Uncle Angus, you of all people ought to know that the devil himself couldn't stop me from accepting that challenge."

"Nay, lad. Yoor only part in this be tae sign th' order fer th' combat. 'Tis meself who'll fight it."

"Over my hacked and bloodied corpse you will. You prevented me from having at him twelve years ago, but you'll not—"

"I will! An' fer th' same reason—tae keep ye fray be-cumin' a 'hacked an' bloodied corpse.' I ken ye too well, lad. Yoor thinkin' tae simply disarm him—hopin' maybe a few good knocks'll jar sum reason back inta his skull. But 'tis nay th' way Ian'll play this. He's crazy, aye. Crazy like a fox! I can see it in his eyes, now that he's finally found his voice. He's oot fer blood, I'm thinkin', an' tae destroy th' whole clan throo yoorself. His son oor nay, he aims tae finish ye. An' he can do it 'cause he kens ye couldna return th' favor. Ye still love him, lad, fer all his madness. If it came to it, ye'd ne'r be able tae strike a fatal blow. Ye canna kill yoor own father."

"But you *can* kill your own brother, I suppose?"

"Aye. 'Tis nay like we've e'er been close—bein' reared in separate worlds as i'twere. If Cain survived th' experience, I'll wager I can."

"Cain didn't survive it very well, if I recall correctly. Anyway, what makes you think you'd be the victor? You're a powerful man, but so is he. And he's a harder man, for he was raised a Comanche. In case you've forgotten how they fight, let me remind you. 'Tis a subject I know well. I was Comanche, myself, remember—before I traded that life in exchange for Heather. My father's people were born for battle. They fight to win!"

"Aye. 'Tis why most of 'em, save th' MacAllister mix-breeds on our land, be herded onta reservations now, like sheep."

"Your sarcasm is unnecessary. I'm not talking Indian politics here. I'm trying to warn you. Whatever's suddenly possessed him, the man's not responsible for his actions. Give him half a chance and Wild Horse will carve you up like a Highland steer!"

"I'm nay steer, laddie—I'm a bull! An' Scots stock dinna carve sae easy. Highlanders fight tae win, too. Besides which, tae th' challenged—that'll be me—goes the choice o' weapons. An' fer all his battle skill, Ian—oor

Wild Horse, if ye prefer—has little held a claymore in his hand. Whilst I was fair born wi' one in mine."

Too much explained too quickly . . .

The tangle that had been building in Dorcas's head since landing in Texas was unraveling faster than she could keep track of the threads. Which made it all the more curious that the one thing uppermost in her mind right then was not any of the big answers she had just been given, but a new, small, and seemingly insignificant question.

Claymores? Hadn't she heard someone else mention claymores recently? But where? And why?

The reply, with all its implications, hit suddenly, like a bucket of ice water down the back, only seconds before Alan said in that low growl she had already learned signaled the end of a conversation, "No. After all you, your-self, have taught me of MacAllister honor, I'll not allow that. I'll write and sign the order, but I'll handle this myself—and it'll be done fairly. Heather was my wife, and that makes this my fight."

There was, apparently, nothing more for Angus to say.

Dorcas listened to booted steps crossing the hardwood floor, listened to the desk drawer sliding open and the scraping of pen on paper. . . . Listened to it all as if she was hearing her own death warrant being signed. Be-cause that was what it suddenly felt like. Could she have found the words to stop him? she wondered moments later. Would she have been able to get them past that awful lump in her throat?

She never found out. A sledgehammer fist on the back of a black-haired head saved her the trouble.

"I'm sorry, lad," Angus said, catching his unconscious nephew before he hit the floor. "But Heather wuz my daughter afore she wuz yoor bride. An' there be too much at stake here. I'll hafta do this my way."

* * *

Exactly what his way was, Dorcas didn't even want to take the time to consider as she fumbled into the forest-green gown she had worn the night of the storm. It was an interesting question, of course. But not nearly so interesting as where Angus had carried Alan, and what he had put in the lamp oil that had made her so drowsy and dizzy before she had realized what was happening and blown the light out.

That last question, however, was also an answer—or at least part of one. It told her how she had been drugged her first night and day at the castle, if not why. Though the why was easy enough to guess. Angus must have done it to keep her quiet while Alan was away.

And where had Alan been during that time?

Most likely riding the range with the MacAllister Comanche who lived on this land. Chasing after mad Ian, perhaps, or tracking down bandits like the ones they had captured that morning.

They were obviously some sort of unofficial police force for the area, the keyword there being *unofficial*. Heaven knew, in wild country like this their services were needed. Although, she had to admit, some might not see it exactly that way. From a strictly legal perspective, there was often very little, if any, difference between avenging angels and lynch mobs. Hence, Simon Elliott's warning—the warning she had yet to deliver.

It was all so clear really, Dorcas was astounded she hadn't deduced any of it sooner. No doubt she would have, she told herself, if she had been less . . . well, distracted by . . . ah . . . other concerns. But naturally, with all the fighting going on in the castle's early years, there would also have been a certain amount of intermarriage. Highland lasses captured by fierce Plains warriors. Native women taken by Scotsmen . . .

She now realized that Alan, himself was the descendant of such a union. No wonder he spoke Comanche, dressed Comanche, rode Comanche, called himself a Comanche. He had Comanche blood and had lived with them before joining the Highland side of his heritage to marry his castle-bred cousin.

And that answered two more interesting but unrelated questions—why the Scottish branch of his family viewed him as something of a dark horse and why he had felt that she should be able to give up her own plans in order to be his wife.

Because he had made the same sacrifice once himself.

Of course, it was easier for men. Females often had to relinquish self-sovereignty to be wives, but husbands— whether they wore trousers or breechclouts—rarely had to give up very much for marriage. Though Alan had given up more than most, Dorcas supposed. It told her the one thing about him that she might never have guessed otherwise.

He wasn't a rake, after all. Comanche, Highlander, or something in between, Alan MacAllister was that curious breed of human generally referred to as a romantic.

Whether he even realized it or not himself, that was why he had galloped her out to the spring that first wild night. He just hadn't been able to resist playing Lancelot rescuing Guinevere. And that was why he had rushed their wedding—it was so much more romantic to spontaneously swing a girl over the side of a castle rampart than it was to court her slow and staid. That was the reason for those satin sheets, for these fairy-tale frocks. This was where his tenderness came from.

And this is why I can't accept his declaration of love, Dorcas thought, feeling as if her heart was being squeezed in a vise.

Romantics always made declarations like that, didn't they? They actually believed them, too—at least while they were declaring them. That was part of the moonlight-and-roses aura of romance. But as her aunt

235

had often said, roses always wilted eventually, and moonlight soon gave way to the harsh light of day, and . . .

"And I can't believe I'm standing here worrying about any of this now, when there's a murder about to be committed and the MacAllisters may lose their way of life because of it!" she declared.

For that matter, she couldn't believe she was standing there worrying whether the MacAllisters and their ancient traditions continued or not. It was just as Aunt Matilda had always cautioned her—emotions got in the way of clear thinking.

"No, not clear thinking. Emotions get in the way of thinking, period!" she amended aloud, moving through the gathering shadows toward the desk. She didn't expect the order to still be there. Angus would have taken that with him, but . . .

"Ahhh!" A small sigh of satisfaction pierced the air as Dorcas carefully lifted the freshly used sheet of blotting paper and carried it over to the dresser. The imprint of the words were in reverse, but by holding the paper up to the dresser's large mirror and squinting a bit, she could just make out what Alan had written.

It was very like him, actually—short and to the point, with few details and fewer explanations—and therefore no help whatsoever. Alan was not the verbose, poet sort of romantic. He was the act-now, talk-later (if you were lucky) type. Other than the date at the top and Alan's signature at the bottom, all the order stated was that Ian MacAllister, also known as Wild Horse, was granted a trial by combat for the crime of murder, to be carried out in the great hall in due accordance with MacAllister law.

Marvelous.

No naming of who would fight Ian in this combat, no mention of what weapons could or could not be used. It didn't even state a specific hour for the contest, so she had no idea how much time she had to try to prevent it. She also had no idea how she was going to get out of the blasted bedroom.

That was another question that had recently been answered: the question of what had happened to the key she had remembered being in the door three nights earlier. The key that had been there when she had gone out in search of food. The key that had not been there when she had returned unknowingly married (sort of). She now knew who had taken it.

Angus had. She knew that because he had used it to lock her in when he had left a short while before with Alan hanging over his grizzly-bear back like a sack of seed potatoes ready for planting in the earth.

And I do *hope that's not too appropriate an image*, Dorcas thought, the pressure in her chest suddenly tightening like a clenched fist. Alan was only unconscious, wasn't he? She *had* seen him breathing, hadn't she, when she'd peeked from beneath the bedclothes?

"Yes, of course I did! And if I don't stop thinking things like that, I may just as well relight the lamp and drug myself into a stupor, because that's all I'll be good for," she muttered on her way to peer out one of the room's two windows.

It was sheer insanity, she knew, for a person with her terror of heights, but she had this stomach-churning notion that she might be able to climb out by knotting the sheets together. There was one distinct drawback to that plan, though—besides the drawback that she would probably have a heart attack if she attempted it. There was the problem of what to do with Rosa, who was still asleep and too young to either be lowered from windows or left alone. That was a question Dorcas didn't have an answer for yet.

When she reached the window, however, she found

the answer to a different question—one she had almost forgotten about. It was a thin burnished metal answer barely four inches long, lying in the center of the deep windowsill, and—considering the circumstances of its original disappearance—surrounded not too surprisingly by what looked like pawprints in the sill's dust.

It was the key the cat had stolen from her when she'd been shut in the tower. It fit the lock in the bedchamber door like Cinderella's foot fit the glass slipper.

Which was really no surprise either, Dorcas realized on closer inspection of her find. What it was, specifically, was a skeleton key. It could probably open every door in the castle. Just as it had once sprung all the locks in Dr. Earnshaw's Philadelphia laboratory that long-ago afternoon she had spied it on his desk and he had let her test it.

That was the surprise—the fact that she had a childhood acquaintance with this crafty old piece of iron mongery. There was little doubt that it was the same key. If nothing else, she could identify it by the oddly styled *E* etched on its handle. It stood for Earnshaw, didn't it? No, that had been her original assumption, but it had been wrong. The *E* stood for Elizabeth, Dorcas corrected herself, as the skeleton key opened something besides the bedchamber door. Just holding it had unlocked memories that had been shut away in the back of her mind for over a decade.

"Elizabeth was my mother's name," Dr. Earnshaw had explained that muggy summer afternoon. "She died when I was still in dresses, I'm afraid. And ever after, until his own death not too many years later, my father wore this key on a chain around his neck."

"To remind him of her?"

"No, child. The image he held of her in his mind and soul was too clear to need any outside embellishments. But this key had once helped save both their lives, and it was one of the few things that came with them when they left their homes to move East. My father said he wore it to keep it safe. But I suspect it was simply to remind himself that the unique bond he and my mother shared was worth everything they had had to give up for each other."

It had seemed both a perplexing and slightly suspicious notion to Dorcas's six-year-old proprieties. "What do you mean, Dr. Earnshaw? Did they really have to give up that much?" she had asked as he lifted her onto his lap.

"Well, now, I'm not sure," he had begun in that special tone of voice that let her know there was a good story on the way. "Why don't I tell you about them and let you judge that point for yourself? The heat's made us too lazy for anything else today, and we still have nearly an hour before Matilda comes for you."

The story had taken most of an hour, too. And it *had* been a good one—full of heroes and villains and magical adventure—just like the ones in the fairy-tale books Aunt Matilda never wanted her to read. The only problem was that the heat had made her more than lazy that afternoon. It had made her downright drowsy. She had dozed off just at the most exciting part and never did hear how the story ended. Not on any conscious level, at least.

The little girl had awoken from her nap to the low buzz of Earnshaw and her aunt's voices; but it had sounded as though they were arguing, so she had taken the diplomatic route and kept her eyes and mouth closed. Adults always disagreed about the silliest things; it was better to steer clear, if one could. She might even have drifted back to sleep. That was what she had thought at the time, anyway. The conversation had made so little sense to her young ears, she had decided then that it had all been a dream and had promptly filed it away under things-not-to-think-about. Now, however, that file had been unlocked.

Poised at the bedchamber door, the telltale key cold in her hand and the memory of that day hot in her mind, Dorcas found herself listening to that argument again with an understanding that was almost electrifying in its impact. She could hear Dr. Earnshaw and her aunt's voices as if they were standing there in the shadowy room with her.

"Really, Zachary, we've been over this before. Dorcas is my responsibility and I am raising her to be an independent person who sees life as it is. So I would appreciate it if you would stop regaling her with these stories of yours. I tell her one thing, then you fill her head with all this romantic nonsense. It's confusing the child!"

"Not half as much as you confuse me, Matilda. You didn't always think romance was nonsense, you know."

"That may be true. But then, I never thought, either, that a man who had pledged himself to one woman would come back from war married to another. Which proves my point, doesn't it? I don't want Dorcas falling into the same trap I did."

"And I don't want to hear anything about traps when you know full well who the trapped one was. I've told you how it was with Caroline and me."

"Yes, Zachary, that's another of your romantic adventure tales, isn't it? About how you were wounded and lost behind Confederate lines? And Caroline's family shielded you and nursed you? Of course, you never suspected their ulterior motives, did you? You never guessed that she had already been . . . shall we say *compromised* by one Union officer, and they were looking for another one to pick up the slack, as it were."

"Matilda, they saved my life. I didn't—"

"You didn't have to find yourself in such a ticklish spot to begin with! That's what you didn't have to do. I

begged you not to go to that horrid war. I did everything—everything I could think of to keep you here.
Good heavens, Zachary, four-fifths of the other men who
were drafted paid for a substitute. Why did you have to
be one of the few who wouldn't?"

"Because my father did not raise me to pay another
man to fight my battles for me."

"Oh, that's right. Your personal honor was at stake. I
remember that now. Excuse me for forgetting it a moment while I was selfishly contemplating my personal
honor."

"Matilda—"

"No, don't say anything. I'm not making fun of you,
Zachary, really I'm not. I admire you very much. I know
you believe in what you do—especially at the time you're
doing it. In your own way, you're a truly noble man. It
was noble of you to go to war when you didn't have to.
Noble to accept responsibility for another man's child—"

"Damn it, Matilda, I want to accept responsibility for
my own child! Caroline and her son have been dead for
over a year now. Can't you forgive what happened and
let me finally make things right between us?"

"I'm sorry, Zachary, but I haven't the vaguest notion
what you're talking about."

"Oh, no? Who do you think this is asleep on my lap,
then—Goldilocks, exhausted after her tryst with the
three bears?"

"Honestly! If you're referring to Dorcas, you're being
ridiculous. Dorcas is my *niece* and you know it. I love
her, naturally, but the only reason I've had the privilege
of raising her is because my late brother appointed me
his infant daughter's guardian in his will. This child has
absolutely nothing to do with you."

"Of course not. That's why, even though she looks like
you in all other respects, she just happens to have the
same dark green eyes as my mother and myself."

"What does that prove? Odd coincidences occur all the time."

"Perhaps. But I've a still odder one for you, Matilda. I did a little investigating recently in the coroner's records at the courthouse. And I discovered that your brother's wife—Dorcas's mother, presumably—died of influenza nearly three months before Dorcas was born. How do you explain that?"

"I don't. I don't have to explain anything to you, Zachary. You relinquished all claim to my explanations the day you married your blossoming Southern belle—without even a thought, apparently, that you might have left me in a similarly flowering state. I still consider you a valued friend and colleague, though. And I am genuinely sorry Caroline and her little Beauregard died. I can imagine that it must be lonely for you now. But you really can't expect Dorcas and me to take their places. You see? This is what happens when you allow yourself to become romantically entangled with someone. They always leave you, one way or another. That's why I can't be bothered with such nonsense anymore. I have better things to do with my life. And I'm going to make certain that Dorcas has better things to do with her life, as well. I'll thank you to remember that."

"All right, Matilda, we'll do it your way. You're wrong about Caroline. I was far lonelier while she was alive than I am now. But you're right about everything else—especially about our friendship. For the sake of that and our professional relationship, I won't mention this matter again. And I promise I'll never make any claims on Dorcas. Your honor may not have been safe with me before, but it is now; you can rest easy on that. I realize you view me as an incurable romantic—and possibly I am. But romance takes a lot of different forms, you know. Most men in my position, I think, would feel that they loved the woman too much ever to be simply friends with her . . . but I love you so much, my dear, I'll take you any way I can get you."

Of all the curious concepts to have roiling around in one's skull at such a curiously momentous time, Dorcas thought, her brain feeling a bit too much like a squirrel chasing its own tail.

Not that she was contemplating squirrels, exactly—even if she was tilting slightly toward the nutty side. She was remembering something she had once heard about another member of the wild kingdom. She was thinking about giraffes. Or a book about giraffes, anyway, and a little girl who had been asked to give an oral report on it.

The girl had read the text, then stood up in front of her class and stated with great solemnity, "This book told me more about giraffes than I wanted to know."

That was what Dorcas was really thinking right then—that she had just figured out a lot more than she had ever wanted to know. She had received answers to questions she hadn't even realized existed. Questions and answers that she could have lived a very long, productive, and satisfying life never knowing anything about.

No, that wasn't correct. It was always better to know the truth; she honestly believed that. It was just that the timing was so off. She had more pressing things to deal with. The truth had picked an extremely awkward moment to poke its awkward head up out of its deep, dark, awkwardly placed hole. If it saw its shadow, would she have six more weeks of wintry confusion? she wondered a little maniacally. . . . *Now, that* was *nuts.*

And the nuts, of course, brought her full circle to squirrels. And a sudden, dizzy awareness of why her thoughts were all going bushy-tailed.

"Oh, my God!" she sputtered, lunging for the bedside table as the sickly sweet odor she had been inhaling finally became potent enough to penetrate the last logically functioning part of her consciousness. "Where are those scissors I had last night?"

Still on the table, thank goodness . . . On the table next to the lamp. The not quite extinguished lamp with its still smoldering wick wafting drugged vapors into her face. She bent over it and scorched her fingers knocking the hot chimney free from its base and onto the floor in a tinkling shatter of glass. A hasty twist of the lamp's key, a hastier slash of the scissors, and the smoking part of the wick landed among the chimney shards, to be ground into a soot spot under the toe of a trembling slippered foot. A second foot joined in wobbly rhythm with the first as Dorcas pivoted and stumbled toward the already unlocked door to pull it open and let in some cleaner air from the drafty passageway beyond.

What blew in instead, however, was a tidy tartan frock, covered by a grease-spattered white apron and topped by a very startled, apple-cheeked face.

"Oh! Beggin' yoor pardon, m'lady. Master Angus sed ye wuz feelin' puny like an' sent me tae make sure ye wuz safe abed," Enid MacAllister lied.

At least, Dorcas assumed it was a lie, because the surprised maid had just removed a handkerchief from her nose and mouth, implying that she had been warned about the lamp fumes and, therefore, had to suspect something underhanded, regardless of what else Angus might have told her.

"Ye dinna look a'tall well, m'lady," Enid improvised, as Dorcas stood staring at her, trying to decide her next move.

It might work, she was thinking. They were the same height, though the girl was a bit plump. But it was a loose-fitting frock anyway, and the cap would be handy for hiding her short hair. It would certainly allow her to move about more discreetly. People rarely looked very closely at scullery maids.

"Let me help ye oota yoor gown an' back oonder th' covers, m'lady."

"Thank you," Dorcas said politely as Enid made good on her kind offer. "And now I'll help you out of yours!"

If the young maid had been startled at seeing m'lady awake and on her feet at the door, she was stunned by the sudden fist that connected with her rosy dimple— stunned cold.

It surprised Dorcas almost as much. She had expected the job to take more than one blow. Whoever would have guessed such a sturdy-looking lass to have a glass jaw? she mused with a slight head shake as she stood at the desk in her new maid's uniform, scratching out an apology:

> *Please excuse me for having to punch you, but I could not be sure of your motives, nor could I spare the time for negotiations. In exchange for your attire, I am giving you this lime taffeta gown. If you let out the seams a bit, it should fit you very well, and the color will highlight the roses in your cheeks.*
> *Sincerely, Dorcas . . .*

She paused a moment and then quickly finished the signature *E. MacAllister*. She wasn't entirely certain about the MacAllister yet, but the middle initial seemed a safe bet. This *E*, unlike the one on the key, did stand for *Earnshaw*. And as she hurried about the room, placing a pillow under Enid's head, a quilt on top of her, and the letter and gown beside her, she prayed quietly that the wonderful but stubborn woman who had raised her would forgive the acknowledgment.

"I'm sorry," Dorcas murmured aloud, hoping that her mother's spirit could hear and understand. "I know you were trying to protect me from the trap that caught you, but, the thing is, I don't believe you realized exactly what trap you had fallen into. You thought love was the trap. But what really snared you was your own fear of loss. You let pain and pride make you cynical. You dug a wound in yourself so deep that you never were able to fully climb out of it. And I'm sorry, but I don't want to make the same mistake. I hope you'll forgive me . . . Mother . . . but I think I'd rather take my chances with love. It may be short-lived, as you said it was, but is a sunset any less real or beautiful, any less precious, because it only lasts a few moments? I guess that makes me sound like all the other so-called fools you always warned me about, doesn't it? It makes me sound like a hopeless romantic."

"No, child, not hopeless. Hope*ful*. It makes you sound a lot like me, in fact."

A large lump suddenly filling her throat, Dorcas's gaze shot to the open doorway and a pair of eyes as green as her own.

"I knew you must have inherited something from me besides your mathematical abilities," Zachary Earnshaw added, with the smile that must have captured Matilda Jeffries's heart years before.

It certainly melted Dorcas's at that instant.

"Don't forget the eyes," she managed to squeeze out past the lump, as her feet somehow navigated the several steps into his open arms.

"Ah, but those aren't entirely mine," the man said, gathering his daughter close. "We both get those from my mother."

"I know. Elizabeth MacAllister—or Elspeth, if you prefer the Scottish version. She was the one who freed the Panther and nearly got burned as a witch, right?"

"My goodness—that old story? You know, as many times as my father told it to me when I was a boy, I never was quite sure I believed him. Fancy you remembering it after all this time." Earnshaw chuckled.

So did Dorcas, but her laugh was more on the hysterical side.

"Remember it? I've practically *lived* it these past days! Being here where it all happened must have dredged it up out of my subconscious. I've been having so many bizarre dreams about it, I thought I was going insane— or worse—until Elspeth's skeleton key finally unlocked my memory," she said, and abruptly found herself held at arm's length.

"You have my mother's key? I've been looking high and low for that," she was told. "I placed it in the base of one of our electric lights on a whim. I was curious to see whether the battery's voltage was enough to magnetize it. But before I could take it out again, Simon had disappeared with the blasted contraption, and I haven't seen the lamp or the key since. Where did you find it?"

"On the sill. But don't ask me how it got there," Dorcas answered, slipping out of his grasp and turning half away. The movement was partly so she could gesture toward the window, but more because it gave her an excuse to avoid the searching green eyes peering down at her. All things considered, she had decided to take Angus's advice and say no more about black cats. Not that she had the slightest anxiety regarding the creature herself—or about Earnshaw's reaction if she mentioned it to him. Her father would understand the truth of the cat as well as she did, being the one who had told her the story in the first place. But she was beginning to suspect that the castle's walls had ears.

And I'm allergic to smoke, she thought, wondering briefly if the MacAllisters' private legal code still included the burning of witches. After all, if it allowed such quaint old customs as trials by combat . . .

"Oh, my God—I'm wasting time! Uncle Angus is planning on killing someone with a claymore!"

She said it at exactly the same instant Earnshaw said,

"All right, we'll forget the key for now, but would you mind telling me why you're dressed as a scullery maid and Enid is asleep on the floor?"

Their voices overlapped, so each only half heard the other.

"What's this about Angus and a claymore?" he asked.

"She's not asleep. She's unconscious," Dorcas answered the second part of his first question because that was the only part of it she had caught. She answered in perfect unison with his second inquiry, so she missed that one completely.

"The little Mexican girl in the bed is asleep though," she added quickly, gathering herself for a lunge out of the room. "Or at this point she may just be drugged on lamp oil. Would you please stay with her? I have to find where Angus has taken Alan—"

She was hauled back by her apron strings before she had even cleared the door.

"Dorcas Matilda, either you have fallen into the beer again or there is something very odd in the works. You know, I came up here in the first place simply to assure myself you were all right. I heard someone being locked in the prison tower a short while ago, and with your recent history, I was half afraid it might have been you. Now, I would like some explanations, young lady. You are not going anywhere until I understand what is happening."

"The minute I find out, I'll let you know!" she promised, wriggling out of the stained apron and tearing down the passageway. Now that she knew where Alan was, there wasn't a moment to lose.

Chapter Twelve

Was it the lingering influence of the drugged lamp vapors fogging the edges of her consciousness and making her reckless? Possibly. But it was more the inner lamp that had recently been lit, illuminating for her who she really was. And her father would forgive her for leaving him in the dust of confusion back there: it was exactly the sort of thing he would have done himself. She was a lot like him.

Her aunt—her mother, that was—had tried to push her into a different mold, one that she thought would keep her daughter safe from the hurt she had experienced. But it had been about as successful as a bird trying to teach her offspring how *not* to fly. Because the fact of the matter was, that prim, proper, safe, little mold had been alien to Matilda herself.

There had never truly been anything safe or proper about Matilda Jeffries. She had flaunted convention right from the start by choosing a very esoteric career for herself. And when marriage to the man she loved had seemed to be cut off from her, she had channeled all her energies into that career. She had always taken too many risks with her research. That was why the final experiment had ended in that fatal blast. It just wasn't in her to stick to safe routes. She was too independent. Too adventurous. And too romantic.

But she never did stop loving my father, Dorcas thought, as she hurried through the shadowed passages. *Her pride wouldn't let her marry him, but their friendship was always unique. After that one blunder, neither of them ever did look at anyone else. In their own, unconventional way, they stayed faithful to each other to the last. Good heavens! I grew up with a beautiful example of true romance and never even realized it until now.*

The apple doesn't fall far from the tree, though, does it? This is why I've been acting as I have—helping Leslie and Flora elope and . . . and all the rest. Hypnotism be damned! No one has been making me do a blasted thing that I didn't really want to. I'm not possessed. I'm not going insane. I'm just in love.

Which might possibly amount to the same thing, she realized, her heart sinking through the floor as one shadow larger than all the rest suddenly blocked the stairway to the prison tower.

"Enid? Have ye done as I bid?"

"A-aye, sir. 'Tis sleepin' like a bairn she be. She'll nay wake 'til morn, I'll wager," Dorcas mumbled, keeping her face well lowered under the shade of her ruffled maid's cap and hoping that checking on herself was all that Enid had been bid to do.

"Good lass. Ye can return tae yoor duties now."

"Aye, sir." Bobbing a quick curtsey, the girl turned toward the passage she thought led to the inner courtyard where the kitchens were, breathing a small sigh of relief as she did.

The sigh was a little premature, however.

"Where ye headin', lassie? Ye'll nay find yoor pots tha' way."

She wouldn't? Damn!

"Ah . . . aye, sir. I wuz gang fer a fresh apron furst. Me oother one wuz too greezy, i'twas," she improvised without turning around.

"Aye? I'd been ponderin' th' lack of it, I had. But ye'll nay find th' laundry there, neither."

"I . . . I wuz gang tae me chamber fer one, maybe?"

"I think ye were gang fer yoor bridegroom," Angus said with a grin, spinning her to face him with one hand while the other one whipped the cap off her short curls. "I'll take ye tae him, shall I?"

"Thank you very much, but I wouldn't want you to trouble yourself when I'm sure I can find my own way. I *have* been there before, you know," Dorcas pointed out, as a heavy grip on her wrist began hauling her roughly up the stairs.

" 'Tis nay trouble, Dorie dear."

"Mr. MacAllister—Uncle Angus—*Wait!*" she cried, frantically trying to hold back. It was as easy as trying to hold back summer's heat or winter's cold. "You can't go through with this combat! You don't realize the danger!"

" 'Tis nay danger neither. Nane fer me, anyways. Nay man can stand agenst me an' a claymore."

"But that's just it! What if Ian is innocent?"

" 'Tis whut th' combat's fer, ain't it? Tae decide whether he be innocent oor nay."

"If you're certain of winning, all it will decide is that you're a murderer!"

"If I win, he's guilty, an' there's th' end o' it. 'Tis MacAllister law. I dinna ken why ye'd want tae spare 'im, but ye'll nay do it. Save yoor breath, lass."

"You fool! I'm trying to save *you!* MacAllister law may not be as secure as you think it is! This castle is being watched by the state—did you know that? Your private code has been under some heavy suspicion, apparently. Officials will be riding in tomorrow to collect the Garcias' murderers, and I was told to warn you that if there's any sign of claymore justice when they arrive, you people could face some harsh penalties yourselves!" Dorcas shot at him, and then wondered if she had shot a little too far, too fast.

The look on Angus's face as he snapped her over the top step and against the door to the tower room was not the look of an angry or vengeful man. It was the look of a suddenly concerned one. Which could be far more dangerous, she realized.

"Ye'd best explain yoorself, lassie," he said with deathly quiet. "Who's been spyin' on us? Who gave ye such a message?"

Would it hurt to tell? The man's cover had already been more or less blown, after all. . . .

"M-mr. Elliott—I mean, Captain Elliott," she answered, trying not to wince as Angus's grip bit into her wrist. "He's a Texas Ranger!"

His response was miles away from the one she had been hoping for. His expression quickly shifting into a disheartening blend of amusement and scorn, the Scotsman threw back his big bushy head and roared with laughter.

"Ahh, yoor as daft as Ian! Oor ye've been inta th' vats again. That dandy's nay more a Ranger than I'm an Englishman!" he scoffed, twisting his key sharply in the lock. "In wi' ye! I'll let ye both oot when I've finished this business."

"You're the one who's daft! And when Captain Elliott gets back here, you're going to have a vat load of explaining to do! I wouldn't want to be in your kilt!" she shouted, as he shoved her into the musty dark chamber and slammed shut the door with enough force to knock her spinning like a drunken top toward the opposite wall. She was saved by a flung-out arm only inches from kissing the adobe.

"If there's a spot of trouble to be found, you'll land in the center, won't you?" a husky voice whispered close to her ear.

Instantly forgetting all else in a wash of relief that he truly was unharmed, Dorcas pressed herself fervently against the body that voice came from.

"*You're* my center," she half sobbed, kissing a startled pair of lips instead of the rough wall she had almost hit.

It was the very first kiss she had ever initiated between them. And the very last thing, apparently, that Alan had expected—or needed—just then.

"Dorcas, this is hardly the . . . What's gotten into . . . Have you fallen into another vat of beer?" he finally managed to strain out against her mouth—having little success disentangling himself from her strangle hold.

What? She could barely see him, but this was Alan, wasn't it? she wondered, pulling back just enough to try to read his expression in the dim light. The figure in her arms didn't exactly sound or act like Alan, but it certainly felt like Alan.

"Do you know you're the third person to accuse me of that? Why does everyone think I'm drunk?" she complained.

"I don't know," he said hoarsely. "Could it have anything to do with the fact that you're making wild claims, getting yourself locked up, throwing yourself at men, and dressing as a . . ." He squinted down at her. "Scullery maid, is it?"

"This is Enid's gown. I traded her the lime taffeta for it," she mumbled into his shoulder. "I think I got the best part of the bargain, though. This is a lot more comfortable than those frilly things you prefer me in."

"Actually, I prefer you out of them."

Ah, now that sounded like Alan.

Tilting back her head, she grinned up at him. "I should think you'd want to kiss your wife after she went to so much trouble to free you."

"No one's free yet, dear," he countered, straining as far away from her as the short chain of the wall manacle would allow. "And you seem to have forgotten that you're a bit too young to be anyone's wife right now."

That shows how much you know, she thought, deciding that the explanation could wait. There was something perversely irresistible about the current situation after all the tricks he had been playing. Pushing close again, she slid her arms around the back of his neck.

"That's not what you said when you insisted on marrying me," she murmured, inching his head down to hers.

"Dorcas . . . please . . . That was a mistake. One I'm trying to atone for now. But you're not making it very easy."

"I'm not trying to. Come on, Alan, it's only a kiss. Don't tell me you've never been kissed before," she coaxed, using a line she had heard elsewhere once.

"That's not funny. And you'll be sorry if you keep this up, lass."

"I doubt it."

"You've picked one hell of a time to change your attitude, you know that?" He groaned as her lips grazed seductively against his. But he was losing the battle. She could feel it even as she could feel his free arm losing the battle to keep from curling tightly around her waist.

"I'm warning you." He breathed raggedly, all his muscles suddenly tensing like a spring about to snap. "Don't do this."

"Do what?"

"Kiss me . . ."

"If you insist," she said, her lips pressing home.

The spring burst wide open. All around her, in fact, as both his arms pulled her completely off her feet and into a kiss that was like a dream and an awakening all in one. It stormed through her like a heavenly blast, sucking the breath straight out of her and spiraling all her thoughts into a glorious rainbow whirl. Their kisses, even when she had fought them, had been indescribably ecstatic. Now that she was fully open to the experience, it was indescribably indescribable. The words simply hadn't been invented yet that could say what that kiss released in her.

Nor her anger when she discovered that their positions had been reversed and she was the one chained fast to the adobe wall.

"Wh-what! You—I—" she sputtered, nearly bloodying her wrist in a furious attempt to jerk free.

"Stop that or you'll hurt yourself," Alan ordered. "I did warn you, you know. This cell was designed for women prisoners. I knew I'd be able to spring the catch on that manacle; it was never intended to hold anyone my size. But it ought to keep you out of trouble while I discover what the devil's going on around here."

Striding quickly to the door, he peered carefully through the grill a moment before backing up a pace and landing two sharp, flat-footed kicks on the lock. It swung open with creaking of hinges.

"I knew I'd be able to spring the latch on that, too," he said, turning back to her with a grin. "Though I'm glad I had my boots on. That sort of thing's a wee bit uncomfortable in moccasins."

"I can imagine," she said darkly, glowering through the gloom at him. "But it was unnecessary, in any case. I have a key, you scoundrel."

"Is that what that was? I thought I felt something long and hard down the front of your frock."

"Yes, I thought I felt something long and hard on you, too," Dorcas stated dryly, and was rewarded by a sight she never thought she would see—Alan blushing deep red under his tan. Even in the dim light, it was obvious.

"Heaven forgive me for corrupting a minor," he muttered to himself, angling awkwardly away. "Ah . . ." He cleared his throat. "Dorcas, I wasn't going to mention this just now, but . . ."

Oh, God, now what? He wouldn't meet her eyes? That was something she had seen before.

"But under the circumstances, I think I'd better set the record straight between us."

What circumstances? What record? For the first time since she had arrived at the castle, things were finally clear in her own mind. *What needed straightening?*

"You were right about me, I think. I have been a complete cad."

No! She'd been wrong—she knew that now!

"And I think the only way I can make amends is to . . . well, as soon as I can arrange it, I'll send you back to Philadelphia," he said, swinging out the door.

"But I don't want to go!"

Damn this manacle! It wouldn't let her reach him and he was already in the passage. . . .

"Come back here and finish this!" she demanded.

His silhouette reappeared in the doorway and she let out a small sigh of relief. Then nearly choked on it at his words.

"Dear, that's what I just told you. This is finished. You're free to go."

"Of course I'm free. That's why I'm standing here shackled to the wall."

"That's a temporary precaution to keep you safe. You'll be out of it before you know it—and then I'll put you on the first train heading East."

It was ridiculous. Hadn't he heard her?

She tried it again, speaking as calmly and clearly as she could. "Alan, haven't you been listening? I do not want to go."

Finally . . . He was finally looking at her. And it didn't help one blasted little bit, because there seemed to be nothing but pity in that look. *Pity? Dear God, this wasn't ridiculous after all. It was a bleeding nightmare!*

"That's just it, dear. You're too young to know what you really want," he said softly. "This ruddy combat—or the reason for it, anyway—has reminded me of that. Locked up here, I've been remembering how things were between Heather and me."

Oh, no, was that it? He'd realized he was still in love with Angus's daughter? Heaven help her, how could she compete with a memory?

"The fact is, I never should have married Heather. We'd nothing in common save what you referred to as animal attraction—the kind that burns itself out quickly. But we were too young to realize that. Plus, we had Uncle Angus egging us on. He wanted the match to secure the MacAllister rights. There's one rather touchy clause in our pact with Texas, you see. Our arrangement holds only so long as a direct legal descendant of the original laird is residing at the castle and acting as clan head. 'Twas the government's way of someday ending the deal, I suspect—not that it matters at present. The point is, there are only two people today who can fill that position—myself and my father. And he'd no interest in the job, even when he was sane."

"What about Angus? Don't brothers count?"

"Not when they're illegitimate, they don't. My uncle wasn't supposed to be illegitimate, mind you. 'Twas a wee oversight of my grandfather's. When Laird Stuart was captured by Comanche years ago, he fathered my father on one of their women, the daughter of a powerful warrior. He married her, too—Highland style—to make her feel better about it. But to make himself feel better when he was eventually ransomed back, he took a MacAllister bride and fathered Angus. Only that marriage wasn't legal, because he already had a Comanche wife. Bigamy is not a Highland tradition, you understand. I suppose he thought no one would ever find out about his first son, but the truth did come out . . . only not 'til my father was nearly grown.

"They brought him here to the castle and tried to make him stay by marrying him to Molly's daughter, Rowena. She was an extremely bonny lass, and I think he honestly did love her, but he'd been born and bred Comanche. The MacAllisters got him too late. He couldn't tolerate life here, so shortly after I was born, he packed the three of us up and rejoined his tribe. The thing was, Rowena had been born and bred MacAllister, and she couldn't tolerate life with the Comanche. He cared for her happiness enough to let her return to the castle without him, and I spent my childhood split between both worlds— half my time here and half with my father's people. The year I was fifteen, though, my mother died. Wild Horse came for her burial; when he left, I went with him. And I didn't see these walls again 'til I was nearly eighteen."

The same age I am now, Dorcas thought, beginning to smell where this might be leading and not finding the odor particularly promising. Still, he was trying to explain himself and that was something, she supposed. Something of a wonder, actually. This was the longest flow of words she had ever had out of him at any one time. Only it seemed as though it might be on the verge of running dry, and that wouldn't help her any.

"You came back to marry your cousin?" she quickly prompted, trying to re-prime the pump.

It worked, but not quite as she had expected.

"I came back for her wedding, anyway," Alan answered flatly. "Heather was going to marry Geordie."

"The brewer?" That was a puzzle piece she had never expected. How did that fit in?

"Aye. My father and I had just returned for a visit. Angus was tickled pink about it—though I didn't guess at first 'twas because Grandfather Stuart had recently died and a new resident laird was needed to continue the pact. I thought he was just glad to see me. He'd always been a fond uncle in his own way. 'Twas a bit of a sore spot with my father. Wild Horse hadn't appreciated Angus trying to make me a good MacAllister, while he was trying to make me a good Comanche."

The feeling had probably been mutual with Angus, Dorcas thought absently. But how had Alan ended up with Heather if the girl had been engaged to another man? Unless . . . well, it was a rather romantic notion—forbidden fruit and all that.

"It was a trap, really—Heather's betrothal to Geordie. Uncle Angus knew she and I had had a powerful adolescent attraction to each other. He never wanted her to marry Geordie, but the moment I was back on Mac-Allister land, he consented to the match. To make me jealous, I realized later. Or so I'd not have too much time to consider the consequences. However 'twas meant, it worked. I galloped here the morning of the wedding. Heather took one look at me and never a backward glance at that poor idiot Geordie. She and I exchanged vows instead . . . and sealed our own separate dooms by doing so."

This was becoming ridiculous again. He looked as if he'd been breaking his back with guilt over something that wasn't really his fault. And worse than that, he was trying to use this against her—against *them*—as though the two situations had anything in common.

"Alan, I realize I'm not exactly an expert on this subject, but it seems to me that teenage boys never consider the consequences of . . . of that sort of attraction, no matter how much time they have," she said, and immediately wished she had choked on the words before they were out. The expression on his face told her that she had simply given him more fuel for his own argument.

"That's precisely my point. Young people haven't enough experience to understand their desires," he said in the fatherly tone that was beginning to make her teeth grate. "Dorcas, I'm trying to spare you from falling into the same trap I did."

Oh, God, that was almost the same thing her mother had said years ago. But her mother had been wrong then. And Alan was, too.

"Love isn't a trap! It's a release," Dorcas stated definitely, not certain why she was so positive about that but knowing that she was.

"I agree. But physical desires can be a trap."

That tone again. Wasn't there anything she could say to break through the wall he'd thrown up around himself?

"You said that this was more than physical desire!"

"It is . . . for me," he admitted, but in a voice that refused to give any ground.

"It is for me, too," she pleaded.

"You can't be sure of that."

Was there just a slight shift in his tone? A hint of anger? Cynicism? Bruised ego?

That could be it, she thought, as a flash of intuition struck her. After all—romantic passion notwithstanding—a girl who could so easily turn her back on one man to marry another . . . There was one way to break down that wall and find out. But she would have to use the heavy field artillery to do it.

"Well, how am I supposed to be sure, then? What do you want me to do? Run out and play footsie with a few dozen other men so I can come back here and say I've made enough comparisons to know that you're the one

I want?" she suggested, looking for all the world as if she was seriously considering the idea. "I'm a scientist, remember. I understand the value of experimentation."

A bit too much gunpowder in the cannon, perhaps? The wall not only broke—it practically exploded in her face.

"I may have to keep you locked up, at that—to protect you from yourself!" he growled, lunging across the cell and gripping her upper arms. He caught himself just short of giving her a shake, abruptly dropping his hands and swinging away into the deeper shadows, so she couldn't see his expression. "Maybe if I'd locked Heather up she'd be alive today," he said barely audibly. He seemed to be speaking to himself, but Dorcas responded anyway.

"I'm not Heather. I never even thought of a man before you. And if you've changed your mind about me, I'll simply go back to my original plan. You know I'd never intended marrying anyone to begin with. I was expecting to be an old maid," she said softly.

"I haven't changed my mind," he said huskily, turning back to face her. "My mind was certain the instant you landed in my arms."

"Mine, too. It just took me a little longer to realize it."

Straining forward as far as the manacle would allow, she stretched out her free hand to him. With a heavy sigh, like that of a man who had just lost a battle he had never wanted to fight in the first place, Alan reached for it and enclosed the slender fingers in the warmth of his own.

"I'd like to believe that, dear, but—"

"But nothing!" She cut him off, tightly lacing her fingers through his when he tried to pull away. "You believed it before I did. You're the one who kept telling me how I felt. Remember?"

"That was before I knew how young you were."

"But I'm still the same person. If my feelings were true a few hours ago, they're still true! Why is it so impossible for you to accept that? It can't be because of anything I've done. Is it something you've remembered about Heather? What *is* it?" she asked desperately as he untangled his hand from hers and started stony-faced for the door, signaling that the discussion was over.

No, it's not, Dorcas thought.

"Was Heather unfaithful to you?"

The question halted him in midstride, stiffening his back and shoulders, but not quite enough to turn him around.

"Dorcas, I've no more time for this—"

"Was she? Is that why you can't trust me?"

That brought him around.

"Good God, no—you're nothing like her! And it's not that I don't trust you. It's just that . . ."

"You've convinced yourself I'm too young to know what I'm doing," she finished for him.

He didn't have to answer. The expression on his face as he turned toward the passage once more said aye plainly enough.

"Then you're a bloody hypocrite! You call yourself a Comanche, but I happen to know that Comanche girls usually marry at about the age of sixteen. I'm nearly two years older than that and you still view me as a child! A real Comanche wouldn't think so! You're more Mac-Allister than you care to admit, Laird Alan!" Dorcas shouted after him. And listened with satisfaction to his booted steps returning to the cell.

"For that matter, so am I," she added, unable to resist a smug grin at the bare-chested figure framed tensely in the doorway.

"More of your surprises?" he asked warily.

"The biggest yet." And the grin stretched into a smile of shamelessly malicious glee.

Which sent him straight down the passage again.

"Tell me later, then. I haven't the time or energy for any more shocks right now," he called back.

The taut manacle chain twanged like a heavy iron bowstring as her own shock caused her to nearly dislocate a shoulder as she lunged forward.

"Alan, wait! I need to tell you this!"

"Later."

"No, now! Come back here!"

"I'll return for you as soon as I can."

"Alan, *please!* This is important! *Alan . . .*"

Throwing back her head, Dorcas screamed bloody murder at the top of her lungs. Actually, she screamed, "Help" at the top of her lungs, but it probably sounded like bloody murder to Alan. He must have taken the stairs four at a time to arrive back in the cell faster than a lightning flash.

"What kept you so long?" she asked as he loomed over her, breathing hard from the charge.

"What the devil's the matter with you?" he countered, his eyes rapidly scanning the chamber and seeing nothing amiss.

"A rat!" she improvised, realizing he was on the verge of abandoning her once more. "It was huge! And it had fangs and claws and it was foaming at the mouth and it tried to run up my skirt and—*There it is!*"

Shrieking, she flattened herself against him, whipping her free arm tightly about his waist and latching on to the back of his belt with a death grip.

Straining to peer over his shoulder at where she had gestured, he said irritably, " 'Tis only a mouse. Now let go."

"Well, it looked like a rat to me," she grumbled into his chest, while discreetly jerking on her manacle. "How can I see what anything is in these shadows? And by the way, our marriage is legal. I had my father's consent."

"Dorcas, let go of m—what consent?"

"Not what. Who. It's a long story and I've only just discovered it myself, but Dr. Earnshaw is my father," she quickly explained, clinging to him like a leech with one arm while the other tried to jar open the manacle. "Since he witnessed our vows and gave his blessing afterward— even though I didn't realize what he meant at the time—I assume that means I had parental permission and therefore, I *am* your wife. Put *that* in your peace pipe and smoke it, Big Chief Know-it-all," she finished, just as the manacle trick worked and both her arms wrapped snugly around him.

His own pulled her completely off her feet and on a level with his hot, glittering glare.

"In that case you'd best hope I'm as MacAllister as you said," he warned, his voice husky and his breath warm on her face. "Comanche beat their wives for insolence."

"Are you threatening me, Chief?"

"Would it do any good if I was, Dorcas Matilda MacAllister?"

"Not one blessed bit." She grinned, electric chills that had nothing to do with fear tingling up and down her spine. "Your threats have no power over me anymore."

"I don't recall that they ever did."

"You're right. So you're stuck with this insolent, pale-face squaw whether you like it or not. To get rid of me at this point, you'd have to divorce me. And I'd never agree to that—not even if you hung me off the ramparts again."

"I hope you honestly mean those words, dear, because to end this union I'd have to *drop* you off a rampart. Or leap from one myself. The MacAllister code doesn't allow for divorce. Our marriages are for life."

Electric chills froze instantly to ice. "Oh, no . . ."

"Dorcas? What is it? What's wrong?" His amber gaze widened in pained confusion, then shuttered down into

264

a closed, cynical stare as she shoved free from his arms and turned sharply toward the window.

"Bloody hell," he cursed under his breath. "Even Heather didn't get tired of me this quickly."

"Don't be an idiot," she scolded, her mind moving faster than her feet as she paced from the window to the opposite wall and back. "I just need a minute to think."

"About what? Dorcas—"

"Hush. I've almost got it."

"You're going to get it, if you don't—"

"Oh, my God, *that's* why she was killed!" Stopping short in the center of the cell, she whirled to face him. "Since you couldn't divorce, it was the only way he could keep you here and ensure the birth of a legal heir to secure the MacAllister pact."

"What? My father's never cared if the pact continued or not."

"I can imagine. But Angus cares very much."

"If you're suggesting that—"

"Well, it makes a certain sense, doesn't it?" she said, cutting him off. "He must have known how unhappy you were with Heather. He reads you like a book—anyone can see that. Did he know about her . . . um . . . indiscretions, too?"

"That's your second reference to that," he said tightly. "What makes you so sure she was unfaithful?"

"I'm not. I'm only guessing. Are you telling me now that she wasn't?"

His hard-muscled chest heaved with a harder sigh. "Hell, no. She changed men oftener than most women change their stockings. And Angus was fully aware of it—along with everyone else in a twenty-mile radius—since she rarely bothered to hide her . . . indiscretions, as you so politely put it. He kept calling it 'youthful high spirits'—said she'd outgrow it if I'd take a strap to her. But I . . . "

"Of course you couldn't. You're hardly the wife-beater type," Dorcas finished for him. "For that matter, neither are most Comanche—despite your comment to the contrary," she added absently.

"You seem pretty sure of that, dear. Where does your information on Comanche come from?"

"From stories my father told me when I was small," she answered, sorry she'd made the digression in the first place and hoping he wouldn't pursue it.

But Alan's curiosity had been piqued.

"And where did our Eastern-born Dr. Earnshaw get his information?"

"From his father." *And you wouldn't believe the rest of it, even if I had the time to tell you right now,* she thought, staring over his shoulder at a curiously iridescent spider adding another lacy tapestry to the dusky, web-hung walls.

"It might have been an accident—Heather's death, I mean," she reflected aloud, as the spider danced in and out of its threads. "He might only have meant to give her the beating he thought you should, but it got out of hand. She fell and hit her head or something, and—"

"Dorcas, you do realize that you're talking about a man killing his own daughter, don't you?"

"I'm talking about a man who was raised to be the laird here himself, until the discovery of your father's birth knocked him down a rung. MacAllister pride must have been fed to him along with his mother's milk. I think he'd do anything he had to protect the clan's rights. You didn't see the horrified look on his face before he threw me in here, but did you hear what I had just warned him of—that those rights might be in jeopardy?"

"The entire castle probably heard you, dear, but—"

"But that's my point! He must have been equally horrified that the rights would die out with you—that any heirs Heather produced would carry the doubt of illegitimacy. Or that you would become so disgusted, you'd leave for good."

"I was disgusted, all right. But I'd given my word I'd stay," Alan stated, his eyes locking hard with hers.

"I believe you," she told him, holding the banked force of his gaze. "But I don't think Angus did. He thought you had already run out on him the day of the murder."

"And what makes you think that?" he asked.

"You. When you said Angus told you that Heather felt she was running away *with* you. Why would he say that unless he thought you had left? And where could he have gotten the idea except from Heather herself? It's why you feel responsible for her death, isn't it? You *had* threatened her with leaving, so when you disappeared that morning—probably just to ride off some steam—she foolishly assumed you'd carried out that threat, chased after you at Angus's urging, and—"

"Why do you say foolishly?"

"Don't ask silly questions. If she'd understood you half as well as I do, she'd have known how empty your threats are." Dorcas grinned up into the shadowy face glowering down at her. "You growl like a lion, Alan, but underneath you're just a big, purring pussycat."

"I'm doomed." He groaned, the glower dissolving into a wry grin of his own. "For I can see who's going to be wearing the pants in this family, now that my secret's out."

"I should hope so. And maybe you'll think twice now, before swinging a girl off the ramparts," she said sternly. "Don't worry about it too much, though. I'll pretend you're in charge, for the sake of appearances."

"Thank you. I'd appreciate that," he said, reaching forward and cupping both her hands in a warm grip. "And I appreciate your fascinating deductions as well. But aren't you forgetting one small detail?"

The hands between his stiffened slightly. "What?"

"That there's no mystery about Heather's death in the first place. We've always known who killed her and why. It was a clear-cut act of insane rage. Though I suspect, in his own mind, he might have felt he was avenging me for her infidelities."

Yes, you would suspect that—it would give you a double reason for your own guilt, Dorcas thought. Honestly! The man was almost too gallant for his own good.

Not to mention hers. That was why he had nearly sent her packing. It had probably seemed the only honorable action he could take—the chivalrous idiot. He was the sort who would cut off his own nose if he considered it to be spiting his integrity, she mused, and fought back a sudden chill as the thought triggered a completely unrelated image in her mind—the image of a dawn-lit face minus one of its central features.

"My father always had something of a temper, you see," Alan was explaining, the tightening of his hands around hers the only sign of his inner tension. "Though no one would ever have thought him capable of an act like that. If he'd had the least fear for her safety, Angus wouldn't have sent Heather with him that day."

"Angus knew they were together, then?"

"Aye. Wild Horse had arrived at the castle looking for me an hour or so after I'd left. 'Twas how they discovered I was gone. It worried my father that I might have run off without speaking to him first, so he agreed to track me. And Angus insisted that he take Heather with him. Grandmother Molly thinks it might have been my father's head wound that tipped him over the edge. He was barely conscious when Angus found him near the body, and bloodied from crown to chin. It looked as if Heather must have struggled and shot him with his own revolver before he overpowered her. She was a sturdy lass."

"Growing up with brothers like hers, she would have

had to be. . . . But something's not right with that story. If Wild Horse killed her in a burst of homicidal insanity, but the insanity was caused by a wound she had given him after he had already attacked her . . . do you see what I'm getting at?"

"No," he said, his hands tightening slightly. "Because, as much as I'd love to believe otherwise, my father *is* insane. He's spent these past years little better than a zombie. An occupant of our dungeon, true, for light distresses him—but a prisoner primarily of his own mind. That's why we've not been able to deal with this before. According to MacAllister law, the accused has to make a plea of guilty or not guilty to be tried and sentenced, and Wild Horse would say neither. The only word he's spoken from then till now has been *beer*."

"Beer?" It brought her thoughts up short for a moment. "Why would he ask for beer? Is he that fond of the stuff?"

"He hates it, in fact. Always has, but even more so since the murder. Offer him a mug and he flies into a rage. Uncle Angus does it occasionally, just so he'll get some exercise."

"Uncle Angus has been trying to keep your father fit, has he? That figures," Dorcas said, agitatedly attempting to pull her hands free and finding them held fast. "I must say, this whole affair has worked out very conveniently for him. Not only did Heather's death free you to marry again and produce unquestionably legitimate heirs, but blaming it on Wild Horse—supposedly gone mad—gave him a perfect excuse to keep your father here as a puppet laird, just in case something happened to you before he could arrange a new match. I wouldn't be surprised if the reason your father hasn't spoken is because Angus has been keeping him drugged. And maybe that's why he's been wandering, too. I gather he's only been leaving his cell since I've been here, right?" she asked, and flew on without waiting for an answer. "Now that you're finally remarried, your uncle doesn't need a backup anymore, and he may feel that it's too dangerous to keep Wild Horse alive any longer. So Angus is the one who's been chasing him off, hoping he'd get himself lost or killed. But since that hasn't happened, he's manipulated this combat instead, to get rid of him that way. Or maybe—"

"Or maybe you're making yourself hysterical again with imaginings—like your giant rat," Alan smoothly cut her off. "Now listen to me; I did hear everything you told my uncle and, unlike him, I can believe we've had a Ranger at the castle. I've seen Smoke on horseback and he rides far too well for a dandy, as Angus called him. But as for the rest of this . . . Dorcas, you saw my father this morning, with the bloodlust in his eyes. He came after you, for God's sake!"

"What does that prove? We *all* had bloodlust in our eyes this morning! I shot one of those swine myself, and I'd never even fired a gun before. Does that make me insane?"

"You don't really want me to answer that, do you?"

"Alan, I'm serious! I think your father simply stumbled onto that horror by accident, the way I did, and was trying to help."

"By attempting to kill you?"

"Yes! Because he had seen me in the yard with the others before you arrived. I didn't realize he had at the time, but I think now that he must have. Wild Horse mistook me for part of that band. I stampeded the horses to keep those murderers from getting away, but if I'd been one of them, I could just as easily have done it to create a cover for my own escape. And the way Rosa was screaming, he probably thought I was stealing her. *That's* why he chased me!"

Well, it *did* make a certain sense, she thought, remembering how Wild Horse hadn't even arrived on the scene until after she and Kathy had plunged into the thick of it under cover of Captain Elliott's wild charge. Were all Texas Rangers such daredevils? she wondered, still trying to decide whether Simon was a hero or a fool. Whatever had he been thinking in that silver-studded saddle of his? That very fancy, very large, and very heavy saddle . . .

A pair of green eyes suddenly narrowed in the gloom.

Why *had* Captain Elliott appeared outside the corral the previous night? If he had been coming to stop her and Kathy, he wouldn't have bothered hauling his tack with him, would he? He'd have been planning on herding them straight back inside. For that matter, why had he, of all the people at the castle, been the one to receive Alan's message that evening? And had that message actually been for her, or had her part of it merely been a postscript?

It was beginning to look as though the appropriately nicknamed Smoke really had been heading out on a moonlight ride when he had been bushwhacked by the equally well named Cat Kildare. But where had he been intending to ride before Pedro and Kid Connors reshuffled his plans for him? To a meeting with a quasilegal posse of mixed-blood Comanche Highlanders led by one of the most infuriating men alive?

No. Scratch that. He wasn't one of the most infuriating men alive. He was *the* most infuriating man—alive or dead!

And he must have read in those flashing emerald eyes that he was perilously close to becoming the latter, for he hastily released her hands and began cautiously backing toward the door.

"Damn you," Dorcas said, advancing toward him. "Just how long were you going to stand there letting me try to convince you of all the things you already knew?"

"Like what?" Alan stalled, a wary smile touching his lips and a warier look filling his eyes.

"For starters, like the fact that Smoke Elliott is a lawman—one you've secretly been cooperating with, so the pact is in no real danger after all. Your father may not be insane. And you don't think he's a murderer any more than I do!"

"Ah, but I never argued with you about Smoke being a Ranger, now did I, dear?"

"No, but you called him Smoke before I had ever mentioned his nickname."

"Was that where I made my mistake?" he muttered half to himself, stepping backward into the passage.

"Your mistake," she hissed through tightly clenched teeth, "was in thinking you could play me for an idiot!"

"Never! An idiot is absolutely the last thing I've ever considered you. It astounds me, the way you manage to deduce so much from so little. 'Tis just that I wanted your thoughts on the matter—to give me a bit more ammunition for my coming fight. And I've noticed that you do seem to come up with your most creative ideas when under fire, as it were. I was simply playing devil's advocate to stimulate your—"

He broke off quickly to deflect her hand as she swung at him, catching it neatly and planting a warm kiss in the center of her palm. "I'd be careful of that. Remember what happened the last time you tried to slap me," he said, grinning.

"Get out! Leave me alone, you . . . you . . ." Words failed her as she yanked her hand free and shoved hard at his chest. Grabbing for the door the instant he was clear of it, she slammed it shut in his face, completely forgetting, in her rage, that she was on the wrong side of it. It was the scraping of the key re-securing the lock that reminded her.

"Aye, dear. I'm afraid I'll have to for a bit. I've some

tricky business to deal with now, and I'd prefer you well clear of it," Alan apologized through the grill. " 'Twas nice of Uncle Angus to leave the key in the lock, though," he added, deftly pocketing it. "Makes me feel doubly bad about the trap I've decided to set for him. Your thinking my father and I were twins gave me the idea for it, in fact. We do seem much alike, I suppose—save for the nose. His was broken in a Pawnee raid years ago; that's why it looks rather like a squashed potato. But our claymore combats are fought in partial armor, you see. And with my helmet's visor down, I daresay Uncle Angus'll never suspect 'tis me inside it."

Before she could gather enough breath for a good, solid scream, he was down the passage, down the steps, and downright depressingly out of earshot.

Bloody hell, Dorcas thought, borrowing the curse from the dark-haired cause of it, and nearly giving in to tears until she remembered her own key. Fishing it out of her bodice, she swiftly felt for the keyhole on her side of the door.

And felt.

And felt.

And felt . . .

"Bloody hell!" she sobbed aloud as she realized why her grandmother Elspeth hadn't been able to use her skeleton key to save herself when she had been imprisoned in this same tower.

A one-holed lock. It could only be opened from the outside.

Or had that been done since Elspeth's time? No, she remembered now. That was part of the story. A part the Castle MacAllisters had never realized, in fact, having never found out about the key.

Elspeth's cat Caliban had initially been shut in the tower with her, and to alert her lover of her danger, she had ripped loose the hem of her frock and used it to tie

273

her secret key around the cat's neck. The tree had been so much smaller then; Caliban had had to leap down almost one-and-a-half stories to reach its top branches. But he had made it to the ground, outmaneuvered several pairs of kilted legs, and, somehow, found his way to the Comanche encampment where Jeremy Earnshaw was staying with his blood brother, the Panther.

"Otherwise Elspeth would have been burned, never having the chance to produce Zachary Earnshaw, who helped produce me, thereby allowing me the chance to be here and go through the whole nightmare all over again," Dorcas mumbled to herself, sinking down onto one of the chamber's main furnishings—the pile of straw so musty she was sure it hadn't been changed since her grandmother's stay.

"Though, of course, there are a few minor modifications in my situation," she continued, hurriedly vacating the straw when several mice and one genuine rat ran out of it. "Elspeth was here awaiting her own death and worrying whether a particular man would be able to rescue her in time. I'm here awaiting a particular man's death and worrying if I'll be able to escape in time to kill him first for being so impossibly pigheaded!"

Alan had no idea what he was walking into. And worse than that, neither did she. There was a trap being set, all right—she could feel it. But whether it was being baited by Alan or *for* him, she no longer had any idea.

"I thought I finally had everything so neatly pieced together, but it's all breaking apart on me," she complained, staring at the iridescent spider again, but seeing, perversely, only taunting images of squashed potatoes floating in vats of sticky brown beer.

"Why did Uncle Angus ever suspect Alan?"

It was back in the bedchamber, wasn't it, that Alan had told her how, when Angus had first found Heather's body with Wild Horse nearby, he had thought, for one awful moment, that he was looking at his nephew? But if Angus knew Wild Horse and Heather were together, why would he make such a mistake? Unless . . .

"Well, that explains the beer, anyway. I guess I owe Uncle Angus an apology," she muttered, kicking through the straw and upsetting several more rodents as she paced anxiously about the cell.

Someone else had obviously been out on the prairie that day. Someone who was probably a better shot than he was a card player and who had mistaken Wild Horse for his son even before Angus had. Then, to cover his own act of vengeance, that same someone had arrived back at the castle with a full-blown story of how he had seen Alan and Heather engaged in some heated conflict— that it had looked as though they were on the verge of killing one another. A ridiculous story, of course, but it had been good enough to send the already worried Angus riding out to survey the situation for himself.

"What's really ridiculous, though, is that the idiot is still telling that story to any new ears he can catch across the poker table. If it wasn't so appalling, it would be comical," Dorcas mused aloud, reaching down to scratch between velvet ears as four black paws fell into step alongside her.

"Not now, angel, I'm trying to think. Why don't you make yourself useful and chase some of these mice. Their squeaking is starting to annoy me-*ee!*" she finished on a startled squeak herself.

"Hello, Caliban. I suppose I should have been expecting you to show up about now."

He purred as she scooped him into a mutually satisfying hug.

"My father once told me all about you incredibly clever little wildcats with the courage of panthers and a life span of thirty or more years, but I never quite believed him until now. Did you know there aren't any of you left

275

in Scotland? You may be the last of your kind. Is that why you've lived so long, because you can't bear for your breed to die out? I've heard that some of your relatives actually made it to forty, but you must be over fifty by now. That's like a person living well past a hundred. No wonder they all think you're a demon!" she said, shaking her head as Elspeth's cat leapt out of her arms and padded to the window.

Her stomach suddenly feeling like a lead weight, Dorcas padded after him. The tree was her only option, of course. She had realized that the moment she'd discovered the skeleton key wouldn't get her out of the cell.

"Yes, I suppose I've been expecting this—Caliban! What's the matter with you?"

Back arched in front of the window, he was blocking her exit from it, hissing and spitting as if he thought he really was a demon.

"Believe me, I'm well aware that even if I survive the climb, the final drop will probably kill me. But at least it'll be faster than being tortured to death in the dungeon. Which is undoubtedly what Uncle Angus will do to me, if I let him carve Alan up with a claymore. I appreciate your concern, but there's nothing else I can do. So be a good boy and get out of the way."

Tucking up her skirts to protect them from the branches and lowering her eyes to protect them from the sight of her own coming demise, she fumbled the agitated cat aside, squirmed through the window crevice, and blindly grappled her way down . . . down . . . dizzyingly down to the last, long leap.

She gasped when that leap landed her, once again, in a waiting pair of muscular MacAllister Comanche arms.

"Alan!"

"Guess again," a rusty voice said close to her ear.

Very slowly, as if delay itself might change what she knew she would see, Dorcas opened her eyes and peered up into the dusky face of Wild Horse—a face that seemed to be superimposed, for an instant, over another, covering it like a translucent mask. The underlying image was gone almost before she could blink, but it had been visible long enough for her to be certain it was a face she had seen twice before. Once that morning, when her wits were too scattered to fully recognize it, and once in an old tintype of his parents her father had shown her—the same day, in fact, he had told her the story of Elspeth and the Panther.

"I don't have to guess. I know who you are," she whispered, realizing that all her original fears had been correct. There *was* a diabolical presence and a form of possession at work here. Someone *had* been toying with her mind. And a trap had been set for an unwary quarry. It was all just as she had suspected. The only point she had missed somehow was that this evening's quarry would turn out to be herself.

"You're a perversion. A paradox. A freak of fate," she told him. "How it happened, I can hardly even imagine— and I know more of the story than most—but you're Jeremy Earnshaw's mind in Wild Horse's body. That's who you are."

"Clever girl," he said, lowering her to her feet and resting his hands on her shoulders. "Now you get to ask me a question."

"Only one?"

The face above hers stretched into a mirthless grin. "Well, one for starters. And we'll see where that leads us."

I know where it's leading, Dorcas thought, staring up at him and realizing that she was looking straight into the eyes of genuine, cold-blooded insanity.

"Then, for starters, I want to know where Wild Horse is," she said, amazing herself that she could speak the words so calmly, when her heart seemed to be trying to hammer its way out through her throat.

The grin twisted into a slight frown. "You disappoint me. I was hoping you would ask who *you* were. . . . Well, no matter." He shrugged. "This question is a good one, too. And one I'm anxious to find an answer for it myself. Where do any of us go when we die?"

"Are you telling me he . . . his mind and spirit, that is, are . . . gone?"

"That's a second question, by the way, and it's really my turn now. But, yes," he replied, "the former occupant of this fleshy prison is no longer with us. He escaped it the night you arrived. A lucky coincidence for me, since I had just managed to escape from my own beastly confinement in that wretched piece of metal. I was able to enter his body at the exact moment his mind departed, but right before his heart stopped beating . . . Though, if I'd realized what I was getting myself into, I might have thought twice about it. Did you know there's a bullet lodged in this brain?" he asked, his left hand bearing down harder on her shoulder as the right tangled in Wild Horse's thick forelock. "How the man survived so long with what little mind he must have had left can only be one of the Devil's miracles. The poor fellow must have suffered the most hellish headaches. I know I've had one since being in here," he murmured, wincing with the obvious pain of it. "Fortunately, it'll soon be over."

"You're not planning on staying, then?" Dorcas asked, her eyes flickering upward and quickly down again, as a slight rustling overhead drew her attention for an instant.

"A *third* question? Oh, well, I suppose I can afford to be generous." He sighed. "No, I'll shortly be free of earthly aches. I'm going to cut this walking torture chamber's throat and release myself into blessed oblivion," he explained, his hands beginning to shift. "But first I'm going to perform the same favor for you, my dear, darling . . . *disloyal Elspeth!*"

Before she could even gasp, his grip was biting into her windpipe and razor-sharp steel glinted a deadly arc upward from his belt sheath to her throat.

"I promised you this would happen, didn't I, if you chose that heathen over me?" he hissed, making a slow practice slice from one ear to the other with the blade held a hairsbreadth from her flesh. "The thought of sending you to hell has been my only solace during these endless, empty years of blackness and cold—the only thing that's kept my mind functioning through its torment. I could have killed you almost any time these past days, you know. I was planning on killing you this morning at that ranch I followed you to . . . but I decided I wanted you to remember, first, who you were. I wanted you to know the anguish of what you and your Comanche lover did to me!"

"They did nothing to you!" Dorcas managed to get out, her voice barely more than a rasp and her eyes darting frantically from his to the lower branches of the tree. "You did it to yourself when you secretly told the MacAllisters who had freed their prisoner. Then you sealed it by trying to kill Elspeth yourself, when she was helpless at the stake. The Panther did the only thing he could to save her. And he paid dearly for it. They both paid! But I'm not her. I'm only her granddaughter. Can't you see that? I'm *not* Elspeth!"

"You may be right. . . . Perhaps Jezebel would be a more appropriate name for you."

Jerking her half off her feet, he swung the knife back for the fatal stroke, quoting righteously, "Thou shalt not suffer a witch to live . . ."

His words became an unholy scream as the witch's demon dropped out of the tree onto his head.

The grip on her throat released, and Dorcas stumbled

backward, grappling a dizzy moment for breath and balance. Then, like a snared bird escaping through a sudden break in the net, she turned and flew across the castle's dark, deserted inner yard toward the gate to the outer court. Toward a blaze of torches where she doubted her attacker would follow. Toward a circle of fierce-eyed kilted men gathered to witness an ancient ritual. Toward clashing claymores, old grievances, and fresh fears. Toward Alan, in the center of it all.

Only . . .

He wasn't.

Bursting from the inner to the outer courtyard, she staggered to a gasping halt. The torches, fierce eyes, ancient ritual, and grievances were there as expected. But the fear was her own, because in the center of it all stood a large stake piled high about with smoking brush. And tied to it was a girl not too unlike herself, who kept flickering in and out of the picture like a candle flame nearly snuffed by a draft.

Was this an illusion created by Jeremy Earnshaw? One of the mind-control tricks he had learned from the Panther, before blind jealousy twisted friendship into hate?

It might be. For she thought she could feel his will prickling at the edge of her consciousness, just as she had felt it before these past days. Was he trying to goad her back through the gate? Back through the dark? Back into the arms of death? This had to be some kind of hypnotic projection. It was too like those muddled memories and dreams she now realized he had been using to manipulate and confuse her. But it wouldn't work, Dorcas told herself, setting her feet and her resolve. She would deny this vision as she had the others.

She was still denying it even as several sets of heavy hands grabbed her and began dragging her toward the stake. It was an unusually tactile vision, apparently.

"Nice of her tae spare us th' bother o'fetchin' her, ain't

it? I'd check th' vats, tho, if I wurr ye, Geordie. No tellin'
whut mischief she wuz makin' on th' way here." One of
the visions laughed. "She feels dry enoof, but witches can
spoil beer wi' a look, sae I've hurd."

"Shut yoor face, ye blatherin' arse! If·ye make mock
o' this, sum'll suspect tain't real."

Real? . . . As an opiate-soaked rag was stuffed into her
mouth, Dorcas knew it was all too real. Digging in her
heels, she began a furious and ultimately futile battle to
break free, scarcely noticing when her bodice ripped and
a slender piece of iron dropped out. Not even certain she
had seen the flash of black that retrieved it and streaked
off, until she heard someone cry out.

"There be more proof of her sorceries! D'ye see?"

"See whut?"

"Th' demon! Air ye blind?"

"Nay, but ye mun be. 'Tis nuthin' there."

" 'Tis th' demon, I tell ye!"

"Ahh, yoor daft."

"Daft, am I? 'Tis Satan desertin' his own!"

"Run, Caliban!"

The last was from her, as she dislodged the sickly
sweet gag for a moment. Though where her furred em-
issary was going with the key . . . *Alan?* she wondered,
and tossed hope aside with the thought.

Wherever he was, Alan wouldn't know what the key
meant or even that it was from her. Her father would
recognize it, but she doubted he would relate it to a murderous replay of history like this. As far as she could
figure, there was only one soul nearby who would be able
to read that small metal message, as he had once before.
But would the cat dare take it to him? He might, if he
thought it was the only chance to spare her.

He'd be right, too, she realized wretchedly, as thick
cords lashed her tightly to the stake. Jeremy Earnshaw
in Wild Horse's powerful body probably would be able

to free her. And a slashed throat would be easier than a slow, agonizing burn.

"Clever girl, Jezebel. I'm coming!"

The words sounded clearly in her head at the same instant murky billows of smoke swirled up, choking and blinding her, and the courtyard exploded in earsplitting pandemonium.

Screaming out a warning, she watched in horror as two forms collided in a locking of limbs and minds that nearly tore her own skull apart with its force. Suffocating in the smoke and blinded by terror, she never knew when it was over, or who had pushed to her side, until her sliced bonds dropped away and she fell forward out of a nightmare into the sound of his voice calling her name. . . .

"Dorcas!"

Chapter Thirteen

"All right, if someone will oblige me with a drumroll," Kathleen Kildare was saying, as the evening shadows deepened in the castle's inner court, "I'll attempt to repeat this tangled little epic and see if I've gotten all the threads sorted out."

Dorcas humored her with a halfhearted thrumming of fingers against the side of the wooden bench they were stationed on. Tucked between a wall and the end of the main keep's entrance ramp, it provided a welcome spot to enjoy the sunset breezes without being on public display. Neither female was much in the mood for company at the moment, beyond the company they could offer each other.

"First," Kathy began, after dramatically clearing her throat. "First . . . and I hope you'll forgive me for starting with the part that concerns myself . . . first"—she raised one forefinger higher—"Captain Simon Elliott of the Texas Rangers, better known as Smoke because of his inscrutable and cryptic ways—though if you ask me, it's really more because being near him makes a person want to break out in fits of coughing. At least, that's how he affects me . . . Anyway, he did not come here initially to spy on yours truly, much as it pains me to admit such a ruthless and undeserved slight to my professional ego. Nor did he come merely to aid Dr. Earnshaw. The insufferable Mr. Wizard does have a scientific background, is a former student of Dr. Earnshaw's, and has been assisting him, but all that was actually just a convenient cover for his true purpose. His true purpose being to discreetly observe castle life from the inside.

"Because . . ." The forefinger shot skyward a melodramatic moment before plummeting into her lap. "Because some overly zealous official at the state capital had received an anonymous letter claiming that Clan MacAllister has been taking too much upon itself, legally speaking, and advising that its special pact with Texas ought to be dissolved before the clan instigated a revolution. Or something equally embarrassing.

"We now know, of course, that provocative little warning was penned by Geordie. And the only thing that surprises me about that," she inserted thoughtfully, "is the idea that the imbecile knew how to write, in the first place.

"At any rate," she continued with a brief shake of her head, "That is why our brewer, with a little help from some of his best customers, organized that lovely barbecue for you last night. Taking advantage of the fact that most of the clan would be occupied far from the outer court with a trial by combat in the great hall, and having overheard enough of your shouting match with Uncle Angus to know that Captain Elliott would be arriving this morning with a marshal and deputies, he decided to give the authorities such a *hot* demonstration of clan tradition that it would *scotch* the whole pact for good—if you'll pardon the puns.

"Not because Geordie was anti-traditionalist, mind you, but because he was anti-Alan and Angus. He'd been wanting to pull the entire MacAllister hierarchy apart since the day Heather jilted him for Alan. Probably the only intelligent thing that poor girl ever did, too . . . though if he'd known you had guessed the truth about him, he would have had an even better reason. I find that wonderfully ironic, by the way—the fact that he didn't realize you had already pegged him for Heather's death and was trying to dispose of you anyway.

"Which . . ." The hand flitted up again for an instant, this time with the second finger joining the first. "Which brings us to Act Two, subtitled *What Really Happened on the Prairie that Day.*

"Unfortunately, we'll never be able to confront him with it, since he tripped into his own bonfire last night and went off like a Roman candle when one of his drunken cronies tried to put him out by dumping whiskey on him—very clumsy of them both, I must say—but it's certain now that Geordie was the one who murdered Heather, having first shot Wild Horse, thinking he was Alan, and leaving him for dead a short ways off.

"Aside from the other evidence—such as motive and that asinine story of his—what makes it certain is Wild Horse calling for beer all those years when he hates beer. With his mind virtually destroyed by his wound, it was the only way he had of naming the true culprit. Instead of saying 'Geordie the Brewer,' he just kept saying *beer*—an obvious clue, really. Alan probably would have caught it himself if he hadn't been so intent on suspecting his uncle—just as you did for awhile, and for the same reasons.

"All that came out during the combat, naturally. It's a pity you were so busy being burned at the stake that you missed it. I thoroughly enjoyed it. Especially the look on Uncle Angus's face when he realized it was Alan he had been trying to skewer.

"Not that the battle lasted very long. Having been taught claymore fighting by Angus himself, Alan knew all the old bear's tricks and had him disarmed within a dozen or so strokes. Then, for an entertaining few moments, the accusations clashed louder than their claymores—until Angus managed to convince Alan of his innocence by swearing it on the sacred honor of the clan.

"It was all so preposterous, I had to bite my tongue to keep from laughing out loud. I mean, the idea of Angus being a murderer! If either of you had asked me, I could have assured you he wasn't the type. He does have sort of a criminal nature, but it's more my sort. Uncle Angus is a master manipulator—a con artist." She grinned. "He'll grab any opportunity and twist it to his own advantage if he can. That's why you ended up here, even though you weren't the bride he'd ordered. He needed Alan married to produce an heir to continue the Mac-Allister line. You presented yourself, so he grabbed you. And then—knowing his nephew very well, apparently—he locked you in the tower, a rebellious captive, to clinch the deal. After all, what gallant knight in his right mind can resist falling in love with a beautiful and spirited damsel in distress? . . . Although I imagine the damsel turned out to be a bit more spirited than either of them had anticipated. You *are* something of a wild card, you know, Dorcas.

"As for the combat . . ." She launched blithely back into the tale. "At least it cleared the air between Alan and Angus. And it ended well enough—except for that one hairy moment when Alan was nearly crushed. I honestly think Uncle Angus is more dangerous in a friendly, forgiving mood than he is when he's angry. The man's hugs are lethal! For a second there, I expected Alan to pass out from lack of oxygen. He'd gone gray as a ghost and was staring over Angus's shoulder as if he'd just seen one, too. Then, all of a sudden—and without a word to anyone, mind you—he shoved free, snatched up his claymore, and went tearing out of the hall as if he'd been shot from a cannon.

"The rest of us stood there with our mouths hanging open, not knowing what to make of it, until Angus grabbed up his claymore, too, and went charging after him, bellowing the MacAllister battle cry. Which, of course, mobilized the entire assembly.

"We were too late to do much, though. By the time Angus and the rest of us reached the outer court, Alan had already turned it upside down and was cutting you free from the stake. Geordie was hardly more than a grease spot by then, and Wild Horse lay where Alan had thrown him. It appears he was the victim of a sudden heart attack. Molly said he was probably dead before he hit the ground.

"Which rolls us straight into Act Three, and the disturbing idea that Molly was more correct than she realized." Kathy sighed, holding three digits aloft.

"Wild Horse was dead before he hit the ground—several days' worth of before, in fact. Wild Horse—or what little was left of him by that time—had died not too long after you first arrived here. It was another who . . . who . . . Oh, I can't believe I'm actually going to say this," she groaned, "but it was someone else in Wild Horse's body who died last night when that body suddenly gave out.

"Which proves Molly correct again, I suppose—or half correct, anyway. Because somehow she knew the Panther had escaped death. She thought he had managed it through Caliban. Now it appears as if he did send his mind and spirit outward right before they destroyed his physical form—but not into the cat. And he didn't do it to save himself, either . . . he did it to save Elspeth.

"That's the part of the story Molly never knew—how insanely jealous Jeremy Earnshaw was. His desire for Elspeth was so possessive, he couldn't tolerate the idea of her even looking at another man. When she nursed the Panther all those weeks and then helped him escape, Jeremy thought she had done it out of passion for the man— that she had betrayed him with his own blood brother— and he vowed revenge.

"It was Jeremy who secretly informed Laird Stuart who had freed the Panther and denounced Elspeth as a witch. Not that he wanted the MacAllisters to kill her— he wanted that privilege for himself—but he knew the Panther would feel honor bound to save the woman who had previously saved him, and Jeremy planned to use the hysteria of that rescue as a cover to murder her and the Panther both.

"He had it all very neatly figured: Stick close by the Panther through the battle, pretend to stumble on the way to the stake, and pull his supposed rival down onto his knife. Then dart up again and slit Elspeth's throat, making it look as though his blade had simply slipped while he was trying to cut her free.

"What he intended after that we'll never know, however, because he never got that far. The Panther foiled him in round one by deflecting his knife thrust during that phony stumble. It hit Jeremy instead, sending his nose flying. That's how you managed to recognize him, even in Wild Horse's shell. The blow left a mark, apparently, that scarred not only his body but his spirit. Very symbolic, if you ask me, since what he had been trying to do was rather like cutting off one's nose to spite one's face.

"As for the rest of it, the Panther was now aware of Jeremy's true intentions but in a dismal position to stop him, with kilts and claymores swarming all over him. As he went down beneath them, he took a desperate chance on the only weapon he had left—his mind. Which seems to have been every bit as powerful as rumored. Perhaps more so.

"That horrible moment Molly remembers so well, with the echoing war cry and the bloodied frontiersman reeling madly toward Elspeth, then suddenly righting himself, cutting her off the stake and leaping onto a horse with her in his arms, was when it happened. But it wasn't Elspeth's frontiersman rescuing her at that moment. It wasn't a traitor and a jealous lover who moved East with her to keep her safe, who married her and fathered her son. It was a friend whose undying devotion caused him to give up his very identity.

"It was the Panther who, with that final scream, had thrown his entire consciousness forward and straight into Jeremy Earnshaw.

"And that's the end of the story," she finished, leaning wearily but triumphantly back. "Did I leave anything out?"

Only the part I didn't mention—the part about Jeremy's mind ending up trapped in Elspeth's key, which he'd been wearing around his neck when the Panther pushed him out of his body. It was probably the unstable voltage of the lamp the key had been placed in that suddenly released him. But you were so nice about accepting everything else, I didn't have the heart to inflict that part on you, Dorcas answered silently.

"Not a thing," she complimented aloud. "I can tell that you honestly do understand it all now."

"No. Not one single, solitary, syllable of it," Kathy declared. "But please . . ." Her hand lifted one final time in a gesture of appeal. "Let's not go over it again. After listening to you mulling it over for hours and hearing myself recite it twice, I don't think I can possibly bear another encore this evening. I just want to take one of

Molly's headache potions and escape into dreamless sleep. You ought to do the same."

Heaving one of her more dramatically executed sighs, she pulled forward and rose a little rockily to her feet.

"Don't sit here brooding too long. Alan will be back soon, I'm sure. A person can only ride so much of this prairie and then he has to come home. You'll be able to sort everything out when he does. Just because he wouldn't discuss anything last night, wouldn't stay in the room with you, and has been rather mysteriously gone since dawn doesn't necessarily mean that anything is wrong. You worry too much," she said, reaching out and ruffling Dorcas's cropped curls.

"You know, I'm almost sorry that Molly has taken over caring for Rosa, because having her to look after right now would, at least, give you something else to think about. But you have your father to thank for that, I suppose—he being the one who delivered Rosa to that eager Scottish pixie after you left her with him last night. Now that Molly has her clutches on the child, I doubt you'll get her back before she's twenty. It's a question of like being attracted to like. Molly and Rosa are so similar in size . . . Ah, that's better! I finally got a smile out of you. Hold that pose, and remember that laugh lines are always attractive, but worrying simply gives you crow's feet."

Looking as though no crow would dare leave its imprint on her own face, Kathy landed one more pat on the blond curls and ascended the ramp into the keep, causing Dorcas to wonder briefly just what she had up her elegant puffed sleeve—besides her derringer, of course. She knew Kathy had to be plotting something. Wanted for a remarkable assortment of creatively performed con games, her position was a little too precarious at the moment to warrant such calm behavior otherwise.

Angus had promised that he could pay any fines and

legally arrange for her to spend any incarceration she might be facing in the protective shadow of Castle MacAllister. But the exchange for such leniency was marrying one of his sons. And the alternative to it was being hauled in by Captain Elliott for what would probably turn out to be a short trial and a long prison term.

Why the latter hadn't already happened, in fact, was something to be considered. Kathy claimed that she had been on her way to breakfast that morning when Simon had returned with the wagons and men to cart off the prairie pirates. And when she had inadvertently stumbled upon him and a marshal just outside the kitchen, and the marshal had seemed on the verge of recognizing her, Simon had quickly introduced her as Mary Mac-Allister, lately arrived from Boston, and directed the other lawman's attention elsewhere. She had said it was because Elliott wanted the glory of bringing her in all for himself, but somehow Dorcas didn't think that kind of glory was quite what Captain Elliott was after.

And what am I after? she wondered.

Easy answers to a few last uneasy questions? An end to depressing doubts and growing anxiety? A Rock of Gibraltar embrace holding her close?

"Actually, if I can just have that last, I'd cheerfully forego everything else," she pleaded aloud, bowing her head over fervently clasped hands. "I wouldn't even care where he's been or why he left me the way he did. If I can just have him safely back, I'll never need another thing."

"Granted," a husky voice replied from several feet in front of her. "I've always wanted to be the answer to a lovely lady's prayer."

Suddenly blurred by hot tears of relief, green eyes gazed up into amber gold. Widened . . . blinked . . . and narrowed into an I-should-have-guessed-it-sooner stare. There were *four* amber orbs glittering down at her. And she hadn't fallen into any vats recently, either.

Well, this answered the question of how Alan had realized her danger the previous night. Although it raised some new ones.

"I suppose you think you've been very clever," she said. She was not addressing the tall figure in the linen shirt, suede vest, and incorrigibly form-fitting trousers, however. "Come here, you little—What's got into him?"

Dropping her outstretched hands in bewilderment, she sank back onto the bench as Caliban leapt off Alan's muscular shoulder, darted through a hole in a nearby wall, and disappeared from view.

"Him? Whatever are you talking about?" Grinning like a cat himself, Alan sank down next to her, pressing his thigh provocatively against hers.

"I suppose you think you've been clever, too. You might have told me you and he were friends. It would have saved me a lot of worry last night," she said. She stifled a gasp as his arm deliberately brushed her breast.

What the . . . ?

It wasn't that the attention was unwelcome—rather the opposite, actually. But all things considered, it was a trifle . . . suspicious.

"What's the matter?" he asked, matching her inch-for-inch as she began scooting nervously away from him. "Your husband has been gone all day and he doesn't even get a kiss for his return?"

Dorcas, you're being an idiot, she told herself, trying not to flinch as his hands slipped warmly about her waist, catching her before she tumbled right off the end of the bench. This was exactly what she had been longing for, wasn't it?

"I'm sorry. It's just that after the way you behaved last night . . . I guess I'm a bit confused," she offered, forcing a smile at her own sudden fancies. Ridiculous fancies, really, about incongruous things: too convenient heart attacks; too easy answers to prayers; a too familiar amber gaze that somehow didn't seem quite so familiar anymore . . . "I must still be suffering from smoke inhalation. It's making me imagine odd things."

It has to be that, she thought, relaxing into his hold as he pulled her close. This was definitely Alan, after all—outside and in. She could feel his unmistakable energy as clearly as she could feel the rest of him. Alan's arms . . . Alan's chest . . . Alan's lips . . .

"Never mind about last night," those sensuous lips murmured. "I was only tired and upset. I didn't know what I was saying."

Something with the weight of a stone plummeted straight down to her heels. It was her heart. Because no one could have known what Alan had said the previous night. That was the whole wretched point. He hadn't *said* anything. After carrying her, choking and dazed and desperate for him, back to their room, he had simply left her there with Kathy and Molly and a flustered chambermaid. He hadn't said a word to any of them. He hadn't even offered a backward glance.

Oh, I do hate being right so often, she moaned inwardly, feeling her blood turn to ice as his embrace tightened.

"How did you do this?" she demanded, bracing her hands against that granite chest and straining backward as Alan's lips sought to possess hers.

A low chuckle rumbled in her ears—from Alan's throat, but not from Alan. "You're a clever girl. Figure it out for yourself."

I already have. It's what I've been worrying about all day, she thought, the murky questions and their suddenly too clear answers hitting her like a fist.

Herself at the stake . . . Alan storming like the wrath of God into the outer court . . . everyone startled by the sight of a bloodied Wild Horse leaping out of the shadows and onto his son's back . . . and no one save herself and the two combatants themselves realizing that the struggle was more mental than physical. Alan had thrown the man off and he'd dropped lifeless to the ground.

"But it wasn't an ordinary heart attack," she said aloud. "If Wild Horse's heart had been that fragile, it would have quit the same time, or even before, his brain did, and you never would have had the chance to make use of him. The reason his body died last night is because you abandoned it during the fight. Without a mind inside to keep it functioning, it simply stopped."

And that is why Alan was so strange and withdrawn afterward, she added silently. Because, by then, he had been under some sort of internal siege, trying to shove out the consciousness that had invaded his.

"This will never work, you know. Even if you kill me now to keep me from telling, Angus and the others will still recognize that you're not Alan," she warned, her voice barely above a whisper.

"Oh, I hardly think so." Jeremy Earnshaw grinned down at her as Alan's arms held her fast. "I've had a very instructive day in here, picking this body's brain clean. I probably know more about your miserable mix-breed husband than he knows himself. I certainly know enough to give a convincing show that I'm Alan MacAllister. As for killing you . . . now *why* would I want to do that?" he asked, looking mildly wounded that she could even suggest such a thing.

"You're so clever—you figure it out," Dorcas said, her muscles starting to ache from the tension of trying to push free.

"Mmm . . . Yes, I do understand your point. But if I'm prepared to let bygones be bygones, I don't see why you can't," he said amiably. "I'll admit I made a mistake last night, but I couldn't think clearly with that body's beastly headache hammering away at me. I just wasn't myself. I haven't been totally myself for quite some time," he said, chuckling at his own joke. "I'm beginning to feel very much at home in this fine, healthy form, however. Especially since discovering that it's from my enemy's own bloodline. Did you know that your husband's redskinned grandmother was the Panther's daughter? That's where he got these curious eyes from. The literal translation of his Comanche name, Eyes of the Cat, is He who has eyes like the Panther. I find it tremendously gratifying having possession of this body . . . since its great-grandfather had possession of mine for so long. It's such poetic justice. Don't you agree?"

"No."

The grin beaming down at her hardened into a tight line. "Ah, well, you will, my girl. You'll learn to agree with whatever I say or do—quickly and without question. That's the other part of my justice, you see. As the sins of the parents are visited on the children, I'm going to make you pay for your trollop grandmother's crimes. That's why I won't kill you. That would be far too easy. What I am going to do," he whispered seductively into her ear, "is make your life a living hell from now on."

"You're too late," she whispered back, abruptly going limp against him in a seeming numbness of despair. "With Alan gone, my life's worse than hell already. If you won't kill me, I'll simply kill myself."

"Now what would be the fun of that?" he asked, one hand tangling roughly in her hair and jerking her face back up to his. "You wouldn't want to destroy all my hopes of hearing you beg for mercy night after night, would you? I've been so looking forward to it."

"You'll be looking forever if you expect to get any begging out of me. Dead people are beyond begging."

"Such melodrama! Would it convince you to stay alive if I told you that your lover still lives, too? Whether or not he stays that way, however, depends upon you. Any more foolishness and I'll toss his sleeping mind into a cockroach and crush it under the heel of his own boot."

"Sleeping?" It was exactly the information she had been trying to goad out of him, but she gave no sign of it. "Is that how you gained control, then?"

"Oh, I would have managed it in any case. I learned mind control from a master, after all; I was taught by the Panther himself. But Alan's exhaustion did make things easier. The moron ran himself and his stallion ragged today, trying to gallop me out of his head—and then fell asleep when he stopped for a moment to drink! That's when I moved to the front. Lucky thing, too, or he might have toppled face-first into that spring and drowned."

"How very convenient," she murmured, letting herself sink closer into him, as those no longer familiar eyes gleamed wolfishly into hers. "But what makes you think he won't do the same to you when you fall asleep?"

"Because I'm not referring to an ordinary slumber. This is more like a coma." He chuckled again. "And I can keep him in it 'til doomsday!"

I wonder . . . He had fallen asleep, had he? It sounded so simple, almost like something one would read about in a fairy tale. Scenes from Cinderella . . . Snow White . . . Sleeping Beauty . . . drifted curiously past her inner eye, as a ravenous mouth ground painfully down and powerful arms squeezed her in a vise.

Alan's arms . . .

Alan's lips . . .

Jeremy Earnshaw's kiss—hungry, tortured, terrifyingly tragic.

Her own kiss in response—searing, searching, screaming into his head with the full force of her love—

Alan MacAllister! Wake up, blast it!

And a blast it was, as two minds raged together, locking horns on the edge of oblivion—writhing, twisting, straining, tumbling—until one tried furiously to kick loose and was knocked inescapably over the brink into eternity. And the remaining one completed a kiss that made his wife feel that she had just fallen out of the arms of Hell straight into the heart of Paradise.

"Dorcas?"

As the clouds cleared, pulses slowed, and two souls finally surfaced for air, those well-known amber eyes stared down in stunned bewilderment.

"Dorcas, what the devil are you doing all the way out here?"

"I was thirsty and wanted a nice, cool drink of spring water," she said, unsure whether to laugh, cry, or kiss him again. She attempted all three simultaneously.

The combination jolted their recipient into a full though slightly soggy awareness of where he was.

"Good God," he breathed, dragging himself reluctantly out of the second embrace to gaze at Dorcas clinging to his neck, the adobe towers standing sentinel in the evening sky. A minor commotion was just beginning at the long ramp up to the keep. Then he looked back at the one part of it all that seemed to hold any real interest for him: two emerald green eyes shining ecstatically into his.

"I feel as if I've just fought my way through a bloody nightmare," he muttered, only just beginning to realize that he had. "And I'm half thinking I'd like to do the whole thing over again, simply for the pure joy of waking and seeing you."

"Well, we could repeat the waking part," she offered, sliding closer to him. "I woke you with a kiss, you know."

"Was that a kiss?" He chuckled softly, shifting his own position to better meet hers. "It felt like a keg of gunpowder going off inside me."

"The best kisses are supposed to feel like that, aren't they?" Burying her fingers in his hair, she began drawing his head down to hers. "Anyway, it did the trick. Welcome back, Sleeping Beauty."

Her words halted his descent barely a breath above her mouth.

"Men aren't supposed to be beautiful, dear," she was informed, with a teasing nip at her lower lip. "There's only one beauty here. And I'm looking at her."

"Then you're wasting precious moments that could be spent kissing her," he was warmly informed in return.

"Ah, *witnesses*—exactly what we need!" a delighted voice informed the world at large.

Or was that statement more specifically for the benefit of the person trudging down the ramp a short pace ahead of the voice? A tall, well-built, well-dressed man with smoky gray eyes that were really smoking at that moment.

"Dorcas, guess what? Simon has asked me to marry him and I've accepted!"

"I have not!"

"Oh, all right. If you're going to quibble, perhaps I *did* exaggerate that part a teensy bit," Kathy Kildare conceded with a slight pout as she pulled herself and Elliott to a dramatic halt before the bench. "But the rest is true." She quickly brightened. "I *have* agreed to marry you— whose ever idea it was—so why split hairs? It's such a perfect solution. If I marry you, I won't be able to marry any of Angus's toads—I mean sons. And you're not the sort of man to cart his own wife off to prison—"

"Aren't I?"

Her laughter rippled like spring rain. Soaking him to the skin, if one were to judge by his expression.

"Honestly, Smoke darling, don't be dim. You're far too much of a gentleman for that. Besides, it would tarnish your sterling reputation to have Mrs. Simon Elliott behind bars. So let's have no more dillydallying. You know you're mad for me anyway, you silly thing."

"Once again, you've gotten part of it right, little girl," he said, grinning dangerously. "I am definitely mad."

Her only response was to level the derringer she held on him and recite clearly, "I, Kathleen Kildare, promise to be your wife, Simon Elliott. . . . Was that adequate, Laird Alan?" she asked with a guileless batting of blue eyes.

" 'Twill serve," he replied, a slight twitching at the corners of his mouth.

"You're a big help," the other man said.

"Don't be such a grouch," Kathy chided him. "It's your turn now."

"And what if I refuse?" That slow grin mocked her. "You're not really looking for a murder charge, are you?"

"Of course not." The aim of the derringer deliberately dropped to a point several inches below his navel. "Who said anything about murder? I wouldn't kill you, honey boy—just *maim* you." She smiled sweetly. "Now make up your mind. It's either marry me or forget about women altogether."

The slow grin abruptly relaxed into a long, low laugh. "Oh, what the hell. We're hardly talking a bona-fide union, anyway. You do realize that don't you, pussycat— that a contract agreed to under duress isn't legally binding?"

"Ah . . . Simon—" Alan began.

"Please! No comments from the peanut gallery," Simon said, waving him off. "Since you've obviously no intention of helping here, MacAllister, just let me get it over with. . . . I, Simon Elliott, promise to be your husband, Kathleen Kildare. Now give me that damned derringer!" he ordered, latching on to her wrist with one hand while swiftly plucking the weapon loose with the other. "You are under arrest, Miss Kildare!"

"Mrs. Elliott," she corrected, unperturbed. "Threat or no, it's a proper marriage under MacAllister law. To make it otherwise, Alan would have to declare his own wedding invalid, since he employed . . . um . . . similar tactics."

"Aye, lad. I did try to warn you."

"I'm afraid you've put your foot in it, Captain Elliott." Dorcas grinned, unable to resist telling him the same thing he had once told her.

"Very cute." He grinned wryly back. "Why don't you come kiss the groom, then, Lady Dorcas? Perhaps we could start a new tradition."

"Not if you want to keep your front teeth, laddie," Alan said, with the biggest grin of all. "I'd be thinking of kissing your own bonny bride if I were you."

"Oh . . . Do I *have* to?" Simon asked, his grin going sour.

"Absolutely not!" Kathy assured him, suddenly the soul of accommodation. "You don't have to do anything of the kind. I've always thought it a rather tiresome custom, myself. And so unhygenic. Why—"

"On the other hand," he said, pivoting sharply and raking her from head to toe with a look that had sent sterner females than herself scurrying for the smelling salts, "seeing as we *are* married, I suppose it'll have to happen sooner or later."

"There's no need to be hasty about it. Later is fine with me," she said, nervously backing away as he stalked toward her. "I'd been thinking more in terms of a . . . a Platonic sort of marriage, anyway. Have you read much Plato, by any chance?" she inquired hopefully.

"Tons of him. I generally read a lot at night, you see— to help me sleep. Of course, now that I have a wife, I'll have something else to do to help me sleep. Won't I, *Mrs. Elliott?*"

"Oh, God," Mrs. Elliott gulped, turning to flee just a little too late. Leaning away with all her weight, she was reeled back by a granite grip on her forearm. "You know, maybe this wasn't such a wonderful idea after all," she tried weakly.

"On the contrary, it's beginning to appeal to me more and more," a bedroom baritone told her.

By the time he was through kissing her, she looked fried to a cinder—fully smoked (so to speak) and hanging up to dry.

"There! Now you know what you've let yourself in for."

"I do?" Kathy asked vaguely, hanging in his arms like a rag doll.

"Yes. And you'd better get used to it, Mrs. Elliott, because there's a lot more where that came from!"

"There is?" she asked blankly.

"You can bet your bustle there is, pussycat! I'm going to keep you so occupied from now on, you won't have the energy to even think about getting into trouble."

"I won't?"

"Never mind, Kathleen. We'll discuss this again in the morning," he said, swinging her completely off her feet and high against his chest. "For now, just say good night to the MacAllisters and we'll be off to beddy-bye."

Turning a glassy-eyed stare toward Alan and Dorcas, she mumbled obediently, "Good night to the Mac-Allisters and we'll be off to beddy-bye."

"Close enough." Simon chuckled. With a parting grin at the couple on the bench, he carried Kathy up the ramp and into the keep.

"I'm impressed," Alan remarked, gazing after them.

So am I, Dorcas thought, shaking her head at the wink Kathy had shot her over Elliott's shoulder.

"What is that sly little Cat up to now?" she wondered aloud, leaning into a muscular torso as a warm arm began drawing her close.

"Cat?" The arm about her suddenly stiffened. "Bloody

hell, I'd almost forgotten," Alan muttered, sounding as if he wished he had.

"Forgotten what?" Dorcas asked, staring up in concern at a face gone ashen. "You're giving me goose bumps. Whatever's the matter? You look as if you've seen a ghost."

His laugh nearly tumbled them both onto the ground.

"Do you ever get tired of hitting so many bull's-eyes with that well-aimed mind of yours?" he choked out, setting the bench square again.

"Please don't mention anything for a while about minds being *aimed* anywhere," she said flatly.

"I'll agree to that if you'll promise to say nothing of cats or ghosts . . . because that's how I realized your danger last night," he admitted reluctantly. "A big, black tom suddenly appeared in the entrance to the great hall and sat there staring at me. Looking into his eyes, I somehow just knew what was happening in the outer court. . . . But I'm certain no one saw that cat save myself."

This time it was Dorcas's laughter that almost landed them in a heap.

"Oh, don't tell me that you think he's a demon, too! I assumed you knew all about him. Why else would he have been riding around on your shoulder—" she began, then cut herself off.

Why else, indeed?

Oh, I'm such an idiot. That makes twice now he tried to warn me about Jeremy, and twice that I ignored him, she mused silently. *Thank goodness Alan showed better sense!*

Grinning up at him, she explained, "Your castle *is* haunted, but not by some devil spirit in a cat suit. Caliban is more like a guardian angel. An earthly angel, though—a flesh-and-blood one. I'm surprised Molly has never told you his heritage. She must be familiar with his breed. It's very rare and nearly extinct now, but—"

"Dorcas, if you're referring to what I think you are, that cat's breed *is* extinct. My grandmother herself can tell you how—"

"Who? Molly? Oh, my, yes! She's an absolute treasure trove of information. She'll be able to tell you all sorts of fascinating things. You're so lucky to have her for a grandmother-in-law, Dorcas," a cheery voice interjected as its owner leaped lightly off the ramp and ran past carrying a small box. "Do say good-bye to her for me, won't you? And name your daughters after me! You can call them Mary, Cassandra, Monique . . . ."

"Oh, no!" Dorcas exclaimed, scrambling out of Alan's arms and racing after her.

"Dorcas!" he shouted. "What—"

"I have to stop her! That box is the disintegration ray my father's been working on—I'm sure of it!" she shouted back. "Kathy, *wait!* You don't know how to use that!"

"Yes, I do. Simon had it in his room, and when I asked him about it, he explained the whole process to me—the big show-off!" Kathy called over her shoulder. "It's safer than I thought it was, too. It doesn't disintegrate *every*-thing—just certain kinds of rock and sand. I can make a fortune with this!"

"You won't live long enough to make anything!" a disheveled Simon Elliott growled, lunging past Dorcas with remarkable speed, considering the mahogany head-board he was handcuffed to and dragging behind him. "Wait 'til I get my hands on you, you little alley cat!"

"However did he get his ankles free from the foot-board? I'm beginning to believe he *is* a wizard," Kathy muttered, holding the box forward and manipulating several buttons and levers as she darted straight for the nearest wall.

Without a sound, six feet of solid adobe instantly dissolved into a doorway-sized view of the foot bridge spanning the moat and the palisade beyond it.

And without a word, a two-legged cat was across the bridge, through another instant opening in the outer wall, and dashing for the corral, the lord and lady of the castle, a loudly cursing Texas Ranger, and a battered mahogany headboard hot on her heels. Never missing a stride, she vaulted two fences in her Kid Connors trousers and landed smoothly on a glossy black back.

"Thanks for your hospitality, Alan! Good luck with your new life, Dorcas!" she called as her mount sailed over the corral gate. "*Adíos, mi amor*—I'll take good care of Esmeralda for you!"

"Damn . . . Did you hear what she had the nerve to call me? *Mi amor*—her *love*," Simon said, his eyes like thunder clouds as he stared after her. "And the little minx has stolen my horse again!"

That's not all she's taken from you, Dorcas thought, watching him watch his wife disappear into the night. Judging by the man's expression, Dorcas knew Kathy had also stolen his heart. She wasn't sure, though, if Simon fully realized that fact yet.

"Never mind, lad. The best brides are worth a bit of a chase," Alan said, with a wink that turned his own bride bright pink. "As soon as we chop that bed off you, you can borrow my stallion. Even though she has a head start, he ought to be able to catch that wild mare of yours."

"You're right," Simon agreed, still staring intently into the night. "And he can outrun Petunia, too."

"The way he rides, he'll probably catch her before dawn. I hope he won't be too angry with her when he does," Dorcas said, approaching the new entrance in the bailey wall some long, lingering moments later. It had been a slow walk back from the corral—what with the stopping every few steps to kiss and cling and kiss again.

"I hope *she* won't be too angry with *him*," Alan replied, his chuckle rumbling against her as he pulled her into another embrace in the shelter of the wall's opening. "That's one wayward lassie Smoke's tied himself to."

"Tied!" Her eyes flashed accusingly at his. "Is that what marriage means to you? Being *tied* to someone?"

" 'Tis an idea you once had yourself, you know—that marriage is some sort of bondage."

"True," she conceded, beginning to understand where this might be leading as his arms drew her closer. "But I know different now, don't I?"

"Do you, dear? Honestly?"

"What do you think?" she teased, deciding to let him fish for it as long as possible. It was so deliciously cozy, after all, in that snug little tunnel her father's ray had created. And her feet had just discovered a convenient perch that allowed her to meet those captivating amber eyes on their own level—to say nothing of those captivating lips.

"I think . . ." the lips began, and then paused as the eyes blinked in surprise. "I think that either I've just shrunk or you've grown."

"Neither. I'm on a pedestal." She grinned. "There must have been something metal imbedded in this wall."

"Metal?"

"Yes," Dorcas said, instantly sorry she'd mentioned it. "This is a poor moment to discuss it, if you want my opinion, but the ray has no effect on metals. That's why it should be so useful for mining. It can uncover ore and extract it at the same ti-*ime*!" she squealed as he abruptly swung her off the perch and dropped to his knees.

"Alan, wh—"

"Bloody hell, this is it," he breathed, squinting through the shadows at the small iron casket on which she had been standing.

305

Suddenly shivering without even being sure why, she found herself inching away from it, weird prickles crawling over her like bugs and weirder premonitions widening her eyes into moons.

"This is . . . is what?" she choked, her own voice echoing in her ears like a ghost's.

"The Panther's ashes . . . and the cat's."

"No!"

Turning to flee, she felt a warm grip hauling her back by the wrist.

"This is what I was trying to tell you before—that Elspeth's cat never survived her rescue. A stray bullet caught him as he ran through the courtyard that day, and his body was burned along with the Panther's. They put all the ashes in this chest and sealed it into a wall—this wall," Alan said gently, pulling her down beside himself and locking her in an embrace that somehow did nothing to stop her shivering. "Your family couldn't have known that part of the story because it happened after Elspeth was carried off. And my grandmother usually omits it when she tells the tale. She knows the truth, mind you, but she prefers to ignore it. She admired the Panther's bravery and his loyalty to Elspeth so much, it's been a comfort to her all these years to pretend he escaped."

"There was no pretending about it," Dorcas said hollowly.

"Aye, dear. Jeremy wasn't the only one picking brains today, you know. I was able to read his memories even as he was reading mine. I understand now that the Panther did escape . . . but Caliban didn't."

"Then there must be another cat—one who looks like him. Maybe he left offspring. Maybe my cat is his great-great-grandson or something," she insisted, refusing to admit what she already knew was true.

"A nice thought but impossible. There've been no cats at the castle since his time. Most of the clan has a su-

perstitious fear of them . . . although I've been trying to
dispel that fear. I'd like to import some cats to take care
of the rats and mice. You might have noticed we've a
wee bit of a rodent problem here."

"No! *Really?*"

The sudden laughter that poured out of her was a better release than the tears she'd been holding at bay. It
was more cleansing than rain, the sound of it so infec-
tious, it swept Alan straight into its stream, until they
were both laughing so hard they lost their balance and
fell forward in each other's arms, accidentally springing
the lock on the chest and jarring its lid back.

"Oh, no . . . It can't be," she whispered, the laughter
ending abruptly. "Someone must have put it here while
we were seeing Captain Elliott off."

"A possibility, I suppose," Alan said softly, staring
with her into the center of the box. "Who, though?
There's been no one out tonight but us. I doubt anyone
else even knows this wall's been opened. The hole's not
been here a half hour yet. And before that . . ."

"Before that, this chest was sealed in six feet of rock-
hard adobe."

"Aye. For nigh on fifty years."

"It does give one pause, doesn't it?" she murmured,
reaching in and gingerly removing the object they had
been staring at.

"Who was the last person who had it? Your father?"

"No . . . it was me," she answered slowly, the tears
that hadn't come before beginning to land in hot splashes
on her open palm, clinging like dewdrops to what lay
there. "It fell out of my dress in the courtyard. And . . ."

"And Elspeth's cat retrieved it. To bring help for her
granddaughter, as he'd once brought help for her . . . I
know. Because he was still holding it in his mouth when
he came to the great hall to fetch me," Alan said, taking
the key out of her hand and returning it, tears and all, to

the ashes in the chest. "Let's give it back to him, shall we? That way if anyone else needs help in the future, he'll have it handy."

"Aye," Dorcas said, smiling at him through her tears and realizing that Jeremy had almost been right. Children did inherit, it seemed—but not their parents' sins. Elspeth's stubborn kindness, her unshakable insistence on nursing those in need, on carrying light into the dark, and the Panther's sacrifice in response had stirred something that had stretched beyond the grave to bless and protect their descendants.

"But let's not seal this back into the wall," she added, carefully lowering the small casket's lid and refastening its lock. "They should be in a decent grave from now on, with a proper marker, don't you think?"

"The way I'm feeling, dear, I'd like to build them a shrine with marble pillars."

"They might find that a bit ostentatious. A small statue might be nice, though. One of a cat, perhaps? That would work for either the Panther or Caliban, wouldn't it?"

"Only if we put wings on it." He smiled, pulling her to her feet and leading her into the inner court toward the keep. "You weren't that far wrong, you know. You told me he was no demon, but an angel. That may be the truest thing you've ever said."

"You think so, do you?" she asked, her thoughts turning to some unfinished business as, hand in hand, they navigated the softly moonlit yard. "Well, I know something even truer I could tell you."

"And what's that, dear?"

"I'll give you three guesses. One for each word."

It jerked him to a halt just short of the ramp.

"Three words, hmm? But what if I don't want to guess?" he asked, his eyes smoldering down at her like two glowing embers. "What if I just want to hear you say those words?"

"And what if I change my mind and decide not to say them, after all?" she challenged, gazing provocatively back at him.

"In that case, I'll probably be forced to carry you to bed and ravish you within an inch of your life."

"We've an interesting predicament here, then. Because I could take that as an inducement to keep my mouth closed."

"By God, you're right. I hadn't thought of it that way."

"Still, just to keep things fair, what's the alternative? What will you do if I *do* say them?"

"Definitely carry you to bed and ravish you within an inch of your life."

"Well, then, I really can't see that I've much of a choice, have I?"

"None at all," he stated, quickly swinging her high against his chest and striding up the ramp.

"Good." She grinned, winding her arms snugly about his neck. "Because I *do* love you, Alan MacAllister! Long after the rest of creation is a burnt-out cinder, my love for you will still be here, shining out like a star!"

"It'll be a twin star, Dorcas Matilda, for I'll be shining right beside you . . . But that was more than three words, you know."

"I know. I threw the others in as a bonus. Do I get anything extra for them?"

"Aye. I'll kiss you breathless on the way to our room," he promised, covering her mouth with his as he shouldered open the door to the keep.

"Mmmm . . ." she said, thinking how everything that had once seemed so queer and sinister suddenly felt so divinely sensible and right. And how mistaken her father had been when he'd told her that marriage wasn't like math, that there were no formulas she could use to make it come out correctly.

This was the simplest equation, in fact, that she had ever solved. Just take one plus one passionately beating heart, subtract all doubts and fears, multiply by an open awareness and acceptance of soul-shattering love, and your end product could be none other than a glistening abode heaven on earth.

I wonder when Leslie's schooner returns to San Francisco. I'd like to send Flora a big thank-you for making me wear her tartan. She's the sort of girl who'd appreciate a nice gift. And I just happen to know of a lovely French trousseau that ought to suit her perfectly. . . .

"Dorcas? Your knee is hopping like a Mexican jumping bean. What is that brain of yours up to now?" the best part of her heaven murmured against her lips.

"I was just thinking what a wonderful castle this is, and how wonderfully much I adore you!" she murmured back. "And if I can still talk, I'm not breathless yet. So you'd better kiss me some more."

"If you insist." And he matched the action to the phrase.

Nearby, in the flickering shadows, an angel sat watching, blinking golden eyes and grinning like a cat.

Jennie Klassel
She Who Laughs Last

The first time they meet, Prince Jibril captures Lady Syrah's thirteen-year-old heart. The second, nineteen-year-old Syrah kidnaps the prince and deposits him in a coffin. And that is just her first trick. Odorous bedpans, clever disguises, fainting maids, gold coins: all are part of Syrah's daring and brilliant strategy to restore her family's wealth and honor. Tantalizing kisses, forbidden embraces, and heartfelt promises (and her brother's overzealous tall tales!) are not. Who's laughing now? So she frees Jibril. Then the prince vows to discover and marry his outrageous abductress, and Syrah knows at last they'll laugh together.

Reckless Embrace
MADELINE BAKER

Some folks say they are just two kids who should never have met—a girl from the wrong side of town and a half-breed determined to make his mark on the world. Their families fought on opposite sides at the Little Big Horn; there can be no future for them.

But when Black Owl looks at Joey, he sees the most beautiful girl in the world. And when she presses her lips to his, she is finding her way home. In each other's arms, they find a safe haven from a world where hatred and ugliness can only be conquered by the deep, abiding power of courageous love.
